Blurred Lines

Hannah Begbie was born in London. She studied Art History at Cambridge University before working as a talent agent, representing writers and comedians for more than a decade.

Her debut novel, *Mother*, won the Romantic Novelists' Association Joan Hessayon Award for new writing and has been optioned by the BAFTA-winning Clerkenwell Films for adaptation into a television drama.

Hannah lives in London with her husband, a screenwriter, and their two sons.

🐦 @hannahbegbie
📷 @hannahbegbie
f /HannahBegbieAuthor

Also by Hannah Begbie

Mother

Blurred Lines

Hannah Begbie

HarperCollins*Publishers*

HarperCollins*Publishers*
1 London Bridge Street
London SE1 9GF

www.harpercollins.co.uk

Published by HarperCollins*Publishers* 2020
1

A catalogue record for this book
is available from the British Library

ISBN: 978-0-00-828326-1

This novel is entirely a work of fiction.
The names, characters and incidents portrayed in it are
the work of the author's imagination. Any resemblance to
actual persons, living or dead, events or localities is
entirely coincidental.

Set in Sabon LT Std by Palimpsest Book Production Ltd, Falkirk,
Stirlingshire

Printed and bound in Great Britain by CPI Group (UK) Ltd,
Croydon CR0 4YY

MIX
Paper from
responsible sources
FSC
www.fsc.org FSC™ C007454

This book is produced from independently certified FSC™ paper
to ensure responsible forest management.

For more information visit: www.harpercollins.co.uk/green

For my sons, Jack and Griffin

Chapter 1

She feels the sales assistant looking her over, appraising her against the wine that she has delivered to the counter. It is a Burgundy, priced at sixty-five pounds, its provenance declared in elegant loops on a simple label. She couldn't pronounce this *château*, and she suspects this man knows that perfectly well. Look at this woman, with her dull, errant hair and the catalogue-bought black trousers that reach for but never quite achieve a tailored fit: at how her slouch and the crease to her brow clash against the pin-straight, darkly varnished floorboards of this wine shop.

He wraps the bottle in crisp crepe paper, one finger cocked like he is taking an elegant tea, as if to tell her: *this* is how it is done. Granted, her wardrobe, her hairstyle, her whole life cannot be salvaged by a moment of his time, but perhaps the act of witnessing his precision and professionalism and his good taste might, in some small way, chip away at her roughness.

She has pulled this bottle from the shelf because a hand-written card describes it as 'a classic example of the type'. Now she wishes that she had been bolder. That she had chosen something without a ready-made approval, to state firmly that she knows better than this man, than any man, how her desires are best met by grapes, and *terroir*, and time in the bottle. Imagine asking if they had the same wine but from another year. A better year, or worse. Knowing what the sun or the humidity or the rain had done to that corner of France in that year.

Why should she know? Who is asking her to know these things?

'Any tips for drinking it?' she asks, her demeanour easy and friendly, like she's only really filling a spare minute while he wraps the thing. Like she has no need of his opinion, but chooses to seek it anyway. A generous gesture that allows for him to know more about this bottle than simply how to wrap it.

'Are you drinking it straight away?'

She shrugs. She won't be drinking it at all, unless she's asked to share it. And even then, she'd only take a few sips.

'Well don't let it get too warm,' he says. 'Won't hurt to decant it, but it won't struggle straight out of the bottle either. Cash or card?'

Becky hands over her debit card. It is the same colour as when she was at school. The first-savings-account hue of somebody who agonizes over whether sixty-five pounds, which she really cannot afford, is enough to spend on wine for a man who might consider it midweek drinking, a bottle to open mindlessly before rushing off to a weekend away, leaving it to idle and spoil on the kitchen island. Is it enough, a bottle like this, for a man like Matthew?

Matthew pays her pretty well. She can't complain. She knows there are others who make less and are worth far more.

Stop it, she tells herself. You are good at your job. You are.

'Enjoy it!' says the man behind the counter as he hands her the bag. Did he see the dismay in her eyes as the card receipt chattered through? Surely he knows that this is a gift, one meant to impress; a wine that she does not understand, intended for someone whose world she only fleetingly visits.

And yet, his smile seems sincere. Perhaps he is honestly grateful for her custom, even if the wine is wasted on her. The money is real enough.

Matthew taught her that, like so much else about their business: everything is only talk, only a possibility, until somebody writes you a cheque, or cashes one you've written them.

As she exits the shop she holds her head high. Today is a good day. She has come to West London to deliver a gift and the gift has been well-chosen. It will suffice.

Becky passes the wedding-cake white houses of Portobello, takes in the scent of freshly cut stems from an elegant pink-and-orange-painted boutique floristry and the steam-whistle of a barista's coffee machine through lacquered café doors flung wide-open. The weather has finally turned a corner. Her skin actually feels warm for the first time in months and she cannot help but stop for a moment, right there on the street corner, and turn her face to the sun, smiling even as she hopes that no one catches her in the act.

It's a small miracle, she thinks, how an idea can turn into a series of meetings, and then a screenwriter's draft, and now – or at least soon – will become actors and cameras and lights, and conversations in the edit suite. Like watching a foetus growing across a series of ultrasound images.

Tomorrow her yellow brick road takes her to the Cannes Film Festival where she will meet the people who can really *make it happen*. Those who can write cheques, or accept them. Her small idea, gathering supporters, players, financiers.

'We could be shooting this time next year,' Matthew had said at that very first meeting, within a minute of her giving him her seedling of an idea. 'Produce it. I'll back you.'

'But I don't know how,' she'd said, hating herself for confessing her weakness so quickly.

'Nobody does, the first time.'

And with that statement, he'd made it real.

She steps over the cracks in the pavement. She doesn't want to jinx it, not now. Not when everything is so close.

She can see Matthew's terraced stucco villa in the

distance, its pilasters and columns all whiter than white against the leafy green health of the pavement trees. The early evening sun reminds her so much of that party night, when she walked this road, on that occasion without wine but with a Jiffy bag of contracts from the office for him to sign, not expecting to leave with a plan for her future.

'Stay,' he'd said to her as he signed the last of the Post-it-marked pages. 'Come and meet some people.'

She'd been the one to order the canapés and the watermelon martini ingredients for this party, and now she was invited to share in them. To accept them as easy gifts from the waiting staff who circulated in crisp white shirts and black trousers.

Of course she should network. Wasn't that how the world worked? A pretty assistant, charming her way around a beautiful garden, making a name for herself, evading both men's hands and the scrutiny of their wives' tracking gazes.

And yet, despite the fact of her canary-yellow dress candy-striped with orange, and the fact that she'd washed her hair that morning with a shampoo that promised gloss and hold, her head itched and she felt out of step and out of place. Here, the rich looked rich, and the nonconformists wore their asymmetric fringes with confidence. In one corner, a famous actor in shredded jeans and Debbie Harry T-shirt made conversation with an elderly critic turned out in linen suit and white Panama hat and both seemed entirely at ease. Where were the people stuck in between? Uncomfortably halfway to somewhere? Unfinished, barely done with being utter imposters?

She had been relieved when Matthew had interrupted a conversation between her and a grey-haired, mildly known actor – not so much a conversation, really, as a lecture – by asking her to step away with him, into his study. She had felt eyes on them as they vanished back into the house together. There was always that question, for some people, concerning what a man and a woman stepping away together might mean, especially when she was *his*, an employee, and just about still young, and unquestionably ambitious. Despite Matthew's wife and children being there. Despite the way he kissed his wife readily and easily. Of course somebody would make a sly comment, win a cruel quick laugh. Why else go to a party like this?

The walls of Matthew's study were tessellated with black-and-white photographs of his beautiful family playing cricket on a beach in Cornwall. Smooth custom-made oak shelves held his BAFTAs and BIFAs and Oscars and a galaxy of other awards in glass, bronze, Perspex, silver and wood.

'I've got the Universal contracts here as well,' he said. 'Won't be a minute.' He glanced up from the paperwork and caught her looking at his statuettes.

'Pick one up, if you like? The Academy one's pretty heavy,' he said. 'You don't want that kind of thing to take you by surprise on the night.' And then he laughed and she really wasn't sure whether he was mocking her or if he was expressing some kind of belief in her and so she chose, for once, to try to believe the latter. And as a small, rare bubble of confidence grew in her, no doubt lubricated by three glasses of good champagne, she had told him, 'I'm ready, I want to make a film. And I have an idea.'

Approaching his house a year later she still marvels at that moment. How did she do it? It had been like pitching to God, but at least prayers go unanswered. No voice from above outright tells you, *No*. You're at least allowed to keep your hope. Her heart was in her mouth, she feels sick just remembering it, thrumming its beats through her, telling her to be ready for anything – so afraid was she that Matthew would declare how bad her idea, how shameless her decision to pitch now: at a party, of all times! Becky had fought every natural instinct in her body to flee, and pressed on, talking to her boss, this movie producer whose life was stuffed to the gills with box office smashes and blockbuster hits. He had listened to her talk about the Greek tragedy 'Medea' and how it might be remade to speak to modern women, and he had said yes, and then told her to make it for £4 to 5 million, give or take a million for their lead actress who would do it for the prizes, not the payday.

'It's about revenge,' she had told him excitedly, not realizing that you can stop once somebody has said yes. 'Medea sacrifices everything to help Jason achieve his goals. Then, when he's taken all she has to offer, he gets bored and leaves her for another woman. And so Medea gets angry.'

As she spoke, something scalding had coursed through her, with the rush of a furiously filling lock. It didn't take much to connect with this feeling, not really, it was close to the surface wherever she was. 'He believes a woman's anger isn't ever something to worry about,' she said, 'but he underestimates her. Medea takes her revenge.'

It didn't matter that Matthew would never know what had lit that touchpaper inside her. She could see from his half-smile that he was interested in her, and proud of her, and she was already addicted to that feeling.

Becky steps into the road to cross it and a car swerves to avoid her, blaring its horn. Its headlights catch her shins. She steps back, a stomach-twisting jolt of adrenaline waking her up.

On the opposite side of the road an old woman takes pleasure in shaking her head at Becky's near-fatal mistake as a new story sweeps away red carpets and lofted award statuettes: Becky, mother of one, a development assistant with no produced credits, dead in the road. A head full of dreams, but not enough blood left in her veins to keep them there.

It is an old feeling for Becky, the idea that her waking life might be parted from her body. That her body is sometimes simply a place where things happen, sometimes with her, sometimes without.

These are not helpful thoughts.

She feels small and foolish now. She is a woman without real power. A woman who can barely cross a road. She has the favour of a powerful man, and that is all. For all the cocktails and glamorous lunches, it hasn't happened yet, the film hasn't taken off, hasn't been made. It's all just words and expressions of interest. Who on earth does she think she is?

She crosses, safely now, passing the old woman who wants desperately to catch Becky's eye.

Smaller and weaker, she arrives at the side entrance to Matthew's house, electing to take a route she has taken a dozen times before, stepping down a flight of double-height steps to a wooden door, barbed wire all curled at the top like a helix of DNA. The air smells of fresh creosote and good maintenance and charred meat and through a small side window she can see that lights are on deeper inside the house.

She pushes at the door and it opens easily. Why doesn't he worry about crime? All that barbed wire and the door still unlocked; a contradiction, a statement, a *dare*. People seem to come and go here, drifting into Matthew's home like it's an exclusive private members' club. If you turn up and they're having a family meal, a place is set for you straight away – no trouble, no problem. Becky has eaten like that on half a dozen occasions, smiling along with every family joke until her jaw ached with tension.

She pads over a paved area and pushes at another door

into the house, stepping through the dark utility room, rehearsing her lines. No, she can't stay. It's a small thank you for Cannes, a token really. If she stays for a drink, will she be so bold as to propose a toast to their forthcoming trip? Is that hopelessly gauche, wishing aloud for success that Matthew has no need of? Siobhan's laser-guided words hit her again: this is a *very* expensive kind of work experience. Said to her face, to Siobhan's credit, as Siobhan booked two hotel rooms and two sets of flights. Chosen and not chosen. Emboldened by Becky's example, Siobhan is developing her own idea to pitch to Matthew, while also printing up the Cannes travel itineraries.

There is music playing in the kitchen. The lights are on in the hallway, but not in here, where the downlighters are set to low. Becky pauses on the threshold of the room. What if he is home alone? What if he has fallen asleep and now she'll wake him? She regrets not ringing the front doorbell but Matthew is always at pains to say it's only ever the builders and delivery men who do that, and she's more than that to him. Isn't she?

But this is an imposition. What if she walks in on him getting undressed or even, God help her, masturbating? In the *kitchen*? she asks herself. Surely not.

She steps over the threshold into a room that is kitchen and dining room and living room all in one, and each area is generously apportioned. The overall footprint is larger than her entire flat.

The retractable glass wall is closed to the garden but

its formal raised beds are tastefully under-lit. The kitchen features navy walls and a distressed copper breakfast bar with matching taps. Soap in big blue apothecary bottles and stripped, white-painted floorboards. There are half-full wine glasses on the marble worktop.

Becky sets her own wine down on the kitchen island and looks around for paper with which to leave a note. 'Popped in?' 'Sorry I missed you?' Or is she right that it's an imposition, this stealing into a person's home, even if it's allowed, encouraged even?

As the music changes track, in the silence between beats, she thinks she hears something – a breath, or a moan, something like pain perhaps. She can't put a name to it, but her mouth dries and her skin prickles, the fine hairs on her forearms rising.

She wants to flee, but what if it's him, dying? An olive caught in the throat. An allergy he hasn't told her about (not that, she'd know). And in the end, she has to check. Of course she does.

She pads quietly around the wood-burning fireplace that part divides the room. Another noise – this time male and urgent. And, horrified, Becky realizes that she is in proximity to sex.

There is movement. On the floor, on the rug that softens the sofa grouping, their bodies mostly hidden by the furniture. Becky cranes her neck a little. She sees a woman's head, and Matthew on top of her, and the woman is not his wife, cannot be unless Antonia has gone blonde. She notices a tall-heeled foot, black shoe with a red sole, sliding off the rug, onto the flagstone, like a calf's leg slipping outward as it takes a first step.

The woman says something to the man. Her arm goes up – pushing him or reaching for him? He catches her by the wrist and moves that arm back onto the rug – and his breathing, his grunting, deepens. The woman's face contorts. Perhaps close to orgasm. Perhaps uncomfortable.

The woman turns her head and looks straight at Becky. And opens her mouth, as if about to speak – or call out – or warn him – or—

Chapter 2

That night in bed, restless under her covers, Becky goes from hot to cold, aggravated by the duvet's shortness, its longness and finally its mere existence. Window up, window down, she cannot seem to find a simple point of balance between sweating and shivering. She lies on her front, her back, curled up, stretched out, grasping and un-grasping her wrist.

Matthew Kingsman. Oxford man. Family man. Film man. There is a waterlogged feeling in her. Perhaps it is disappointment, though that would be irrational. Matthew is a free agent in a free country. He can do as he pleases, and it is no business of hers.

She tells herself she has been naïve: that people do this all the time. Flings, dalliances, affairs, trust-bending, trust-breaking. There are of course open marriages whose openness isn't advertised to one and all. People have sex with people they shouldn't, all the time, particularly in her industry where everyone is looking at themselves, and if not at themselves then at each other, in the mirror or through a camera or on screen. Bodies attractive enough to sell tickets win easy lays, quick fucks, promotions. She gets it. It shouldn't be news to her. She needs to loosen the fuck up.

Successful people are boundary-benders, boundary-breakers, and maybe it is Becky who should be taking a lesson from this rather than sitting here in judgement. She has so much to learn. She aches under the weight of it, aches at how childish she still is.

All these thoughts ricochet off the sides of her, like a ball in a pinball machine.

She considers for the hundredth time how, with the kitchen lights behind her, she must only have been a silhouette. How she turned and ran so quickly and quietly that perhaps if they were drunk she'll be remembered as something that couldn't have happened. A shadow in the corner of the eye, with nothing there on second glance. She was never there. If he asked – and why would he ever ask? – she would look blankly back and deny everything.

It is none of her business how two people have sex. Some people like to dress up. Some people play rough, hold each other down and tie each other up by the wrists, silence and hurt each other. She knows all that. She's not completely naïve.

At five in the morning, and with just two hours left before it's time to wake Maisie for school, Becky admits defeat and leaves her bed, padding quietly to the kitchen to make a pot of coffee. Maisie will sleep through the kettle whistle, through the smell of coffee, through all of it. Maisie rarely dreams. She sleeps like a child whose days are straightforward, which is precisely how Becky has laboured to arrange them.

Becky breathes in her home and the smell of washing powder and the ghost of last night's chilli and tries to calm the thud-crack in her heart. She looks around her small kitchen and at all the boundaries that surround her in her old East London maisonette; at the low ceilings and narrow rooms, at the double-glazed, triple-locked door that leads out onto a paved patio. At the window grills that slide across and meet in the middle. At the moose-headed coat hook in the hallway that holds her black lycra running top and the pair of creased and dusty wide-legged trousers she'd once worn for weekly self-defence classes at the local gym.

At first, what she learnt there made her feel safer than any triple-locked door. She enjoyed making a fist in a boxing glove so her wrists didn't snap and her tendons didn't bruise, and how to deliver a punch with speed and precision. She had felt reassured and emboldened by the tight wrap of the gloves around her wrists and how they made her arms feel bionic, almost not her own. She had enjoyed the feeling of strength return to her body.

But she abandoned the lessons when she began using her new-found skills in unconstructive ways. There wasn't a local gym class on earth that would teach her the skills she needed to defend her against herself.

Becky tries not to panic about how much she has to

do, how she will manage a day's work, a flight to Cannes and a couple more hours' peppiness for all those new people who will need impressing. All on no sleep whatsoever? Back in her bedroom she lightly folds a dress and rolls up a cotton shirt and two T-shirts. Fills her washbag. Pulls out pants and socks and assembles it all in a pleasing jigsaw inside her carry-on suitcase: two carbon-scented copies of the *Medea* script at its base.

She makes notes on her Cannes meetings, banishing thoughts of that silken hair spilling out onto the kitchen floor, coming up with six ways to pitch her idea to six different kinds of people.

But she knows what she really wants to do and she knows that it is destructive so she fights it, at first holding her own hand lightly, reassuringly, like a friend. And then when the feeling does not subside, gripping her hand tightly, before grasping at the thin skin and raised veins of her own wrist, holding it tight, as if pulling herself back from a fight. She has agreed, in therapy, that standing up to this instinct is a good thing. Succeeding means she has taken her power back, or something like that; but without sleep all those rules are dissolving at their margins, her desires pushing away old decisions.

Surely if she just *does* more, the instinct will leave? She clears the washing basket. Cleans surfaces that already gleam. Lays out an array of jams and breakfast cereals despite the fact she never eats breakfast and her daughter's favourites are firmly established and unflinching.

She means to make a cup of tea next, but somehow before the kettle boils she has opened Scott's Twitter page and she is already on her way to losing the fight.

Becky has two Twitter accounts: one that is her. And one that isn't.

The one that isn't Becky is Melanie. Melanie has a line drawing of a face in the photo caption, all thick and twisty like the pen hasn't been taken off the page. 'Melanie Hasn't Tweeted Yet' but Melanie follows a few people – thirty-seven corporate accounts like BBC News, Sky News, Popbitch, and another dozen or so famous people, including a TV presenter who crossed the Gobi Desert on foot and whose dinner-party speciality is puffer fish. Then there are forty or so 'ordinary people', people who maybe said something funny once or do something unusual or are vocally for or against some issue or other. And she doesn't check on anything they have to say, because all of them – the corporations, the celebrities, the nobodies – are padding to disguise the fact that Melanie is following Scott.

She knows it's overkill, but Becky dreads the slip of a fingertip, an accidental 'like' or retweet of a Scott comment, anything that might tip him off that Becky Shawcross is monitoring him. Safer not to look directly at him.

Scott has changed his main picture again.

Now Scott is in fancy dress, dressed as Elvis in a maroon button-down shirt, the collar of a leather jacket pulled high around his neck and his hair styled like a whip of black treacle.

It's not a picture she has seen before.

Perhaps he has been to a party.

She logs into Facebook, via another fake profile account. He friended her without asking questions. He already had 762 friends. Why not welcome another one? Somebody has tagged him at this party. Elvis lives! A grinning friend of his has slung an arm around Scott's neck. Scott is pouting for the camera in aviators. Not for the first time, he has chosen a costume that allows him to wear sunglasses. He likes to hide his eyes, those giveaway windows to the soul.

She scrolls back through his timeline. She's seen it all before, a thousand times. His whole life is in her head, or at least those parts that she can get at from the safety of her own flat.

Last year Scott purchased a large indoor fish tank. His colleagues appreciated the cupcakes he bought them one afternoon in Soho. He celebrated the birthday of his oldest house plant and 152 people put hearts by it.

Recently drank espresso Martinis with an old friend who'd flown over from Australia. You'd think *he* was Australian, with a name like Scott, but he's English. Like Becky, he was brought up in Hounslow, where the roof tiles vibrate under the flight paths.

And there's one picture of him that kills her every time now. Taken a year or so ago, it's like he's staring right back at her, without the usual sunglasses hiding his eyes, without a care in the world. Without remorse. You don't get that icy-blue finish to the eyes without going into a shop and buying coloured contact lenses, without swaggering in there, your veins running cold with vanity. In the picture, he's got an expensive haircut with bits of white blond at the ends. Becky reckons the colour is officially 'ash blond'. Successful, good-looking, like a boy band member, his hair dipped in ash dye – the ashes of other people. Not a crack in that gorgeous fucking life of his.

She surrenders to it, the scanning and watching distracts her from her twitching hands, from thoughts of the kitchen floor. She'll read him until Maisie stirs, she knows that now, so she scrolls to champagne glasses intertwined and fizzing. She surfs his flat, job, and the people who love him best (a sister in Belgium, some nieces and nephews). No sign of a significant other; that's something, at least.

How easily he lives.

But she is breathing quickly now, the energy inside whipping itself into a hot storm with nowhere to go because it's not enough to see him live his life. It never is. And yet, she has a daughter who relies on her. Everything she wants must be measured against that.

Enough, she tells herself. And so she dresses in jogging bottoms and threads the laces of her running shoes with trembling hands and closes the door behind her with a double then a triple lock. Silently, so as not to wake Maisie, a crackle of worry across her chest about leaving her, but knowing that there are two people to look after. Another edict from another therapist. Self-care. Making time for her.

Becky takes three quick steps, ordering everything inside herself to be quiet, and soon enough she has slipped into a good, quick pace and is running through the streets, heels slamming hard on concrete, landing so as to feel those shockwaves snake up sharp through fibula and tibia. And then, when her chest and muscles ache, she adjusts her gait to save her shin-splints and instead let lungs and thighs scream.

She runs down an alley – she'd never dream of taking it at night and even now, with just the weak morning daylight, she holds her breath in her chest and her keys in her hand like a dagger. Once she's out the other end, she races for the park where round and round and round she will go, pushing herself faster on each lap.

She lets herself have one lap – only one – where she lets Scott fuck her before she cuts his throat.

Then she is so full of shame. It drums in her ears and leaks out of her tear ducts and flecks her mouth with spittle.

She stops running. Finds a tree. Stands with her back to the rough-edged bark and now she cannot stop what she does next. She curls her hand into a fighter's fist, making sure her thumb stays on the outside of her second and third knuckles, exactly as she was taught. Then, at the thought of Scott's flashing smile and icy eyes, at the thought of that woman's hair shining so bright and gold, her arm stretched so long and thin across the rug, her wrist held, she pummels her thigh. Softly at first, like a drum. And soon enough she is thumping her leg, much harder this time, and imagining all her thoughts, all her feelings, being knocked out of her with every beat, like an old-fashioned washer woman pummelling the dirt out of fabric. Nice and clean, washed away and forgotten.

Soon her leg hurts so much she cannot thump it any more. Underneath her jogging bottoms she knows it will be pink where the flesh has been hammered, and that there will be a yellowish tea-wash stain behind that and that soon the pink patch will go purple and black before it too goes yellow tea-wash. She hammers and punches on the same spot because she is trying to stop something but it is a race she is losing and however much she tries to hold it back, she can't: her mind ribbons out like it is being released into the wind, sharp claws at each ribbon's end, thoughts and memories all searching for something, a clue and jigsaw piece, something to make her whole again.

Chapter 3

Becky loves Saturdays. No school all day, and then another day just like it to collapse into after this one's spent.

Today her parents have gone out to the garden centre and left her in peace to enjoy the high-pitched presenters of Saturday morning television as they leap about in front of butter-yellow and sugar-pink backdrops. When Becky is old enough to do this kind of thing, when it is *her* turn to interview people, it will be in her contract that she gets to choose the colour of the sofa – hot pink to offset her lime-green leggings, thank you! She will ideally graduate quickly from children's television into a kind of late teatime, prime-time Saturday slot just after the family game shows. And as a presenter she will have a habit of asking tough and yet elegantly emotional questions like, 'But in the last ana-lysis, how does that actually make you *feel*?' Perhaps while reaching out a warm hand in genuine concern. It will sort of be her *thing*, so that after a while her guests expect it and people will talk about how she was the refreshing opposite of all the old men who do their chat shows.

Becky has a box full of diagrams of the set she will inhabit, drawing each one like a bedroom with four walls. It doesn't occur to her that you need to put the cameras somewhere, so one wall has to be imaginary. She sees no trickery, no special effects. Just a bright, bubblegum reality that is kind enough to welcome her in, whenever she turns on the television.

Charred burgers and relish for lunch today, the classic Saturday meal in the Shawcross household, complete with Dad complaining about broken tongs and Mum saying he should bloody well do something about it then.

Becky goes to the local pool. In the changing room she watches other women's bodies as they get in or out of their costumes. As she walks to the water, she is a catwalk model with all eyes on her. When she dives down, she is a dolphin or a jet-ski or a shark. When she returns home later that afternoon the house smells of hot dogs and frying onions: the conciliatory dish her mum offers her dad after a hard day's arguing.

She calls out from the hallway. 'It stinks in this house. Will someone please open the window? All my clothes are going to smell of gross oil and onions.' Then she runs up the steps to her bedroom, two at a time, in a bid to rescue her party outfit.

Downstairs her mum begins a fresh diatribe on her favourite subject, which is 'being blamed for bloody everything in this house'.

Becky stands at the mirror of her wardrobe in her underwear, wanting to look more sophisticated than she does in these baggy pink cotton knickers bought in bulk by her mum every Christmas. She needs to investigate alternative options. She hates the idea of a G-string, the notion that somehow you are a block of cheddar perpetually on the verge of being halved by a cheese wire. And then there's the sheer hassle she'd get if she actually bought something nice (comfortable cut, bold-coloured lace) and her mother found them in the washing basket. The torrent of questions that would follow! Who was she thinking of impressing with a pair like that? Who the bloody hell did she think she was? Which boy exactly had she impressed so far? And the crowning glory: what precautions was she taking, and did she know that even condoms can't prevent pubic lice from spreading?

Becky lays her outfit out on the bed and her make-up on her side table, so that everything is ready. She loves decorating herself: all that nipping and tucking and flaring and wedging, like taking a sharpened pencil and rubber to your outline and adjusting it accordingly.

She holds up a fluorescent-pink vest top with a spaghetti strap which, because it was bought at a flea market lacking a changing room, is too big and needs adjusting so the lace trim of her bra is not on display. She wreathes strings of beads and trails fake pearls about her neck until she is satisfied with how good the concentric circles look against a plain pink background. Then she takes her jeans

– tight, low-slung, the fashion – and pours herself into them, ramming the zip closed twice before it stays put.

The next bit takes the longest. She outlines and flicks and smudges and colours in cheeks and eyes until she looks a picture: the best, most sophisticated version of herself, she thinks.

Just before she leaves, she stands a few feet away from the threshold of the kitchen rubbing moisturizer into arms that are dry and chlorinated from the pool, watching as her mum lays out a fresh cloth on the table.

Her dad turns to her and laughs, then says, 'You look like you've fallen in the dressing-up box.'

Becky wants to say, *Don't be a dick*, but she won't risk being sent to her room and having her plans cancelled. Instead she settles for a sarcastic smile and a mumbled, 'You're not exactly setting Milan on fire with those Union Jack socks.'

They're not the kind of parents who insist on collecting their child from a party at a set time. They don't suggest it and Becky doesn't ask them to. That's one good thing about them. She'll be home when she's home.

Their party plans had nearly been abandoned because of Mary's summer cold, which Becky would probably have been OK with, if she's honest. But now that Mary is on the up, the only sign of her ailment a lower-than-usual voice, left gravelly by a week's coughing, it's all back on and they're arm in arm, walking down the road from

Mary's house, with Mary pushing and pushing to see if Becky will do a pill with her tonight.

Mary is Irish and favours wearing pinafore dresses with band T-shirts rumpled up underneath. She is extremely persuasive. Her hair is terracotta red out of a packet which emphasizes the china white of her skin, which in turn emphasizes the rings of dark under her eyes which are there because she has to get up earlier than her body wants to, she says, which is one more crime that the education system has to answer for. Mary feels that the school week compounds the problem of weekends, which should ideally involve missing at least one whole night's sleep.

'So? Are you going to do one with me or not?'

Mary believes that, as friends, you go down together and you come up together. If it's a good pill then you have a fellow traveller for the night, and if it's a bad pill then you don't die alone.

Today, Mary is disappointed about an unsupportive government and disappointed with the bags under her eyes, and Becky can't quite bear to add to the tally, at least not yet, so she says: 'Yeah, maybe I'll take a pill. We'll see. Yeah, go on then.'

Mary whoops because it is only a party when you are guaranteed to have fun and not die alone. Then she takes out two cigarettes, lights them both and hands Becky one as if smoking cigarettes together is the best way of sealing this deal of *togetherness*.

It is Saturday night and Becky is feeling good. Her skin

feels lit with magpie-bright colours and sparkles, and it fits well. At this moment, walking arm in arm with her best friend, everything is as it should be.

Oh, to have a photograph of that moment, the time before the rest of it happened.

To have that to come back to, to tell yourself: you are still in there, that girl with flying hair and a newly lit cigarette and a whole weekend, a whole life, laid out for the taking. She is not lost to you. Imagine yourself back into that skin and feel the closeness of the fit. Persuade yourself.

But you are not watched by anything other than a fat, ginger housecat, which moments after you pass him forgets you for a rat-rustle in the bushes nearby.

Chapter 4

Becky sits at her kitchen table, skull resting in her hands, the sweat of her running kit rapidly cooling. Suddenly she shakes her head from side to side, like she is trying to unblock water from her ear canals.

Her hands shake as she reaches for her cup of sugar-sweetened tea. There are only minutes left before her daughter rises, before she must pack it all away, every messy part of herself, and instead shower and emerge into the office day clean and effective and capable of more than she feels. And in twelve hours she touches down in Cannes and will need to find yet more energy from somewhere to be extraordinary. Impressive. So much better than her ordinary self.

Her phone dings. Siobhan from the office.

Becky has known her for three years now and they have their taller-than-average heights in common, along with a history of photocopying, office organizing, script reading, and attending to the needs and wants of Matthew. All the things Becky is now shedding.

Something's going down. Advise turning up on time . . .

Ding

. . . early. Ideally? M is in a weird mood. Wants to talk to us.

Becky's body tenses instinctively, her stomach drawing in as if she is about to be punched there.

Immediately, she thinks: I am to blame for seeing something that wasn't my business. There would be no point in telling herself that blame is an irrational response – what she feels in that moment comes unbidden, from a place that is fossilized in her bones.

I am to blame for entering his space without permission.

All that time spent preparing for Cannes: choosing and rolling and folding and packing things to decorate herself with: the pretty clothes and the jewel-toned make-up and the bangles and necklaces and perfume. The shameful, wasteful vanity of it all. He'll cancel the trip, and then sack her from her job. All those years she worked, wasted. All the studying and handbook-reading between toddler meals and screaming baby put-me-downs and pick-me-ups. The evening courses and coursework threaded between hastily arranged pieces of childcare. Not to mention the hours spent reading novels, watching television programmes and films, not for pleasure but to educate herself: studying story construction and characters. Feeling surprised and comforted when some characters sunk into her bones, enough to make her laugh and cry and scream with frustration and sometimes, if she was really lucky, to feel their presence for days and months after . . . What did people call it? Characters that *stayed with you*, like a good friend, a true friend who holds your hand at a time of need.

One night, after watching a film about a woman who had fought against the odds to find happiness, all this feeling brimmed out of her and onto the page in the form of a well-worded letter addressed to the Soho townhouse offices of the film's producer, Matthew Kingsman.

I want to work for you more than anything. I too want to bring stories to people that make them feel what you make them feel: less alone.

It had all been so hard-fought. And soon it would all be gone because she had put herself in the wrong place at the wrong time.

She slaps her own wrist. Stupid girl.

'Hey, Mum.' Maisie is standing at the doorway to the kitchen in bare feet and white and blue tartan pyjamas – brushed cotton, a Christmas present from Becky – the ropes of her bathrobe hanging down, brushing the floor gently, vines in the wind. 'Are you all right?'

Becky wipes at her cheeks with flat palms, like she is applying moisturizer. 'Yes, absolutely fine.' Reassuring people was something she learnt to do many years ago. One trick amongst many.

Another one: fill a silence with a question of your own.

'How long did you stay up revising?'

'I don't know,' says Maisie. 'Late?'

'It's important to get some rest as well. You can't think properly if you're not getting enough sleep.'

'You want me to add *resting* to my already massive timetable?'

Becky smiles. She likes Maisie's sharp edges. They'll keep her safe, she hopes. Not an easy walkover, a girl who'll puncture your feet as you attempt it. 'What are you working on?'

'I was doing my physics revision. How long have you been up for?'

'Do you study the atom bomb?'

'You mean fission bombs?'

'I have no idea! If I'd studied them I might be able to answer that . . .'

'Anyway, no, we don't. In our school that's probably more of an ethics thing than a science thing.'

'I just always thought it was interesting. A tennis-ball-sized thing flattening a whole city.'

'Morning, Mum! Can I have some breakfast before we talk about the end of the world?'

Becky smiles and sets about sorting Maisie's breakfast.

'I don't want you to stress about your exams.'

'Yes you do! I know I need a scholarship to stay at sixth-form and those ten A grades at GCSE aren't going to magically achieve themselves.'

'Just don't let it get on top of you.'

'I actually slept really well. Did you go to bed? You look rubbish.'

'Really building my confidence before Cannes.'

'It's not like you're an actress. You don't have to look sexy for anyone.'

'True. Well, I'll cling to that, shall I?'

'Yep.'

Maisie levels her out. She always has done. There have been times, many of them, that without a child to hold onto she might have fallen off the edge of the world. And here, like a miracle, is a smart-mouthed funny young girl, living under the same roof, loving her more or less unconditionally. Even when she first pushed a pram around the park, round and around, when she thought she could actually *feel* the gazes land on her soul, heavy with judgement – a feckless teenager with a mewling newborn, a mistake that'll no doubt be paid for by the state – even then just looking down at her soothed her, pushed her agony to the sides, made space in her for her heart to beat.

Now teenager-mother and baby have morphed to become mother and teenager. And often they are mistaken for sisters – they are almost the same height, have the same long mousy brown hair, the same strong thin nose. Maisie's eyes are darker and a little larger. Her skin tans in the sun where Becky's burns. But these are small differences. 'Cut from the same cloth,' Maisie's grandfather is fond of saying. 'Not much of you in there, Adam, and thank Christ for that!' Adam, adored by his father all his life, affects outrage before claiming that Maisie has his hairy arms. Becky watches on fondly as they all collapse into more laughter. The joke varies. Sometimes Adam claims she's going to have his size twelve feet, sometimes it's his sticky-out ears, but the form is unchanging.

Sometimes as the shtick begins Adam meets Becky's eyes and there is a private understanding before the lines play on. Maisie loves it. Sometimes she prompts it, asking Grandpa T who she looks like, feigning innocence but already grinning in anticipation of which mutant body part Adam will claim for her inheritance.

'Sorry to have to be away,' says Becky.

'No offence, but it's non-stop pizza when you're gone so there's not going to be many tears shed.'

'I'm going to ask Adam to make a salad.'

'OK. He can make it and then we'll both sit there admiring it while we eat our pizzas.'

Becky smiles and her phone dings again. Siobhan:

Scratch that. He is in a really CRAP mood. Something is UP. How long does it take you to pack anyways?

'Can I go to a sleepover tonight?'

'Definitely not. It's a school night.'

'Mum.'

'No.'

The silence that falls is plugged with the jet rush of the tap as Becky fills the kettle. She arranges tea bag and mug. Her clothes are stiffening with drying salt.

'I've got to go, Mais,' Becky says. 'I only said I'd be half an hour late so I could get myself sorted for this afternoon and so far neither of us has showered or eaten.'

'How come you get cocktails in the sun with little umbrellas and bits of pineapple and sexy people dressed in Armani and I can't even go to a boring sleepover?'

'School night. I admire your tenacity but you're not going to magically persuade me that Wednesday is followed by Sunday.' Becky smiles and ruffles her daughter's hair. 'Anyway, I thought you were working towards buying those trainers? Put in more revision time instead of going out and you'll be a step closer to earning them. What are they called again? The Nike neon wattage . . .'

Maisie rolls her eyes. 'Volt, Mum. Volt is the colour of the trainer, not its electrical charge.'

'Great, the point is they're so painfully hip that everyone will want to be your friend then you'll never be short of an invitation so why not wait . . .'

'Nice try but I'm fine with the invite I've got right now. Come on, Mum, please let me go? Only one boy is going to be there. He hardly counts.'

'Definitely not. And it's not about boys.'

A lie, but an easy one.

Becky takes some bread out of its cellophane bag and lines up two slices next to each other, all the while surveying the line of texts on her phone screen. Her stomach turns slowly at the slick of butter across the bread and twists in irritation at the congealed and messy blackcurrant jam refusing to spread tidily.

'Who's Scott?'

The question freezes Becky. How is it even possible that Maisie is asking it? Her laptop is closed. She's always careful to log out and delete and tidy it all away. Becky is glad that she is facing away from her daughter.

Even with years of practice, in moments like this she can be read.

'He was an explorer. Died at the South Pole.'

'Funny. Ish. Seriously, are you thinking about dating this guy?'

'Which guy?'

When Maisie says his name – his full name – Becky feels like she has been cornered. Nowhere left to run.

'Where'd you hear his name?'

'You asked me to fix our rubbish Wi-Fi.'

'And . . .?'

'And so I logged into the router to see if anyone's squatting on our connection and there wasn't, but what there is is lots of visits to his Twitter and his Facebook and I was like, that's a bit obsessive, Mum!'

Becky attempts to look calm. Blithe, she tells herself. Unruffled. Everything has to be weighed now. If Maisie asks Adam about Scott, any lie that she tells now will be easily unknotted. Something close to the truth is required.

'He's a guy I knew when I was younger. School days.'

'He's a *sexy* guy you used to know!'

'Not my type.'

'Why are you looking at him then?'

'I was curious. He was one of those kids you wonder where he'll end up. It's a big bit of my job, taking real people and then making up endings. Sometimes I'll think about someone I once knew and decide how their story ended and then look them up just to see if I was right.'

'Oh my God, that's so weird.'

'I'm good at it!'

'No, you need a better hobby than Facebook-stalking people to see if you're good at making up stories.'

'Fine. Get me a basketball for my birthday.'

Maisie looks up. 'I actually thought for a moment you might be thinking of going on a date. And I was like . . . good! At last.'

'I'm not against dating. I'm just really busy.'

'Yeah, but soon all the women your age . . .'

'My age? I'm only thirty-two!'

'Yes, like I said, soon women your age are going to be getting married and having kids . . .'

'Jumped the gun there, did I?'

'Mum. You need to get in there before all the good ones get taken. Go on a date again.'

Maisie takes the plate of bread from her mum's hands and kisses her cheek. 'And don't mess it all up by saying you've got a daughter. I know that's a buzzkill. Get them hooked first, and then drop the clanger that is me.'

'Begin with a lot of lying?'

'That's how online dating works! A lot of small lies, big exaggerations and some massive omissions, like: *I've got a teenage daughter*.'

'And when I bring them over?'

'Say I'm the maid.'

Becky laughs now, right from the gut. It feels like it has set off chemicals through her brain and soul.

'I'm just saying, you don't always need to be so honest from, like, the first minute.'

'Thanks for the advice,' Becky says. 'You're too wise.'

'So.' Maisie picks up a slice of bread and for a moment gets distracted by some sticky blackcurrants tumbling off the side. 'I've given you excellent advice, cheered you up . . . quid pro quo.'

Becky knows exactly what's coming and she can't help it but she laughs again – all that confidence and persistence Maisie has. Armour against the bad things that will surely happen to her.

'So can I go to the sleepover?'

'Where is it?' Becky leans against the kitchen cupboard and folds her arms, smiling.

'Not far. Islington.'

'Whose house?'

'Jules' house. Lily and Eva are going as well.' Maisie is braiding a long section of hair now, eyes focused on her work and evading her mother's searching gaze.

'Is Jules a boy or a girl?'

'He's a boy from school.'

'Is he someone's boyfriend?'

'Lily likes him.'

'And who does Jules like?'

'Oh my God. This isn't healthy. You need to be dating.'

'Don't avoid the question.'

For a moment Maisie looks like she's going to sulk like she used to when she was five or six. But perhaps sensing there is a battle still worth winning, she finds a way to let it go.

'I think he likes me.'

'And what do you think?'

'I think Lily's one of my best friends.'

'Could be quite a complicated evening.'

'Not really.'

'Can we talk about drugs?'

'I'm not selling you drugs. You have to stop asking me, Mum.'

'Are you going to do drugs?'

'Do you mean, when I'm trying to get another scholarship am I going to wreck my *cerebellum* for the sake of what the kids are calling "a high"?'

It's not what Becky means. She wants to ask: *Will anyone drug you? Will you lose your sense of who you are? What if you're attacked? Will you be unsafe? Who will prey on you?* But instead she says:

'Yes.'

'I'll have some wine and maybe a smoke but that's it. I'm not really up for getting expelled.'

Maisie's school is beautiful to look at, expensive to attend, and prides itself on a newly strict drugs policy brought in after a sixth-former got caught dealing coke to fifth years. It is a red-brick and sandstone confection of buildings with soaring arches and narrow windows and turrets curled skyward, like an Oxford college. There are playing fields for rugby and hockey, where a fete is held every summer. Every day there are three hot options for lunch, three cold, plus an extensive salad bar including vegan, dairy-free and gluten-free choices. Maisie is there on a full scholarship and, even so, the annual bill for uniform and extracurricular classes and school trips leaves Becky swearing in disbelief and saying things she never thought would come out of her mouth, like 'There has to be a cheaper way to play lacrosse.'

Becky always feels the gulf between her and other parents, but Maisie seems not to notice it.

The last time Becky went to a parents' evening at the school, someone mistook her for a sixth-former and asked her for directions.

Ding, Siobhan: Brace, brace

'Mum, can I? I'll have my own room. Jules is going to sleep in a different room.'

'I don't care whether he sleeps in Glasgow.'

'His parents will be there. You can call his mum if you want to discuss my revision schedule with her.' The veer into acid sarcasm. The assumption of disappointment. 'Mum, come on, I'll be the odd one out if I have to say my *mummy* won't let me go.'

Siobhan, ding. Where are you? Seriously, BRACE.

'Oh for fuck sake, Siobhan, I'm coming,' Becky shouts at her phone.

Maisie is startled.

'I have to shower,' says Becky to Maisie. 'I'll talk to Adam about the sleepover.'

She wants to be bold and brave, a pirate queen of a mother who encourages her daughter to take risks and trust her friends and strike out for the horizon set on gathering experiences. But every map marks monsters where the known lands end, and how can Becky be there to unwrap every tentacle, to declaw and defang, to empty the new world of snakes and sharks so that her daughter can wander through it, imagining her own courage, but never having to test it?

Chapter 5

Hampstead, London
13 September 2003

Mary whoops a greeting to someone Becky has never met before which sends a curious surge of panic and betrayal through her: did Mary mislead her when she said that she didn't know *that* many people going to this party? This is Hampstead, populated by a lot of North London private school kids. These are not their people, but Mary doesn't seem to know that.

Everything around her feels too big, too wide, too loud or too high: oversized drum and bass beats tumble out of the amps, there are paintings on the wall bigger than her fridge and a curling staircase worthy of a stage set. A vase on a plinth: Becky has no idea of how to exist in the same space as a plinth, and then it occurs to her that perhaps the truth of it is that none of these things are too grand or too big. Rather she in fact is too lowly and too small – which is an irony, a conundrum, a conflict, a terrible clash in her mind, because when Becky looks around she knows she is far from small. She is, without doubt, the tallest girl there. She is always the tallest girl everywhere, never feeling as imposing as she knows she looks.

A girl with a tiny waist, goth-black hair and electric-pink lipstick turns to Mary and says in the sweetest sing-song voice that she loves her dress. Then Mary yammers on about the shop she bought it at and just like that the two of them are friends, moving on to name all the people they might have in common. Becky doesn't quite catch every word and instead she just hovers and watches – watches how Mary's confidence shines from inside her like a disco ball. She wants to stop time and take Mary aside and ask her flat out: *How do you do it? How do you draw people to you like that?*

Soon Mary and Becky are the girls hanging out with a group of five boys. The boys' voices are louder than the girls' and their volume makes Becky feel like they have more to say, even though there are times she listens to their name-calling and football scores and feels like this assumption might not prove true, in the cold light of day. There is, she notices, an asymmetry to every conversation. Mary always says things to get Brendan to listen to her, and Brendan wants his friends to laugh at his jokes. Becky soon realizes that the best things she could say will be things that are funny or interesting, making her a cool friend, or to tell stories that cast Mary in a favourable light. This realization makes it hard to say anything at all, so she settles for watching things play out.

Mary has been friends with Brendan a long time and

in the last year Brendan's currency has begun to rise, what with his new haircut (short at the back and a forelock at the front which he is able to jerk away from his eyes without having to touch it) and a subtle yet clear change in his choice of clothes (bomber jacket especially appealing). Mary has decided to explore the possibility that she and Brendan could be more than just friends. Tonight is about edging further in his direction while at the same time not having to make that attempt solo.

Becky is her Sherpa. There to hold the luggage when Mary summits.

It's not that Becky doesn't enjoy being part of this group of people who are increasingly the subject of scrutiny, what with their nice haircuts and confidence and how together they look like a sort of rock band. But there is a limit to how *other* Becky is prepared to become. She knows she isn't girly and bubbly and entertaining, nor quite loud enough or tomboy enough or confident enough to be one of the lads. What then, does she bring to the party?

'You look hot,' Brendan says, and Becky is so caught up in her thoughts that she thinks he is talking to someone else. He is wearing black jeans and DM boots and a black 'Lemonheads' T-shirt. He jerks his hair clear of his face: there is something oddly flattering about the gesture, thinks Becky, like he can be bothered to clear the path for a conversation with *her*.

She realizes that Brendan has said these words too loudly, in earshot of the other boys – almost as if he needed one of them to hear him say it more than he wanted Becky to hear it. Is this how it's done? Showing the world what you mean to do before you do it. Is this what confident boys do?

Very quietly she says, 'Thank you.'

Brendan then turns away to talk to someone else and Becky knows that her subdued response hasn't given him enough to get his teeth into. She has failed a personality test that she hadn't chosen to take. Will he tell Mary? Will she laugh? What did he mean by it anyway? Was he just trying to be nice? Is *hot* a word that he uses ten times a day, for anyone, meaning anything?

Becky feels light-headed. She hasn't eaten since lunch because her jeans don't allow for anything other than a flat and therefore empty stomach, but until she can track down some booze to numb the hunger pangs, a cigarette will have to do. She slides one out of the box, suddenly feeling grateful for an action that allows her to bow her head and hide from Brendan and the rest of the room for a moment. She sparks it up, lighter metal scuffing her sore thumb pad, the smoke hitting the back of her throat. The unwelcome taste of coal. But she inhales deeply anyway, elbows bent in at the waist, one forearm slung protectively across her middle, watching Mary talk to the pink-lipsticked girl. The combination of nicotine and hunger is making her feel nauseous. Vomiting on the floor in front of everyone would be totally mortifying but at least it would give her a legitimate excuse to go home.

'Having a shit time yet?'

She turns to find the speaker leaning back on the same bit of wall as her, grinning. Just the sight of Adam's sweet smile and the radically diminished size of his otherwise egg-large eyes under the thick-lens glasses makes her feel instantly better. He is wearing a woollen sleeveless jumper, like he does whatever the weather, and the collar of his shirt is thin and un-ironed and poking out of the top. He is skinny and into computer programs and indie rock and there isn't anyone else at their school much like him. Most boys at their school wear the same brand of everything, making choosing a different colour their sole mark of personality.

'Sight for sore eyes and all that,' he says.

'And you. That's a particularly thin collar you're wearing this evening. I assume you're on the pull?'

'That's a particularly large number of necklaces around your neck. Selling them for spare change?'

'Bitch,' she says, and they both laugh. 'Seriously, why didn't you tell me you were coming to this thing? You knew I was.'

'Thought I'd leave you dangling over the abyss.'

'The abyss sucks.'

'Well here I am now. Massive party times.' He says it deadpan and she laughs.

'Who do you know here?'

'Who *don't* I know.'

'Seriously?'

'Natalie. We used to go in the paddling pool together. When we were five.'

'And you swapped digits and stayed in touch?'

'Actually we are still mates. She's a gamer.'

'Adam, you can't use that word any more. She's a *homosexual*.'

'Well played, Shawcross. Got the gay/gamer gag in before midnight. Who did you come with?'

'Mary.'

'Yeah, I mean who does Mary know?'

'A guy called Brendan.'

'That prick?' Adam nods toward Brendan, who is finding it a challenge to add an extra turn-up to the bottom of his jeans because his hair keeps getting in the way. 'I don't know why she bothers.'

'You're just jealous.'

She says it as a joke but a shadow passes across Adam's face before his face breaks into a smile. 'Yeah, you're right. I want the floppy hair but sadly mine stays out of my eyes on its own.'

'You can get hair products that'll make sure it stays in your eyes.'

'I've tried them all. They do nothing for me.'

Adam offers her a drink from a clear glass bottle. Becky sniffs it suspiciously.

'It's a bit of everything. A mongrel spirit, like myself.'

'I'll try anything once.'

Becky takes a swig, and then another. Any hunger,

46

nausea and nerves dissolve like sugar in hot tea and soon she is smiling at Adam, thank God for Adam, feeling warmer, better, looser, so much more herself.

'Technically you're trying everything once, when you drink that,' he says.

'Did you put that orange one in there?' She feels her fingers tingle and her spirits lift a little higher so she drinks more of this disgusting, glorious, magical medicine.

'If it was in my mum's cabinet, I decanted it.'

'That's genuinely the worst cocktail I've ever tried.'

'That's crushing, given you only usually drink in London's finest cocktail bars. Another swallow? Go wild.'

'I probably shouldn't drink too much more. I said I'd take a pill with Mary.'

'Oh my God, you're so cool.'

'Don't be judgy.'

'No, really, Becky. I was going to go home early but now I want to see you do the special MDMA dancing.'

'Thank you for your support.'

'Always.'

'Do you want to do it with us?'

'Obviously I'd join you if it didn't mean associating myself with a group of people that look like a manufactured popular music band.'

'Popular music? Your snobbery knows no bounds. Anyway, Brendan's wearing a Lemonheads T-shirt. You two might completely love each other if you got to know each other.'

'That's my greatest fear of doing pills.'

'Not dehydrating and dying?'

'That'd be fine. But, no, it's telling Brendan he's *actually a really great guy*. Chills me to the core.'

Becky laughs again. They smile at each other, Adam holding her gaze a split second too long. Not long enough to necessarily interpret as anything more than a minor rest in their conversation, but also not short enough to be entirely sure that this is what's going on. It happens between them sometimes. But it's OK. It's acceptable. Largely ignorable.

He breaks the spell with a change in smile. 'You'll be fine. Just keep the ambulance on speed dial. *Ciao* and all that.' He swings on his heel to leave her.

'Wait,' she says. 'How about a movie night next week? *Back to the Future*, popcorn, I can smuggle some beers from my dad. My house?'

'Sure,' he says, without turning round. 'That would be fine. Enjoy the party and . . . just be careful none of them miss their footing and fall on you. Those are some beefy public school types you're hanging out with now. Scrum down, Shawcross.'

Becky finds some beers on a side table, gets drunk, and watches other people get drunk. She grasps her bottle and tells herself that she can see how alcohol floods the systems of the people around her, making their movements looser, sloppier and more animated. One girl slams her palms against the chest of a boy far taller than her and although she looks angry and sad, he is laughing as he tries to bring her round to his way of thinking. He draws her to him and she thumps his chest with her fists until she gives up and curls into him, laughing.

A girl with corkscrew hair sways and gyrates like no one is watching, or something like that. Becky feels both embarrassed and jealous, watching her dance like she is at a warehouse rave, weaving her arms in between strips of blue and green light.

Mary is talking to Brendan who is standing over her – his arm positioned in a way that makes it look like he is bolstering the wall, as if he is as essential as a ceiling joist. Mary is waving her hands, clearly telling a story that means absolutely everything to her, and she is delighted, in her element, because Brendan is looking at her and laughing and no doubt appreciating her pretty Irish eyes.

As if she hadn't already known it, this confirms everything for Becky. Soon it is extremely unlikely that she will see Mary for the rest of the night. Despite all their promises it isn't practical for them to do everything together. They are not Siamese twins. Mary is fun, which is why she is laughing with a boy she really likes. Becky is more introverted, harder to like, she thinks. It occurs to Becky that after tonight Mary may not in fact need her around any more. Having played her role as wingman she will be made redundant, a needless adjunct once Brendan is at the heart of Mary's life. And then where will Becky belong?

It is no good for Becky to have these thoughts – not at this party, in this house where she doesn't know anyone. But what can she do? She can't afford a cab home on her own. Should she find a corner and try to sleep?

She lights another cigarette as Mary walks out of the room holding Brendan's hand.

How embarrassing to feel so sad about something so small, a friend going off with a boy. Instead of what?

She wonders about the night bus. She can afford that. What's the route? And can she bear it, drunk and alone and, yes, quite close to crying now?

She feels a hand at her back and a pathetic sense of gratitude rises in her that someone wants to talk.

'Hey,' Scott says.

He is tall, blond, good-looking. A friend of Brendan's. Not quite in his group but not out of it either. One of those people who move around and seem to know how to get along with everyone.

'There's a game of Spin the Bottle going on upstairs. Mary and Brendan sent me to get you. We've got all the "stuff" up there.'

'Spin the Bottle?'

'Yeah, it's retro. No obligations. You could just do a pill.'

'What if the bottle says I have to do heroin?'

He doesn't get her joke fast enough to laugh at it. She wishes she could take it back.

'So do you want to come?'

Suddenly she knows that, more than anything, she is fed up with standing here with her thoughts. She wants to climb out of her head and have some fun.

This will fill some hours.

To think that she could have chosen the arduous night bus journey. The chances are she'd have made it home uncomfortable and tired, but safe and sound and awake enough the next day to enjoy her mum's Sunday roast. But then again, she could also have fallen asleep on the top deck and found herself at the depot miles from anywhere, lost and vulnerable.

Followed home.

Or worse.

As it is, she stays at the party. She drains her beer bottle to its last tasteless drop, looks at Scott and tells him, 'I'm game.'

Chapter 6

The sky is blue in Soho this morning, and the sun casts a clear clean light across a street lined with fabric shops, one after the other, their fronts thrown open and piled high with rolls of cotton and acrylic, satin and lace. The food stalls are still skeletons, too early to be stacked with vats, rolls and wraps for the lunchtime crowd. Soho's entertainment village is populated by film execs whose heads are full of the edit, TV producers whose minds are bending with budget cuts and the interns in Converse and skinny jeans feeling so hashtag-blessed.

Becky kicks through a messy pile of plane tree bark and fuzz balls on the pavement outside the office, a red-brick townhouse on a square just south of tourist-choked Oxford Street. Her tired eyes itch with pollen and pollution, her nerves still jangling after Maisie's disgruntled departure for the school bus.

Over the years she has worked for Matthew, she has perfected the art of placating him, knowing whether his grumps are down to hunger or thirst or aggravation with a bullish agent who is fighting for more money and more rights. She takes satisfaction in the feeling that she is somehow unique, being both soother and gatekeeper for a man as special as he. But being the cause of Matthew's problems? That's new to her.

How will he raise it with her? 'Last night, as I was shagging a young woman on my rug . . .?' Will he take her aside and say they like rough sex? What is the etiquette here?

Siobhan is standing at the bottom of the staircase ready to greet her, clasping a telephone in each hand. 'Am I glad to see you? Yes, I am,' she says. 'He's been on my back and now he's locked himself in his office again and I've got about forty things that need his attention. I'm going to make him an extra-milky coffee and slip a beta blocker in there.'

Becky likes to think that Siobhan is still mostly pleased for her about *Medea* going on the slate, because they went to the pub a few days after it happened and drank too many pints and Siobhan proposed a toast of congratulation before going on to say how much she needed to change her life so she didn't feel such a failure. She came in with white-blonde hair the next day and that seemed to settle it.

One floor up, their office is painted white, with a little exposed brickwork to lend texture, and a nice long-leafed palm all tangled in fairy lights at the entrance to the fireplace, done for Christmas one year and then left because Matthew liked it. Only three of them are full-time but many more desks stand ready for production requirements. One such desk serves as a surface for stacked scripts and another as a place to lay out headshots of potential cast: long necks, long hair, high cheekbones, big eyes, soulful looks.

Matthew's own office at the end of the floor is screened with glass walls and blinds. Becky looks at it anxiously. Matthew is inside it.

Siobhan grabs the phone on her desk before the door to the stairs has even swung shut. 'David, I'm sorry, I did tell him you'd called. Yes, yes, I know . . . hold on.' She presses her hand to the receiver. 'It's David Barraclough from Total Agents. Matthew's been avoiding this call all morning. David is like, *fever* pitch angry.'

'Really? But he's so nice.'

DB, they call him: the linen-suited, salt-and-pepper-haired agent to a scrolling list of A-list actors whose careers he has launched and whose offspring he later calls godchildren. Becky recently took him for lunch at a tapas restaurant on Dean Street to discuss *Medea* casting ideas over half a carafe of red, chorizo and squid which she only occasionally sipped and picked at while he did most of the talking. He told lots of stories, some about the days he and Matthew were junior agents together, and she had encouraged it all by laughing along. Their lunch finished without any real business done but with DB feeling the warm fuzz of having been listened to, and that was everything that lunch needed to achieve. A success, by all accounts.

Siobhan throws up a hand as the voice on the end of the line rants on.

'Hand it over, I'll give it a go.' Becky takes the phone from her, smiling. 'Hello, DB! It's Becky. I'm so sorry you're having to chase Matthew. It's crazy with Cannes at the moment. Is it anything I can help with?'

'He *needs* to call me.'

'He definitely will. And while I have you, in terms of *Medea* I think we're closing in on our lead actress. Hoping to pin her down at Cannes, and then we'll have someone for your men to cast against. You'll be top of the list, of course.'

'Matthew knows what I'm calling about. Tell him to stop avoiding my calls and get him on the phone to me.'

He hangs up and Becky holds out the receiver. She feels ants under her skin – scared, perhaps, that she may have somehow made things worse.

'What's that about?' Becky says to Siobhan.

'I dunno but he's having a bad day about something. Maybe one of Matthew's little lies about shooting schedules caught up with him. So anyway, listen to this. I emailed a new idea to Matthew over the weekend.'

Something feels off. It's a small office and they are all aware of which calls need avoiding, delaying or returning within the hour. Aware of any conflict over contracts, pressure on production, egos, fallings-out, ground to be made up . . . And DB and Matthew have never had a falling-out before. At least not as long as she has worked there.

'So it's kind of *Beaches* but funnier, but really more like *The Hangover* only sadder, with really upbeat yet emotional music, actually probably more like if *Watership Down* was actually happy?'

'Sounds good.' Becky is biting her fingernails, one so much it stings.

'Two female leads so, you know, on trend, pretty topical. I'm thinking Aniston. Go big, or go home. And then I'm thinking Emilia Cosvelinos. More classical, but she is bankable now with the Scorsese film coming out and I think she'll add real weight to the crying scenes. What do you think?'

'Sounds great.'

Becky has barely been listening, but Siobhan's face fills with sunshine and she claps her hands together. 'Exactly!'

At that moment, Matthew opens the door to his office and waves them in. 'Let's get started.' The volume of his voice makes Becky jump and her heart shudders with the thought that *this is it, the end*.

The two of them take their places on the olive velvet sofa opposite Matthew's desk, so low that he appears to be on a raised stage looking down at them. His office smells so faintly of whisky that it might not be whisky at all. And coffee, drying in the heat, at the bottom of the cup. The smell of the place, the way it looks, it could be a normal morning at the office, the stage set for the start of business: windows closed, blinds pulled down over the glass walls in preparation for a private meeting, books straightened and arranged in the cases so they descend in shapes like flights of steps. Apart from his computer, he keeps an entirely clean desk: blade, fineliner pens in one drawer, pending contracts in another. Scripts piled into a cupboard, titles inked onto their spines. Everything must have its place: stacked, stored, tidied and hidden away.

'Travel arrangements for Cannes,' he says.

Is this how he's going to do it? Work through the list towards her? Siobhan rattles off flight names and departure times.

'Calls,' he says.

'DB called again,' says Siobhan. 'He sounds fucked-off.'

'Thank you. Noted.' The subject is closed.

'He's called five times,' says Siobhan.

'And he can call again, if he likes. I'll speak to him when I get round to it.'

Siobhan tucks the borders of her script outline neatly behind her notepad but recovers quickly, saying, 'Did you manage to get to the Deal cottage this weekend?' because this is always her strategy for deflecting the energy from a conversation that has caused him stress, like telling a child to think of nice things like beaches and sweets before they go to sleep at night.

Matthew is studying something intensely on his phone, glasses balanced at the end of his nose. He doesn't reply immediately but when he does he says, 'Yes. The weather was lovely. The jasmine is out.'

His gaze is nowhere near Becky. It is dissociated, disinterested, so far from her that she might not be there at all . . .

He looks up at her suddenly, as if he's sensed the beam of her thoughts on him – his brow still furrowed, his eyes narrowed. He takes a deep breath and reorientates himself by saying, 'Tux?'

'Waiting for you at the hotel,' Becky says, laying down the order confirmation sheet in front of him.

'Accreditation passes?'

'Waiting for you at the hotel,' says Siobhan.

'Good,' he says. 'Becky, have you got yours? You'll need them for all screenings and parties.'

'Yes,' says Becky, looking away from Siobhan instinctively, feeling uncomfortable that she is the one who gets to go to the ball.

'Have you confirmed all our meetings with the actors tomorrow? You should get Jenifer Palmer and Sarah Pastor on the list. Both look the part.'

'Yes, all set.'

'On which note,' says Siobhan, more quietly than usual, 'I just wondered whether you'd had a chance to look at my film idea so you can, I don't know, maybe give it to someone you know who might be visiting the festival and might sort of like it?'

'It's interesting,' he says, which Becky knows means it's not interesting *enough*, but before the conversation can progress further his mobile rings and without looking at either of them he waves them out of the office like he is directing traffic. He waits for them to step outside before he answers.

Becky is the last to leave. She hears him say, 'Yes, David.'

The two wait outside. Siobhan sat at her desk, Becky perched on the edge, waiting to be called back in.

'Fuck, he's in such a bad mood.' The door buzzes and Siobhan picks up on speaker, '*Bonjour?*'

'Siobhan, it's Antonia, can you let me in?'

'Er, sure.' Siobhan presses the buzzer and looks at Becky, shrugging.

Antonia sometimes calls the office more times in one day than she does her own child (a tall and gawky boy called Bart) and Becky knows this because Antonia tells her this. She calls Becky to co-ordinate stuff or just to remind her that she needs to usher Matthew out of the office on time because they are popping down to the Deal cottage for the weekend and want to miss the worst of the weekend traffic. Antonia gets Pucci scarves and spa weekends for her birthday from Matthew that have been researched and paid for on his credit card, by Becky, and Antonia knows this because Becky needs to check in advance that Antonia doesn't have allergic skin reactions to mud wraps and whether she – discreetly, of course – would like Becky to secure her an appointment with that special Botox man everyone always raves about.

Antonia enters the room in a cloud of expensive perfume. Her black and silver hair is tangled in a bun and strands have escaped everywhere. The shape it makes, tested through time to work with the curve of her face, is both messy and yet impossibly stylish. Her hairstyle works with the linen dress (a tailored and loose cut, only a few crumples) which in turn works with her leather sandals (one gold strip across the place where fine foot bones fan) and buffed sandstone calves. She is expensive and lovely and perfectly curated for a warm spring day.

She is also, most definitely, feeling harassed. Her face is drawn and her words quick. 'Becky. Siobhan. Where is he? He's not picking up the phone to me.'

Becky answers. 'He's in his office. On a call. Won't be long. Can I make you a coffee while you wait?'

'No, thank you, I need to talk to him.'

'I don't think he'll be long.'

'I mean now.'

Becky feels an instinctive need to give Matthew the space and privacy for his call with DB. It's what she's paid to do. But Antonia is glaring at her.

'OK, sure,' she says. 'Let me pop in and get him off the phone.'

Becky moves quickly, perhaps to get ahead of anything Antonia might be planning on doing, like bursting into the office. She pushes Matthew's door open and hears the words, 'She misinterpreted that. That's not what happened at all.'

He looks up, cheeks flushed a deep pink.

Becky just has time to mouth the word 'Antonia' and for Matthew's face to arrange itself in a way that Becky has never seen before. Something almost childish: both beseeching and perturbed. But before she has a chance to enquire, Antonia moves past her. 'Thank you, Becky. I'll take it from here. What the fuck are you playing at? In our house?'

Becky backs out quickly and sees the door is shut firmly behind her.

Siobhan whistles through her teeth like a bomb flying through the air. Then for a short time they listen to Antonia and Matthew's raised voices behind the door, nothing distinct enough for them to understand exactly what the argument is about but enough for it to become clear to Becky that it might concern the woman on the floor of their well-appointed kitchen.

Becky fights the urge to cower under her own arms as if that were protection enough from the explosion that will surely come. And, as the net of aggravated people surrounding Matthew widens, Becky fears he will take his frustration out on her by frog-marching her out of the office saying she stepped over one too many boundaries. She saw him part-stripped of his clothes in his own home and part-stripped of his dignity and composure in the office and it's too hard to maintain a professional façade after that kind of thing.

Becky finds herself googling her boss's name, wanting to know the identity of the woman getting between such a couple.

She feels afraid of what might happen next and yet also relieved that someone other than her knows about the woman on the kitchen floor. Surely Becky can afford to forget what she saw now that it's clearly just business between husband and wife?

She takes hold of her own wrist, lightly, instinctively, and bends the joint at small angles, back and forth, back and forth so that it aches a little.

Antonia leaves very suddenly and in silence.

Matthew appears in the doorway of his office.

'Where were we?' he says. 'Siobhan. Yes. Your film outline. The idea doesn't hold together. It's muddled. But that casting idea you had. Emilia Cosvelinos?'

'Yes?' Siobhan's eyes brighten with hope.

'She's a great idea for Becky's film. She'll be in Cannes promoting her Scorsese movie, we should get a breakfast booked in with her. I'm mates with the agent. I'll put the call in. He'll go out to bat for us if Emilia bites – but she won't bite unless it's fucking irresistible and if the Scorsese film's as good as everyone's saying it is, then she'll want an Oscar for whatever she does next. It's worth a shot.'

Becky squirms with discomfort. 'Mightn't it be better if you pitched it to her, Matthew?' she says, trying to put some space between her and what is happening. 'As your idea. I mean, you've won Oscars for actresses—'

'No. I like the project. But you love it. It's your baby. That goes a long way with actors. Pitch her like you pitched me and you'll do fine. Right, that's it. Siobhan, can you get our man from IcePR on the line.' It's not a request. 'I need to speak with him as soon as possible. Tell him it's urgent.'

Matthew used to be in PR. Telling a story, spinning a story, knowing when to take the heat off one character and put it on another: such a transferrable skillset for the film industry.

'I'll call him right away,' Siobhan says quietly.

Becky's house is on the way to City Airport so she plans a quick trip home to collect her things. She arrives to the sweet, steamy scent of pancakes on the skillet. It is the food that Maisie and Adam make together every time he comes to stay, their most enduring ritual. They mix it up in terms of the recipe – made extra fluffy with egg whites, coconut and banana added, criss-crossed with candied bacon – but always they have pancakes.

Adam's chocolate-coloured leather weekend bag has been dumped at the top of the stairs next to a pair of unlaced Campers, worn in and bashed up to the perfect fit and level of comfort. She can hear Maisie and Adam talking in the kitchen, giggling their way through the rambling conversations they specialize in. Adam and Maisie are masters of mimicry together: if Adam is Kermit, Maisie will reach for her best Miss Piggy. Neither of them would ever say it, but clearly they don't like it if Becky tries to join in. So that's become the tacit rule when they're all together. Becky speaks with just the one voice; Adam and Maisie are multitudes.

She doesn't have long to get her things and catch her flight, but she still takes a moment to enjoy the sound they make together, then peeks in to see that Maisie is back in her pyjamas, school done with. Right now she is moving photographs around the surface of their fridge, like pieces of a jigsaw. Every few weeks she takes new photos, prints and sticks them here, leaving only a loyal few old-timers by the handle. A faded colour one of her being bathed as a baby in the kitchen sink at the Hounslow house, just before the two of them moved with Becky's mum. Another favoured photo is of the three of them together, Becky and Adam standing at either end of a low mossy log while ten-year-old Maisie steps along using a stick for balance, her great high-wire act.

Adam tips batter from a metal bowl into the frying pan.

'Is there one for me?'

Adam's face lights up when he sees Becky, and that's a lovely thing. Not for the first time the thought rushes in: how might it be to be smiled at that way every night? To come home, kick off your shoes, and for there already to be conversation in the kitchen and somebody else taking care of dinner?

'These are genuine buttermilk pancakes,' he says. 'How many d'you want?'

'They're an eight,' adds Maisie. They started ranking pancakes five years ago. To begin with they had a log book, but while that's long since been abandoned, the need to allocate marks has endured.

'Just the one, please.'

Adam may have aged – of course he must have – but to Becky his face is the same now as it was at school. Kind, curious and easy to read despite his efforts. His buttoned-up skinny-fit shirts give the impression of him being a well-turned-out kind of guy, but she knows the cupboards and drawers of his Shoreditch apartment are total chaos. His jeans, like his face, are unchanging, always bought from the same website in the same size, same shade of indigo, a replacement sought once the old pair has faded and thinned at the knees. He's as loyal to his jeans as his friends.

'Adam dumped Brooke,' chirps Maisie. 'She offered to get the cover of his favourite magazine, *Men's Health*, tattooed onto her back to try to make him love her.'

Adam erupts into laughter. '*Men's Health* isn't my favourite magazine!'

'She got as far as inking the title across her shoulder blades.'

'Sorry to hear that,' Becky says.

'About what? Brooke's shoulders?' Maisie loves being in the middle of any conversation when they are all together. She's grown up that way, thinks Becky. It might have done her good to have a sibling. And then she thinks, it's not too late for her to have a sibling, is it? Becky's only thirty-two after all so there's still plenty of time, a decade perhaps . . . And then she has to remind herself to put those thoughts down and concentrate on what's in front of her. A pancake bubbling over heat. A plane to catch.

'How did you do it?' demands Maisie. 'Gory details. Come on.'

'I don't find break-ups easy . . .' Adam blushes.

'No one does but come on, she was planning your interiors. You had to pull the trigger.'

'I didn't really read that as a sign she might want to stay,' he says. 'I thought it was handy because, you know, she had good taste. I thought she enjoyed picking out blinds.'

Maisie slaps her forehead in delighted disbelief.

'Was she American, with a name like Brooke?' asks Becky.

'Tell her the surname!' crows Maisie. 'What was her surname, Dad?'

'Waters,' says Adam, sheepish, as if he'd named her himself.

'Brooke Waters!' howls Maisie. 'Damn, girl! Headline for the week: Adam's Waters broke.'

'Hey, Maisie,' says Adam. 'Can you go into my bag and grab the blueberries I bought?'

'Yep, I'll be a minute OK? Got to get sorted for tonight first.' She takes a few steps toward Becky and pecks her on the cheek. 'You're amazing, my hero, I totally love you.' Then she wanders out, answering her phone on the way.

'Thanks for keeping an eye on her tonight. I appreciate it.' Becky stifles a yawn and looks round the kitchen trying to remember where she put her travel-sized sun cream.

'What stuff is she getting sorted? Are you guys doing something fun tonight? Bowling . . .'

'Well no,' Adam looks up, perplexed. 'The sleepover?'

'At Jules' house? I told her she couldn't go to that until we'd discussed it.'

'Oh, I'm sorry, I thought you'd . . . the way it . . .'

Becky's chest tightens. 'I said no to her.' Her whole body is tense now. 'She's playing us off against each other, Adam, she—'

'Hold on a minute,' he says. 'When she said there was a sleepover I asked her questions like who's there, what time are you going. I suppose I assumed she was already going . . . we were talking about other things at the same time: hash-browns and climbing walls.' The two of them do go off on tangents. 'I can't quite remember how the conversation went but it's possible she thought we'd already spoken.'

Becky is a combination of anxious and irritated. 'Why did you assume anything? Didn't you think I might have some concerns about her staying at a stranger's house?'

'It's not that, the last thing I wanted to do was . . . I just thought you'd made a call on it already because, well, honestly? It all sounds fine to me.'

'But I've never met this guy . . . Jules, or whatever. What if . . .'

'I have.'

'You have?'

'Yes, he's nice. He's sweet. Totally unthreatening. I'd be

67

more worried about him. He looks malnourished: Maisie could take him down in five seconds flat.'

There is a silence as Adam watches Becky's fingers flick over her cuticles in quick and silent clicks then dart to the silk skin on her wrist and back again. He knows what she's thinking.

'She's a sensible kid, Becky,' he says eventually.

'I know that. But I was a sensible kid before that night in the Hampstead house.'

'That was different. You were . . . no one could have predicted . . . This is so different. Sober school night, parents down the corridor, the girls sharing a room. It's not a party, they won't even be drinking. It's all good, I honestly think it's all good.'

But he sees from her expression that she's not convinced and so he continues, 'She's growing up quickly. If we box her away from what everyone else is doing she'll do it anyway and then won't tell us about it.' Becky bows her head. Knows he's right. 'We have to trust her.' He's sweet to put it that way when what he means is that *Becky* is the one that must trust.

'It's not Maisie I don't trust. It's other people.'

'So let's make Jules wear a monitoring device?' says Adam brightly, hauling them both back into the present. 'With the capacity to shock him remotely?'

'You really think he's OK?'

'He's passionate about the polar ice caps and Dinosaur Junior. That makes him more than fine. Come on.' He reaches out for her hand and then lets his arm fall by his side.

'OK, OK, fine.'

He smiles. 'I think it's a good decision. For all of us.'

By *us* he means Becky. Good for her to let go, is what he means. Becky feels her stomach unknot with the feeling that Adam is the net under her tight-rope.

'Right,' she says. 'I think the spare room is all made up . . .'

'That's OK, I won't need it,' says Adam casually, 'I'll go to poker if Maisie's going to be out.'

Becky turns to face him, her stomach knotting all over again. 'Where?'

'Pete's new place in Ladbroke Grove?'

She wouldn't dream of travelling to the opposite side of London in the same situation. She'd get on with stuff at home to quell the anxiety that her daughter was staying in a house she had never before visited, as if knowing the colour of the wallpaper would somehow make Maisie safer. Becky would potter about, phone in her back pocket, just in case Maisie needed to speak to her.

As it is, Becky will be in France and Adam will be in West London. Her jaw tightens. Did he tell Maisie she could go to the sleepover so he'd be free to play poker with his mates? She banishes the thought. It's not useful. He's doing her a favour by being on call; what do they call it, *in loco parentis*?

'But what if something happens?' she says. 'And she

needs to come home and you're not here? It'll take you ages to get to her.'

Adam turns to her, smiling. 'Lily's mum is at the house and Zee can always call me.'

Part of her is scalded with panic: by that time, it will be too late to save Maisie from whatever has happened. And yet another part of her knows that what he's saying is entirely reasonable. If only she were able to feel the same reasoning in her bones, just a fraction of his confidence, an iota of his assurance. She wishes she was more like him.

'OK,' she says quietly. 'OK then.'

'I'll fix that shelf in the hall before I go,' he says, 'then the shelf gets to have a good night too.'

'Thank you,' she says, trying a smile. 'And please, keep your phone on and close to you?'

'Of course I will. And I'll be here when she comes home from school tomorrow. Come on,' he winks. 'This really is fine. Go and have some fun in Cannes.'

Maisie lopes back into the kitchen holding a box of blueberries in one hand and an over-stuffed rucksack in the other.

Too late for Becky to change her mind now, she holds onto her daughter tightly and silently prays for her safety.

'Be asleep by midnight,' she says. 'You've got school. And you can call your dad if there are any problems. Or me. I'll have my phone with me in Cannes. WhatsApp, text, a call, it will all work . . .'

'Yes, yes,' she says quickly, and turns to face Adam. 'You guys are the best.'

She catches the intense concentration and joy in Adam's eyes as he flips a pancake onto her plate: the pleasure of a job well done for the people he most loves. So she can't ask him for everything she might want, and he might not do everything exactly like her, but she feels so lucky for what she has. Things might have spiralled into a row without him there, with Maisie not feeling listened to and Becky the baddie, the mother who fails to trust her daughter.

Adam is her compass. Her confirmation person, her Call in Case of Emergency man. The man her daughter calls Dad. Her best friend. Joint custodian of the great lie at the heart of her life.

Chapter 7

In the weeks after the party Becky can wake in the mornings and for a few moments feel as if she has come to consciousness in her normal, untouched life. But then she remembers the badness, and it fills her heart and mind to the brim. She overflows with it.

It becomes a struggle just to get out of bed.

At first, she gets away with some mornings at home, complaining of a virus and, later, the flu. She insists she doesn't need anything for it but her parents press paracetamol, tea and damp flannels in her direction. Weekends come and go but her usual trips to the pool are dropped and she can no longer countenance the bright and bouncy happiness of Saturday morning television presenters. She chooses to watch soaps instead, passively allowing their stories and characters to slide past her thoughts and feelings.

She hides her body in baggy clothes. She avoids the mirror, as if it might talk to her. She just wants to sleep.

After a fortnight of this her mum declares this period of

supposed ill health as having gone on 'far too long'. Becky is sent to a doctor who diagnoses glandular fever. This buys her another four months of staying in bed, watching television and avoiding food, until her mum begins to mistrust this diagnosis – having come from a generation that does not trust an illness with undefined edges and blurred duration and no brand-name pharmaceutical pill to cure it.

She insists on tests for Becky: blood and urine.

Becky goes to the GP surgery to get her results, alone. Just her and the doctor in his airless, disinfectant-scented, steel-and-chipped-Formica office. The words bend her reality. She thinks that she is losing her mind and that she is instead simply sitting in a maths lesson, studying a Venn diagram of symptoms for depression and pregnancy, looking where the circles bisect. Depression is the blue circle, pregnancy is the red circle, and there she is, all mixed up in the middle, as purple as a bruise.

Then, she cries a lot.

Time slips past her. The abortion clinic judges that she is well past twenty-four weeks pregnant. They offer to try to make an exception for her but they need to confer with their lawyers. She never goes back. She can't talk to anyone.

In the end, Adam is the first person she tells about what is growing inside her. He hasn't stopped coming round to her house, asking to see her, even though she always says no. Mary gave up weeks ago.

Adam holds her in his arms, asking nothing of her, simply being her friend.

Soon after, like it has been biding its time, waiting to be brought out into the open, the size and shape of Becky's body betrays her and she becomes the example to be avoided, the beaming red sign for how wrong things can go.

People give her a wide berth in the school corridor, like she's got a contagious illness.

Adam walks her to and from school and holds back her hair when she is sick on her shoes outside the school gates.

Sometimes he says that if she ever wants to talk, then he is there for her.

At home she eats very little and then goes straight to bed and watches television. It's easy at first, when her dad isn't talking to her and her mum is smoking a lot at the kitchen table. Becky just has to endure the times between when her dad makes tea and leaves the room, if she is in it, and the times he conveniently finishes eating as soon as she arrives at the table.

But it becomes less easy to shut herself away as her parents' responses grow more vocal and persistent, like a cancer metastasizing. Her father, in particular, who has spent a lifetime calling pop stars and actresses in short skirts 'harlots' and 'sluts', becomes consumed with the idea of his daughter having underage sex as a leisure pursuit. He fills with rage and shouts things like: *How could you be so irresponsible?* Becky finds this response particularly unjust and excruciatingly painful, sinking further into a kind of listless, inward blame – the very worst form of rage. As if it wasn't enough to watch her belly fill to the brim with her own shame, she has to add her father's to the mix as well.

Then come the endless stream of questions – questions that sound more like accusations: *Did it happen at home? In our home? How many of them have there been?*

They receive a congratulations card from a neighbour and a helium balloon printed with the words: *You're going to be grandparents!* Her father bursts it with the tip of a carving knife.

She stops going to school.

She can't read. She just wants to watch those soaps on television, to be held in the soft bubble of other people's mistakes, conflict and intrigues.

Her mum and dad stand in the doorway of her bedroom, faces pinched with anger. They ask her the same questions every day.

Who did this to you?

Who is its father?

Chapter 8

It had been a post on Scott's Instagram account that gave her the idea for her film.

Judging by his Twitter and Facebook, Scott had been in Birmingham for a weekend of clubbing and drinking with a friend of his. The next day he'd visited an art gallery in an attempt, he quipped in his caption, to experience more than the city's capacity to get you really drunk. LOL Scott. His favourite painting had been one of Medea, made by an artist called Frederick Sandys. He took a snap and posted it on Instagram. Just one more image in a cluster of his weekend shots.

Becky had been transfixed by it. Wreathed in red coral necklaces, with desperate eyes, and an obsessively incanting mouth, Medea looks away as she makes her poison. To where does she look? The hours ahead of her? To infamy and damnation?

Becky had lost a whole afternoon to it. Medea. Studying the image, reading the play's text. Some lines, over and over: *Here are the women with ancient anger in their veins.*

She obsessed over why this picture, of all the pictures in the gallery, had spoken to Scott: did he wonder if she, Becky, was still out there, coming for him some day? His own personal Medea, unstoppable in her rage. She had known within minutes that this character was one she needed to advocate for: in her research, she saw more meaning in Medea than she'd found in many years of therapy.

Her updated version would be a message to Scott that the consequence of what he did would never leave him, and a warning to men that their crimes against women, the injustice of their contempt for women, might be challenged. These men lacked her vision for pain. They could imagine her only as outcast and beaten, once they had no need for her. She was meant to be used, spent, and discarded.

But Medea would show them what power lies at the heart of rage.

These were some of the things Becky said to the screenwriter she hired and instructed to see what she saw.

Medea is Becky's conduit, her dark avatar, her brutish foot soldier. Her outrage, her violated body, her sorrow, her magnet for the smashed and long-dispersed pieces of her self.

She must not let Medea down.

She is doing a good job for her, so far. She has leapt through another flaming hoop, having touched-down, checked-in and changed into an outfit suitable for her first night in Cannes.

And now, she stands on a stretch of grass in the forecourt of her hotel (five star, Matthew says literally everyone stays there) at the ready, surrounded by palm trees and steak-red beach umbrellas, swimming pool still as a mineral-blue pane of glass, looking out at the Croisette: the stage for the world's most famous film festival.

Scott had been here two summers ago, holidaying on a roof-top apartment over-looking the sea. *Sweltering,* he'd called it. Posted a picture of a charred black and grey steak he'd barbecued on the terrace: *I present you minute steak, cooked for ten minutes! Maths fail!* Becky had spent ages tying up the visual clues and identifying the exact location of his apartment: distance to the beach, position of the palm trees, amenities – micro-wave, hairdryer, Wi-Fi, barbecue (charcoal included) – and the final giveaway outside the entrance to his apartments, the yellow and blue neon sign, *Croisette corner! So Hollywood-Boulevard! I heart this sign for my kitchen wall!* It was easy after that. Google maps for a more specific location. Scrolling the interiors of nearby apartments on a rental website. *Bingo* she'd said as she matched it all up with the images he'd posted; green snooker ball rug in the living room, shining subway tiles in the kitchen. A call to the rental office to check the *exact* address. *Just checking to see how central the location? Fabulous apartment!*

She'd left it there. For a few days it had been enough but then, as the sludgy feelings sunk back in, she'd returned to the computer and searched Skyscanner for flights, thinking: *What if I got on that 6am EasyJet flight? Arrived on the Croisette, waited for someone to let me into the main apartment (lost my key card!), lift to the twelfth floor, bing bong – hello there, he says, answering the door with an espresso cup in one hand – barely finished his sentence before I'm in and driving him through with his own fucking serrated steak knife. Don't wait around. Back on 3pm flight. Home for an omelette and an early night.*

She feels her heart-rate increase, her skin heat, her eyes prickle. She tells herself she *must* keep her eyes on the present. She is here for herself and her own dreams now. Not him. What did Adam say? *Enjoy yourself!* Well OK then.

And soon she will meet Matthew who flew in on a different airline to her. Having met briefly at City airport, they parted ways at the first-class lounge and she had felt both envy, and then relief at not having to make impressive and professional conversation for the journey.

For a moment she closes her eyes and allows herself to feel the heat of the sun, a favourite habit since childhood, and a rare thing that has survived to travel with her. She listens to single words break through the loud hum of conversation – *yes* and *gorgeous* and *absolutely* – and the happy music tumbling out of a nearby amp. She allows herself to feel at least a little excitement. She is here to bring life to her baby. And yet, as she begins to move across the grass, through lines and curves and collections of people absorbed in their tasks – meetings, a phone call, a laughingly funny conversation – she feels so uneasy.

She doesn't look out of place – she is wearing nice enough clothes, and like them she is draped and looped with her rainbow lanyards of accreditation – but the world plays like it is on an IMAX screen in front of her. She steps almost spaceman-slow through this seemingly flawless world of self-belief that smells of suntan lotion and perfume and cigarette smoke. It sounds like glasses toasting and the soft hollow thunk of a linen-suited back-pat and the same easy laughter she hears when people come into the office to see Matthew and share the warm facts of their relationship – the work projects, dinner parties, play dates and holidays. These are the people who wave diamond-punctured sunglasses and gold-buckled bags and drinks in the air to flag each other down after a few weeks of not seeing each other.

For a moment Becky allows herself to imagine what it must feel like to indulge in appetites so freely. Laughing without concern for volume. Writing cheques without concern for bankruptcy. Drinking negronis without concern for conseqence. Then she checks herself. Wipes a sweating palm down the front of her crumpled, aeroplane-upholstery-smelling cotton T-shirt that she now realizes looks cheap even when worn under a blazer. She is not them! *She* is a woman defined by straight lines, limits and ceilings, not unashamed, unapologetic *appetites,* for God's sake.

She thinks again about Scott. Sixteen years since she last saw him in the flesh.

She thinks about the nameless woman lying on the floor of Matthew's house.

She thinks about Medea, about how she might persuade others to see her as she does, so much more than a villain who murders her own children to punish her husband.

She should go home while she can – this unproduced woman, who makes packed lunches with economy supermarket bread, whose trainer sole is peeling off, whose house carpets need replacing. She can't do this. Of course she can't do this.

But it is the thought of Maisie that stops her from turning back: Becky is wearing one of her tops, a ruffled grass-green favourite of hers. Its smell, of incense and old perfume and Maisie's shampoo, makes her feel like her daughter is close, laughing at her doubts and willing her on as she walks through the hotel's marbled lobby and into an outside bar area: umbrellas down with the sun, now setting on a burnt-orange tinfoil sea all punctured with the rudders and sails of yachts.

The area is crowded: coffee meetings that have turned into pre-dinner Aperol spritz meetings and chats about family, people, politics – non-film subjects and yet still business. It all deepens relationships, generates trust, creates the foundations for a good deal in the future. Becky knows that business is done on every corner and in every bar in Cannes. She knows there are makeshift offices in apartment blocks rented for the week, that the benches, sofas and bars all become workplaces and playgrounds.

No one observes times of day, the standard boundaries for phone calls. She knows because she's been on the receiving end of those calls in previous years: at the office and in the early hours as she sleeps at home. Now she's here, for real, amidst the people who have a good time. The people who have something to sell.

She can see Matthew and another man sitting at the best table – unimpeded view of the sea – arms outstretched across lines of throw pillows, both swiping at their phones as they talk to each other. Could she do that? Break off a conversation to fire off an email? Is it expected of her here?

'Becky!' says Matthew, standing up and then drawing her in for a hug. She cannot remember a time when he has greeted her this way in London. The rules are different here; she must learn them, and fast. 'This is Rebecca Shawcross,' he says to the man he is with. 'Becky works with me,' he adds, while making space for Becky to sit at the end of their padded bench. 'And how are you enjoying sunny Cannes so far?'

'It's so beautiful,' she smiles. She scrabbles for something to say to illustrate her point and finds herself mentally scrolling through Scott's old Instagram feed. 'So many art galleries here,' she says, regretting it immediately. She's not on *her* holidays. The last thing she wants is for these people to think she'll be visiting galleries or even *considering* casual tourism in precious working hours.

'She's about to make her first feature, actually,' Matthew says, and the other man nods. 'We're meeting Emilia Cosvelinos for it tomorrow.'

His voice is warm milk and whisky. He has described her as someone who works *with* and not *for* him and he has used her full name. Pathetic, she thinks, so pathetic, that she feels important to him when he speaks it, as if the name she was given is worth more coming from his mouth. And yet, her legs feel a little stronger and she sits a little taller now.

'Alex is a film critic. Alex Simms?' says Matthew.

'Ah yes,' she says, recognizing him from his byline. 'I love your reviews. Always unsparing, always very funny.'

His shoulders flex a little wider. Becky can tell he's pleased.

'I hope I've spared anyone you know,' he says.

'I think you called Tommy Sheridan's last effort "well-intentioned". He was in the office last week for a meeting. Said he cried for a week, but didn't deny you'd nailed it.'

Alex laughs. Delighted. 'He's a good director but he's got a terrible sweet tooth,' he says.

'I think he'll end up doing musicals and making an absolute fortune,' says Becky.

'You're a hundred per cent right.'

Matthew smiles. And Becky has the odd sensation that she is standing outside her own life, watching a woman in her skin do a half-decent job of this thing which is flirting and flattery and bonding and, she supposes, networking.

Alex is a good deal shorter than her. His eyes are pale and filled with a darting energy that makes him look like a young deer until he smiles, when the fine skin around his eyes concertinas to betray his age. He looks at the ruffle lining her décolletage first, and then meets her eyes second. Becky remembers to give them warmth but without the insinuation of an invitation. Her price isn't ever her own body, but she knows that's by no means the case for those around her.

'So you're meeting with Emilia? I just came out of the screening for her new film actually,' he says.

'How was it?'

'Reviews are embargoed till midnight, but it's five stars. It's going to win everything.'

'What's she like in it?' asks Matthew.

'Yeah, well, what to say . . . she's great. But she's not the lead. She'll get a supporting nod. She'll want the main course next.'

'That's brilliant,' says Becky. 'I think she's incredible.'

'You'll struggle to get her now, my friend.'

She feels Matthew's eyes on her. It's not like it's a test; this is just the back and forth of a conversation, but still. How to say the perfect thing. How to be confident and not frightened, not cocky but still impregnable. Is that what this place wants?

'Well,' says Becky finally, 'I've got something in common with Emilia. We'd both like to see her win Best Actress.'

The journalist grins. 'Good luck with it. See you at the Oscars!'

Matthew waggles his phone. 'Just going to confirm our breakfast with Sam. Back in a jot.' He turns away to make his call and Becky is flooded with discomfort at this reminder of how uncertain their meeting, her only meeting in Cannes, truly is. Not even Matthew can command it take place. Even he might have to flatter and persuade.

A thick and awkward pause lies between her and Alex, now that she is unwatched and they have sole charge of the conversation. All her life any lapse in conversation or round-edged awkwardness has been her doing, she is sure of it. Does she give off something? Some signal she can't herself see or read that tells others that, for all her apparent efforts, she would prefer to be many miles away, probably alone. She must have something more to say to this man. Some clever thing. Some pithy thing to let him say, in a year's time, when *Medea*'s trailer launches, that he knows the producer and she's smart. Going places. Now that he has met her, he can be asked for his opinion of her. What will he say? What can she offer him?

'So you're an art lover?' he says.

'Oh no, not especially.' She squirms, afraid of being caught out, asked about artists and paintings she knows nothing about. Again her thoughts return to Scott's Instagram feed. 'A friend recommended the Bonnard Museum here. Once. A long time ago. I know nothing really.'

He smiles. Amused by something in her. 'Has Matthew shown you the store cupboard yet?'

It is Alex's casual tone that makes Becky unsure about whether she has heard correctly. Is this an industry term she hasn't come across yet? But there is an edge to it. A hint of acid, a subtle probing.

'Our office is tiny. Everything's on shelves.' Lightly evasive, without confessing her confusion.

'Has he shown you the top shelf then?'

'I know the market's bad, but we're not making *that* kind of movie. Not yet.'

It is like she is swimming ahead of something and calling it a game but fearing that if it catches her, the teeth will prove real. He laughs, like he knows that she *knows*, but is only in the mood to play, and only for so long.

'What's your film going to be about then?'

'It's a new take on *Medea*, the Greek play?' She hates that she made this a question.

'The one about the woman who kills her kids?'

'Spoiler alert,' she says wryly.

'Get Richard Curtis to take a pass.'

'The feel-good, lighter side of infanticide. *Honey, I've Killed the Kids*.'

'Quite. Yeah, but seriously, that sounds fucking dark.'

'It is.'

'Woman commits murder,' he says thoughtfully. 'Get it right and it's Oscar-bait though, isn't it?'

'I think there's more to it.'

'Think what you like, it's still going to be the murderous mum movie. Punters think in single sentences, believe me.'

Becky is beginning to find him a little patronizing. She wants to say, *Don't tell me how the punters think*. She wants to say that she actually *works* in the industry: unlike him who simply skirts around its edges, writing about it. But she knows better than to get him off-side, he might review *Medea* one day, and so instead she says: 'James Cameron's single sentence: *Romeo and Juliet on a sinking boat*.'

'A billion dollars later . . .' He laughs.

'*Time-travelling robot tries to kill someone*.' She's good at this game.

He smiles, impressed. 'So what's your *Medea* sentence if it isn't *Mum murders her kids*?'

'Woman struggles with toxic controlling masculinity and discovers that her power lies in being overlooked and underestimated. But the journey breaks her.'

'Maybe don't put that on the poster.'

She laughs.

'You've got Matthew behind it,' continues Alex. 'That's definitely something to put on the poster: *From the guy who's made a bunch of things you liked*. Goes a long way.'

'He's only exec'ing this one.'

Such vanity! Alex spots it in an instant. She sees it in the smirk he can't quite hide in time.

'He's obviously fond of you.'

He passes her a drink from a tray that is going round

and she notices the tan skin covered in a soft down of sun-bleached hair, the curve his forearm makes. She's seen that curve before, the unmistakable shape of a man who works out, a man who likes to possess strength. She thinks of Scott and his trips to the gym and wonders how many more men with bleached hair and vanity running through their honed muscles she can really take.

She puts her lips to the rim of a heavy-bottomed glass and takes a sip, would consider taking a sip or two more – how nice to drink a whole drink right now, just the one, just enough bitter gin and tonic to take the edge off her *sweltering* thoughts – but the liquid is sweet and bubbly and she hates it. Sweet and fizzy and alcoholic, a curious cocktail of childhood and adulthood, neither one nor the other, a confusion of the two. She hates it like she hates the alcohol tang of aftershave.

Anyway, she must remain alert and in control and alcohol won't help that. She glances over at Matthew, willing him to end his call and return to her and get this transaction back on track.

'How long have you known Matthew?' she asks Alex, trying to re-anchor herself. He doesn't bite.

'Don't you think killing your children is quite an extreme form of revenge? I'm just interested in how you'll make an audience not hate her.'

'They might not love her, they might not agree with her actions, but I think they'll understand her. They'll understand her despair at how badly she was treated by her husband. At how she gave Jason stature, children, her love. Then he took it all. Left her with nothing. Just, *discarded* her. What happens doesn't come out of nowhere. She's not a psycho who does the most messed-up thing she can think of. She's utterly wronged.'

'Wronged?'

'Yes?'

'Your mate Tommy probably felt wronged after the reviews he got for *In Golden Square*. Didn't go out and butcher his family though, did he? Let me know if I've got that wrong. I'd have to write him an apology.'

Becky feels her foundations shift. She hasn't got anything solid after all. She has a whole script and yet suddenly it's all blown into nothing substantial, and so easily. She sees the reviews forming. 'Implausible.' 'Unlikeable.'

'Haneke gets away with it every time,' she smiles. 'People butchered in their homes. Cutting their throats for effect. He doesn't worry about making people likeable. He says: this is who we might be, if we strip the rest away.'

'I fucking hate Haneke films.'

'No you don't. I read your review of *Caché*. You gave it four stars.'

His mouth curls into a half-smile. 'It's a four- or five-star film. I still hated it.'

'So maybe you'll hate my *Medea* but still give it an OK review.'

'It certainly sounds well-intentioned.'

'I'll join forces with Tommy and pay to have you killed.'

He laughs. Clinks her glass with his own. 'Biggest compliment you can pay a critic, threatening to dismember them. It's only then that we know you actually give a shit about what we say.'

She sees it then, beyond his confidence, the part of him that is both vain *and* anxious. He is courted here only because his reviews are read. But he wants more than that. She understands that. When he teases her, her discomfort flatters him. The moment his opinion can't touch her, he'll hate her instead, albeit from a new distance. Is it only women who have to work this hard? she wonders. Or is it just that the exchange between men is more straightforward? Is it the possibility of sex that makes it so much more difficult? Medea comes to her again; resolute, cutting away the trappings of her gender, ready to be unloved, loathed even, for all time. Is that bravery, or has she simply lost too much to bother saving anything?

She wonders what she might say to Alex, were the boot on the other foot. But she cannot discount the fact he might review her work in the future and thus she cannot offer him anything, really, beyond a passing entertainment and the threat that, maybe, if her stars align, one day she might matter like Matthew does.

Matthew rejoins them. 'All good,' he says to Becky. Then, to Alex, 'Coming to the party on *Freebird*?'

'What's *Freebird*?' asks Becky.

'Petrovskaya's yacht,' replies Alex. 'Apparently it's been fitted with anti-missile technology.'

'Won't save anyone from a bad review,' quips Becky, and Alex grins.

'She's funny,' says Alex to Matthew. A two-word review, but a good one.

'Did she tell you about *Medea*?'

'Yeah. I'm sure she'll make it work.'

'If the stars align with the right people,' says Matthew. And suddenly Becky feels naked: with these words, she senses the conditionality of Matthew's help. Will he still support the project if the script doesn't attract a glitzy and powerful enough cast? Or if its main financier ends up a little lukewarm on the whole thing and doesn't make it a priority?

If it fails, it will be her failure. That is clear to her.

Isn't that what she wanted? Something she could take absolute ownership of?

But she finds herself remembering how Alex had reduced her idea to something that people might snipe at or look down on and how he'd hooked his fingers into his jeans and bent his arms to make himself look bigger and wider, as he did it. And she remembers Matthew's words again, allowing herself to feel the full force of what failure might bring. The exposure. The isolation. The fear, and the shame.

Becky excuses herself. She locks herself in a nearby toilet cubicle. Sits down on the seat, legs bent, leaning over with her head in her hands, as if she is about to be sick. She is so angry when tears come despite her efforts. They will leave her eyes red. For the rest of the evening she will look like a woman who has been crying. Soon she has cried enough to have blown her nose three times.

When she walks out of the cubicle thankfully the room is quiet. But at the far end of a row of pink-marbled sinks one other woman stands bent like a flower toward the mirror, fixing her lipstick. Her hair is cropped, her eyes fine and free of make-up. Becks recognizes her immediately. She is Sharon McManus, a director known for her big attitude and her low budgets. Becky has met her once before, briefly, at a festival gala. She doubts she is remembered. Sharon's film *Relics from the Near Future* has screened today and been deemed a success. Becky recalls the photos on Deadline; like everyone, Becky toggles between being at the festival and reading about it, so that she'll know where she is. On stage, taking questions afterwards, Sharon had raised both her arms and kicked out a leg, dressed half in flowers and half in sharp-suited lines: half like a woman and half like a man. The way Sharon kissed her lead actress? She looked so content, like the puzzle of her life is completed in such moments.

Becky walks to the sink and runs the tap, pressing cool damp tissues to her puffy eyes. Perhaps they can be saved. She can hear the conversation outside getting louder, bolshier – nearing the pitch of the summertime pavement crowds outside a pub at closing.

'Boy trouble?' says Sharon.

'That'd be nice.'

'I heard you blowing your nose. Very unladylike. I was impressed.'

'Oh God. Sorry.'

'No, fuck that. Trumpet it out. Don't go dabbing it away now.'

Becky could, perhaps, paper the cracks with jokes, and then run to her room. But she feels the place inside that her crying has hollowed out and is suddenly too tired to cover up, weave round, edit and hide.

'I just fucked up,' she says.

'How badly?'

'Nobody died but . . . I got asked about something I'm working on and I felt like I couldn't land it. I just allowed myself to be . . . It's my job, my only job, to defend this thing and I let this guy . . .'

'Shit on it?'

'It wasn't even that bad. I just did a rubbish job defending it. And now I feel like I've let someone down.' Medea. 'Even though . . . Even though it doesn't matter to anyone except me.'

'Been there a few times myself.'

Becky feels Sharon assess her. She feels sure she is looking at the running mascara, the tangled mess of hair and lopsided clothes, but that she is doing it with kind eyes while formulating something.

'Never mind,' Becky says. 'I'll just . . . I don't know. Try and learn from it.'

'What are you selling here anyway?'

'It doesn't matter.'

'Come on, I'm asking. I'm not going to shit on it. You've made me curious.'

'Yeah, but now it'd be pitching to a director.'

'What, so you've been crying in there waiting till I need a piss so you can get five minutes at the mirror with me? I mean, if that's your game-plan you're the best fucking producer on the planet. Seriously wily. You've got Tamara Lenkiewa back there too. She'll be needing a shit soon, you could have a crack at her as well.'

Becky laughs at her smudged mascara and puffy eyes. 'Projecting an air of calm authority. A producer who never panics.'

'I know that's what you're meant to be, but it's all bollocks, isn't it? Fucking hell, I look at my mistakes and I'm amazed anyone listens to me on set.'

'And if they don't?'

'They'd get fired, obviously. I'm mean, I'm not having that!' They both laugh now. 'So what else have you made?'

'Nothing as producer. I've been in development.'

'First features are a fucker.'

'I work with Matthew Kingsman and he'll exec it, so it shouldn't be as hard as I seem to be making it.'

'That's a good pedigree to stick on the table.'

'Do you know him?'

'I've done meetings.'

'For anything I'd have worked on? I've been there a long time now.'

'My thing with Matthew Kingsman is, you look at the films he's made and you count how many women he's had helming them.'

'Andrea was on *Eight Lies* until she dropped out,' says Becky.

'However you cut it, he's done north of twenty films and I can name one with a female director, which was *Hellensgard*.'

'He got brought that with Lotta already attached.'

'See, that's even more depressing.'

'He's not a sexist. He hires women. He's got me producing.'

'Still. Back to the one out of twenty directors statistic . . .'

'There aren't that many women directors who can get a film made. I mean, even if you want to back women, if you can't raise money because France or China or whoever hasn't heard of them, then you can't make the film. Believe me, I've gone through the lists hundreds of times. You're rare. You make good films that also make money.'

'Not sure Matthew agrees with you. I went for that Austen film you guys did. Didn't get it.'

'That's a shame. You'd have been great.'

'Might have dodged a bullet. It was all a bit bonnets and blushing in the end. So what's your idea then? Your thing that got shat on?'

Becky has to recalibrate for a moment. Then she plunges in. 'It's based on the ancient Greek myth Medea. It's a contemporary retelling. It's about a woman who takes back her power in a messy and destructive way. It's about that moment when men realize that women can be every bit as dangerous and imaginative and vindictive and proud as the men they know.'

'And what's the story?'

'Men take everything from her. Promise her things and betray her. She kills her own children to destroy their father.'

'It's usually men who do that to their ex-wives.'

'Exactly.'

'And you've got a script?'

'Yes. It needs a bit of work, but it's basically there.'

'Can I read it?'

'That'd be great. I'll send it to you when I'm back in—'

'Send it to me now. I'm on Gmail. It's: Sharon 105 mm.'

'Like the Nikon lens?'

'Exactly.'

Becky has to tap the email address into her phone twice, her hands are shaking so much. She cannot believe she is sending *Medea* to a director as amazing as Sharon. She feels a true fizz of excitement until she catches herself, wondering if it's all a big joke that is being caught on hidden camera, as she attaches the PDF from her Dropbox. Then with one tap it's sent.

'That's my bedtime reading then.' Sharon hugs Becky. 'I've got to go back and be nice to my North American distributers now. Good luck. And chin up.'

'Nice meeting you.'

'Top tip? Don't bother to look like you haven't been crying. Just say you found someone's film really, really moving. Even better if it's their film. They'll buy you drinks all night.'

In the morning when she wakes, in her pretty hotel room facing away from the ocean, there is an email from Sharon waiting for her.

FUCK YEAH I'M IN*

(* terms and conditions apply)

97

Chapter 9

The location for their pitch meeting is the hotel restaurant area, timed for just after the breakfast rush, after the plates and cutlery are gone but when plenty of people are still milling around and chatting over coffee. The restaurant is unremarkable but for its glass walls on all sides that allow patrons to both watch (people, the sea) and be watched. When Becky arrives, Matthew is already there with Emilia, seated at a circular table that makes them particularly noticeable. Becky cannot help but inwardly applaud Matthew's genius: nothing like a very visible meeting with a high-profile actress to get people wondering what *that* was about. What a way to kick off the buzz, thinks Becky.

Matthew is leaning forward over the starched table-cloth and Emilia is leaning backward slightly, tilting her head, either laughing or making space; it's hard to tell from across the room. Becky watches them for a second. It looks like an old dance: alpha man stretching out his arms to command space and pretty girl, like silk, supine, promising she'll be hard to catch. Have they done this before? Have they been lovers once already? She imagines them on Matthew's kitchen floor together, locked into each other, but dismisses it quickly as an unhelpful thought.

Then she finds herself idly wondering whether Matthew has ever thought of her *in that way* before; as someone attractive or alluring or beguiling enough to want to sleep with. She knows that she can look pretty enough, sometimes, with the right make-up and clothes in the right light. It's not as if she finds him physically attractive, she's never wanted to sleep with him *as such*, and yet she still finds herself feeling a little disappointed when she reminds herself that Matthew is a man surrounded by exceptional beauty and talent and charisma and that she has none of those things in any great measure. She finds herself wanting, simply, to have the choice about whether she is thought of *in that way*, or not.

When Becky joins them, there is a heavy pause, almost indiscernible, as if she might have interrupted something. But then Sam, Emilia's agent, also arrives and suddenly everyone is on their feet kissing and bear-hugging and trading congratulations on the reception of her new film.

They take their seats and order coffee. Becky sits opposite Emilia. She is smaller than Becky had imagined, even though she is used to actors being bird-like or doll-like in the flesh. She feels taller than ever, tempted to slouch, to throw away her height like it's unwanted. Her gaze toggles between the actress's bare, milk-white arms and the oversized, widely spaced eyes that take up so much of her face. She is beautiful. And she is dressed down, wearing a black tank top with her punky hair tied up in a loose and messy knot darting out at all angles – pale pink, yellow blonde, platinum – like a tasteful firework. Elegant without trying. Where did she learn how to do that? And she is already bored, her eyes flat, arms resting across her waist. With Matthew alone she looked alive. Now this is work. Becky feels like she has gate-crashed. But perhaps it's only in her head.

'Did you see Yarrow yet?' grins Sam at Matthew in a smooth and tuneful American West Coast accent. 'My God. I looked at that guy and thought, you lucky fucking son of a bitch. You have no idea what you're doing and yet suddenly you're the toast of the festival. And you know what? He doesn't even understand that! Yarrow thinks he deserves it. Fuck me! I saw Jane and she was like: *I'd like to fire him for proving the universe is cosmically unfair, only . . .*'

' . . . She's making ten per cent on that cosmic unfairness,' finishes Matthew.

'My point exactly,' grins Sam. He turns to Emilia, 'You, dear Ems, are that rarest of things. A client I like better the more I get to know her.'

Emilia gives him a small smile.

'You're having a great festival, too, I must say,' says Matthew, addressing Emilia.

'It's Martin's film,' she says, in a low and considered

Texan drawl, making her sound unfazed by anything. 'He gets an easy ride from the critics.' She gives a slow shrug, like success or failure mean very little to her. I'll bet she does a lot of bikram yoga, thinks Becky.

'Not always,' says Sam. 'I've seen Marty take a kicking more than once.'

Sam is dressed in jeans, short enough to display sockless feet in tan leather loafers. Suit jacket and t-shirt. His job is to oil the wheels, smooth the seams and join the cracks, so that his client has a secure platform on which to stand. He is courtier and gatekeeper, turning on a dime between being a bad-ass deal-maker, sensitive confidant and cocktail party wingman. And for all his ice-breaking bonhomie, he never forgets – and never lets anyone else forget – that Emilia is the star, the epicentre of this meeting. Her work quickly dominates the conversation. Her recent gig with Spielberg. How the central heating broke down in a Nepalese hotel when she was shooting at the foot of the Himalayas, and how Sam nearly flew over there himself with a portable heater and bear skins, it got *that bad*, ha ha!

And time is ticking. They'd have less than an hour, Matthew had told her. And nearly all of that has gone. Why is nobody raising *Medea*? Should she do it? Is Matthew silently wondering why on earth she's sitting quietly when she should be pitching the hell out of this actress? She sees it all slipping away and begins to feel nauseous with the smell of bleached tablecloth and the soapy-sweet perfume of an aftershave. No one has committed to anything. They're going through the motions. Emilia probably hasn't read the script yet but has been told it's too late to cancel Matthew, a man who she still wants on her side. But this is now a formality before the next rooftop party. Becky has seen it play out countless times. She has done it herself before, once when a script by a friend of a friend came in and, for the sake of her friendship, she spent an hour trying to tell him that he really couldn't write without sounding anything less than enthused about his writing. *Do you think you might buy it*, he'd asked her, towards the end of the hour. *It needs a few more drafts*, she had said, confident that he'd never get round to that.

'Were you at the gala party?' Emilia asks Becky.

Becky flushes, wondering if she's been staring at the actress without realizing it. 'No, last night I mostly hung out in the loos.'

Emilia laughs.

'The French do a great fucking ladies' toilet, so I'm told,' says Sam.

'Good company?' asks Emilia, rubbing at her kohl-lined eye as if it is gritty and bothering her.

'I didn't mean to spend so much time there. I got talking to a director and we just sort of failed to head back to the bar.'

'Which director?' asks Matthew.

'Sharon McManus.'

'Ah, she's brilliant,' says Sam. 'Love her. Has she done one of yours?' he asks Matthew.

'No. Tried to get her for the Austen thing,' he replies.

Becky shifts uncomfortably in her chair, recalling Sharon's very different version of events. 'She'd have been great for that,' she says: marvelling, not for the first time, at Matthew's capacity to bend the truth in order to reach the finish line. *It's all just talk until the cheque is signed.*

'What do you think of her films?' Becky puts it to Emilia too bluntly. She has given her no way out if Emilia hasn't seen them. Does she need a way out? She's just done a Scorsese film, at the artier end of his spectrum. Does she want to be that kind of actress?

'I loved her early shorts,' says Emilia. 'There was one called *Low Treason* that was really funny and weird. She must have made it for about ten pounds.' The words 'ten pounds' sound strange coming from Emilia. She could so easily have said 'ten bucks'. She likes to be precise, thinks Becky. That matters to this woman. 'I can't remember its name, but she also did a short about two sisters trying to build a submarine.'

'*Blue*,' says Becky.

'That's the one! Both of them wanting to be in charge.'

'Two periscopes!'

'And they end up just staring at each other through them from opposite ends of the submarine, shouting at each other while it sinks. It was smart as well. It was like, Russia and America not remembering that it's all one planet. It was the whole Cold War with two sisters and a bunch of scrap metal.'

'It had that *Dr Strangelove* feel. Absurd and serious.' Becky smiles, remembering it fondly.

'Yeah. That stayed with me. I'm kinda jealous you met her, now.'

'It's free entry to the ladies' loos. You just have to wait to pounce on her. Join me next time.'

'I might do that!' Emilia gives her a big, chalk-white, shiny, straight-toothed grin.

'She wants to do *Medea* as her next film.' Becky addresses this last remark to Matthew, like she's sharing an interesting bit of news. A little update that he might like to know. No big deal.

'Great fit,' says Matthew, picking up the baton smoothly.

'So is that a go thing for you guys?' says Sam.

'A bit of work to do, but it's well on its way,' Matthew replies. He turns to Emilia. 'Look, if it's something you're interested in, we haven't gone to anyone yet and you'd be top of our list for Medea.'

'I've been so busy I'm behind on my reading . . .' Emilia glances at Sam.

'I need to cut more space into your schedule. I'll get onto that. But it's a great piece of work.' Sam nods at his client and turns to Becky. 'And if you put Sharon on it, well, that's a movie.'

'Can I read it and let you know?' says Emilia.

'Of course,' says Matthew. 'We'd be thrilled to talk to you about it.'

'I actually talked to the screenwriter about one of your

performances before he went to draft,' says Becky. 'That moment in *Your Daughter* when you stand at the edge of the sea and then walk in. There was something about the endurance and sacrifice of that character. It really got me. And even though this role isn't anything like that, apart from those things, it was one of the only performance steers I gave him. I thought your work in that scene was incredible.'

Emilia is listening to her now. Really listening.

'If you like,' Becky continues, 'we could even try and find time to sit down with Sharon while we're all here together?' It's a push, but Becky knows that the promise to read something fades fast. Getting into a room with a director you admire – that makes things real.

'That'd be great,' says Emilia.

'I'll hook us all up,' says Sam. 'Let's make a fucking movie, guys!' He raises his coffee cup in a toast, and then four coffee cups meet in mid-air, and Becky hears the blood pounding in her ears.

Sam consults his iPhone. 'We need to get you up to the Peacock Suite for the junket, we're a little late already,' he says to Emilia.

'See you soon,' says Emilia to Becky, giving her a big smile. And then they're gone.

Becky and Matthew sit there in silence for a full minute. Becky is savouring the moment, and hopes that he is, too.

'Sharon McManus it is then,' he says.

'Was that OK? I'd have rather run it by you first.'

'No. Look, Emilia gets it made. You could have my

brother's Labrador directing and someone'd still finance it with Emilia in the lead.'

Disappointment pricks at her. She had wanted to impress Matthew with the value of what she, alone, had brought to the party. 'Do you not rate Sharon?'

'I think she's good. My point is she doesn't have to be better than good. Because you've landed Emilia.'

'Have we?' She feels better again.

'I think so. Sam knows her better than anyone and he's a big fan of the script. He wouldn't roll out all that "let's make a fucking movie" bollocks if he didn't think she was thinking that. I'll call him to check, but I think we can start talking about it.'

'Don't we need to get Sharon to approve Emilia first?'

'No!' Then, softer, 'It's your film. If you want to make Sharon feel like she's in charge, that's up to you. Personally I don't think it hurts for a director to feel like they're coming onto something substantial. Something that will very easily survive them exiting it, if it comes to that. But you have to figure out what works for you and for the situation. It's different every time.'

'But you think we'll get it made?'

'I do. And I need to spend more time hanging out in the toilets. Not a tip anyone's ever given me before.'

'I got lucky.'

'Bollocks. You somehow managed to attach Sharon to your project between pissing and washing your hands. That's a rare talent, Becky.'

She fills with happiness at these words, the ones she's been waiting for. She feels silly for the disappointment she felt earlier. She should know Matthew by now. He always picks his time to roll out a deserved compliment for maximum effect. His eyes are shining and he is still smiling at her in an enquiring way, as if she is an artefact that has caught his eye. She wonders whether she's closer to being more like Emilia, more alluring to him, and in the same thought, the possibility repulses her. Instinctively she takes hold of her own wrist.

'What would you have tabled otherwise? To convince Emilia? Just out of interest?' Matthew's question is so professional that she is torn violently out of her magical, ridiculous thinking.

'She did a fundraiser for a women's refuge back when she was a teenager. Her mum was disowned by her family when Emilia was a baby. The father ran off with another woman and left them with nothing. She's talked about it in a few interviews. I was going to go for a take on Medea as someone who gives love, gives birth, honours her family, and then gets left, disowned, betrayed. Despite having done nothing but try her hardest, men blame and punish her. That was going to be my thing. Try and make it personal.'

'No, I get it.'

'You can't just launch in with all that over an Americano though, can you?'

Matthew laughs. 'Not a bad Plan B though.' They grin

at each other. Thoughts of being alluring now firmly shelved, she likes that she and Matthew are in on this together, side by side, players on the same team. If nothing else, she is on her way to feeling like she is someone *interesting*.

Good news travels fast but rumours fly faster here, where *knowing things* is the one currency everyone understands and values.

Sit somewhere visible, Matthew has told her, *and watch them come to you. That's when you know.* Bringing her in on his secrets now.

So she sits outside a café, sheltered from the sun by a canopy, blue and branded with the insignia of a well-known champagne – drinking black coffee and making notes on the script, anxiously checking her email for a confirmed time and place for Sharon and Emilia to get together. She waits for people to find her and, as Matthew predicted, they do. Two financiers and an actress stop to chat. *Can I read a script? When does casting start? I hear good things. I hear you have the hot project.*

Emilia emails her in person. Their schedules don't work in the next two days, though Sam and Mads – Sharon's agent – have bent themselves in half trying to make it happen, so Emilia's proposing flying to London before she goes home. Cake in Soho? The three of them?

The three of them!

Becky hides a smile at the fleeting image she has of

herself as someone who is invited to summer cocktails on the rooftop of a London private members' club and then, a few months later, to drink whisky sours and cinnamon-spiced mulled wines for the Christmas party season.

Once Matthew rejoins her, even more people stop by – sometimes staying for coffee – greeting them with kisses and sitting close to Becky, as if they know her well. She is his golden girl, the clever one who is making that timely film about women and revenge. Becky sees herself reflected back in other people's faces as they tell her Medea *sounds fabulous. What an exciting package. What a wonderful team. Send me a script. I'll read tonight. I'll read it today.*

She begins to glow from the inside. Can they see her excitement? Is that off-putting? Or does it read as passion for the material, the actress, her director?

Sharon is 'her' director now.

Somebody notes that Becky is kind of what Sharon needs to move up the ladder: like she, Becky, has done Sharon an almighty favour anointing her as the one chosen for her Emilia pic!

The snot-blowing, insecure half-girl in the toilet stall is fading fast:

Becky was only ever there to adjust her eye make-up.

Sharon approached her.

They'd met before.

It was a meeting of minds.

Her eyes were clear and she hadn't been crying.

Let me tell you a story, she'd said, across the marble

hand basin, and Sharon, rapt, had listened to her, Becky Shawcross, protégé and producer.

A woman who gets things done.

Champagne, orders Matthew, and Becky allows him to fill her glass so that the liquid tips giddily over the rim. She drinks the whole thing down in three or four gulps, with everyone around her doing the same, toasting their, *her* success. She allows herself to let go and feel it all; her insides warm with the alcohol, her skin warm with the sunshine, her whole self cocooned and belonging with these interesting people. She is enjoying herself. She is safe. Snooker ball carpets and steak knives have no place in this Cannes, her Cannes. *More champagne,* orders Matthew. And Becky knows that now it has begun, it will never stop.

Chapter 10

Later that night, Becky and Matthew continue their work at a party on the beach – confirming the rumours of Sharon's attachment, speaking positively about Emilia, keeping the energy high with talk of casting and shooting dates – leaning against the bar under swags of rainbow fairy lights and a straw roof, set up like something out of *Cocktail*. Many of the people they have spoken to that afternoon are there, plucking from trays of cocktails and canapés, all courtesy of one of the UK's major film financiers.

The heat and adrenaline and half a bottle of champagne have taken Becky's edges off and now she is taking the first sweet and sharp sip of a mojito, figuring it as the most sensible chaser. She'd forgotten how fabulous and invincible alcohol could make her feel.

'Becky, right?' The woman who has appeared at Becky's side is a little shorter than her and has long dark hair scraped back tight. It is impossible to tell her age; her skin is stretched like cling-film, flat and shining as if it were fresh out of a packet, but then the stories about her go way back. She needs no introduction but gives herself one anyway. 'I'm Madeleine, Sharon McManus's agent. So pleased to meet you.' She grasps Becky's hand. 'Sharon is so looking forward to getting her teeth into *Medea*.'

'I'm thrilled she's come on board.'

'She tells me the updating really works? That it's timely. I'm afraid I haven't read the script yet.'

'Yes, there's the whole toxicity of men and how they don't see women coming because of it.' Becky realizes that she's garbling her words, but it doesn't seem to matter. Not here, with the sea and this cocktail and the heat behind her.

'Is Matthew producing?'

'I'm its producer but it'll be through his company.'

'I see.'

Becky picks up on a fine skein of something she doesn't want to see. Dissent? A problem? What hasn't she thought of?

'I spoke to DB earlier,' says Madeleine cautiously.

'Oh, I love DB,' blurts Becky. Then, remembering his curt words on the phone to her and his anger with Matthew, she speaks in more sober tones. 'He's such a great agent. So tough.'

'We go back a long way,' says Madeleine. 'It's not like in Hollywood where they're all slitting each other's throats before breakfast.' She pauses. 'We talk.'

Becky has no idea where the conversation is going now but she feels the low thrum of dread, something bad is coming. She hopes she's wrong, hopes they'll simply talk about favoured lunch spots. Does she have a DB story that she can table? She thinks hard.

'I saw DB recently, he told me that an ex-client of his came over to his house one Christmas Eve. He was working as an actual Father Christmas in a shopping centre because that was the only work he could get, and he'd got drunk in his costume after work and had come over to shout at DB. Only DB's kids opened the door and were all excited and then this man apparently felt so bad that he went through with it and did his whole routine for the kids in DB's living room.'

'I heard that one,' Madeleine laughs. 'And when one of the kids, Lottie I think it was, asked for a present, the client gave her his cigarettes and DB was like, let me get you some wrapping paper for those!'

'I love DB,' says Becky again, and she really feels it.

'He's rather cross with Matthew. You know that, don't you?'

Becky hesitates as if feeling her way round the edges of a concealed and sheer drop beneath her. 'There were a few calls before we left.'

'Do you know why?'

'Do you?' Becky asks.

'The difference between us is that it doesn't matter to *me* why he's angry. I don't have a film with him . . . But you do, and Matthew's been a rather naughty boy.'

Becky feels the heat of Madeleine's expectant gaze on her as she struggles to link the facts in the right order:

looping back to the woman on Matthew's kitchen floor around to DB's irritation, Antonia's rage and where she finds herself now . . .

'It's clear you don't know,' says Madeleine flatly. 'Well, it's not fair to gossip, but I'd advise you to talk to him. If it really is your movie, you don't want a stink around it. Not when nobody's under contract yet. Sorry to patronize. I'm sure you don't need advice.'

Madeleine detaches herself with a soft squeeze to Becky's forearm before she goes. A message has been delivered, but what is it? A grim grittiness now sits in Becky's belly. Has she done something wrong? Becky feels around those dark discomforting areas, searching for something that could give her new information, feigning distraction at something going on across the bar, trying to push back the energy emerging from a buried and ignored place deep within her, feeling it swell and grow, powered on by alcohol as if it were petrol. Soon she feels that same energy gather to a sharp, metal spade-tip point and begin its work excavating. She sips her drink and tries to think of all the reasons that DB might be angry with Matthew. Mentally she scrolls through DB's client list. Has Matthew dumped one of his actors from a film? Riled him or her with a disrespectful deal?

She tries to remember details about the woman on the floor: her long neck and spun-gold hair. She momentarily catches hold of an image – a chignon-twist – but she can't place exactly where she saw it. Laid out on a table

114

somewhere as a headshot or photograph elsewhere? In a magazine? One of the stills from this week's *Radio Times* television preview about that new drama? But as quickly as the image arrives, it is washed away with the alcohol and the interruption:

'Hey, good to see you. It's all been kicking off for you in the last twenty-four hours, hasn't it?'

It's the journalist from yesterday, Alex. His eyes are a little glazed, and he leans in, enough for her to smell spirits on his breath. 'So this *friend* who recommended, whatever, the galleries here,' he says. 'What was he? Like a *special* friend?'

It takes her a few moments to connect with what he's asking and then she remembers: Scott and the Bonnard Museum. Scott had complained on his Instagram feed that there weren't enough Bonnards in the Bonnard Museum. He'd wanted to see his favourite painting, *Nude In The Bath*, which wasn't there, was never going to be there, actually; something he'd have known if, like Becky, he had bothered to look it up. Becky had stared at the digital image of *Nude In The Bath* for an age. A body in the bath, stretched out for all to see. A woman's body, looking like a corpse. His comments had seemed so mocking and victorious; as if, despite everything, he could still take what he wanted from a woman, ogle and gaze and leer at her body like he fucking owned her, like she existed just to sate one of his many appetites. Becky had slammed her fist so hard on the sideboard that it bruised the soft fleshy bit of her hand, tenderized it like one of Scott's stupid fucking steaks.

Alex leans in again then, suddenly and close, in a way that she had not been expecting.

And she flinches, like he has hit her.

He collects his drink from the bar top behind her and then makes a show of creating a wide berth between them. She can see that he is hurt, because his eyes seem to turn to stone, a dark offence, like she has accused him of something terrible.

'I . . .' There aren't words to explain her reaction so instead she turns and pushes her way toward the outside. Her foot catches on someone's bag strap and she falls to the ground.

The flesh on her upper arm is gathered and pinched and she panics at this sense of being held and caught like a fish on a line, and she tries to shake it off by punching her arm outward in a well-mastered jab. It looks like she is defending herself from something. She looks up at the person holding her and it is Alex, surrounded by a sea of shiny, painted, concerned faces.

'It's OK, God, I'm just trying to help you up,' he says.

She gets to her feet and, before she can stop herself, the panic overwhelms her completely, driving her out of the bar – without a thank you or goodbye or sorry or excuse me. Shame runs cold in her blood at the thought of what people will surely be saying about her now and in the morning: that fledgling producer who doesn't know how to control her appetite for alcohol, *so* drunk, probably got carried with it all, quite embarrassing for the poor girl. Bless.

She runs down to the seashore where lights are bouncing off the water now, where glasses are being clinked for dinner and charcoal burnt to fire orange for fish and meat. She finds a place far from the people and the laughing and the eating. Searches for her phone, knowing she must call him first. He will guide her along the maze as she walks through it, step by step, hoping not to lose her way forever. She dials his number.

Adam answers her call sounding relaxed, but—

'Adam? Adam? Is Maisie OK?' she says.

'What do you mean?'

'Was she OK when she got back from school? After the sleepover. Did she seem herself?' She is wiping the tears roughly from her cheeks with the pads of her fingers.

'She was happy,' he says, his words kind, soft. He knows where she is. 'She had a great time. She's in the living room now doing her coursework . . . You sound . . .'

'I did it again,' she says.

'What do you mean?'

'I let myself relax and . . . I drank. I drank alcohol.'

'Hey, that's OK. It's OK to drink, you know it is.' He pauses. 'What actually happened? How drunk are you?' His voice splits with a new, contained panic. 'Talk to me.'

'No, nothing bad's happened. I just couldn't cope. I had a few drinks, I shouldn't have drunk, I can't do it, I just thought . . . the most basic thing just set me off. Someone reaching for their drink across me. I looked crazy.' She begins to cry.

'It's OK.' His voice is calm, full of relief, full of questions he knows not to ask straight away.

'My film is happening. It's actually going to happen. And I still . . .'

'It's OK. Breathe deep. Come back to the future. Come back. I'm talking to you now. You're safe.'

'I'll never be good enough.'

'You are.'

'I'm not going to be fixed.'

'This is a small part of you. It's not who you are.'

'I just wanted to enjoy the moment. I wanted to celebrate. I wanted to let go. I tried, I really did.' She is crying so much she's not sure he'll be able to understand her.

'It's OK. It's OK.'

'Adam, I'm so angry.'

'Long slow breaths.'

'I fucking hate myself.'

'In through the nose, out through the mouth.'

'Yes, fine,' she says, and when she's calmer they end the call; he, reassured that she will go back to the hotel. But she is not reassured: his words are not enough, they never are, nothing is ever enough. She turns her back on it all, forming a fist, thumping her thighs in time with the crashing waves, harder and harder, the flesh humming with pain from the time before, and the time before that. There will be bruises tomorrow, and more, if she can help it, she thinks, crying, tears spooling down her cheeks, spooling back in time.

Chapter 11

Hampstead, London
13 September 2003

There is barely space to move in the house. People smashed and smoking and wandering and dancing and chatting, perched on sofa arms, five people crammed onto a two-seater. Scott is holding Becky's hand, leading her through the halting, pushing, drink-spilling crowd, to the kitchen, and then to the stairs which they climb to join Mary, Brendan and the others. She has drunk more than she realized. Everything only makes sense in sections.

At the door to the bedroom Becky says something like, 'After you,' and then Scott says, 'Don't mind if I do,' and they laugh and drink some more beer. When he smiles at her, she is pathetically pleased to be proved so wrong about this tall, handsome but lunkish man who has only ever been on the fringes of her world.

Scott takes the lead and pushes at the door into a vast bedroom – white-painted shutters closed tight to the outside world, carpets sprouting grey and soft underfoot, and a pale pink silk coverlet rumpled in a wave over the kingside bed so that it looks like the inside of a conch shell. A blanket chest, a side table, chairs, all pushed up against the walls to accommodate a big group of people – fifteen or twenty, perhaps – all sitting in a circle on the floor, all clogging up the otherwise sophisticated air of this room with their smoke-choked, pheromone-laden, alcohol-tanged teenage breaths.

Alcohol is everywhere. Six-packs, twelve-packs, boxes of beer. Lines of disco-blue and medicine-orange alcopops. At least two people are swigging from champagne bottles, holding the necks lightly and effortlessly as if this is what they do all the time.

This is how things are done here. Try to pay attention, Becky tells herself.

She goes from feeling shot through with delight and confidence – showing teeth and eyes, standing at her real height – to feeling smaller, shorter, duller, greyer, years younger as she looks at this circle of North London teen-agers whose voices are perfectly pitched and cutting, whose laughs are elegant or flirtatious, or barks that fill a room. Becky feels the eyes of the room look her up and down, but she merits no more than a quick glance from anyone. Scott has left her side.

Brendan and Mary sit in a small huddle with two others she does not recognize.

Mary smiles.

'Mate, over here,' Brendan says to Scott, and motions to a space next to him.

121

Scott waves Becky over and, grateful, she squeezes in between Scott and Brendan. She is too big for the too-small space – knees overlapping with a boy either side. She wonders if she should sit outside the circle.

'Hey,' whispers Scott, looking up at her. 'You're flying low.'

Becky glances down and sees the lace of her pants showing in the gape of her jeans zip.

Scott laughs. 'Don't worry about it, you wear it well.'

He hands her a bottle of the disco-blue drink as she tugs at her top to try and cover her pants.

'Let's do this, bitches,' shouts a girl with a nose ring, brandishing an empty champagne bottle.

'Are we seriously still twelve?' mutters a boy in a vintage *Goonies* T-shirt.

'Ground rules?' asks another girl.

'Take turns clockwise. Snog wherever it lands.'

'I'm not getting off with Nick,' says *Goonies* boy.

'You couldn't handle me,' replies a boy Becky assumes must be Nick. 'I'd fucking destroy those thin lips.'

'I'm only playing to watch Nick and Bento get it on,' shouts one of their friends. 'Who needs gay porn?'

'I do,' says a beefy guy, putting his hand up, to gales of laughter. Becky laughs too.

'Come on then,' says nose ring. 'Who's first up?' When nobody volunteers, she shrugs. 'Let the bottle decide!' And with that she spins it.

People track the spinning neck like they are standing

round the wheel of a roulette table. When the bottle comes to a standstill its neck points clearly to Mary. Everyone exclaims as she shields her face theatrically with closed and flattened palms.

'Do it!' commands nose ring. 'Give it a proper shove.'

Mary spins her bottle. It slows and points to Brendan. Mary smiles at Brendan.

'Kiss, kiss,' the teenagers in the circle chant.

'Argh, this is so cringe!' shouts Bento.

'You'll get yours, mate,' laughs Nick.

Mary's eyes are glazed with alcohol and nerves and the excitement of everyone's attention. She crawls on her hands over to Brendan and leans into him. They kiss each other, tentatively at first and then, encouraged by the chants and cries, lunge at each other for a fuller performance.

'Bloody hell,' whispers Scott to Becky, with a nervous laugh.

Brendan and Mary confer then stand up, join hands and step out through the circle toward the door, like a married couple heading up the aisle. Mary turns briefly to address Becky: *Sorry*, she mouths, and then she is gone and Becky knows that she will not see her for the rest of the night.

'Sorry, what exactly am I signing up for?' laughs a red-headed girl.

'Spin it!' shouts someone. 'I want to get laid too!' More laughter.

Becky looks down at the rubber curve of her trainers

and feels more at sea than ever. She takes a huge gulp of her drink because it is something to do other than look anxious. She wants to go now.

With no regard for order, a boy called Nick leans forward and spins the bottle, urging it on, 'Spin, bottle of fate! Show me my sexual destiny!'

The bottle points to nose-ring girl. She shrugs good-naturedly.

Nick lies down next to her, posing and pouting. 'Come on then. Lay it on me, baby!'

Nose-ring girl leans down and gives him a quick kiss. Three seconds at most, no tongues. Raucous cheering and laughter.

'Marry me?' he says to her.

'Next!' she shouts.

The girl sitting next to Nick reaches for it.

One by one they spin and kiss, until it comes to Scott. 'Ah, fuck,' says Scott, dismayed, as the bottle faces him.

'Go on, mate,' calls out a boy in a baseball cap opposite him. 'Good luck. Hope you don't get a minger.'

'Fuck off!' says the red-head. 'We're all beautiful!'

'Only on the inside,' retorts Nick.

When Scott spins the bottle it is with the strength of someone who wants it to ricochet across the carpet, to smash against a skirting board and disappear from the game entirely. But as it makes its final slow revolution, the group cheers and whoops as it comes to land on Becky.

Scott and Becky look at each other and then Becky looks

at the boy in the baseball cap to see if she is deemed a minger.

Scott leans in and kisses her. She is surprised at how soft it is. It's a kiss with good manners. 'Shall we get out while we can?' he whispers to her.

'OK,' she replies.

They get to their feet, to roars of delight. 'Wardrobe, wardrobe!'

'For God's sake use a condom!' shouts Nick, emulating someone's anxious mother.

'How come I only got a kiss? We need to look at the rules,' laughs someone else.

'Spin on!' declares nose ring as Scott holds Becky's hand firmly and leads her away to the walk-in wardrobe, while the whole room raises another cheer. His expression now is not soft, or kind – rather, he looks determined.

Becky realizes that she has agreed to leave one place, but in doing so seems to have agreed to come to this place: a space about the size of a small garage, full of orderly rails of shirts and skirts, lines of shoes and boots. What are the rules of a place like this? There is no bed to lie down on. She hasn't agreed to that. A sliding door has bumped closed on its rails behind them. They can still hear the game being played, people hammering their hands on walls and cupboard doors and knees, like a drumroll as the bottle spins. She can't take off any clothes in here, can she? Does she even want to? She looks at Scott, trying to decide what she wants. Is this at least an answer to the question of how to pass the night, with Adam gone and Mary somewhere with Brendan, perhaps taking her clothes off right now? Is this what she wants?

Scott steps toward her and kisses her, pushing her slightly into a soft wall of coat sleeves. His hand circles one of her wrists.

She closes her eyes and, actually, like the first time he did it, it's sort of OK. He's not really shaving yet and his lips are soft. Like kissing a girl almost, she thinks, and then she asks herself why she's thinking such a weird thing. It's not like this is her first kiss. *Not my first rodeo!* She wishes her mind would stop wandering. Why can't she just concentrate on this or, better, not concentrate on anything?

He slides his other hand onto the waistband of her jeans. She remembers suddenly that she is flying low. He eases away the button above the open zip and she no longer knows what this is, in the middle of all the coats and a mother's best high heels on racks. She feels his fingers reach for the hem of her pants. She breaks off and pulls her wrist out of his light grasp.

'No?' he says.

'I'm not sure,' she says, because the word 'no' on its own is just too stark, too short, too accusatory.

He steps back and she breathes easily again. She does her zip and button back up. He looks ashamed of himself.

'Was that not . . .?'

'No, it's . . . I'm on my period.' An easy enough lie to stop him feeling bad.

'Oh, fuck. Sorry. I should have . . .'

'No, I should have said.'

'It's a really weird game, this whole thing. I just . . . Can you forget about it?'

'Yes.'

They stand there. Where do they go from here? Do they go back to the room? They'll clap. They'll ask questions. Did she blow him like a champion? Did they do it? They won't be able to look sad about anything.

'Do you want to kiss me again?' she says, in the end, because she can't think of another way for things to go.

'Do you want to?'

'I don't mind.' Does he now not want to?

'This whole thing's . . .'

'Yeah, it's weird. I mean, it's a random way to . . . you know. Get off with someone.'

'I think,' says Scott, 'we probably stopped playing it for pretty good reasons. Not that . . . I mean, you're really nice.'

'So are you.'

'It's just that everyone else at this party . . .'

'Yeah, I know!'

'I'm not sure I can face going out there to kiss the rest of them.'

Becky laughs and Scott laughs too, like a new way out of this closet space has just opened up and they've both elected to take it.

'What do we do now?' asks Becky. 'Do we just hide in here until they get bored?'

127

Scott reaches into his jeans pocket and takes out a small brown pill bottle. Unscrews the cap and shakes a pill into his palm. 'I'm going to go down the rabbit hole to see where it leads me,' he says.

'What is it?' she says.

'Just a pill.'

'Curiouser and curiouser,' Becky smiles. 'Mary's meant to be doing one with me later.'

'I've got four. One's for Brendan. He wanted two more. I'm guessing that was for the two of you. You can have yours, if you want?'

'How much are they?'

'Tenner.'

'What are they like?'

'I don't know. I'll let you know in about an hour! I might go and have a dance. Come up on the dancefloor.' He smiles at her. 'Thanks for not being weird about this whole . . . thing . . .' And suddenly she doesn't want him to go. Can she follow him downstairs?

'Can I have mine?' She rummages in her bag for her purse and hands him a ten-pound note.

'Great. We'll come up together. Drug buddies.'

He hands her a pill and she takes it quickly, before she can change her mind.

If Mary can break into new areas, then maybe so can she.

She kisses him on the cheek because she wants to let him know that she is going to be a good time when she's high, and that she's happy with herself and if anything goes wrong he should be a friend to her.

There is a roar outside. *Kiss. Kiss.*

'When we go out there,' he says to her, 'we should say we found another Spin the Bottle group and had an orgy with them.'

She laughs. 'Or we could just stay here for a bit? It's kind of nice. Kind of *Lion, the Witch and the Wardrobe*, you know? We could just push at this bit of wall and see where it goes.'

They both try and push through the wall and when nothing happens they collapse onto the soft carpet in giggles. Soon her head is swimming in ice cream whirls, making shapes like the silken seashell coverlet she saw in the parents' bedroom. They giggle and they paw at each other's faces like kittens and talk a language only the other understands.

Her eyelids flicker, like she might be sick but she doesn't really mind. Her nerves are all tingly.

'Smacky pills,' mumbles Scott.

'What?'

'I'm just . . . Jesus. Ketamine or something.'

She rubs her hands together to send ripples through her.

Out in the bedroom, a girl's voice. 'All right you lot, out you go. No one should be in here. It's my mum and dad's room.'

Becky and Scott giggle quietly, pressing each other's fingers to their lips. They aren't going anywhere.

There is a lot of calling out, a kerfuffle, more shouting: 'Get a move on, Bento!' Before silence finally falls outside.

The light is too bright and then it's out. Maybe she is sick after all. She doesn't know if she is alone. She drinks because she's thirsty and forgets she's swallowing down another sickly sweet alcopop. Her head spins and spins and there is a point where she stops being able to remember images, feelings, anything . . .

Chapter 12

Becky breathes in the smell of her flat. She feels safe here, cocooned in the familiar furniture-polished, washing-powder-marinated mustiness. It is her refuge from the nagging rawness inside about how she crashed clumsily and painfully out of the bar. Her despairing call to Adam. The identity of the woman on Matthew's floor. She smothers her feelings of discomfort with the business of *doing things*, like tamping down a plaster on the sting of freshly scraped skin.

She collects the post from the mat. Does Maisie just step over it? Does she even see it there? She goes to hang her coat and notices that the shelf Adam said he would fix is still sliding toward the floor at a precarious angle, held in place by a single rawlplug. It's unreasonable to feel annoyed – even though he said he'd mend it, Adam isn't her carpenter – but she feels it anyway as she adds the task to an already over-long list of things to be resolved and fixed. She wishes she could confidently outsource these tasks to buy herself some space. Wishes she could outsource her feelings.

In the background the comforting and domestic sounds

of her kitchen filter through: china plates laid down on a wooden table top, the stiff fridge door suctioned open with might, and the springtime bird sound of Adam and Maisie laid over it all.

Maisie laughs. Becky stops to listen, smiling. Forgetting all the tasks that lie ahead.

'It did, it totally did. I'm not lying,' she says. 'Seriously, Lily's place would have an actual cake stand and someone to dust it. But wow, it's awkward when her mum and dad are around. No one talks much, it's like they're in church or something. Lily says they're both obviously waiting for the day that she and her brother leave school so they can file the divorce papers. So I suppose I'm saying thank you, for sparing me a lifetime of seeing you and Mum argue, or at least hate each other silently.'

Becky's stomach tightens. She can almost hear the tangle and speed of Adam's thoughts in the silence that follows.

'It's different here, I mean we're different, it's a different situation,' he says.

Becky lays a flattened palm to her tummy, protective of the place where Maisie began her life.

She thinks of the times she wished her body would split in two. One half to live in, one half to burn. Her hand circles and un-circles the phone in her pocket. She wonders what scorn she can pour on Scott's potential evening plans: a late showing of *Nightmare On Elm Street*? French onion soup at that bistro in Kentish Town? One day she'll do it, one day she'll have the guts to post: *I hope you find*

*glass in your soup, that it cuts your throat and you drown
in your own blood.*

'What do you want to do with these little cakes?' says
Adam.

'Shall we just put them all out on the plate? She'll be
back any minute. Hey, why are you laughing?'

'I just don't understand what's wrong with being called
Danish?' Becky can tell that Adam is speaking the words
through a broad smile.

Maisie sighs. 'I'm not talking about that again.'

'Why is someone calling you Danish an insult, though?'

'It's not the *Danish* thing. He was taking the piss out
of my height. So what that I'm the tallest girl in the class?
I don't give a shit about it. Call me the Great Dane. Viking
girl. Watch me not give a fuck.'

'Language.'

'You know you can height-shame as well as fat-shame?'
Her voice is higher, more agitated now. 'Stop *laughing* at
me!'

'I'm not laughing *at* you. Danish women are famously
beautiful. They are known for their beauty. The Vikings
loved Denmark because all the girls there are really hot.'

'Oh, yeah, lovely. Pillage me now.'

'Jules was probably trying to find a way to compliment
you.'

'No.'

'It takes some men a long time to just say what
they think if it involves feelings. Most of the time boys

take the piss relentlessly out of anyone they fancy.'

'I know, I know. Pulling ponytails. Starts in the play-ground. Jesus,' she says with disdain.

'Adults are big kids at heart. They're worried about their feelings being spotted sometimes. Covering them up lessens the risk of, I don't know, being hurt I suppose.'

Becky folds her arms tight across her chest and looks up at the ceiling.

'It's a stupid strategy.'

'How many times did he call you Danish or a Viking or whatever?'

'All night. I was like, my dad's short and skinny and looks more like he's from Spain than Iceland.'

'I'm the same height as your mum!'

'And she's definitely not Scandi?'

'He's really got inside your head, hasn't he?'

'I really don't care.'

'I believe you.' Adam is deadpan. Becky smiles, pressing a palm to her mouth to stifle a laugh.

'Shut up, Dad!'

'I'm saying I believe you!'

'You're so annoying.'

'If it's any consolation, you take after your mum, and your mum's gorgeous.'

Becky takes her palm away from her mouth and smiles, feeling the warmth of a gentle kind of joy, alongside a strange sense of achievement – like being awarded a certif-icate for something.

'It's not a consolation,' says Maisie. 'I'm still really annoyed with you.'

'With me?'

'Yes, you're being a dick.'

'You're not at all annoyed with Jules, and I'm the problem?'

'That sums it up. And stop laughing!'

Becky enters the kitchen. In an instant Maisie's ferment is forgotten and she flings her arms around her mum. 'We missed you, oh Queen of the movie industry,' she says.

Adam turns to Becky and smiles. 'Seriously, well done. Welcome to your celebration tea party! You're actually going to get a feature film made.'

They hug each other.

'It hasn't happened yet,' she says, looking around the kitchen in awe at how they have decorated it: silver lamé hanging off picture rails and cupboard corners, golden balloons bouncing across the floor. She feels loved. 'But thank you for this. What a lovely way to celebrate a breakthrough.'

Adam, tea cloth flung casually over his shoulder and a smile painted across his flour-dusted face, takes the pile of post from her hands and helps her with her coat. Leafing through it and seeing that only bills remain, he turns to put them in his bag.

'No, don't,' Becky says, taking the envelopes back.

'Let me,' he says, pressing his hand over hers in such a way that is more soft than firm, in such a way that she has to let go.

Hannah Begbie

'Let him, Mum,' shouts Maisie over the scrape of chair leg on tiles. 'I would ideally like to continue having hot showers until we're living off your movie mogul billions.'

'This is the last time, OK? Thank you, but it's the absolute last time.' But Becky is feeling secretly relieved not to have to worry about the bills. And also guilty – at the stab of annoyance she felt when she saw Adam's unfixed shelf. He is her lifeboat, it's so churlish of her to worry about the fact he hasn't repainted the stern.

'So full of pride,' says Adam.

'So much pride and so little money,' chirps Maisie. 'It's fine. I'm going to nail my exams and get my scholarship for sixth-form so at least you won't have to worry about paying the school fees. And I've been thinking,' she continues sombrely, 'you don't have to buy me those Volt trainers, Mum. They are way expensive and I can probably make do with decorating a pair of green-flash with poster paint. It'll be less waste for the landfill and quite retro. I might even start a new trend?'

'You're ridiculous,' laughs Becky. 'Thank you for being thoughtful but we had a deal. Work hard, put the hours in and I will buy you those trainers the day before your first exam. You'll have earned them.'

'If you're sure? It's true that I've been working super-hard and I can nearly spell my whole name now.'

'I simply don't know why they *bother* making you do the exams, love.' Adam is talking in his camp-uncle voice now. 'It's so depressing for the other children.'

'Children ought to be depressed,' counters Maisie, switching into her eco-hippie mode. 'Your generation has fried this planet, man.'

'We didn't know! Nobody knew! We thought ozone layer was very bad layer! We tried make hole in him!'

They continue in this fashion for another minute. Becky is happy just to eat a cupcake and play audience, which is what they want from her. Eventually, when she can get a word in, she asks: 'How was the sleepover?'

'Absolutely fine, thanks.' And when Maisie proffers nothing further, Becky finds herself sunk with disappointment, wanting her to talk about Jules in the way she knows Maisie spoke to Adam.

'No gossip?'

'Everything was supervised and very safe.' I'm a nag, thinks Becky. I'm the not-fun parent with conditions and rules attached to everything. Of course she doesn't want to talk to me about fun stuff.

They sit down and cut the white iced celebration cake.

'Tell me,' says Maisie, 'was it that flamenco top I lent you that got your deal done? Was it the nice little ruffle over a highlighted, sparkling décolletage that reeled in that actress and director? Were they like, that woman has got *serious* taste?' She laughs, picks up her fork and stabs the cake. 'Seriously though, massively pleased for you, Mum.'

'Thanks, my darling.'

Becky reminds herself that this is one of life's joyful moments. She takes her phone out of her pocket and puts it face-down on the sideboard, vowing not to look at it again while she is with her family. One day soon she will delete her Instagram app. Delete him.

'We've been talking about what to do for Dad's birthday. We've been making lists. You'll be proud.'

'So what are you thinking?' says Becky.

'I don't know.' Adam takes a seat next to her. 'Something low key in the evening. At a pub, maybe? The room on top of The Three Bells?'

'It's quite small.'

'I dunno, I went to take a look at it with Kate the Sunday before last. I think it'll be fine. Kate's mate had her thirtieth there.'

'Kate's mate,' says Maisie. 'I'm a fren of Ben. I'm a pal of Hal.'

Becky had seen their friend Kate for lunch since then, and Kate hadn't said anything about it. Becky has no right to information from either of her friends, and more than that, any information proffered shouldn't cause a dent beyond casual curiosity – and yet, something shifts and slips inside her, jarringly making space for new, as yet, unnamed possibilities.

'This is your big 3-2,' she says quickly. 'Why don't you get some of your friends together for a dinner party at your flat?'

'He doesn't want to cook on his own birthday, Mum,' says Maisie.

'Of course he does. He loves cooking.'

'I might have the builders in doing some stuff, I don't know, not sure yet,' says Adam.

'We'll throw you a party, Dad,' says Maisie, and gets up to leave.

'Where are you going?'

'Sorry, Mum. Gotta message Lily about some stuff,' she says, loping out the door.

Becky pours coffee, pressing her hand tight over its lid. She finds herself absorbed in the tiny bubbles sliding over the black water.

'So, have you got any Danish blood?' asks Adam.

'What?'

'Some boy's been teasing Maisie about her height. I think he may have been trying to compliment her, but she's still annoyed.'

'Dad was tall. You'd have to ask him. Oh no you can't: he fucked off to Malaga.'

Adam laughs. There is an awkward pause, something charged in the air. 'Maisie asked me to move in,' he says.

'Of course she did. She loves you.'

'She likes it when we're all together.'

'You know it's not that simple. Remember what happened at Christmas?'

'It was a great Christmas.'

'It really was,' says Becky. 'But the look on her face when the time came for you to go home.'

'I don't really understand. We could avoid all that if I moved in. I could sell my place and buy a townhouse.

139

Two floors for living, one floor each for messing up our private lives. Maisie would love that. I could keep her company when you go on dates. You can criticize my pancakes. And anyway, I hate my flat.'

'Your flat is great. People would die for that flat.'

'I've grown out of it. Exposed brick just looks like someone couldn't be arsed to plaster, and however high the central heating goes, it's still too cold.'

'You need to brighten it up a bit, is all. You need a few plants.'

'Or some human beings.'

'It would be really confusing for her.'

'Why?'

Becky cannot believe he is being so bold. He is suggesting something practical, as if that would be the sum total of it, and yet, what he's talking about . . . If it went wrong, it would shatter them all.

'Maisie needs stability,' she says.

'Maisie needs Nike volt trainers.'

'Seriously, two people bringing home dates?'

'You never have dates,' he says.

'That's a whole other issue.'

'It'd be simpler. She already grew up with us like this.'

'Yes, but living apart.'

'We already spend so much time together.'

'Nobody's taking that away from her. I just think we shouldn't . . . get her hopes up.'

'Hopes?'

'Adam. Come on.'

'What?'

Becky turns away and begins to clear crumbs and stack plates.

'So are you going to talk to me about last night?' he says. 'You sounded terrible.'

'Same old shit. It's worse when I get tired.'

'Well . . .'

'That's all. I'm a bit shattered. That's all it is.'

She can't look at him. He knows her better than anyone else and for a moment she thinks about telling him everything that is inside her head, all the clashes and conflict and suspicions. But what exactly would she be saying? That she thinks something might be wrong? Something has always been wrong. She always thinks that. Where is the news?

'I wish you'd let me help more,' says Adam. 'You're getting really tired. You work too hard.'

'I like working hard. And you've helped enough,' she says. 'I don't want you to have to keep on popping up to pay the bills. She's nearly sixteen, Adam. You should be, I don't know . . . your job is done. Your monumental task! You know I'll never be able to thank you.'

He looks so sad. 'It's hardly a job, Beck. It was never a job. I love you guys.'

'I didn't mean for it to come out like that.'

She gets up from her chair and throws her arms around his neck.

141

When she feels him in her arms now, she feels the edges of a possibility. It's not the first time she's thought about it. If it was clear-cut between them, if they were just recent friends, if their past wasn't so sticky and embedded with complication – then perhaps she'd see things clearer and be prepared to throw the dice on the non-precise nature of what is, or is not, between them.

But she can't afford for it not to work.

So it mustn't be tried.

Adam's phone beeps. He glances at the screen, ignores it.

'Who's that?' asks Becky idly. 'Svetlana who only eats apple crumble? Beth who windsails in dresses? Or Alberta, who keeps getting blocked by Twitter?'

'None of them,' he laughs. 'I'm off internet dating now.' He pauses. 'It's just Kate.'

'Oh, right.'

'Yep.'

'What's she saying?'

'She's just sending over some times for the cinema tonight.'

'Oh, great.'

Becky returns to her chair and they sit in silence. She is sure Adam can hear her heart racing, can read her thoughts like ticker tape across her head. She reaches for something, anything.

'Have your birthday here,' she says. 'It'll be nice. Have your birthday with us and your friends, here. Please.'

Chapter 13

In the lightless hours before dawn, Janette goes to use the toilet for the fourth time. She has a kidney infection that she blames squarely on the stress of her daughter's affliction. She pops her head around Becky's bedroom door, as she has done since she was a child, to check on her. But she finds the room empty.

She searches the other rooms in the house, looking behind curtains and under beds as if playing an age-old game of hide and seek, expecting to find Becky curled up with tea on a sofa or chair – somewhere. The pregnancy seems to have broken Becky's usual patterns of sleep. She has been keeping odd hours, up through the night and sleeping the days away.

Janette opens the back door and checks to see if Becky is sitting out there, under the cold spring stars, but the garden is black and empty; nobody comes to the call of her daughter's name.

Janette calls Adam before she calls the police, because lately Adam is the only friend Becky has allowed to visit

143

her at home. Adam says he'll go and look for her. She's probably gone for a walk, is all.

Janette is able to go back to bed, and begins to allow herself to be annoyed with Becky again. A teenage girl out walking the streets in the early hours! This is exactly the kind of muddle-headed not-thinking that led to her getting pregnant. She has no common sense! No bloody regard for other people, when it comes down to it. Janette's kidneys ache. She vows to call the GP first thing; for antibiotics, yes, those are needed. And to ask – is it normal, sitting up all night? Not seeing anyone? Is she actually depressed and, if so, why can't they just give her a pill for it? Will a pill harm the baby?

Her husband is no use. There is a child growing inside his child, this bright girl who was meant to go on to do this and that, who has chosen instead to be no better than one of those blank-eyed girls with bad skin pushing their squealing brats out of their council estate blocks to collect their benefits. A nothing kind of person who'll likely raise the same. It's like he's forgotten that he loves her, thinks Janette, sipping water as her husband snores beside her. How does that work? Because for all her anger – and there's plenty of that – she couldn't ever forget to love her own daughter. Is that why she's still up? Isn't that why her kidneys hurt?

It is not hard for Adam to find Becky.

She is sitting – bent over, holding her ankles, facing her feet – on the low scarlet step on the highest mustard platform of the topmost climbing frame in the local park. She snaps up, terrified, when Adam says her name from the top rung of the ladder.

She is shivering in the cold night air. He gives her his jumper and his coat and his hat.

He takes the seat next to her, his arm thrown over her shoulders to seal the warmth between the layers of clothes she now wears. It is then that he sees the half-full bottle of neat vodka at her feet.

'That's not ideal,' he murmurs. 'Given you're keeping it.'

'I'm not *keeping* it. I'm giving birth to it. Then someone else can take it.'

'OK. But . . . you know what I'm saying.'

'Too late for that.' She glances back at the bottle with glazed eyes.

'Maybe once is OK. I don't know but . . . it's probably OK.'

'Don't tell me it's OK. Nothing is.'

He looks out at the stars. 'Well. Nice night for it.'

'Did Mum tell you to come out?'

'No, I felt like a dawn trip to the swings and you happened to be here. Which is nice for me.' He doesn't get a smile from her. 'Yeah, she rang me.'

'There's no law against going out.'

'True. It's probably why she called me and not the police.'

'She hates me so much.'

145

'She rang me. Which means she was checking on you at five in the morning. That's not someone who hates you.'

'Yeah, it is. You can hate someone and still have to look after them. I bet there are psychopath murderers whose mums still turn up for prison visits.'

'Isn't that a good thing?'

'I'm not going to know . . .'

'How'd you mean?'

'Whether it turns out decent or . . . a criminal like its father.'

'What?' Adam has gone very still.

'Someone raped me when I was passed out. That's why I'm pregnant.' She looks directly at him. The words feel numb and stripped to her, like they belong to somebody else. 'I don't remember any of it. It happened at that house party in Hampstead.'

Adam says nothing, his eyes just visible in the near-dawn light, wide and horrified.

'I'm really sorry,' he says, finally.

'I think it was Scott . . . it was Scott who raped me. He tried to do something earlier in the evening but I didn't want to. We did a pill instead and . . .'

'And what?'

'I woke up and I'd been . . . I just don't remember anything. Scott was the last person I was with, I think he was there when . . . But I don't know.' After a few minutes have passed and Adam hasn't spoken, Becky says, 'I don't even know if it was definitely against my will because I can't remember, I just can't . . . Like, maybe I said yes?' Another minute passes and Adam touches her hand gently, unfurling it from its tight grip around her own wrist, like she has been trying to conceal something there.

The morning after the party, fingerprint bruises had come up on her wrist, gradually, like a series of little images appearing in a polaroid picture. The bruises have long since disappeared but she still finds herself holding a place that feels branded, laid claim to. Who had done it? Had *she* done it? Had she been the cause of her own pain?

'Can you please just say something?' She says eventually, turning to Adam.

'Sorry.' He is crying. 'I can't believe this is happening.'

She reaches for the bottle at her feet. 'I shouldn't have got so wasted. I was out of it. It wouldn't have happened if I hadn't . . .' She is gritting her teeth and trying not to cry when she hurls the bottle into a high arc. They both watch it smash across a steel upright of the junior swings.

'I didn't go to the police or anything,' she says, a tear tracking her cheek. 'I mean, what would I say? I got drunk and did drugs and blacked out. What are they going to do?'

'Why didn't you get rid of it?' He catches himself. 'Sorry. Fucking stupid question. Ignore me.'

'I was six months when I went to the doctor. I can't

Hannah Begbie

explain it totally. I didn't want it to be real. But I can feel it kick.' Now she begins to cry. 'Before it was just like my period had gone but now I can actually feel it in me. I just want to die.' A great wrenching groaning sound escapes her. It sounds alien. Her misery is absolute. After a moment, Adam puts his arm around her.

'Do you think I'm disgusting?' she asks him. He is shocked by the question. 'It's OK if you do. I just want to know.'

'I don't think you're disgusting. I love you.'

She cries harder at that, at the dreadful kindness of his lie.

'I want to kill him,' she says. 'I don't know what to do,' she cries.

'You'll be OK,' he says.

'What if I love it though?'

'I don't . . .'

'I'm scared I'll give birth and they'll make me hold it and I won't be able to get it away from me. I just want it to be over *now*. I want to die.'

'Don't. Please don't say that.' They are both crying now, holding each other. Months of despair flooding out of her. She knows how thick and toxic it is; she watches his skin fall away as it touches her.

Later she sits on one of the swings, pushing off the asphalt with the toes of her shoes, while he collects the shards of broken glass from the vodka bottle. This is Adam,

148

who drops empty crisp packets on the pavement. She realizes that he's worried a kid will cut themselves on the broken glass.

She has emptied out. Now she has a headache. The sun is not yet up but the sky is lightening. Her mum has called Adam again and they've spoken, Adam talking to her in calm, measured tones.

'Do you think I said anything before it happened? What do you think actually happ—'

'I don't know,' he said. 'In a way it doesn't matter as much as what happens now.'

'Do I go to the police?'

'I think you have to figure out what is best for you. I mean, talking about killing yourself . . . a doctor, a . . .'

'I don't want to be in my body.'

'OK, but you don't want to die. This is . . . this is horrible now, but if you give it time, I know you don't believe me, but you can still have an amazing life. You're funny and you're clever and you're beautiful. You're going to have great things happen. Not just this.'

'I can't do it. I can't do any of it.'

'I'll help.'

'Every day one of my parents asks me who the father is. My dad wants to know who'll pay for it. My mum just— I don't know, I think she just needs to know. And I just say, *I'm not telling you*.'

'Why?'

'I don't want to be that person. I don't want them to

149

look at me like, like that . . . like someone who was stupid enough . . .'

Adam's face stretches with effort and pain, his eyes fill with tears. 'But Becky, none of this is your fault.'

'I went to the party. I got drunk. I didn't say anything. I did a million things that were my fault. And now look at me.'

'It's not like they're going to throw you out. Are they?'

'My dad . . . My dad thinks I just fucked anyone. He doesn't say it but I know he thinks it. He thinks I don't even know the father's name, and that's why I can't say it. Because I'm that kind of a person. He looks at me like, like I'm a slut.'

'That's his problem.'

'I have to live there.'

'Not for long.'

'I can't do it. I'm sorry. I just can't.'

He throws the last of the glass into the bin and returns to her. Facing her, he begins to push her on the swing. There is a wobble in his voice when he asks her, 'What do you mean when you say you *can't do it*?'

She turns to face him: her eyes clear, tearless, determined now. 'I mean that I don't want to be here any more. And I don't even want to talk about it with you because I don't want you to end up feeling bad, like you should have done something to change it, or like you can do something to change it. You can't. Nobody can.'

'You're talking like you're going somewhere . . .'

'It's my fault. I took drugs with him. I should have known.'

'Becky, look at me.'

'I don't want to.' She pushes her feet off the asphalt and swings, her eyes closed now.

'Please hang on a bit longer. Just while we work it out.'

'It's OK.' She cuts him off. 'I will.' But in her flat and firm words, delivered to silence him, he understands that calculation replaces honesty. She has put him on the other side of an invisible wall. Her decisions are being made behind closed eyes.

He is afraid of her unhappiness now, at how deep and impregnable it is. He can't shift it.

'Let me take you home,' he says finally.

'OK,' says Becky. Going through the motions now. She is, he knows in his gut, waiting to be alone again so that she can do what she needs to do to remove herself. He wants to make her promise not to kill herself, but that moment has gone.

Janette opens the front door and lets Adam and Becky in. She didn't go back to bed after Adam called her. She knew she wouldn't sleep a wink.

'Have you been drinking?' she asks. She can smell the vodka.

'No,' says Becky. There is no life in her voice. 'I'm going to go to bed.'

'Let's have a cup of tea first,' says Adam. 'I'm quite

cold.' Becky moves seamlessly towards the kitchen and the kettle. Janette looks at Adam: he sees how frightened she is, and she sees that same set of fears in him. They follow her.

Bill lumbers down the stairs in his dressing gown.

'Bit early, isn't it?' he says to Adam. Adam shrugs.

'Do you want tea?' Janette asks him. 'Becky's making.'

'No.'

'Can I help?' Adam asks Becky. She shakes her head. He sits down.

The kettle boils with a click.

'It's my baby,' says Adam. 'I'm the father. She's been protecting me because she didn't want me to feel like it was up to me to have to sort things out. We made a mistake. And I have to take responsibility for that.'

Becky turns. In her expression, her mother reads the final revealing of a secret.

'You stupid fucking prick!' shouts her father, at Adam. 'You've ruined her life!'

'No, I haven't,' says Adam, firmly. This skinny guy, talking like he's made of iron: how can he be a teenager? 'Becky's going to have a great life. Becky's brilliant. This is just something we've got to get through first.'

Bill takes two steps and punches Adam in the face, knocking him to his knees. Becky cries out and runs to intervene, Janette flies in, and for a moment the four of them are locked in a surreal, wild struggle, blood flowing from Adam's nose and Janette wailing and Becky putting herself between her father and Adam, her father vibrating with rage.

'Coward!' shouts Bill. 'You stitched her up and you let her hang!'

'I know,' says Adam, bleeding down his T-shirt. 'I'll try to be better.'

Afterwards they sit in her bedroom, the two of them, two plugs of toilet paper up his nostrils to stem the bleeding.

'This way you can't kill yourself,' he tells her. 'I know you're my friend and you care about me, at least on some level. And if you kill yourself then I'll always be the cause of it. For your family and my family and everyone we know. So you won't do it.'

'But you'll be the person who got me pregnant. And gave away their child.'

'I can live with that. I can't live with losing you.'

'I don't want you to be making that choice.'

'Tough. I made it. Even if you try and say you don't know who the father is, now they'll think you're lying. To protect me.'

'I can come clean. Tell them what happened to me . . .'

'I don't want you to have to do that. And you don't want to do that. This way's better. Let them blame me. Your dad can hate me. I mean, I don't give a fuck if he does. I can take it.'

'Is your nose broken?'

'I don't think so.' He smiles at her. 'No bad thing if it is. I'll look like a tough guy. The kind who strangles thugs with his cardigan if they make trouble.'

'This thing you're saying, it . . . it isn't something we can take back.'

'I know that.'

'Adam, your mum . . .'

'My mum will be nice about it.'

'It's not just me people will look at differently.'

'I know. Becky, I've thought all that through. It's so much less shit for men. So this is something I can do. Let me do it.'

'My dad will be on at you about everything.'

'Do they know you're going to put the baby up for adoption?'

'Yes.'

'All right, so this is only for a little bit. Just let me be the one whose fault it is. If that's what your dad needs, to stop blaming you. It's easy.'

How is any of this easy? Still, she feels something lift, fractionally. She tests the idea of killing herself: the idea she has run toward and then pushed away for weeks now. And she sees that he is right: she finds that she cannot bear the unfairness of it, as she pictures Adam castigated, blamed, and screamed at for destroying her.

He has trapped her into staying alive. And she hopes against hope now, that maybe he is right about the consequences of that: that someday she will find all this behind her and be glad of her existence again.

She feels the kick against the side of its soft balloon home and she finds herself wondering: does it know her heart?

It's not like it's uncomplicated.

When Adam's parents come round with Adam, and they sit, the six of them, Becky comes close to breaking.

They are so kind. They offer to help out with expenses, like post-natal care. They offer to contribute to Becky getting some help with therapy, if she wants it.

Adam's mum suggests, tearfully, that maybe if Becky changes her mind and decides to keep it then they will help, they'd love it, really they would . . .

'Mum,' says Adam sharply.

'I'm just saying that it would always be loved. I'm sorry, but I have to say that. But I won't say it again. I'm sorry.'

'Becky's going to university,' says Bill. Becky tries to picture herself in Freshers' Week, running riot with her new friends in student halls. But she can't see it. There is no future where she is so light, and free, and rootless.

All she sees is Scott's expression as she steps back from him and he lets go of her wrist. As she readjusts her jeans. Pure disappointment. Had he planned everything from that moment onwards? Was it always going to be her? Would the same have happened with another girl in that room or was it something about her?

'What are the arrangements for the birth?' asks Adam's father. He has brought a notebook with him so that he can capture any to-do items that he agrees to take on. He volunteers to drive Becky and Adam in, when it's time.

'You don't have to be there,' says Becky to Adam, and she means it. In fact, she wants him not to be there. She wants nobody there.

'I'll be there,' says Adam.

'Fucking right you will,' says Bill.

'I'll give you all my mobile number then,' says Adam's dad. 'I read that women often go into labour at night, so . . . I'll bear that in mind.'

'We've cleared the diary,' says Adam's mum, blinking back tears. She wants to ask: *Can I see the baby? Can I hold it? Can I take it home? When it looks like my son, can I refuse to let anyone take it away from us?* And instead, she looks down at her lap.

Two weeks before the baby is due, Bill leaves his family.

One morning, the three of them are sitting round the kitchen table, plates of burnt toast and cups of cold tea in front of them.

Janette leaves the room and comes back in brandishing a thin cardboard box. Janette has spent money on an expensive cream for stretch marks. She thinks it will gee everyone up.

'It'll help her get back to normal,' she says.

Bill stares at the receipt. 'Forty quid? For that?'

'It's a good one. We want her to have a good one, don't we?'

He goes upstairs and Janette calls after him, 'I'm not taking it back. And anyway, you've already taken the top off, so I bloody can't.'

Becky wishes the ground would swallow her up. She wonders if she could move into Adam's parents' house, at least just until this is all over with. And then she remembers the look on his mum's face and that love will ruin everything. Love will persuade and cajole her to keep the criminal's baby and turn one blacked-out moment into the rest of her life.

What if the baby looks like Scott? The thought of it makes her sick.

Bill returns thirty minutes later, carrying a suitcase. He doesn't announce his departure. He just goes.

'Is he going?' Janette asks Becky. 'Is he actually going?'

Janette chases after him, calling him a selfish prick all the way down the street.

When her mother returns to the kitchen, Becky is bent over and throwing up all over the kitchen floor. Janette goes to her quickly and scoops handfuls of her daughter's hair back up and around her neck. 'There, there,' she says. 'There, there.'

Adam comes round and they sit on her bed watching eighties comedy movies, eating popcorn. They don't talk much. What is there to say now? They are waiting out their lie together.

Word has got out at school. Mary gets in touch to say: Adam??!

Becky doesn't reply.

'Have you seen Scott?' she asks Adam.

'No,' he says. 'I'm not even sure he knows.'

Here comes life. This screaming, wriggling, red-faced hungry thing. Becky feeds her, only because it seems cruel not to. The milk is there. Her breasts hurt. The baby latches on. The tightness of the connection surprises her. The baby's other hand rests on her breast.

She looks nothing like Scott.

None of them are meant to come, not Janette or Adam's parents, but they come anyway. And what can she do? Turn them away?

On the face of it, Adam looks like a little boy himself. All that steel going. He wants to protect her and he doesn't know how.

Janette holds the child and its tiny red fingers clamp round her little finger. 'I can't believe your dad's missing this,' she says, blunt to anything but the truth of what she feels.

Adam's mother changes the baby's nappy, with quick expert movements.

'You haven't forgotten anything, have you?' says Adam's dad.

'You don't,' she replies, stooping to kiss the baby's belly. 'Are you going to hold her?' she asks Adam.

And the moment Becky sees Adam kissing the child's head, holding her in his arms, she knows without doubt that something catastrophic has happened.

They have all fallen in love, and so fast.

It will fall to her to cut these ties. To break one, two, three, four hearts, not including her own. To hand this baby over to someone else, someone who will smell unfamiliar. Who can offer her a bottle where she had a breast. Will the child remember?

'Do you give her a name or do the other people do it?' Adam's mother is doing her best not to cry as she asks it.

'Maisie,' says Becky. The name comes unbidden. From out of nowhere, like the child herself.

'It means pearl,' says Adam. 'From the Greek.'

'*Margarites*,' says Adam's dad, himself born half-Greek on his mother's side. And bearing a name now, the baby adds another stitch. It is one thing to give away an unwanted child; it is another to give away Maisie.

Becky looks to Adam, willing him to be resolute where she fears she won't be. Tell them all it's time to go. Begin the arrangements. Strip away her name, gifted in a moment of weakness, of instinct. Take it back; it's not hers. The child, the name, none belong to her. Take them away now.

Maisie opens her eyes and blinks. Her lips move. The beginnings of a cry. The baby is handed back to Becky and Becky looks at him, silently pleading: doesn't he know what to do any more? He has been so certain.

Maisie latches onto Becky's other breast and begins to feed again.

'She's going to be tall like you,' says Adam.

Becky's bones ache with exhaustion. She reaches for the last thing she can find.

'Adam,' she says. 'Don't you realize? If I keep her, you've got a daughter for the rest of your life.'

Let him decide.

If he can carry that weight, she'll carry hers.

'OK,' says Adam.

'No,' says Becky. 'Listen to what I'm saying.'

'I know what you're saying,' he says. 'If you want to keep her, I'll try my best to be a good dad.'

It is incomprehensible, this offer. This stupid, kind, too-generous teenage boy. He doesn't know what he's doing. He's making her decide.

'Keep her.' It spills out of Janette, who has lost a husband but gained a granddaughter, and who finds that she cannot now lose her too.

'We'll help,' says Adam's father to Adam.

'You don't have to decide now,' says Adam to Becky. 'You can change your mind any time, if you think about it.'

The people from the agency tell Adam much the same. People change their minds all the time, he reports back. Sometimes forever, sometimes only for a few months.

'She needs to smell your skin as well, son,' says Adam's dad, who has done all the reading, despite the situation. 'That's how she recognizes you to begin with.' So Adam peels off his T-shirt and holds Maisie against his skinny chest. He rocks her gently, cradling her head and neck, kissing her cheek. It comes easily to him. Of course it does, thinks Becky. He's generous with this as with everything else.

For a moment she thinks: look at everything that Scott is missing here. Maisie is hers alone. Scott doesn't exist in the baby's universe, and never will. Becky feels knowledge harden into the kind of secrets that are kept forever. She'll never tell. And so Scott will never face justice. She cannot have one and keep the other.

Maisie falls asleep in Adam's arms as he sings a low, private song to her.

Later, Janette does what she can with the night feeds and nappies between the extra shift work she has to do, covering the mortgage on her own now that Bill isn't coming back.

On a good week for Becky, Adam visits often, bringing cakes and pies and lasagnas from his mother, changing nappies, rocking the baby, walking and playing with the baby while Becky sleeps off the long nights of feeding. He falls asleep with Maisie on his chest before returning home. But there are days at a time when he doesn't come, and it's those days Becky finds the hardest and loneliest – missing him bitterly on those occasions for the lightness and warmth he brings, for the break in tedium. But she doesn't complain, it would be so ungrateful to make a fuss when he has his own future to build, what with exams and coursework and an on-off girlfriend called Charlie with pneumatic tits and good Nike Air Max.

He's been so generous already with his time and his friendship. She can't complain. Her loneliness isn't his fault. It's hers.

They throw a party at Adam's parents' house on Christmas Day, and his dad roasts a turkey with all the trimmings. With his mum and dad and Becky's mum and the baby, they are six.

Adam takes his A-levels and declines to go to university. Becky suspects that he is concerned with leaving them, though he denies it.

He leaves college with his accountancy qualifications and a good group of friends who like music festivals and pub lunches and getting high, sometimes. Later he starts a business of his own, and still he comes to the house, plays with the toddler, their little girl, bringing lunch and dinner, paying bills, bringing a steady stream of nappies, and later new clothes, so that Becky almost never has to buy anything like that. And the days he doesn't come? Glastonbury, and most other summer weekends when there are barbecues or park gatherings. On weekday pub nights and long periods of study. She gets it: she and Maisie are just happy to see him whenever he gets a moment.

She continues to battle loneliness: no one her age is in a similar situation and all the women who are have careers and husbands and mortgages. She's stuck in a no man's land, but Adam doesn't need to be brought down with talk of that.

Becky wonders when he will turn around and say, *Right, it's time now, we should tell people the truth*. But Adam's parents love their granddaughter too and all of them are banking memories of Maisie's first words and steps, like they are precious treasure.

'No rush. Perhaps let's not,' says Adam, when she asks him about it. 'She's my Maisie now. That'll never change now.'

Maisie is at school the day Grandma Janette dies.

Becky finds her, lying on the carpet of the living room.

Everyone grieves, a layer of their Russian doll family removed.

Bill does not come to the funeral.

Adam's parents do, of course. They organize most of it.

Becky thinks she is to blame for breaking up her parents' marriage, for her mother having to take on double shifts to pay the mortgage, for keeping her up through long nights of baby-screaming and later bed-wetting. For everything that caused her heart to give out.

Becky cries and cries and hugs Maisie tighter, with all her love: this precious child who has come into their lives at such a cost.

* * *

When Maisie has just a few more years of primary school left, Adam sits Becky down to talk about the future.

'I've got money now,' he says. 'Not endless money, but enough so if you want to retrain or something you can. I can pay for some childcare. And there's my mum and dad.'

'I can't have you pay for my whole life, Adam. It feels really wrong.'

'That's the point. I want you to find something you really love to do so you can feel less reliant on me. I don't want you to feel like you need me around. I want you to want me around. It's honestly not about the money.'

'I just . . . Whatever you say about it, I find it hard to get past how much you've done for us when you didn't need to do any of it. Wouldn't life be easier for you if you didn't have to spend time visiting us?'

'I don't *have* to do anything. Maisie's the best thing in my life, Becky. She's not an obligation. She's not an inconvenience. I absolutely love her, more than anything in the world.'

She is so relieved to hear him say it.

She knows it's true, but she likes to hear him say it from time to time. It keeps her feeling safe.

Soon, Maisie and Becky move from her old family home into a new place, a maisonette near good schools, and closer to where Adam lives in Shoreditch. Becky takes adult education courses and applies for internships with heartfelt letters written to those people whose work she admires. She's still young, only twenty-four herself. Somehow, between them all, they make it work.

The day Matthew hires her as his PA, with the promise of a move into feature film development if she does her time and proves her worth, Becky finds herself standing outside the central London office, employed, with the sun out, a script to write a report on in her bag, an overpriced coffee in her hand, and she realizes that Adam was right, in the early hours of that kids' playground in Hounslow. She has a life that she loves, after all.

A piece of long-held tension drops away.

That evening, after Maisie is long since tucked-up and asleep, she opens her new laptop – a congratulatory gift from Adam – and for the first time Googles his name:

Scott.

Chapter 14

Less than an hour after returning home from Cannes, Becky finds herself sitting in the back of a company-account black cab, her handbag still cluttered with boarding pass pieces, torn luggage labels, a free mini-bag of airline pretzels, napkins. She has been summoned back to the office, torn away from Maisie and Adam and their cupcakes.

'Where are you?' Matthew had asked. He had flown back on a flight even earlier than hers to catch his son Bart before he left on the school trip to Venice. 'Sorry, but I need you back at the office as soon as you can manage.'

As Becky's cab swings past the oversized-headphone-and-satchel-wearing walkers of Old Street, she inflicts tiny mutilations to her body – straightening her hair where it will not be straightened with tugs to the skull, pulling at her looped silver earrings so the lobes stretch and sting. She is anxious. She copes badly with the threat of bad news in a vacuum. What has she done? How has she messed up?

She taps hard at her phone and finds an image of Scott,

grinning madly with freshly bleached hair. Nominated for an award now! Oh Scott, the gods keep on giving! Something about being the best something in something to do with finance? Who cares what exactly, the point is he looks like the cat that got the cream, the Olympian gold medallist, Zeus, Neptune, Caesar – so smug with his new Tom Ford sunglasses balanced on his head, questioning: *But what to wear on the big night?*

Body bag? Thinks Becky, toggling to Google Maps, typing in his office address and watching (not for the first time) the thick blue-lined route appear, running hot and fast like a vein through London. She could go there now, couldn't she? Later today, perhaps, or tomorrow when she's worked out exactly what she will say. Something like: *Did you hold me down as you fucked me? You hurt me, you know.* She could get her answers, she could, but then what? A police investigation? They'd have to believe her first! And what to tell Adam? What to tell Maisie? What if Scott denied it?

Her head hurts. No, she tells herself, she must focus on the present. She has something more immediate she needs answers to. And so she taps at her phone again, plugging in her name, the company's name, Matthew's name, into Google, into Twitter, into Instagram. She has done this a hundred times, tracking word of mouth on film releases, writing up reports on how trailers have landed, how various stars are talked about. She knows her way around.

She finds what she is dreading.

The fractured images she had been trying to marshal the previous night in Cannes when Sharon's agent had grasped her arm – *It's clear you don't know* – now coalesce into a toxic jigsaw.

Blonde chignon. The long neck. That face. Lapis-blue eyes.

Amber Heath.

Client of DB's.

The woman on Matthew's kitchen floor.

Becky stares at the name again, and the first search result. A clip, hosted on an entertainment news website – one that carries breaking gossip, publishes intrusive photos and catty rumours and no doubt makes a ton of money; adverts, cookies, signs and banners flashing over the text. She impatiently swipes it all away as if clearing away the dirt to reveal the name on a headstone, and presses play.

The footage appears to have been recorded on an iPhone. Perhaps shot by an opportunistic reporter. It is jerky, obviously hand-held as the questioner follows a man emerging from a bar and heading down a busy night-time street in central London. Becky recognizes him as a minor actor, but she can't place him exactly. Was he the special advisor in that BBC drama about the disgraced MP? Or the school teacher in that ITV comedy?

Her brain glitches and jumps, her eyes only able to dart and identify key words, unable to follow the flow of a sentence:

Kingfisher Films. Matthew Kingsman. A relationship with the actress Amber Heath. Alleges that . . .

She plays the clip.

I'd hardly call rape a relationship.

The words come out loud and aggressive, her phone on top volume. Her first instinct is to glance up at the cab driver to see what he's heard, then find the mute button to stop him from hearing more.

She plays it again and reads the words that ticker tape along the bottom: *I'd hardly call rape a relationship.*

The man in the clip has large, clean-cut features, is dressed in a long beige trench coat and dandyish loafers. An air of sozzled camp about him. The reporter seems to have chased him down the street to ask his questions, perhaps that's why his answers are so blunt.

'Are the rumours about your friend Amber true?'

'Yes, she's gorgeous, it's true.'

'Is she having a relationship with Matthew Kingsman?'

'I'd hardly call a rape a relationship.'

'What?'

'No comment. Kingsman's a nasty little bitch. That's my last word on the subject of that tosser.'

'Are they not together then?'

'You're being boring now. Go on, piss off.'

The man waves the reporter away, knocking the phone out of his hand.

The footage ends there.

Her mouth dry, Becky skims the blog post's text. The

man in the video is identified as one of Amber's best friends, fellow actor and noted *bon vivant* Ollie Hennessy. An update on the article says that Hennessy has clarified that he spoke out of turn and that he apologizes for having a big, drunk mouth.

It's far from being a retraction.

David Barraclough, Amber Heath's agent at Total Agents, has been asked for a comment but hasn't replied to the website's overtures.

Becky looks behind her, out of the grey-dusted rear window, as if she's being followed. The traffic is moving fast and she struggles to calculate how long she'll need between alerting the driver, the cab making a safe stop, the wait for the door's red light, opening the door and vomiting onto the pavement.

DB. Such a nice man. Such a nice lunch they had together. She looks at his client list online. Amber is a relatively small fish. Becky tries to remember: had DB pitched Amber before? Perhaps for a supporting part in something that fell apart days before shooting was due to begin? Perhaps Amber maybe even came in to meet for it? Becky tries to think back but the panic is making it hard to ground her thoughts. Was Matthew there? Did he offer an opinion?

She tries to search her phone for more information, each movement cumbersome, clumsy, misdirected and slow now that her hands seem not to be working properly.

Twitter has picked up on the story. Questions being thrown about.

She thinks about Amber's blonde hair spread across Matthew's floor. That same hair tamed and tied up in chignons on red carpets and plaited in the pages of celebrity magazines.

Becky closes her eyes and tries to remember precisely what she saw but all she can see is the blue-veined path on the map flashing its crooked line.

The cab swings left and a motorbike comes for them, swerves at the last minute to avoid the collision and skids away.

Regent Street gives way to a narrow maze of Soho streets with shoppers and workers idly walking the narrow pavements, blackened and sticky outside pubs where beer spilt from the night before traps ash and litter and diesel fumes.

'Here,' she says, when the black cab gets to Soho Square. She pays and waves away her change. Can't think about that. Lands on the pavement, still bent from exiting the cab, no time to hold her hair back, her head tips forward and then, yes, she vomits. Her hair swings into the sick, like vines in the breeze.

It hits the pavement and someone passing by in new white trainers leaps away from the splat, squeaking dramatically at his friend, before they both laugh. 'Drunk or pregnant or both?' says one to the other, loudly, as they walk on.

It had looked like pleasure and pain, on Amber's face. How could she know which was which? Held or pinned down? Rough sex or rape?

She uses the aeroplane napkin from her bag to wipe glossy spittle from around her mouth. Pours water from the aeroplane bottle onto her hair where vomit has caught it, until it runs clean. Her legs are rippling. Don't cry again, she tells herself. Now is not the time.

Siobhan is waiting for her at the front door of their building.

'There you are, thank bloody hell for that. Have you seen?'

'About Amber Heath? Yes, I've just watched it. What's going on?'

'I don't know. He's holed himself away until you get here.' So in they go.

Matthew opens his office door and leans out, hand still attached to the doorknob like he's in a strong wind and needs something to anchor himself to. Becky's heart hammers against her chest wall, piston-quick. Matthew is pale and drawn, his layer of tan wiped away in a matter of hours. And she feels sorry for him.

She and Siobhan step forward.

'Just you,' Matthew says to Becky. 'Siobhan, mind the phones, please. Take messages, say I'm in meetings all day,' he says. 'Becky, in here, please.'

Becky steps into his office. He closes the door behind her. Becky just has time to glimpse Siobhan's expression before it shuts. Envious and wondering.

'Take a pew.'

Becky takes her seat on the sofa. Matthew takes the

low Modernist leather armchair he favours in this set-up. He sits back, swings one leg over the other, grasping the wireless landline phone in one hand and his mobile in the other. Is this what a man accused of rape looks like?

She silently presses her fingers against each other like she is rubbing butter through flour, waiting for his cue.

'There's a story,' he says. 'An actress has made some false accusations about me.'

She realizes she had been expecting him to confess to some kind of crime. When he doesn't, she is more relieved than she thought possible. Yes, she thinks. Of course it isn't true.

'Have you seen the clip?'

'I had a look for company news once Siobhan called me. There's lots of good stuff about *Medea* out there as well.' She means for it to sound balanced, like the media situation might somehow tot up to being a neither-good neither-bad kind of day. She realizes immediately how ridiculous that sounds.

'So, yes, it's not quite Amber making the allegation but her mate, Hennessy. I'm not sure it makes a difference, really. Once it's out there it's out there. I have to decide whether to go after him for slander, or make a statement and let it fizzle out. It's hard to know exactly what's best. Do you know him, Hennessy?'

'Not personally.'

'He's not a great actor. If I sue him, it'll be catnip for him. He'll be in the papers every day for weeks. Darren at IcePR agrees. We're thinking it might be better just to weather it . . .'

'Why would he even say that?'

'What? That I raped her?'

Becky nods.

'Perhaps she told him that.'

'Why would she say that though?'

'Bitter, perhaps? I turned her down for a big part she thought was hers. Maybe it's a kind of revenge.'

'So she planned for Ollie to blurt it out like that?'

'Come on. You know how often photographers just "happen" to be there when an actor does or says something they'd like to have recorded. We've worked on those things ourselves.'

She can feel her heartbeat thrumming in her ears. *Did he or didn't he or did he or didn't he.* She has to hold it together. 'I . . . I . . . What would you like from me, Matthew?'

'Your advice and then your help with making this go away. You and I have work riding on this. IcePR are great but I need a sounding board. I'm not going to blame you if this doesn't go my way, if that's what you're asking.'

'No! God, no. Not at all. Of course, I'll do anything I can.'

'Great.'

He looks tired and lost and not at all like a criminal. She feels sorry for this man who has paid her wages, who bothers to send Maisie birthday cards and who asked after her that time she had pneumonia, wished her well during exams.

She knows he won't have eaten – he never eats when he's stressed – so she takes the bottle of water and the pretzels she's been given on the plane out of her bag. Lays them on the table.

He ignores them both and lights a cigarette. 'You'll need to take care of yourself.' He pauses. 'I've spent the morning talking to financiers, casting directors, the whole shooting match for the rest of our slate. They're all good, all calm. No one's worried. But *Medea* is vulnerable. It's got those strong themes and . . . I don't want a stupid bit of gossip surrounding me to affect your film's shot at getting made.' Becky understands immediately that there is a deal being made here. 'So what do you think I should do?'

'About *Medea*?'

'About the whole thing. With *Medea* I can make sure my name's off the press for it. You can talk to Emilia and Sharon and reassure them.'

'The film wouldn't exist without your support. It doesn't seem fair.'

'Fair?' His tone is brusque, scathing almost. 'Learn to recognize a favour when it's being offered to you. And learn to take it when you need it. You need to protect yourself and your work. Don't ever assume that justice will somehow prevail and make everything OK. Good men lose everything, all the time. Women, too.'

'Yes.' She nods. 'What should I say if Sharon or Emilia ask me about it?'

'Don't make it a questionable statement. You get in early and say: *This is what has happened and this is what we're doing about it.* Make them feel special that you even bothered to consider them.'

She notices that this is exactly what is happening now. He has not denied the allegations but then why would he need to? Never apologize. Never explain. Let everyone else do the talking, let everyone else tie themselves in knots.

'All actors care about is how they are perceived,' Matthew continues. 'How their own careers are standing up. That's all. You have to have the conversations. You pitch it with calm and confidence? It'll be a conversation, forgotten in five minutes, absorbed into a busy schedule. Can you do that?'

'Wouldn't it be better coming from you?'

'God no.' He almost laughs as he says it. 'You're good, you're smart, you can do it.'

'It must be hard on you. All this.'

'You'll get it too, one day, Becky. There's a lot of have and have-nots in this business. Not everyone can be talented. Human beings who are failing love nothing more than to tear someone off the top spot, back down to their level. You're not up there unless someone's trying to drag you down.'

'So I'm telling them that this person, this actress, is

someone you turned down for a role, who thought she'd been offered it, and who probably bitched about you to a friend of hers, and the friend then misspoke about it because he's a drama queen who loves attention.'

'Throw in a joke about vengeful women. Medea. There must be something in the water.' He laughs, but he is not laughing. 'But yes, your version works. Any more questions?'

'No. I'll start making those calls.' Becky finds herself almost looking forward to making those calls, to convincing Emilia and Sharon of how they need to think about this. She finds herself looking forward to the moment she can call him and say, *It's fine, it's done* – to making him proud of her.

'You *do* have another question. Be honest.'

'I don't . . .'

'Surely you want to know if I've slept with Amber? *I'd* be asking that question.'

For a moment he lets that hang there and she wonders if she is being challenged to confess: *I was there, I saw you, I know you've fucked her. But I don't know what it meant, what I saw.*

'The answer is yes, I have,' says Matthew. And these are the words that seal the deal for Becky. An explanation for the two being together on the kitchen floor. He isn't trying to lie to her. She feels a flood of relief, a tension easing that she hadn't fully acknowledged. 'I've cheated on Antonia before. We've muddled through. Antonia has also . . . I'm sorry. Probably you don't want to hear any of this. A middle-aged couple's assorted indiscretions. But I want to be straight with you.'

'Matthew, you don't owe me, you know, I hope you don't . . .'

'We've always kept it between us. But now . . . I mean, what do I say? Do I tell the press: *No, not true, never been alone with Amber?* That fiction would crumble quickly and then I'd look like a liar. I would be proven a liar. But if the alternative is telling them, *Yes, we've fucked but it was consensual?* Then I ruin my family. I have to ask myself, who do I *owe* the truth to? To my wife I owe the ability to hold her head up in front of our friends. I owe my children their family. I owe Amber . . . less than any one of those people. I didn't owe her that part either. And I owe the press nothing at all, though they don't like settling for that. And then I suppose I have to ask myself, what do I owe you, Becky?'

This time she assumes that the question is rhetorical and that she can afford to sit in silence and wait to be given his answer. But instead he sits back, and she realizes that he may, after all, be waiting for her.

'You've supported my whole career,' she tells him. 'You don't owe me anything. It's me who owes you.'

Matthew's eyes fill with tears. He takes Becky's hand. 'Thank you. I know how it costs friends to weather this kind of thing together. But you don't forget the ones who stick by you. I promise you that. You walk over glass for *those* friends, for the rest of your life. Believe me.'

It is the first time he has ever referred to her as his friend.

After a moment he releases her and, as if a little ashamed of his show of feeling, rises and walks to his desk to check a notebook. Becky guesses that he's not really looking at anything, but that he simply doesn't know how to end their meeting. As an employee he told her when the meeting is over; as her friend, how is it done?

'If you don't mind, I'm going to call Sharon now,' Becky volunteers.

'Good. Let me know when you've done it and I'll set up a nice dinner for us all – just you and me, Emilia and Sharon – so we can celebrate properly. I'll take you all to a place that's just opened in Fitzrovia. Private room. Have Siobhan look for a date we can all do.'

He is back to business. He reaches for the phone on his desk and, without looking up at her again, expertly taps in a long number. An American number, she guesses.

She slips out of his office and goes to her own desk as Matthew's friend and fellow producer. In the trenches together, doing what they do – putting out fires and making room for magic. It is her and Matthew together now; they are the people with projects on the line. In the middle of all this ugliness, has she somehow been promoted? Is that actually what is happening now? she wonders, feeling the granules of the favour she is doing him dissolve into water. Transaction complete.

She feels such relief there is an explanation for it all,

and just the slightest knot in her stomach at his genius, his sleight of hand: how he has turned the shape in her head, the possibility of a woman who was receiving something she did not want, into the woman who was not getting enough of what she wanted.

She looks out of the window and sees the clouds form animal shapes, or just clouds. The man is a magician, an alchemist, a god.

Chapter 15

A few days later, Becky is gingerly lifting hot mugs and plates from the dishwasher back into their homes. She is tired after last night when she, Matthew, Sharon and Emilia met to share toasts and successes, stories and champagne at a new gloss-black-tabled Japanese restaurant in town. The mood had been upbeat, those unpleasant allegations dispatched with, far in advance.

They had eaten diver scallops, Wagyu beef and mountains of sashimi. Sharon told them about getting stuck halfway up Mount Kenya with the giardia bacteria multiplying in her gut. The night ended with too many tequila slammers, which Becky managed to avoid by pretending she had a call to make. Out on the pavement after midnight, they had all turned to their Uber apps, high and happy and bonded.

'The potatoes! We've got to get the potatoes on!' Maisie's voice rises in amusement and frustration. 'Come on Mum, that's your job.' She is grasping a vegetable peeler in wet hands and looking annoyed enough to use it on her mother.

Becky looks up, disorientated. 'Sorry, yes.'

'I worry about you sometimes.'

Becky smiles. 'What's to worry about? Other than this mountain of food to chop and slice and fry and boil in time for your dad's friends.' The kitchen table is a mountain range of stuffed shopping bags. Becky rams a few items into cupboards, bending cardboard corners to fit, and switches on the kettle. 'I forgot the streamers, and the balloons, and I meant to do a banner. I was going to write *Happy Birthday You Old Bastard*, in glitter – but he'll have to make do with a *15 Today* badge.'

'Did Matthew talk about Amber last night?'

Becky keeps moving, and has to work to pull all the surprise out of her voice.

'Amber Heath? No, he didn't.' She keeps her voice breezy, turns away to the cupboards and pulls out salts and spicing and rubs. 'Can you pass me that . . . that thing?' She motions to a spatula. 'She's just an actress trying to drum up some attention while she works out her disappointment at losing a role. Storm in a teacup. We had better things to talk about.'

But try as she might, in the last few days Becky has struggled to find any kind of peace, finding herself battling between an image of Amber between castings and gym visits and lunches and beauty appointments, strategizing and wringing the situation for all the publicity she can get – and another image of Amber broken and barely able to get out of bed. An online gossip outlet has recently published a picture of her in tracksuit bottoms and over-sized sunglasses, hair scruffed up in a bun, which could cover both the realities Becky is imagining.

Things come back to gnaw at her. DB's anger with Matthew. Antonia storming in to see him long before any story broke online. And her own skittish memories of seeing Amber there, her mouth opening as if to say something to the woman she must have seen in the kitchen. What had she intended to say?

Becky clasps a palm to her stomach where it twists and complains, and reaches for a clean chopping board from the dishwasher. A carving knife, positioned blade up, catches the end of her finger and a bead of blood forms at the tip. 'Shit,' she says.

'Language!'

Maisie speedily hands her a folded clump of kitchen towel which Becky squeezes around her finger. Fleetingly her focus shifts and Becky finds herself understanding the calm relief that people report after cutting themselves.

Then she files that feeling away.

'Jules the Viking is going to be at Lily's and I said I'd pop by after dinner,' says Maisie. 'I hope that's OK? Your lot'll be on to the crap jokes and beer pong by then.'

'Be back before eleven.' Becky begins peeling, awkwardly navigating the potato skins with her kitchen-towel-bandaged finger. 'What is he, exactly?'

'What do you mean? Like, is he a werewolf? What are you asking?' She is smiling, messing with her mum. 'Relax.

He's my friend.' Maisie is in a bouncy mood, full of questions tonight, and just when Becky is hoping for some quiet. 'When you and Dad dated . . .' Maisie begins again.

'We never dated. We just liked each other for a bit.'

'Enough to have me. So obviously it was meant to be on some level, you lucky people.'

'What did you want to ask me?'

'So Jules called me his Viking Queen yesterday. What do you think that means?'

'It means he believes you are royalty and also that you are a member of a sea-faring race of warriors from—'

'Don't even try to be more annoying than me. Be serious.'

Becky can hear the girlish insecurity in Maisie's voice, the need to know what this boy is thinking about her. She almost regrets teasing her: what if Maisie stops talking to her? Then how will she keep her safe? But Becky also thinks that Jules sounds bombastic and full of machismo, the kind of boy who is looking to get his rocks off at Glastonbury in an expensive tent bought for the occasion by his parents, who have positively encouraged he go, seeing it as a passport to adventure. All the while, Jules is probably planning how to get the pills and dreaming of deflowering someone like Maisie, perhaps Maisie herself, on the built-in groundsheet floor of his expensive tent.

She wants to tell her daughter that, whatever it is Jules means by his comment, she is without doubt so much better than this probably disappointing teen lothario, who is busy hiding a galaxy of insecurities behind his new leather jacket and his long hair and his loud voice.

'If he's teasing you? If he's giving you nicknames? It means he's thinking about you.'

'Did you and Dad have nicknames for each other?'

'I called him my Viking King, as it so happens.'

'Mum!'

'Sorry. Um, I don't know, really. I've forgotten so much from back then already. I think I always called him Adam. He didn't, I don't know, he didn't project a need for nick-naming. Does that make sense? Like, some people end up with ten nicknames given to them by ten different people. But others just get their birth name.'

Maisie has lost interest. There is something else she needs to press on her mother.

'There's this spare ticket for Glastonbury going round,' she says. 'He hasn't offered it to me yet but Lily thinks he will.'

'No. You're not going.'

'Give me three reasons.'

'Pills and amphetamines and vodka.'

'Mum, nobody does speed any more. It's not 1975.'

'Toilets, then.'

'I think I'd survive them. Two hundred thousand people seem to manage it each year. I'll get one of those portable travel things that women can wee into standing up, if you're really stressing about it.'

'You're not old enough for a festival.'

'How come the other parents think their kids are old enough then?'

Becky's phone rings, flashing Sharon's name up on the screen.

'Hold on, I have to take this,' she says to her daughter, clamping the phone between face and neck, wiping grimy and wet hands on a tea cloth, heart thumping with anxiety. 'Sharon! How are you? How's the head? Wasn't last night fun? No, I understand . . . Yes, I think that's normal but you don't need to worry. He simply wouldn't mention it. He finds it very difficult. It's hard to have someone say those things . . . Yes, he's got a lot of dignity.'

Becky turns away from her daughter, who is scraping the white seeds from the core of a pepper and straining to listen.

'Amber has a bit of a track record of making false allegations,' Becky says. 'It's really unfair that some people would condemn him without any proof. It's like they used to drown witches – no evidence, just one person's word and your life's taken from you.'

How very unlike herself she sounds, Becky thinks, turning around as if she can feel the beam of Maisie's gaze burn into her. She sounds too loud, too vehement. Becky wipes grime from her eyes. She is tired, stressed, she thinks. She is not herself. She must get more sleep.

Becky turns back, steps further away and comes to a

standstill at the kitchen doorway, looking out into the hallway.

'Of course I understand. I can tell you that he absolutely . . . no . . . no, he is appalled by the accusations. Absolutely appalled, of course he is. But the thing is, Amber hasn't said anything. It's actually some drunk, show-off friend of hers who was probably recycling a second-hand rumour about the wrong person. The bottom line for me is that I couldn't work for a man who I believe might do anything like that.'

Becky leans against the doorframe and struggles to find something to hold onto, something more than the painted wood beneath her fingers that would not yield or break were she to thump and slam at it.

'I'll see you at the FilmFour meeting next week,' she says. 'Yes, it's very exciting. If we can get them on side we could be shooting this side of Christmas.' Her fists clench and her thoughts turn to *Medea*. The call ends.

She can feel Maisie's eyes on the back of her head.

'You sounded pretty worked up,' her daughter says.

'I am. It's cruel, lobbing accusations at someone without proof.'

'Yeah . . .'

'What?'

'Like . . . isn't there no smoke without a fire?'

'Such overused words. Why bother with the justice system then? What, we can just throw people into jail on the say-so of their pissed-off neighbours or vengeful exes?

I know, what about if someone said, *I saw Maisie kill someone. Or maybe someone who looked a bit like Maisie. She was tall anyway.* Off you go then, Maisie. See you in twenty years. Is that enough smoke?'

Maisie looks a little shocked. Says quietly, 'So why would the actress make something like that up?'

'We have no idea what she thinks! She hasn't said a word to anyone. It's her moon-faced stupid twat friend who's been ruining lives so he can get his fifteen seconds of fame.'

'It's fifteen *minutes* of fame.'

'Whatever.'

'Who were you talking to just now?'

'Oh. The, um. The director.' A flash of something catches her eye. 'What are those on your feet?'

'Nike Volt Utility Trainers?' Maisie replies sheepishly.

'I know that,' she snaps. 'Where did you get them from?'

'Uh . . . Dad bought them for me?'

'They were supposed to be a reward for working hard.'

'He gave them to me as an early birthday present this morning because he said I was working hard already.'

'He shouldn't have done that.' Becky shouts. She wanted to buy her daughter those trainers. She wanted her daughter to learn the value of hard work. She didn't want to feel so undermined. And now all these *questions* Maisie has for her.

Becky looks up and sees the surprise, more a low level of fear, in her daughter's eyes and pulls herself up. She shouldn't be punishing Maisie for Adam's actions, or for asking questions. None of it is her fault.

She promises herself she'll bring up the trainers with Adam. At the right time, she will.

After a pause Maisie says, 'Is she worried about it?'

'Is who worried about what?' Becky snaps again, unable to help herself.

'The director,' Maisie says quietly.

'Everyone's worried about it. If Sharon or Emilia walk off, we don't have a film. And after that it's a film that anyone with *decency* wouldn't touch with a bargepole. And then you don't *ever* have a film again. And it's years of my life down the plughole. And I'll probably get fired as well. So, yes, I'm a bit worried.'

Maisie nods slowly. 'Amber is obviously a nutter.'

'Who knows what she's like? She should pick her friends a bit more carefully. I'll say that about her.'

An hour later Becky's phone pings.

Matthew has given an interview at the request of a journalist looking at the story for a major entertainment news outlet.

Becky sits and reads it carefully.

Matthew tells the journalist that nobody has formally approached him about these allegations. The police certainly haven't been in touch. He knows as much as everyone else, which is to say very little indeed. But he's heard from enough concerned friends now to decide that he has to speak out: *before baseless rumours become baseless facts and real damage is done.*

He mentions how he is hesitant about talking freely when several sensitive subjects are raised by the allegations and moreover when Amber herself hasn't said anything about them.

The journalist asks him if he'd like to comment on Amber's reputation for being difficult on the set of her last film, possibly due to mental health issues?

Matthew chides his interviewer. It's not really fair to discuss someone's private life, and besides, mental illness is heavily stigmatized already. It shouldn't be raised to tar someone as a liar.

Anyway . . . When Matthew last saw Amber it was for a work thing. He felt she seemed a little altered and rather aggressive with him. He now wishes he'd done more to reach out and help but; *as ever, work swamped me.*

Becky pictures sedation needles and strait-jackets and a mask over Amber's face with metal rods that look like teeth.

I could have done more to help. I regret that I didn't act to help her.

He concludes by saying that he has tried to reach out to Amber to talk to her, but hasn't succeeded. He wants to wish her well, and to urge people involved in spreading malicious rumours, both at his expense and at Amber's, to reflect before they join the feeding frenzy. *We all gossip. That's human nature*, says Matthew. He's been telling stories for decades now. He knows how quickly a good one travels. But there's a crucial difference between fact and fiction. Or at least, there ought to be.

There is a picture, lifted from a professional photographers' online portfolio, of Matthew looking tanned and at ease with his family in the living room of their house. Piano in the corner. Black and white.

The journalist quotes some anonymous sources:

One says she's *vengeful*.

The other, a film producer, name withheld, mentions that Amber made a pass at him for a part.

The journalist finishes with ruminative remarks about stories and storytellers that echo Matthew's points.

The article is written by Alex Simms.

Becky Googles his picture and, as she suspected, this is the same Alex she met in Cannes. Matthew's old mucker. His passport to the best parties.

Becky's hands are cold and they quiver at the edge of the phone.

She wonders whether she wouldn't just do the same if she was in trouble: call a friend and get them to help out, corroborate her point of view. Give the world her truth, as she saw it.

You walk over glass for friends like that.

Becky runs a quick search on Amber Heath and finds that off the back of Matthew's statement 'mentioning' her mental wellbeing, other stories have been mushrooming all over the internet in the last few hours.

Becky swipes through the pictures of Amber Heath tripping up, wearing short skirts, shocking-pink bra straps loose and hanging, falling out of cars – outside night clubs and restaurants. As much as they could get of her body without it being inappropriate or illegal to print. Elastic long limbs and bloodshot eyes and messed-up hair. She looks so young in the pictures, early twenties, perhaps – chubbier then, and just breaking out.

An ex-boyfriend of Amber Heath's, who used to supply the highs, talks about why he broke it off and why he thinks Amber is trying to stitch this producer up.

Emotional. Ambitious. Someone who would do anything to feed her ambition.

There's a blurred cameraphone picture of her cutting a line, fishnet tights and garter, legs crossed over, white of the kneecap captured by the flash. It's grey and white, pixelated, almost, but apparently it's definitely her.

Here is one of Amber and Ollie in a car together, trying to shield themselves from paparazzi flashes. The piece that accompanies it asks questions about calling time on 'anonymous sources' and goes on to list dozens of whispers about Amber. If it means to defend her, it just ends up looking like a compendium of Amber's worst hits.

Matthew is spinning Amber, Becky thinks – twisting and rolling her and leaving her to hang by her threads, a dancing skeleton puppet tangled in its own strings.

'What are you reading, Mum? They're going to be here soon, have we done everything on the list?' Maisie is flitting around the kitchen, stirring this, poking that. She looks up at Becky, trying to understand her inaction, frowns. 'What's wrong?'

'Matthew's released a statement calling into question Amber's mental wellbeing,' Becky says.

Maisie looks confused. 'But she probably is a bit unstable. You even said . . .'

'And now everyone's jumped on her as someone who is messy and . . .'

Maisie can't see the spark of the touchpaper as it lights within Becky. Her mother has been tipped back into a past where she is unable to get out of bed, toggling between tears and panic, unable to take prescription antidepressants because of the baby growing inside her. Her mother is diving between that memory and the image she most feared: Amber's life arrested. Unable to get out of her own bed.

'They don't have to judge her mental stability in the papers!' says Becky, tears pricking her eyes. 'Like somehow it, and therefore *she*, is to blame for the thing that's made her feel bad. She doesn't deserve to have this splashed about everywhere. Nobody will hire her again.'

Damaged, damaged, damage.

Done with this body.

The thoughts come despite Becky's resistance.

She takes a deep breath and tries to swallow back her tears and anger.

'Mum? Are you OK? Can you even hear me? Oh my God, why are you crying?'

She hates herself. She thinks of the miserable-looking girl on the kitchen floor pinned underneath Matthew. She sees now that she was pushing him away and yes, he pinned her arm back, holding her down at the wrist. Now Becky cries for her. She cries and she cries and she cries and thinks she must do something, she must do something about all this.

'I'm gonna call Dad,' says Maisie.

'Don't. I'm OK.'

'You're being weird.'

'I just feel really sad for her. And angry. She didn't cause this situation. A man decided to talk about her. It's not fair.'

Becky puts a palm over her mouth, gasping silently as a piece of the past dislodges and slips inside her. Who is she to judge when she did the very same thing?

She crammed the gap in her history with the most readily available story. Inside her mind she condemned Scott for a crime without either trial or evidence, and she thinks, at speed, the thoughts crash into themselves, she must at least try and get that evidence now. What if she followed that blue-veined line to his office and tore the fucking tuxedo that he's planning on wearing to his awards ceremony right off its hanger? Stamped and spat on it? Would it help her live her life in peace to know what the truth of all of it is? Whatever the fall-out, surely it's worth risking for peace of mind?

* * *

As Maisie makes the finishing touches to the table before the guests arrive, she pushes her phone into Becky's hand. 'Sorry, Mum, but there's more.'

Someone has got hold of a picture of Becky, Sharon, Emilia and Matthew eating together at the window table of the restaurant, laughing and joking.

Hadn't Matthew talked about a private room? Instead, they'd been led to a table at the front of the restaurant.

The female employee and newly minted producer, the maverick female director with impeccable feminist credentials, and the celebrated young actress making waves in highbrow cinema. Sitting with Matthew. Unwittingly vouching for him, every time they laugh and pass food to one another.

Chapter 16

'Ads . . . I need to talk to you.' Becky's hand rests on the door latch, having let the last of their guests out of the house. But she hasn't yet committed to her words and they are quiet and slight and she thinks they might go unheard. And perhaps that would be for the best.

'Happy Birthday to me,' sings Adam, making a small drunken pilgrimage from table to sink with a single plate – sauce and fork teetering on its edge. It's painful to watch, mostly because she is stone-cold sober, but also because it will take them ages to clear up his way. She watches him drop the plate into a large pan of water.

'Oops,' he says, as brown foam splashes over the edge. The pan had been soaking after he'd drunkenly promised to make everyone caramels for pudding. He'd poured half a bag of sugar and some water into her best pan, put it on a high heat and turned the contents into a shining gold gloop. In the moments he was performing his victory dance, much to the amusement of the crowd, the caramel had stuck blackly and viciously to the bottom of the pan. The pan was unsalvageable really but Becky had thrown it quickly under the tap, like treating a burn on human skin, stifling her frustration and the urge to say anything because, along with most other items in that kitchen (and now Maisie's new trainers) Adam had sweetly and generously paid for it. It would have been churlish to say anything at the time, churlish even to say anything now, on a night when he is happy and humming contentedly, basking in the glow of having spent an evening surrounded by his oldest friends.

And so she'd let her annoyance dissolve. Besides, the pan had been a good, momentary distraction from her worry that their guests would ask her about Matthew. But they live and work in different worlds and it didn't come up. Maybe, she thinks, it's not really a story outside the industry? And as they all talked about haircuts and politics and that time they went camping (Becky wasn't there, she'd been caring for Maisie after she had her tonsils out), she was working out when and how to share the burden with Adam after everyone else had gone home to their beds.

She needs to talk to someone, and he is her someone.

As she watches Adam take on the portering of the next plate, she has got as far as planning her apology for not saying anything sooner, and how she feels ashamed for that, but that also no one can be sure of what really happened.

Please just let me talk.

He'll want to protect her. He'll tell her to exit and leave her film behind. She'll end up talking about how hard it

197

is to get a film like that made, a film that you actually care about deeply. Something that might even matter.

She doesn't need that conversation. She knows all that.

She also wants to tell him about how she is longing to visit Scott to get the answers she needs, and to that one he will certainly say absolutely not, that it risks Maisie finding out, risks chaos and destabilization for all of them.

'Did you want to talk to me?' He zigzags his way back toward the sink and his phone dings a text message. He pulls it out of his back pocket and narrows his eyes to focus on the screen. His hair is ruffled, his shirt loosened at the waist, his eyes are still and bright: Becky doesn't think she's seen him look so happy. 'It's Zee. She's on her way home,' he says. 'Lazy Maisie, she never ever pays me, for the waaaays, I plaaaaays, the bassooooooooon!' Adam turns and grins at Becky. 'Fuck I'm drunk.'

'Good. Birthday achieved.' Becky checks her own phone, expecting the same words. Finds nothing.

His phone dings again before he's had a chance to put it away and his face creases up in laughter when he looks at the screen.

'What?'

'Jules bought her a Viking hat. Look.'

She glances at his phone, finding no amusement in the foam confection balanced on her daughter's head. This is why she is the less fun one, the nagging one. Because she wants information and Adam wants jokes, so Adam gets both and she gets nothing. Her mood has soured with envy and she can't help herself when she says, 'You shouldn't have bought her those trainers, it was my—'

'I'm sorry,' he says, all eyes and regret. 'I only want her to be happy.'

'But I was trying to teach her the value of working hard to earn what you want,' she says more softly, chastened by his quick apology. 'Not just getting it all when you click your fingers.'

'Because we all know the world doesn't work like that.' He smiles but there is an edge to what he's saying. 'She can't be all cynicism, Becks. The world can also be a good and generous place. It can drop things in your lap when you're least expecting it and it's good for the soul to know that. Right?'

She's not sure whether she's more bothered by the removal of an opportunity to teach her daughter something, or the feeling that she's been undermined by him. She should pursue these grievances really, to avoid it all happening again and yet she runs out of steam at the sight of his broad and warm smile. Then she can't help but be won over by his good intentions and ability to look at the bigger picture in a way she always fails to. And his generosity, like a little kid giving away all his sweets in the playground. And it's his birthday. On balance she decides to drop it.

'You wanted to talk to me. I'm here,' says Adam, the smile still on his face. 'All ears. What's *really* going on in that head of yours?' He takes two empty wine glasses from her hands, places them by the sink and turns her to face him. They look at each other, a moment too long perhaps, in low light and smiles. 'Thank you,' he says, and she thinks she sees his eyes try to focus below the influence of all that booze. 'Thank you for hosting tonight. It was really fun. I had so much fun.'

He is brimming with wellbeing and the moment is so joyful that she can't bring herself to destroy it with further conflict about Matthew and Scott and how any decisions made could seismically reshuffle their carefully balanced life together.

'I had a nice time, too,' she says.

He never seems to have a list of problematic 'issues' in the same way she does. Never seems to run out of steam, or kindness, whereas, she seems to have to ration both. Why is that? Was that always the case?

And now, a moment passes through and they both feel its flashing edges, the thrum of its warm heart, the sparkle of its energy – impossible not to, what with them playing house, having these conversations about the family, sharing a kitchen late at night, catching up after a dinner party. Just like husband and wife. He is still holding her arms gently, still looking into her eyes when he says, 'I realized something tonight . . .'

She thinks about his kindness and generosity, his wisdom, how much his friends love him, how much he loves her daughter, how he is the one she can talk to about her day, her mundane life.

'I think that I really need to talk to Kate,' he says.

'Why?'

The scaffolding behind her smile melts and too late she realizes that this is not the question she meant to ask out loud.

Becky had been watching Kate that night, between courses and conversations, Kate had worn a top that Becky had never seen before: scarlet, one-shoulder, with a black lightning flash motif, the kind that draws attention and appreciative comments. And she had a new haircut. Again, drawing appreciative comments.

Also new: Kate had tried not to look at Adam when he was talking, like she didn't want to be caught out listening to him.

'We went bowling last night and it was nice. We get on really well.'

'Of course you do, you've always got on well.' She feels her powerlessness.

They are meant to be a platonic group of friends, now. All the 'trying each other on', all the sleeping together and alliances made and broken, had taken place while they did their accountancy exams and broke out into the world of jobs, together. All that had taken place while Becky was still in the muggy sleepless haze of baby and toddler. By the time Adam had introduced Becky, the wild times had calmed into pub visits and dinners and the occasional weekend spent together. Their fondness for each other is familial and friendly – not special, not romantic. That's the rule.

'I guess I'm finding it confusing, these hanging-out things that sort of feel like dates but never turn into . . . dates. I mean, we left the bowling alley holding hands last night and I didn't even know what it meant.'

'Right.'

He shrugs. Her response is unhelpful. 'Well I don't know, I just need to talk to her about it, I suppose. What do you think?'

'Why do you need to talk to her? Don't you know what you want?'

She feels like her feet are trying to stay anchored to the ground as she controls a kite that wants to take flight without her.

Adam and Kate. Jules and Maisie. New relationships, growing up toward the sun, all green shoots, while all she feels is her own rotten roots diseasing everything and pulling her back.

'You've got to know exactly what you want before you ask a woman a question like that.' Her words sound accusatory now and the smile on Adam's face struggles to beam as brightly. 'You can't just sound things out. Surely you know that? If you talk to her about this thing that you're wondering about, that you *think* is between you, then you're basically saying that you think about her as someone without her clothes on. You can't *ever* undo that. It's like if I told you I'd murdered someone in my past. You'd never, ever be able to forget that about me.'

'I don't know about that. I'd forgive you anything.'

Would he?

He squints at her. 'Becks?'

'What?'

'Have you murdered someone?'

'Not yet.'

His grin widens. 'I just feel like you're trying to steer the conversation around to telling me you've murdered someone.'

'You'll be the first to know when it happens.'

'Is that because I'll be the person it's happening to?'

'Most likely.'

'So you don't think I should talk to her?'

She looks away, thinks about busying herself with the dishes. 'I didn't say that. I just pointed out that there are some things you can't undo.'

'You sound like you've thought it through. More than I have, at least.'

His words are disconcertingly calm and she thinks she can see a smile in him. 'Not really, I haven't thought about it at all, not at all in fact, I just . . .'

Adam drains a half-empty wine glass on the table. His lips are lightly pixelated with black from the red wine. 'What did you want to talk to me about again?'

'Nothing. It doesn't matter. And you should speak to Kate, if that's what you want. I just think you can't have everything. You can't want to move us all into a house together and then start going out with Kate. That would be ridiculous. That would be too much. For Maisie. It

would be destabilizing. She won't deal with that level of
. . . whatever.'

'You were completely opposed to the idea of us moving
in,' he laughs. 'I thought that was off the table.'

'Well, if it wasn't, it probably should be, now that you're
marrying Kate.'

Adam is laughing a lot now but inside she feels a
pure and shocking panic at the thought of losing even
an hour of his friendship and his kindness, to Kate. His
focus elsewhere. She wants to ask him for his advice,
wants to tell him what's been happening now, wants
him to help her decode her past from her present, but
now it is as if there is someone else standing in the room
with them.

They look at each other for a moment, and then her
phone buzzes in her pocket. She has set up a Google Alert
for breaking news relating to Amber Heath. And now here
it is.

Amber has spoken, typed words on a white notes app
page, attached as two images to a single tweet that just
says 'My statement':

*My mental health is good at the moment. I am not a
mad woman making wild accusations. I wish Ollie hadn't
said anything, honestly. I didn't get to decide any of this
but now I've got photographers camped outside my flat
and ex-boyfriends getting offered crazy money to tell
journalists I'm a nasty manipulative piece of shit.*

Matthew Kingsman is making statements about me in the press so I will make mine and then that can be that.

I have gone to the police today and reported that I was raped at a house belonging to a man in the film industry. It was not consensual. We had drunk a lot and we kissed on the sofa but then I wanted to stop. I told him that in clear words. He raped me on his living-room floor. I tried to push him off. I never once said yes. I said no a lot of times. That's all I can say about that.

I think there was a witness. Someone came in and I saw them see us. I think it was a woman.

If she reads this, I am begging you, can you please come forward? If only to say I'm not crazy and I'm not putting it on for whatever reason.

I am not going to make any more comments on this. Any further enquiries can go via my agent David Barraclough at Total Agents. In the meantime, if you have even a bit of humanity, can you now please leave me and my friends and family alone?

If you are the woman who saw me, you can call the police direct if you don't want to speak to David. Please, just don't say nothing.

Becky tries to breathe deeply, relax her face, will her eyes to beam normality. 'I have to get to bed.'

'Wait. We were talking. I thought we could have a bit of that rhubarb gin Kate gave me?'

'What?' She feels a flash of annoyance at how Kate has even managed to infiltrate what they might drink together. 'No, sorry, I have to work early in the morning,' she says. He looks crestfallen, but she can't focus on him. Only Amber now. 'Leave the washing up and I'll do it tomorrow.'

As she hammers up the stairs, statistics float in and out, unbidden, half-remembered from stories and reports that she has read over the years.

Approximately ninety per cent of those who are raped know the perpetrator prior to the offence. Does that put Becky in the remaining ten per cent? Or the ninety per cent? She has never known. She has never felt she belonged anywhere inside those numbers.

She locks herself in the bathroom, sliding her back down the door and huddling there, next to the warmth of the radiator. Clutches her phone close, reading back and forth, again and again, pulling out the possibilities between the reported facts like they are already there, writ large for everyone to see.

Online they are speculating that the witness was Matthew's wife. What's her name? Charlotte? Anne? Antonia.

There are only two people in the world who know for certain that 'the woman in the kitchen' wasn't Antonia. Becky, and Antonia.

Does Matthew know it was her?

Amber saw enough to know that it was a woman

looking at her. Will she identify Becky from the press picture of the restaurant?

Was there CCTV footage of her entering Matthew's house? How long is that kept? Will the police really go to those lengths?

The man in the wine shop. Why did she have to make small talk with him? Why not simply buy the thing and leave? Why couldn't she do that?

Her credit card will prove she was there. Surely the police wouldn't look there . . .

She doesn't know what to do.

Should she come forward and say she was there?

If asked, should she say she got all the way to Matthew's door perhaps, but turned back? Never went inside. Would that be enough?

But if she came forward now she'd put her own livelihood at risk, the career she's been building, Medea, her growing reputation. And what would Maisie think of her if she found out? It would create problems just at a time when they both need to be focused and stable. She must be stable.

She thinks of the burnt pan and the Volt trainers, those petty things she'd been concerned about earlier in the evening, and what Adam said: maybe he was right when he said the universe puts good things and good people in your path. It's important to be able to honour that.

Matthew has been so kind and generous this past year,

she'd be nowhere without him. Surely Becky owes him more than going to the police and reporting what she may, or may not, have seen? Surely she owes him so much more than a betrayal?

Can she say nothing?

Chapter 17

The next evening, Becky slices through mushrooms, peppers, onions – far more than she needs for the recipe, but she finds the rocking motion of the knife soothing, the clean cut through skins, satisfying. She throws the vegetables into the wok. She can at least do this. She can at least feed her daughter well. The oil spits onto the backs of her hands and she lets it, feeling the scatter of needle-prick stings through her skin. The sound of the doorbell wrenches her out of this thing, this controlled stupor.

'Mum, it's for you,' Maisie calls out, before returning to her piles of books and notes in the living room.

'Rebecca Shawcross?' asks the young man at the doorstep, glancing at his phone screen.

She is expecting a package to sign for: contracts or new bound scripts from the office, or perhaps that hand-made photo album she'd ordered for Maisie's birthday. Here at last.

'Can I help you with something?' She wipes her palms down her jeans.

He glances up at her with pale green, watchful eyes, circled with dry flaking skin and red patches. He looks like an iguana, she thinks. 'I'm from *The Sun* newspaper,' he says. 'I need a quote.'

She grips the doorframe with one hand to control the anxious quiver that has set itself waving through her blood. 'What about?'

'The allegations made by Amber Heath against Matthew Kingsman.'

She thinks the fire engine-red T-shirt he is wearing is too bright and that his wax jacket has too many pockets. He looks like the pixelated screen of a computer game and why won't her thoughts stop skirting, tripping, glitching?

'I don't think any allegations have been made, have they?'

'Yeah, all right, she didn't outright name him, but everyone knows she's talking about Matthew Kingsman.'

'So what's your question?' she says impatiently.

'Amber Heath seems to be alleging,' he is speaking slowly, as if to a very young child, 'that she was raped by Matthew Kingsman. Do you have any comment about that?'

'She *seems* to be alleging?'

'Do you have a comment about it?'

'I'm not going to comment on rumours and gossip. Nobody should.'

The doorframe in her grip feels like a monumental shield.

'What about your film?'

'What about it?'

'I heard it's fallen apart over this.'

'That's not true. And look, I know this is your job, so I'm not being an arsehole about it, but I can't spend all day going through everything that's not true in the world. So we should probably leave it there. Thanks.'

She closes the door on him.

Is it true? Has her film died?

She rests her forehead against the cool, painted wood but it does nothing to stop the waters from rising around her. Adam is leaving them, heading for Kate's bed. Her film is shrivelling into dust. She has no map, no boundary, no place to go, no beacon, no co-ordinates with which to navigate her past, present and future, and there is no end in sight for her anger and sadness. She has a void. She has toxic grime. She fears these will swell, now that their bounds are fraying, like an aggressive cancer, an unwanted, metastasizing thing piling on weight and kicking against her from her own insides.

How to hold onto her film, save Matthew, save the company and save herself? Her mind tingles and crackles with only small, weak possibilities. She doesn't have anything good. Isn't it her job to solve this?

'When's dinner?' calls Maisie, but Becky doesn't know what to say in response. She can't think about food, routine, basic needs like hunger or thirst or exhaustion. She runs quickly and quietly up the stairs and closes the door so as not to make a sound. Through the bedroom window she can see the journalist leaning against a car bonnet, tapping something into his mobile phone.

She needs guidance. Needs not to feel so alone in her fear.

She dials Matthew's mobile number.

'Matthew, I . . .' She wants to ask him is it true, is her film really dead? 'There's a journalist at my door wanting a quote about you. About Amber.'

There is a pause on the line and she wonders whether he is angry with her for calling him. Whether she's done the wrong thing by adding to his worries. She should be able to handle this.

'You have to ignore him, if you can, ignore him.'

Had she ignored him enough? Had she said too much?

'How long is this going to last?' she says.

'I don't know. This hasn't happened to me before.' There is a tightness and anger edging his voice.

'I'm not complaining,' she says quickly. 'I know this is horrendous for you. I just wanted to ask, I mean I don't know, what to, you know, I didn't say, well, what should I say?'

'I don't know. Nice things!' He sounds almost amused. 'Tell the truth, Becky. Say that's not the man you know. I just spoke to Pips.' He is solemn now, talking about Pips, Matthew's pet name for his son Bart, a year younger than Maisie. 'Someone tried to talk to him as he came home from school.'

'Oh God. They're such shits.'

Becky can't help but picture it. The child being asked those questions: *Is the man who loves you also a man who holds down women who are not your mother, and rapes them on the same rug where you still open your birthday present?*

'Pips is so upset.' There is a wobble in Matthew's voice, and it is this that fills her with rage that this arrogant and bloodthirsty journalist is taking up space, her space, outside her house.

She hangs up. Hammers down the steps. Opens the door with so much force the joint of her arm stretches and burns with pain.

'Matthew Kingsman is a good man,' she spits. 'He's a family man who loves his wife and kids. He's worked hard over decades to build a company that supports talented film-makers. He invests in women as staff and in telling women's stories on screen. I've never seen anything to make me doubt him. These allegations are terribly hurtful and destructive and people should think twice before acting judge, jury and executioner.'

'Were you the woman in the kitchen?' he says.

'Was I the what?'

'The witness.'

'This is ridiculous. I'm not going to be part of a witch-hunt. Goodbye.'

* * *

The alerts come in for *The Sun on Sunday* online story the next morning and it's worse than she imagined. There's a large photo of Becky walking into work: earphones in, collar up on a denim jacket, bag slung across her shoulders. She remembers the outfit, the day, but she hadn't seen a photographer. Where had he been hiding? Had there been others?

They write that she has denied being 'the woman in the kitchen'. Siobhan's had the same treatment.

She realizes that she has chosen a side, in typed and reported words she can read back to herself, that tens of thousands of others can read. She can't be in the house any more where the air is too close to breathe and it feels like everything is watching her, listening to her.

'Maisie,' she calls up the stairs. 'I have to go, I have to go for a run.'

Maisie emerges from the living room, concern clouding her face. 'I thought we were about to have breakfast together? I thought we were making—'

'I'm sorry, you'll have to make toast. I've run out of time. I have to get out, I'm sorry, I just . . .'

Becky makes her way gingerly through the hallway. Laces up trainers. She doesn't bother replacing her tracksuit bottoms with running trousers. Doesn't say any more, just runs out into the early morning sun, past the window where her daughter is standing and watching her.

She threads through people on the pavements, going far too slow.

214

She has become not the woman in the kitchen. Another lifelong lie to commit to. She has done it once, she can do it again. She knows how to hide the feel of it. She can do this.

She needs to get to the park quicker than this. She speeds up, brushes shoulders with a harassed mother pushing a pram: enough for the woman to spin round and accuse Becky of terrible manners with only a look in her eyes.

She tells herself to calm down. Hears Matthew's reasoning voice. What does she owe the newspapers? For them it's a scoop, some sales. They don't care. The people she owes are the boss who believed in her, the daughter whose home needs to be paid for, the film she has worked so hard to bring into life and which wants to say something important about women. These are real things and they are worth protecting.

Maybe this is OK.

A child's scream drives itself through her skin.

Did Matthew's PR people reach out to Amber? Did they offer her a deal for a more cheerful rebuttal, *Oh that, that's all fine!* In exchange for working again? For money, maybe? A deal she maybe turned down?

Did Alex's stories of her emotional and physical *messiness* only follow when she refused?

What does Amber know?

She glances around the park. The pink Lycra-clad jogger, the khaki-coated dog walker, the dog itself, they're all judging her. Of course they are.

215

She didn't know, she wants to say to them all, she didn't know what the woman on the floor of that kitchen was feeling.

She runs faster now, fast enough for the sides of her lungs to hurt and gasp and rasp.

She had fled from the kitchen that Sunday afternoon, embarrassed to have been caught seeing Matthew with a woman who wasn't his wife. That was all. That's all she saw, all she thought she saw.

Becky pictures Pips in tears on his bed, his father made monstrous to him, and Matthew desperate to console him, to convince him that there are liars in the world. Liars who can reach out and harm you and who need to be fought.

She runs through the aches in her lungs. She wants to test the limits of her legs and her heart, to see how far her body can carry her before it starts to feel light and faint, for the edges of her vision to go cloudy white before everything fades to a pinpoint and then black.

Is Becky strong enough for the fight? She feels the question like a prosecutor's interrogation. Perhaps she is. She should be. She doesn't think she is.

Rebecca Shawcross denies being the woman in the kitchen and has launched a strongly worded defence of the man she credits as 'investing in women as staff and in telling women's stories on screen.' She said, 'I've never seen anything to make me doubt him.'

Once at home, she races to the bathroom. Locks the

door behind her with one hand while scrolling through her phone with the other.

Twitter friends post on their timelines that they know Rebecca and believe her. She is a good woman and a talented producer and deserves better than this shit-show.

Does she? Does she deserve better? She switches to Scott's Instagram account before she allows the thought to take root further.

Scott is modelling different outfits for THE BIG NIGHT on his feed. *Monochrome suit and tie? Nothing says style like black and white. Or fluoro-green T-shirt and jacket, perhaps. Dare to stand out?*

She grits her teeth. 'Dare to stand out?' she hisses, and types beneath his post:

I hate you, I fucking hate you so much, I hate you I hate you I hate you

But even as she watches the words appear she knows they are empty, pointless, not enough, never enough and so she stops.

Delete, delete, delete

She opens the bathroom medicine cabinet and finds the nail scissors.

She sits on the edge of the bath, eyes closed, breathing hard still from the exertion of exercise and the adrenaline tracking hot and alive through her veins.

She rolls down her joggers, then makes a tiny cut on the inside of her thigh, a V-shaped snip, the shape of a baby bird's beak. Blood pours out of its mouth.

Chapter 18

Monday morning she wakes as dawn is breaking, after only a few hours' sleep.

It's not yet eight a.m. when she turns on her phone and picks up one message from Emilia's agent, Sam, asking her to call, and a second from Matthew summoning her to his house for a *catch-up*.

Maisie, home for a planned revision day, returns from the corner shop with milk and a copy of *The Sun*.

'They've laid out ten suspects for "the woman in the kitchen",' she says, hair fallen either side of a paler than usual face. 'Lily just messaged me the article. Told me she'd seen the actual paper. Said I should get one for the archives. To show my grandchildren.' She looks up from beneath her hair. 'One of the suspects is you.'

Becky swallows and smiles. She can do this for her daughter. She can be calm and reassuring.

'Yes,' she says. 'But it's fine. Obviously it's not me. And look, everyone they've got has denied it. Only Matthew's wife hasn't, but she hasn't said anything to

218

anyone. And come on!' She tries a laugh. 'They've even put Julia Roberts in as a potential suspect! That's hilarious.'

'She was in London and she's a friend of his,' Maisie says quietly.

'Wouldn't you recognize the world-famous star of *Pretty Woman* and *Notting Hill* and a million other things if she was standing over you, *watching* you? This is completely stupid.'

'How many of these people do you know?'

'I don't know why this is still a story,' says Becky, affecting growing irritation.

'It's a weird thing to make up though, isn't it? Why would you make up something like that?' Maisie crosses her arms across her chest.

'I don't know. Maybe she wants to sound credible, claiming there was a witness, even if there wasn't. That way people think they're waiting for proof that they'll end up getting, instead of it being what it is, which is ultimately her word against his.'

'That's, like, most rapes, isn't it? He said, she said?'

Becky has had versions of this conversation before. She spent six months working with a psychotherapist building up to being able to talk about sex, consent and personal safety without breaking down. She practised, like she was training for a marathon. She wants sex for her daughter to be loving or playful or fun, and safe. She doesn't want her to feel used or discarded or belittled.

She doesn't want her daughter to feel the fear that has sat heavy on her own shoulders all these years.

But now Becky struggles to remember those lessons as she affects to study the newspaper carefully. There is her picture – at the beginning of the second row: an old black-and-white shot, taken from an online graduation brochure for an evening class in film-making at the local university. It's woefully out of date but up until now there's been no reason for her picture to be on the internet at all. In this picture, her hair is shorter, her eyes less lined, her choice of clothes still resolutely teenage. The woman she is now hides behind long hair and slightly better clothes, instead of baggy clothes and walls.

'God. I've aged badly,' Becky says, trying for a laugh. 'I can't believe you've spent money buying this paper. You're funding trash. This is a paper that used to publish photos of women with their tits out to help men get through the day without looking at soft porn. I'm not sure anyone should be taking lectures from this lot on women's issues.'

But Maisie doesn't pick up on the thread that might otherwise direct the conversation down another path and instead she says quietly, almost childishly, 'Mum?'

'Yes?'

'I really hate that you're in the papers for a story about someone getting raped.'

'Nobody was raped.'

'I *know* that. But it's still a story about that.'

'I don't like it either. It'll blow over.'

'OK. I fucking hate Amber Heath.'

'Language.'

'Sorry.'

'I'm sorry if this is hard on you at school. Just remember that . . . this isn't me. It's a story about someone I work with.'

'OK.'

'Focus on your revision.'

'I will. Are we going to be all right if the company goes under?'

'Why would it go under?'

'If nobody wants to work with Matthew any more.'

'That wouldn't be very fair, would it?'

'The world's not fair. You've said that, like, a million times.'

'I know, I'm sorry, I'm really trying to be less cynical. Here, look at my new smile.' She grins but Maisie is unconvinced. 'Look, please don't worry. I can always get another job.'

'Are you going to?'

'No. I want to make my film. I've put a lot into that. I can't walk away from that. And besides, I completely love my job. Shouldn't that count for something? Why should I have to lose all that over a story that has nothing to do with me?'

'Can I meet Emilia?'

'You can come to set and hang out, absolutely.'

'Can I bring Jules?'

Becky's phone rings. It's Sam, Emilia's agent, again. She diverts the call. 'I have to get going,' she says quickly. 'Maybe work on your chemistry or Spanish today?'

'*Sì.*'

'Oh, very good. Chemistry it is then.' Becky kisses her quickly, puts the paper under her arm, and heads for the shower.

Becky is on her way to Matthew's house in an Uber when she returns Sam's call.

'Hey there, rock star,' he says. 'How've you been?'

It must be the middle of the night but agents in LA seem to be as on call as doctors, and despite the hour Sam sounds like he's been playing tennis, drinking green juice and generally having a great time. Like this call is just one more thing he's *super looking forward to*, even when the next thing he has to say is going to be bad news.

'I'm great!' she says. 'And what about you?'

'You know, I never bitch to my British friends because I know you guys have to tolerate a lot of bad weather on top of whatever's going on in your lives, so I'm going to say all good.' Sam laughs. And then he's down to business. 'OK, so we need to talk about these rumours. And let me first say that Emilia loves you, loves Sharon, loves the project, OK? But she's a little, shall we say, a little *twitchy.*'

'I understand her anxiety, I do, but what's going on
. . .' She glances up at the driver and lowers her voice to
a stage whisper. 'It's just hot air. It's bullshit.'

'OK, sure, and I'm the first person to stand up for
Matthew, but we have to be honest that even if it's bullshit,
it's bullshit that's not going away, you know?'

'If I thought there was truth in these rumours, I wouldn't
be anywhere near this project.'

'It's Matthew's project though. It's his company.'

'His name's not on it.'

'You work for him! People aren't going to be fooled
by that shit. You're his girl.'

Becky feels her phone slip in the sweat on her palm.
She covers it with her other hand as Sam continues to
talk and says to the driver, 'I'll jump out here.'

She is still a few streets away from where she needs
to be and the route to Matthew's house is horribly
familiar.

'People are believing women, Sam,' says Becky, louder
than she intended. 'That's a thing in our culture right now.
Believe me when I say this film is watertight for your
client.'

There is the wine shop. She crosses the road to avoid
it, and half-turns her head away in case the man from
that afternoon is in there.

'And I think that helps, I honestly do!' says Sam. 'But,
cards on the table, if Emilia turns round to me tomorrow
and asks me outright if she should do this, I'm fucking

223

torn. She loves it and I love it but let's be honest, it's not a payday for her, so what's it about? It's an awards movie. She gets a Best Actress nomination out of this. But if it turns into the film about feminism that a male rapist made . . . you hear what I'm saying? That film doesn't get distribution, let alone a run at awards season. It's bad. And what's worse than that is if she goes ahead and does the film even though the story is on the table. We could cut it back a little, say she was under contract already and believes in due process, blah blah, but it'd still look bad, and all for zero upside. You see what I'm saying here?'

'I don't know what else to say.'

'Well you need to think, friend, because what I need from you is something very smart and substantial to tell to my client, otherwise the thing I'm left saying is all the stuff I just laid out. And by the way, I'm only even having this conversation because I like Matthew a lot and because I think you have a big future as a producer. If it was anyone else I'd tell Emilia to bail already and be done with it. Fuck knows she has other options.'

'I hear you.'

'Cool, but what am I hearing from you?'

Becky is dizzy. She wants to ask for time. She wants to lie down. She needs a day – a week, maybe more – to figure out a way through this mess. She feels like a squash ball getting smashed around the court, flying at all angles. And Sam wants his answer or everything collapses.

She stops and leans against a garden wall, taking a deep

breath. Even as the clock ticks and Sam waits, she can't help but wonder whether Scott has ever had to justify himself so thoroughly for his actions in his entire life. Had another woman suffered at his hands since he touched her? She burns with shame and anger at her own weakness and inaction.

Then she straightens her spine, stands to her tallest height, plants her feet firmly on the ground.

'First and foremost,' she says, 'this film is going to matter to women. It's a call to women everywhere to stand up for justice. How much would it suck if, of all things, gossip about a *man* derailed that? I don't think any of us should feel good about letting go of a film like *Medea* over something like that. How does doing another superhero film shift the conversation? Really? So that's the first thing. Secondly, tell her that Sharon's nobody's fool and nobody's little woman either and she's still on the film. Emilia can sit behind that if she needs to. She's not going to throw a great female director under the bus over an unproven rumour. That wouldn't be very sisterly now, would it?'

'Sharon's definitely still on it?'

'One hundred per cent.'

'OK, that's good. Because if Sharon bails then Emilia will too. You get that, right?'

'Yes, I get that.'

'OK, that's solid. And can I tell Emilia that you're looking at ways to potentially remove the project from Matthew and Kingfisher?'

She pauses. 'We can try to position it like it was never really one of his things in the first place, but I'm not taking the film away.'

'All right. So you're going down if he goes down, huh?'

'What?'

'If you're not cutting ties, you're staying tied to him. It's admirable, man. A true fucking friend, for sure. He'd better write you the biggest fucking Christmas bonus of his life.'

'I owe him a lot.'

Scott must pay. Someone must pay.

'OK. Cool. I think we're done here. Great talking with you, cowgirl. Go get 'em!'

'Bye, Sam. Send Emilia my love.'

With perfect timing, she has reached Matthew's front door. This time, she rings the doorbell and waits.

Chapter 19

'Instant?' Antonia says. 'Hope that's all right?' She fills the kettle to the top. 'There's been no time to do a proper shop. People, lawyers, in and out. I don't know where I am any more.'

Becky is now fairly certain that the morning Antonia whirlwinded into the office she was confronting Matthew about his indiscretions with Amber. It's only now, as Becky recalls how much rage and determination were set in the creases of Antonia's face, that she thinks maybe this was less shock than the signs of a woman who'd had enough. How had she found out? Had Matthew said something to her? What had he told her? But then why burst into the office to confront him? Is that not the action of a woman who has been given the awful truth by a third party and then rushes to confirm it?

For a fleeting, absurd moment, Becky wonders if she might not have been the only person to walk in on that scene. Plenty of their friends wander in and out. What if another woman, a friend of Antonia's, walked in and out just as she had done? And called Antonia the next morning, to relate what she had seen? Then Becky would not have had to exist in this story. Erased from the scene, scrubbed out in post-production like an anachronism removed from the frames of a period drama. Gone, and so much lighter for her absence.

As Antonia moves between kettle and coffee and milk, she shows no sign of letting up on the diligence and care with which she talks about her husband. There is no reference to any indiscretion or other such thing. Instead, this is a crisis inflicted on them from beyond their gates.

'Matthew is attached to his phone. He's really suffering with spondylitis now, with his neck bent at that angle the whole time. I'm sure he'll be out in a moment but it's wall-to-wall calls. But you know that. Of course you do.'

Antonia turns, leans back against the butler's sink with both palms bolstering her. 'He's not sleeping, I'm not sleeping. We were both shuffling around the kitchen in our dressing gowns last night before dawn. Like the living dead.'

Antonia's eyes change, like storm clouds passing and in that moment Becky sees that Antonia has thought of something that cannot be voiced, cannot be shared. Becky is, after all, an employee.

'It makes it all the more important to have good people around you, times like these,' says Antonia instead. 'Makes all the difference. So thank you, Rebecca.'

'It's nothing.'

'No, it means a lot to him. And to me.'

'He's been so supportive through my whole career. I mean, he *is* my career. I'd never let him down.' Becky's eyes travel to the sofa grouping. The rug.

Antonia passes her the mug of coffee. 'I do wish I had something else to offer you.'

'This is perfect. Thank you.'

Close up, the tension in Antonia's body is manifest. Her face is drawn and pale. She holds herself as if she has a glass globe on her shoulders instead of a head. But above all else she holds herself like she still has her dignity. Despite these accusations of her husband's infidelity, possibly his violent infidelity, she is calm. There will be no plates thrown by Antonia. Not in front of the children, not in front of the staff. Becky knows a little about that herself, the battle to look poised when inside it is all waves threatening to engulf you, filling the lungs and mouth.

Becky wonders whether Antonia has seen the words written by trolls on Twitter and in the blog posts. The comments under clips of Amber's films on YouTube.

Becky remembers pushing Maisie in her pram, past a group of schoolkids two years below her. Hearing the word 'slut' mock-whispered and then their laughter. Knowing that she wouldn't turn, wouldn't shout, wouldn't protest it. She had tried to walk taller. She had forced herself not to speed up. Don't let them see that they've hurt you. Don't give them anything. Not so much as a flinch. And with her back to them, while her pace went unchanged, unhurried, her face was free to twist into an agony of shame and anger and sadness. Antonia knows all this, thinks Becky. She knows which parts of her Becky can see and she has decided which other parts she'll show her. The rest can only be guessed at.

How are Antonia and Matthew, truly, walking in their kitchen at dawn? Stepping around that rug?

She watches Antonia try to open a packet of Fox's chocolate biscuits wrapped in matt-navy foil. Her fingers are long and thin and she is wearing one particularly striking ring, an almond-shaped sapphire circled with tiny diamonds. To Becky, it looks like the Death Star surrounded by angels. Becky wonders how Antonia would seem, clad in Medea's robes. How would she wear her face, if allowed to be all rage, all revenge, all agony?

'Here, let me,' Becky says, taking the packet from Antonia. 'These are Maisie's favourites. There's a bit of a knack to it.'

'I'll look and learn.'

Maybe it's this small kindness that prompts Antonia to unlock another layer of her private hell to Becky.

'Bart is having a horrible time, having to side-step the press every time he leaves the house. He's very sensible, he's a good boy, he's got used to saying, *No comment.* I think it's just awful how these people feel that they can do that to somebody. I feel sorry for them. They can't have much else in their lives.'

Becky knows that Antonia won't ever say anything to her about Matthew and Amber's historic or recent indiscretions. Perhaps she has tried to wipe it from her mind entirely, knowing that their marriage, the business, the family, everything that they have built together, must now be protected. Fought for. And if there are casualties, well, so be it.

'Have you ever met this girl?' asks Antonia.

'Who?'

'Amber Heath.'

'No,' says Becky, fixating on the sheen of the fridge. 'I think that what it is, I think that maybe . . . everyone's looking for their moment in the sun? It's an industry mostly made up of people who haven't made it, or are realizing that they won't make it. I think Amber was probably starting to feel like she was old news and wasn't going to be someone who gets big parts. And now she's in the papers. In a twisted way she's probably got what she wanted, on some level. If that makes sense.'

'You can see why I hired her, can't you?' says Matthew, entering the room from deeper in the house. He is wearing a white linen shirt, unbuttoned twice. 'Becky already knows more about how things work than people who've made ten films.'

And in the brief and uncomfortable gap when it is clear she will not come to him, he walks to her instead, throws his arms round her, the cool edge of the phone in his hand digging into her as he hugs her like an old friend. She notices that he smells of soap and roses. He steps back from her, smiling, working just as hard as Antonia to be the exact version of Matthew Kingsman that the moment requires. 'How's the doorstepping going at your end of things?'

Like they're the two ends of the situation, her and Matthew. A problem shared, equitably and easily. 'Nothing more since *The Sun*.'

'I think you've done a great job. Your character reference was, well, what can I say? Five stars.'

'I'm glad if it was a help,' she says quietly.

'Anyway, I think it's all on its way out.'

'It is?' Antonia's face softens. Her eyes shine, perhaps there is a tear; she certainly looks as if she might cry and Becky knows that this will be the only evidence of Antonia's storm.

'Yes.' Matthew steps toward his wife and puts his arm around her. 'There isn't enough of a story for it to get any more traction. The stuff about the witness this morning? It's all a bit *CSI*. The police *obviously* aren't going to do anything. Amber's had her moment in the sun. I'm fairly confident, by the way, that she won't be landing a good gig for quite a while. She's burnt more bridges than she knew existed, pulling this stunt.'

'It's unforgivable, really,' says Antonia.

'I spoke to Sam,' says Becky. 'I think *Medea* might make it through if the story starts to go away like you say it will.'

'Let's spare Antonia the boring stuff. We'll talk in my study.'

'I was saying thank you to Becky,' says Antonia. She wipes under her eyes with the pads of her fingers and fixes Becky with a strong, determined gaze, dredged up from the silt. Her eyes are sun-warm with gratitude. 'It probably hasn't been easy for her either.'

'It's nothing,' says Becky.

'Will you stay for lunch?' says Antonia.

'Thank you, no, I can't. I've got to get back to the office.'

'Right, let's move things along,' says Matthew. 'To the bat cave.'

'Darling, I'll put lunch on the table for one-ish,' Antonia calls after them brightly, a weight lifted from her on his promise of a return to normality, or something that looks like it.

A walk down a wood-panelled corridor. Matthew leads Becky further into the heart of the house than she has ever been before: into a red-wine-carpeted room lined with bookcases and more wood panels, varnished darkly. A cumbersome moss-green leather-topped desk sits in the middle of the room, flanked by two padded red leather chairs, high-back seats fastened to their frames with lines of brass buttons. She stands at the perimeter a little breathless, a little anxious that there might not be enough air to breathe the further she ventures inside this crypt that smells of old hide and damp pages, of furniture polish and freshly brewed coffee.

'The story heading into the nationals could have gone a radically different way,' Matthew says, not going for the desk and instead slumping back into one of his study's plump, old-world armchairs. 'I've had three people from IcePR working on this and I think it's almost safe to say we've won the conversation.'

'I saw a lot of stories by that guy Alex you introduced me to.'

'Yeah, he's one of the good ones.'

'How does it work? Do you pay them?'

'It's not quite as blunt as that. But everyone gets rewarded eventually. It's an ecosystem. The smart ones understand that. Why do you ask?'

'Only because I want to learn.'

She steps into the room and perches at the edge of one of the red leather chairs.

'You may well call this experience educational. Not sure I wanted to be the case study, but there we are.'

'So once the stories dry up, is it all over?'

'The damage limitation part's over, but then there's a bit of rebuilding to do. You can't do that immediately. It makes you look reactive and fraudulent. But in due course we'll probably spend some money on mental health and actors: you know, how it's a hard trade, not enough support for the vulnerable, body-shaming, etcetera. I don't know if it's a foundation or funding the right charity or opening up a conversation, but we'll take a quiet lead on it, build it into a nice healthy debate.'

'Doesn't that just make people think about the story all over again?'

'Yes, you don't want to get it wrong. But if you do it right, it shows you're confident enough about it to engage with empathy. The message is, you had a brush with a mentally ill actress who really needed help more than anything, and you've reflected, and the experience has changed you and you'd like to do something to help. That looks like strength and compassion. The guys at Ice will get a proper plan written up and costed.'

'How much will it cost you?'

'Personally? Probably quarter of a million or so. Depends what we do, but I told them to look at that budget range.'

'Good to get people talking about stuff. Issues that need to change. Doing good. I guess that's the upside of what you're going through.' She wipes at her damp forehead with the back of her hand.

'I agree. It'll be money well-spent. Just not under the kind of circumstances I'd have wished for.'

They sit in silence for a while and she wonders whether this is the moment to say something . . .

'You were saying about Emilia?' he says.

'Yes. I spoke to Sam. I think if the story dies down and Sharon stays on board then we'll get through it with Emilia still up for it.'

'I've had some very special conversations with Sharon's agent,' laughs Matthew wryly. 'Let's just say that Sharon's going to get a much better deal than I'd have signed a month ago.'

'So Sharon's definitely staying on?'

'Of course she is. It's a proper A-list rising star, an Oscar-bait script, and a budget where she can afford a real crew and all those cranes that directors dream about. It's all that, versus a malicious rumour that's going to be forgotten by the time she's in cinemas. She's not stupid.'

Matthew walks toward a wooden cabinet in the corner of the room, a brass key sticking out of its keyhole. He takes out two tumblers – *Drink Me*, thinks Becky – their surfaces shining and jagged like they have been overlaid with the smashed cubes of car window glass. He sloshes whisky into both and hands one to Becky.

'Ice?'

'No thanks.'

'Well then, here's to you. Your passion for your project. And on a personal note, your loyalty to me continues to move me deeply.'

She turns the words *passion* and *loyalty* around in her head as she allows the whisky to touch her lips but go no further. She won't ever make that mistake again. Anyway, she hates whisky and its peaty, arrogant smell. It reminds her of her father. It's the smell of verdicts passed and judgements given. An airless drink that listens only to the sound of its own voice.

'Maisie will be so proud of you when you get this film

made.' He says it as if he has sensed she needs some anchoring and reassurance. 'It's a wonderful feeling, to have your child see your work. It's how they come to know you in a whole different way.'

He takes a drink. 'And it will be made, I guarantee you that. No matter what happens, even if we lose Emilia and Sharon, even if I have to pay for the thing myself, that film will get made. It's a story that needs to be told.' He lays his glass down on a coaster. 'I couldn't forgive myself if my own stupidity fucked it up for you after you'd landed it in Cannes.'

The smile he gives her is one that demands to be reciprocated.

And she does smile back, but only mildly, and he drinks again. 'It can't be easy for you, all this,' he says. 'I had another casting thought. I was thinking of getting my friend Simon Bach to play Jason. What do you think? He'll do it if I ask. But it's your film. Your choice.'

'Yes,' she says, feeling her eyes light up as if she's taking receipt of a gift-wrapped box. Simon Bach. Gained the respect of audiences and financiers for choosing high-quality art-house films that ended up outperforming more commercial ventures. He progressed into Marvel, other franchises, always ones that were reviewed well and made millions at the box office. A little older than Emilia. Rugged, blue-eyed, tanned. Dates the A-list world. Rumoured to be gay and worth a fortune.

'I think that would be great.' Presents, favours. All

reciprocal, aren't they? 'Sorry, Matthew, is there a window in here? Can we open a window?'

Matthew opens a window a crack.

'Do you want to talk to Sharon about him then?' He is all deference with her. 'You don't need him to get it made, but you'll get a lot more money with him on board. Asia and both the Americas love him.'

'I'm the woman that Amber saw,' says Becky.

'I know.'

Becky is near tears. She wonders if she needs to bother hiding them now.

'CCTV loop. It's very discreet but the insurers demanded it as part of the cover for some of our paintings. It downloads in real time to a server. Wipes after twenty-four hours. I'm really sorry you walked in on that little scene. Can I ask what you were doing?'

'I wanted to give you a bottle of wine to say thanks.'

'For what?'

'For taking me to Cannes. Believing in me.'

'Ah, right.'

'I took the bottle away with me. Sorry.'

He laughs. He actually laughs. 'Yes, I can see why you did that. Well, I hope you drank it. And I'm sorry that you walked in on . . . that whole scene. It must have been horrible seeing your boss like that. I wanted to raise it with you but part of me hoped you'd run off thinking it was Antonia and me together.'

'Matthew, I have to ask . . .' She speaks quickly; she

doesn't want to lose her nerve or this chance to ask the questions that will surely put her mind at rest.

'Anything.'

'What happened? What did I see?'

'You want me to tell you what *you* saw?'

'You know what I mean.'

'Why don't you tell me how things looked from your point of view and I'll fill in the gaps?'

'No,' she says, feeling a pinch of anger at this game. 'I just want you to tell me what happened.' It is perhaps the first time she has ever outright refused him. Overruled him. If there's a flicker of irritation from him at this insubordination, he hides it well.

'It's exactly as I told you,' he says. 'Amber and I had a fling a while back. I was clear with her. Or at least, I thought I was clear about what it was and what it wasn't. I was never going to leave Antonia. I love Antonia. I have many faults but I'm also very clear about people. I'm loyal, in my way. And believe me, Becky, after you've done three or four films, you'll be sitting here again telling me how unbelievably tame a discreetly conducted affair is compared to what you'll have seen. Co-stars posting runners at the entrance to the film lot, to tip them off about putting their clothes back on before wives and husbands turn up. The whole crew knows the co-stars are banging each other, but their partners don't and probably never will. You will see some things, believe me.'

He shifts in his chair. Part of her wants to say, *Yes, and, so?* But she doesn't, she doesn't want to miss a thing.

'So what does a beautiful young actress like Amber want with an old man like me? It's a question you might well ask. I took her away on a few nice weekends. And I suppose she thought that I'd give her a good part in something. That was never the deal, I mean, there was no "deal", but I'd be feigning naivety to think otherwise, wouldn't I? It's something she wants and it's something I can offer. The truth is – and this is rather shaming for me, but let's have honesty now – if I'd liked her better then I probably would have been coming to you and suggesting you consider her, not for Medea, obviously, but for one of the smaller but substantial roles. But I started to find her quite tiresome. That's a horrible thing to say, isn't it? Easier to claim that my conscience about Antonia flared up, but that would be self-serving. I just found her a bit grating. She had mood swings and our last time together she was in a particularly difficult spot, and I ended up thinking, this is not any fun at all, really, is it? This girl obviously needs a boyfriend, someone who'll be there for her more than on the odd night here and there. I can never offer her that, but that's obviously what she wants from me. We sat up and talked for hours about everything she found difficult, all her anxieties, everything she felt sad about. And when I got back I decided I had to break it off, for both our sakes. And so I did.

'I don't flatter myself that she was in love with me,

but I do think she needed someone. And she'd decided, just as I was pulling away, that I was the answer. I didn't know all of this when I told her. Some of this came out then and there and, anyway, the upshot was she accused me of betraying her. Of lying to her. Leading her on and all that. I actually told her that I felt she needed some help and I offered to pay for her to see someone, a therapist, for weekly sessions. Not as a pay-off. I genuinely thought she needed that. And I have the money.'

Becky waits patiently for Matthew to refill his glass. She is careful not to move and she bids her breath be shallow and soundless, as if she were hiding from someone, or something. She doesn't want anything to distract Matthew from telling her these things: these facts or jigsaw pieces or whatever. She must drink them in and commit them to memory with all the concentration she can muster.

'She came to the office to try and see me,' he says. 'And at that point I was quite concerned, if I'm honest. Here is this very unstable girl, telling me that I have left her hanging, without explanations. That I have made her depressed. That she worries she can't act any more and it's all because of how I have treated her. Quite difficult stuff. And I was really on the spot then. You know how many people we know who work near our office. Actress with mascara running down her face, shouting at a producer? We know how that looks. If I had put her in something then I could have at least said she was upset about being left on the cutting-room floor but . . . Anyway. I told her we'd make

241

time and I knew that Antonia and the kids would be away for a night in the next week so I told her, *Come to my house then and we'll go over everything. I'll hear what you have to say and I'll try to help you.* But it wasn't going to be a resuming of play. Nothing like that. Would you like a top-up?'

'No, thank you,' she says. She is struggling to keep a clear head, what with the effort of listening and committing to memory and the worry of hearing things wrong. And the heat. Oh, the heat.

'I think I might.' Matthew returns to the cabinet and drains his glass before adding another splash then taking his seat again. 'Amber came over and she seemed rather sanguine about everything. We agreed that we had had some good times together but that it could never have gone anywhere. I told her that I thought she needed more than I could offer and she actually agreed with that. I made us some food, we had some drinks. And, God, I just felt so relieved about the whole thing. I'd really worried she was going to turn out like some kind of crazy stalker, hounding me, but she was very charming. It was like she wasn't trying so hard any more. So I thought, well, let's try and help this girl.

'And we sat on the sofa and we drank some more and talked about movies and how actresses build their careers and what kind of opportunities there are out there. It felt constructive. It turns out I actually do know one or two things about the business and I was happy to share them.

I don't know how much we ended up drinking and I couldn't tell you how long we sat there for. And then she made a pass at me.

'If you're going to condemn me, and look, I condemn myself, then that was the moment to have some backbone and say, *No, we're not going to do that. Sit and talk, yes. But the rest is over with.* And I protested a little but not very strongly. Now, I have to ask a very awkward question. Because I'm committed to being utterly honest with you here about what happened and what was in my head, but equally I don't want to embarrass you with the grisly details, so would you rather I gloss over things or can I speak freely?'

'Speak freely,' she says, because what else could she say?

'OK. Well, what happened was, she got onto my lap and I realized, or rather she made me realize, that she had no underwear on beneath her dress. Sorry. And it was this very odd moment for me, because for me it was all organic. It was just sort of happening. But for her, she'd come without underwear, or she'd slipped away to take it off, which made it a seduction. Does that make sense?'

Becky finds herself saying *Yes* not because it would make sense to her in that situation but because he is telling the story as if it would make sense to *him*, a man with expectations and appetites. And if she said *No*? She wouldn't hear what happened next.

'And so I was caught,' he continues. 'I wanted to sleep

243

with her but I could also see that this was nothing but trouble for me. And bear in mind that I was drunk, too, by then. This is sort of what I can recall. And what happened next was . . . Well, it's really hard to explain. And I feel terribly ashamed of it.'

She feels a slight caving inward, at how the admission of a weakness makes her warm toward him. We all make mistakes.

'We began to have sex on the sofa,' he says, 'and then she looked me in the eye and said, "I knew you still loved me," and I thought, fuck, oh God, this is terrible. How do I convince her, after everything, this whole evening we've had and what we're doing together now? And my idea then was to try to show her that I didn't love her. To make her feel certain that I didn't have any feelings for her, so that maybe she'd hate me for it, but at least she'd be free of this . . . terrible delusion. And I had her on the floor and I told her, *No, I don't love you. You're cheaper than a whore.* And she wouldn't believe me! She thought it was a game. So I kept on. I felt I had to show her. I insulted her. I belittled her. And eventually I think she did believe me. But it was all happening so fast. I don't know if she ever said *Stop* or anything like that. But at some point I know she pushed at me and called me some terrible name and I wouldn't let her go because I needed her to know that her opinions didn't matter to me. It was a kind of theatre. I couldn't think of anything else.

'And then afterwards she was crying and I desperately wanted to say, *Look, I'm so sorry, I just needed you to understand that I don't love you and telling you that I only liked you wasn't working.*'

Becky is rapt. An audience member in the theatre, a cinema, at home on the sofa. 'It's good you were upfront with her again. No room for ambiguity there.'

'Well and then she asked me to call her a cab and I did that,' he says. 'We didn't talk much while we waited for it to come.'

'What more was there to say between the two of you?'

'Exactly. But then she said she'd never forgive me for what I'd said and I said I didn't expect her to. I put her in the taxi and I wished her well. And that was that. Well, then DB called me the next day and went off at me, saying Amber had called saying I'd assaulted her. And Antonia – well, you were there when she came to the office, weren't you?'

'Yes, that looked . . . it must have been awful.'

'Amber had emailed her.'

'Oh God.'

'And then I realized, I think I got this wrong.' Matthew laughs, but it is an authentically despairing sound. 'I told DB, *No, this is about me cutting things off with her.* And the idea that I'd "assaulted" Amber was, well, I couldn't even take that in. Is there any world in which she might have honestly thought that? How could she strip off her underwear, seduce me, and then call it an assault? But of course I'd said all those things to her. I'd aimed to destroy that idea, that I loved her, and I'd done it while we were having sex with each other. It seems like an insane idea.'

'We all do stupid things under pressure.'

'I swear at the time I thought, *This is what I have to do to make her see.*

'I called her, after I spoke with DB and after I'd talked to Antonia. I told Amber, *Look, I'm sorry for how I was. I didn't mean to hurt you. I just wanted you to see that I'm not in love. It's never going to work the way you wanted it to work.* And I told her that I was weak and I bitterly regretted how I'd gone about things, but that I hoped maybe in time we'd find a way through it to be friends. She listened to me, she said that she got it and she accepted my apology and that was the end of it. She said she couldn't imagine wanting to be my friend. I said I understood but that I hoped one day that would change. And I meant it.

'And then we were off to Cannes. And I thought, God, I have a mountain to climb to mend fences with lovely old DB and my darling wife, who deserves so much better than an email from . . . But if I can do that, and maybe put in a quiet word for Amber somewhere where she won't know it was me, maybe I can begin to dig myself out and learn from this. And Cannes is such a bubble. And this time it was you who was the star attraction. You're so talented.'

Becky bows her head and blushes at the compliment.

'I could sit back and just admire watching you work. It reminded me of so many things I realized I needed to reconnect with Passion for the work. A hunger to push against your limits. I flew back full of joy, like I'd been given a second chance. I sat down – Antonia will tell you, she watched me do it – and I wrote a list of everything I hadn't done that I'd once wanted to. Books I love, plays to take forward. I was pulling books off shelves, childhood reading, with a hunger to do better again. To be more than the cliché of a complacent producer finding more pleasure in the attentions of a young actress than in the work. The work is harder by far, but it's what nourishes you in the end. I'd forgotten that.'

She remembers the first letter she wrote him asking for a job. It was his passion for story she had seen shine through in everything he produced. She had wanted the same for herself.

'Yes,' she said. 'Yes.'

'And then everything caved in. As you know. And I realized that maybe there would be no second chance after all. And with its loss would go . . . your film, your hopes. Antonia's. My children's. My reputation. Friendships with DB and a few others. I'd indulged in the hubris of trying to convince a lover that she is not loved, even as we made love – and the price to be paid for that was everything.

'I've fought it with everything. I have tried to protect you, and my family, and my employees, and myself.'

'So much to take on.'

'I don't wish Amber ill but I wish to God she'd step forward and take it back. But of course she won't. Because I broke something between us with such cruelty. And so of course she hates me.'

'Hate is such a strong word . . .'

'If I could disentangle the rest of you from this, I would. I hope you know that. I'd take my punishment. But that has proved impossible. So now I have to work to atone, where I can, and protect the ones I love, if I can.

'I know that when you said nothing about seeing us that night, when you said to the reporters that you were never here – those choices were an act of love. I imagine you might have found it difficult at times. You're a good person. You must have wondered about me. Could I have done what Amber said I did? Did you know me at all? In my most hopeful moments, I believe you made those choices because you do know me. You know that I could never be violent. Predatory. I can't make you believe that, I accept that. But I can hope. And I can acknowledge it. You've been a friend to me, is the simplest way of putting it. You have chosen to believe the best of me and at a cost to yourself, perhaps.'

'You've been so wonderful to me. You're the reason I'm doing everything I ever dreamt of doing.'

'Sam texted me to say you'd refused to cut ties with me, even if it meant seeing your movie break apart. And I know that film means everything to you. So I know you've been asked to count the cost of our friendship.

And it's amazing to me that you've done that and you've decided, yes, the cost is worth bearing.'

Matthew wipes a tear away from his eyes. 'We'll get through this, but it won't be the same as before. I know you won't forget what I've told you today and sometimes I'll feel humiliated by that. Ashamed. Well, so be it. But other changes will be better. I can't ever again think of you as my employee. We'll figure something out but I hope we'll produce together. I'll support you, of course, but I have seen who you are. I know you've got talent but you've got more than that. I want to help you take flight. It's not a debt, Becky. It's atonement. It's clarity. It's . . . simply a determination to do better from now on. To deserve the friendship you've shown me. And I'll see that through.'

'I know you will,' she says, and she picks up her full glass. 'To friendship,' she says.

'To friendship,' Matthew says, before they both raise their glasses and put them to their lips at the same time – the best way to seal this thing, this *togetherness*. She allows the whisky to pass through her lips and flow over her tongue. It is warm and it stings.

Then Matthew turns around and pushes the window wide open for the outside air to finally rush in.

Chapter 20

Becky sleeps, but her dreams feel as vivid and urgent as her waking life: a thousand images, cracked and distorted, like an old television being tuned, passing through the channels and back again.

She wakes to the soft cotton of a heavy duvet holding her down on a mattress dampened with her sweat. She has dreamt of being trapped in a maze made of strings of beads, coloured candyfloss pink and chalk green, like the ones she'd worn to the party at the Hampstead house. Scott's white-toothed smile. The fray of his jumper at a tanned neck. She was trapped, unable to find a route out, but worse was the sound of her own voice. From somewhere above is the mewling, childish sound of her own crying, that played its soundtrack over the images and, in time, brought her back to waking.

She gets to the office that morning, late, dragging herself to the doors with slow and heavy steps. Her mind feels blank, her heart heavy, her soul on the floor, drained by the effort of simply being.

She makes her calls and writes her emails in the hot

and airless office that smells of printer ink and coffee. Siobhan is also subdued. There is none of the usual trickling chat between the two of them, a happy flow of words that usually cuts through their heavy workloads.

Becky edits a press release entitled: *Kingfisher Films announce the attachment of Simon Bach to forthcoming feature* Medea.

More emails pile in, many of them from Sharon: a meeting with a casting agent, script notes to consider, and an upcoming face-to-face about heads of department (now *who best* for set design, lighting, graphics, the edit?). Becky's job now is to answer and solve or defer and deflect. To keep the dream she fought so hard for moving, moving, moving.

Simon Bach said: 'I am so looking forward to joining the dream team that is Sharon, Emilia and Becky. These are three passionate, clever and fabulous beacons of progressive film-making. The story they have to tell is vital and I could not be more thrilled that they've invited me along for the ride.'

Becky Shawcross said: 'I am over the moon that Simon has agreed to play the role of Jason in our forthcoming production. He brings magic to everything he does.'

Further notes to editors: with MEDEA, Kingfisher Films will be one of the first UK film companies to implement an 'inclusion rider' across the whole production, ensuring that during pre-production,

*production and post-production both cast and crew
fully reflect British society in terms of gender, BAME
identity, sexuality and disability status.*

Becky stares down at her own quote. It's too short. It's
a bit flat. Can she really not think of anything else to say
about this actor?

'Have you ever even met him?' asks Siobhan. 'He makes
it sounds like you've all been camping together. Had a
fabulous night on magic mushrooms under the stars and
are planning to buy a holiday house *together*.'

'That's just actors, isn't it? Best friends by day two on
set, cry at the wrap party, don't bother replying to each
other's emails the following week.'

'He and Matthew are good mates, aren't they? They
worked together on that Russian sports film. Matthew's
really pulling it out of the bag for you, isn't he?'

But it's not a question.

'He hasn't done that much,' Becky insists. 'I've been
making all the calls and doing all the meetings. Besides,
it's a good role for Simon.'

'Chill,' says Siobhan. 'I'm just saying he's obviously
going above and beyond because he totally loves you.'

'He totally loves the film.'

'Come on. You're his number one girl since you testified
in his defence.'

'*Testified*?'

'You know what I mean.'

'Well what else would I have done?'

'Don't get me wrong, I'd have done exactly the same.'

Becky looks up, face flushing hot with shame at the memory of giving too much, anything, to that iguana-faced *Sun* reporter.

'While we're here.' Siobhan places her hands on both her hips. 'I want you to know that I don't need to be mollycoddled. Yes, I dropped Emilia into both your minds as a casting suggestion, yes it was kind of genius on my part, but it's not like I own her. I'm happy she's attached to your film. It's good for all of us. But it sucked to find out the news online. Like one of the civilians. You could have just texted me.'

'I'm sorry.' Becky's face burns a degree warmer. 'I've been preoccupied.'

'Throw me a bone here! I'm stuck doing, like, ninety per cent of the shit stuff and you're planning how many ballgowns you need for awards season.'

'I'm thinking five?'

'Seriously though. Don't get too grand.'

'I was being thoughtless, I'm sorry. All the stuff in the papers has been freaking me out a bit.'

'Well,' Siobhan says, reaching into the filing cabinet and pulling out a bottle of pitch-black nail polish. 'With great power comes great responsibility.' She has no tools, no nail polish remover; she smudges her nail borders, botches the job and yet, cracks on. 'God I love this colour. It's so goddam goth,' she says. 'Yeah, all that stuff in the papers with you was heavy. Not sure

I'd like my face in *The Sun*. I'd prefer the *Guardian*, to be honest.'

'A better class of witch-hunt?'

'If someone's going to accuse me of terrible things, I want them using really long words so my mum won't understand when she reads it.'

'That's very strategic.'

'*Strategic* is a good example of what I'm talking about. That's a classic *Guardian* word.'

'Can you look at this press release for me? I'm doing a shit job.'

'Which bit are you struggling with?'

'My own quote.'

Siobhan laughs. 'I'm putting: *Becky says, I like eating dropped pasta off the floor.*'

'That's better than what I've got. Oh God,' Becky slaps a palm to her forehead. 'I've been so busy, I've completely forgotten to do the expenses. Would you mind? Please?'

'Because I'm not busy at all.'

'I'll make it up to you.'

'I want to play Jason in your movie then.' She blows along a row of nails. 'I'm going to put that in the press release now. *If Simon dies before cameras roll, the part will be played by Siobhan.* At the very least you owe me a pint and a sharing platter.'

'I know you won't let me forget.'

Becky hands over the print-out. She begins to pack her phone and some other papers into her bag.

'Going somewhere?'

'I'm taking Maisie to Camber for her birthday. I'm having a couple of days off.' Becky clocks Siobhan's raised eyebrows and speaks quickly. 'It's her sixteenth, a special one, and besides, I can't keep on ditching her whenever work gets crazy. I've done that a lot recently.'

Siobhan tries a smile, but it is effortful, far from her usual wide-eyed generosity.

'So do you want me to do the expenses because you're busy being a hotshot producer, or because you're fucking off on holiday? I'm finding it hard to keep up.'

'Both. Please, do me this favour?'

Siobhan doesn't answer the question and instead asks, 'Where are you staying then?'

'A place in Kent that was recommended to me.'

'Who by?'

'Matthew.'

'Oh how bloody lovely for you and your good hair.'

'Thanks, it needs all the support it can get,' Becky says, trying to steer them back to their usual chatty rhythms.

'And does that support come from a hair salon, or does Matthew trim it himself?'

'Simon Bach did it, actually. He's playing my haircut in my next film so . . .'

'Can I be honest actually?' Siobhan says, her smile now entirely flatlined. 'This is all a bit fucking galling given I started work here before you. I get that *Medea* was your idea, but doing your expenses while Matthew gives you foot rubs and sends private chefs to prepare your morning porridge like you're Beyoncé?'

'It's not forever. It's just while he's feeling bad that he nearly fucked up my film.'

'I thought the whole thing was a totally baseless rumour?'

'It was. But nobody was accusing *me* of being their rapist. I'm having to fend off reporters while keeping my work going, I'm—'

'Wow, I'm going to get one of my mates to bang him just so I can tell the papers it never happened and then get a private jet off him.'

Becky doesn't laugh like she's meant to.

Siobhan shrugs defensively. 'If that's what it takes, right? Until then, how's about a big old-fashioned "Thank you" for agreeing to do all your work while you sun yourself on Kingsman-recommended sun-loungers?'

Yes, there is a definite edge to her.

'Thank you, Siobhan. I'll let Maisie know I only managed to get away because you're a lovely, kind person.'

'And sexy and talented.'

'And because you always smell amazing.'

'Fingernails?'

'Very witchy.'

'I want you to credit my fingernails for your whole mini-break.'

'Will do.'

And with that, Becky hurries out of the office, towards the chauffeur-driven car waiting outside the building, that Matthew has laid on to drive her and her family out of the city in style and comfort.

Chapter 21

Becky leans against reception waiting for their paperwork to be completed and their key cards to be issued, fingers pinched round the bottom of a champagne glass, absorbing the low light and neutrals, the peaceful string music, the interior water feature of tiny rocks and bonsai. She breathes it all in like clean mountain air, allowing herself to feel hope that a break, a change in place and pace, could really, genuinely, be what she needs. Her own childhood family holidays in Rye and Camber Sands weren't exactly sunshine, Snakes and Ladders and sea-salted skin – there were arguments and feuds and a lot of being alone. She can do better, can't she? Surely she can.

She's already made a start by building a dam against the fretful toxic sludge that seeps through Twitter, Instagram, the *Daily Mail*, the *Guardian*, YouTube and the blogs. She's closed down every unhelpful window and app on her phone, determining that she will leave the speculation about Amber well alone and that she will leave Scott well alone to get on with his preening and preparation, while she spends proper time with her family.

And yet, she has already spent the journey to Camber Sands fretting over Maisie. Her classmates have been making digs about the fact that Becky was in the papers. Maisie tells Becky that she batted them away 'like annoying flies', but what remains at the end of the conversation and stays with Becky for some time after is a sense of her daughter collecting battle scars. She saw her daughter's sad eyes in the rear view mirror and Becky blamed herself for it.

But now Maisie and Adam seem to be happily fussing over a luggage label, discussing when they should set their alarms for pancakes and eggs the next morning, and maybe there is hope after all. Let it be simple. Let it be fun. Let nobody ask her about Amber ever again.

The receptionist, dressed like a health spa specialist, in a cream tabard, looks up and smiles at Becky. 'Breakfast will be served from eight and I'll need your credit card for any incidentals.'

Becky hands it over. 'Can you put the rooms on this one too?'

'Everything's paid for. By Matthew Kingsman.'

Becky hesitates then glances around her, as if someone's watching her. When she's sure no one is, she says, 'Are you sure about that?'

'You just need to pay for any incidentals.'

She pulls her sleeves over her fists. 'Honestly? I'd rather pay for the whole thing if that's all right.'

'It's all done, all gone through. Is there a . . .' She checks a sheet of paper by her keyboard. 'Is there a Maisie Shawcross with you?'

'Yes? Why? Do you need her?'

'Please.'

Becky turns to Maisie. Thinks twice. 'Hold on, can I ask what it's about?'

'Of course.' The receptionist hands the sheet of paper to Becky. It reads:

Dear Maisie, Please enjoy a trip away in this hotel, all expenses paid. If you'd like to try horse riding on the beach tomorrow, just ask and they'll arrange it. Have a great birthday. If you grow up anything like your mum then you'll be an amazing human being. Best birthday wishes, Matthew Kingsman.'

Becky folds the paper in four and drops it into her handbag. She is shivering. The air-con is up too high.

All presents are reciprocal. Aren't they?

Her mind is shivering now, darting all over the place like it can't find a place to settle, or hide. She takes the paper out of her bag and throws it in the bin like it's contaminated. She doesn't immediately untangle the details of *why*: all she knows is she doesn't want Matthew's promises within an inch of her daughter.

Maisie runs over, Adam in her wake. 'This place is amazing, Mum! They have an omelette bar at breakfast.'

'Traitor,' growls Adam behind her. 'We are pancake

260

people. Don't go chasing after other round foods at breakfast. No bagels. No omelettes. Definitely no pizzas.'

'Omelettes get folded in half.'

'That's because they're sneaky!' shouts Adam, collapsing Maisie into giggles.

'Mais,' says Becky, 'can you go to the bar and order us three nice cocktails?' She hands her a credit card. 'Make sure you pay for them on this. Oh, and non-alcoholic.'

'Coming right up.'

'What's up?' Adam says as they watch Maisie skip to the bar with its low-lit oceanic lighting. 'You're tense.'

'Matthew's paid for the whole thing,' she says quietly.

'Wow, that's generous,' he says. 'And that's a . . . problem?'

She wants to tell him everything: for it to pour out of her like news headlines racing across the bottom of the screen. But instead she is silent.

'I'm disappointed not to be allowed to pay for it,' says Becky. 'For the first time in ages I can treat her, properly, you know?'

This is also the truth. She had wanted to make up for the things Maisie lost along the way – all the missed bags of sweets, magazine subscriptions, school trips to Sorrento and Venice. She could have asked Adam for the money for all of that, but she didn't. He'd done so much already.

'And, you know,' her throat tightens at the memory of those Volt trainers he paid for, 'I wanted to show Maisie this time: *Look, this is what hard work gets you.*'

'I understand.' He smiles. 'But I'm sure Maisie will find a dozen other ways to nearly bankrupt you this weekend, if that's what you're after.'

But Becky doesn't really hear him. She glances at the bin and then at her daughter taking receipt of an enormous citric-orange cocktail, a delighted smile painted across her face. Becky's stomach contracts. She does not think of all the positive ways in which her daughter might see her: as a bold, young producer, someone who tackles big issues, someone who understands characters and stories and story-tellers. In that moment, all Becky sees is what she's passed down to her daughter: toxic offerings and her own shame – repackaged, reconstituted, nothing to do with her and yet, still, the shame that is having a mother who is spoken about in the same sentence as the words *sexual harassment*.

Becky feels like such a fraud standing there on the soft marl carpet. She feels . . . dirty.

Adam leans in, his shoulder brushing Becky's, as if he senses she needs reassurance. They are touching each other in the way they have contrived so many times in the past – through doorways, knees brushing under the table – always moving away, snooker balls glancing against each other, but this time is different. This time they are both aware of entering each other's space and how the atmos-phere is warmer and more magnetic there.

She turns to him and says, 'I think I want to leave.'

Maisie has arranged the cocktails on a low table and is examining a leaflet.

'If you don't want the boss paying,' says Adam. 'I'll pay. She's really happy. Look at her.'

'No, it's not that. You don't need to do that. Please don't do that.' She wants for them to run from here and pitch their own moth-eaten bell tent in a field near the beach, to buy a portable barbecue and beers, to sit by a fire and sing eighties power ballads. 'I feel spoiled. It's making me uncomfortable.'

'Your daughter is extremely comfortable with it, I must say.'

'So should I just suck it up?'

'Yes, Becks. Try to suck up all the free luxury pampering. And if you can't handle it, I'll scout around for a bin for you to sleep in.'

She laughs, and it produces tears. 'God. I don't know what's *wrong* with me.'

'Working too hard?'

'I should be grateful, shouldn't I?'

'You should try and enjoy it.'

She considers Adam's point: how Maisie would feel to have something so nice given to her and then taken away in less than ten minutes. And what reason could Becky then offer her for such mean-spiritedness?

'Look at it this way,' says Adam, equitably. 'From Maisie's point of view she's being spoiled and pampered for a special birthday. That's a nice thing, isn't it?'

It's only later that Becky comes back to what he has said: did Adam talk about Maisie's point of view because,

263

from his, it looks different? Like a bribe. Like blood money. He'd be too careful to say it outright. She wants so much to know what he thinks but doesn't know where to begin or even if she should.

She decides to ignore it all. To be in the moment.

Half an hour later, they meet poolside in the spa complex. The water is untouched. Gemstone blue. Adam and Becky lie on loungers, wrapped in chalk-white waffle robes, gazing up at black-veined marble and gold-stuccoed ceilings.

'That is a lot of money to spend on a ceiling,' says Adam, but Becky's not ready to joke about the money. The money is the problem.

Maisie leaps into the water and emerges, hair shining like the wet skin of a seal. 'Are you coming in? It's amazing! I mean, obviously it's amazing.'

'In a minute,' replies Adam, standing up and letting his robe fall off his shoulders. 'I'm going to have a relax. Beckles, are you all set to relax? Can I get you anything to increase your relaxation?'

'No, thank you,' says Becky, lifting her hands off the side of the lounger as if they are covered in something sticky. 'There used to be a place that sold chocolate pancakes in the car park at Camber Sands. Shall we walk there later and get some? If it still exists?'

Adam pushes his lounger closer to hers. 'Sorry, I couldn't hear what you were saying over all the Bach and birdsong.' He is wearing navy trunks and a T-shirt that falls nicely across his shoulders, over his chest and down his stomach. 'Something about pancakes in a car park?'

'I'd just like to get out of here. Wouldn't you?'

'Poolside luxury or car park?' He weighs them up with open palms. 'It's a tough one, but the pool wins. Anyway, it doesn't look like Maisie's going anywhere.'

Becky looks up and sees Maisie leaning against the poolside at the far end, arms folded over each other, talking to a boy on a lounger whose age Becky cannot determine. When did the boy even arrive? Did Maisie wish for him? Is that how her sixteenth is going to work?

'That boy has got very defined abs,' she says.

'You like a defined ab, do you? How do you rate a good circulatory system and correctly working organs?'

'Very attractive.'

'Thanks. I feel less terrible about my abs now.'

'What abs?'

'Such cruelty. This is why you'll die bitter and alone.'

Silence.

'That,' says Adam, 'sounded a lot more fun and teasing in my head.'

'It's fine. It's true.'

'It's not true.'

'Speaking of dying alone, what did you decide to do about Kate?' She keeps it light. Nonchalant. Like she barely cares.

'I'm sorry about the other night. I was quite drunk when I was saying all that.'

'Don't be ridiculous. You can tell me anything.' She doesn't add that she reserves the right to agonize about some of those things for hours. For days. She wants him to be honest with her. She can't make him afraid to tell her the truth.

'We went to the pub the night before last. I didn't even have to bring it up. She'd obviously been thinking the same. She put it on the table.'

Becky shuts her eyes and allows this information to sink through her, like a stone dropped into dark water and landing in mud, a slower sinking for the final inch towards burial.

'She said she had feelings for me,' he says.

'Oh yes, what kind of feelings? Tired feelings, hungry feelings, sad feelings?' She doesn't open her eyes because she fears that if he sees them, they will betray her.

There is a long and heavy silence, during which Becky makes a wish of her own. Can she please find a way to connect with him, one last time before Kate is confirmed as a *thing* in his life, one last time before they can never go back to the way they were before? Can she make him promise not to leave them, even if he's going to leave her?

'So what did you say to that?' says Becky, quietly, opening her eyes again.

'Well, do you want to know what she said first?'

'Not really,' Becky laughs.

'I'll tell you anyway. It needs that context. She said she had feelings for me. She said she's been in love with me for about a year.'

'That was around the time you got those new skinny indigo jeans, wasn't it?'

'We always knew those jeans had power. You said it at the time.'

'So when's the wedding?'

'It was actually a very hard conversation.'

'It's a big decision. Vegas or Clapham?'

'Please. Becks. I'm trying to tell you this.' She glances down as she feels his hand touch her. Feels the warmth and insistence that transmits itself through skin and flesh and blood on its journey to her heart. She dares herself to look up at him and fails the challenge. 'I told her that I didn't feel the same way. I'd thought I might feel the same way, but I realized it was more like I was willing it to happen, if that makes sense.'

'It makes sense.'

'I don't love her.'

'Good.'

'What does that mean?' he asks, after falling silent for a moment.

'I don't know,' says Becky.

'Do you really not know?'

But Adam's words are carried up through the peppermint-scented steam puffing from an open steam-room door, interrupted by the gleeful laughs coming from the swimming pool and finally forgotten as Becky turns her attention to what is playing out in front of her: Maisie and the boy, who is now by her side in the pool, both leaning on their forearms, speaking into the tiles before turning to face each other. Laughing again.

'If you're thinking of getting a cocktail, I'm in,' she says, not taking her eyes off this scene. As if she might miss something crucial if she did.

Adam looks at her for a moment, then lets his head drop a little, disheartened perhaps. 'What's your poison?'

Their laughter is getting louder. The boy is leaning in further to show Maisie something on his arm and Becky cranes to see what. Then Adam lightly touches the top of Becky's wrist to get her attention and she leaps out of her skin.

'Woah,' he says. 'Sorry, I didn't mean to . . .' She looks at him like he's just appeared. 'I just wanted to know what you'd like to drink?'

'I don't know, nothing, I don't want anything.'

'Right, I'll just get the one.' He pauses. 'Becks? They're just talking.' The pool water splashes over the edge as one of them showers the other in a playful game. 'Let her have her fun before you send in the lifeguards.'

She blushes, looking over to Maisie, feeling caught in idiocy.

She waits for Adam to depart for the bar before she stands up. She can see the alchemy happening between boy and girl in a swimming pool, the magical violet and emerald and silver mist passing between their lips, swirling in a vortex around their two bodies, the *Wizard of Oz* twister that takes away the house. There is no time to waste, she must interrupt now, and break the spell before it is complete.

Becky stands at the pool's edge. 'Come on, Mais, we're going for an early dinner.'

Maisie keeps her eyes fixed on the pool tiles. 'What? It's not even five. Can I meet you later? I'm kind of having a nice time swimming.'

'Sorry, chick. We're going now, and you're coming with us.' Becky tries so hard to sound light and casual, but she is declaring a done deal. Maisie will hate her, but the alternative is worse: giving her trust to someone who will steal from her. 'We're going to have fish and chips in Dungeness.'

'You can go. I could just stay. I'm not even that hungry.'

Becky squints at the boy in the pool, and he takes her steely gaze as his cue to swim away.

'Here, I'll give you a pull-up,' says Becky.

'Jesus, Mum . . .' Maisie hisses at her like an aggravated snake as she pulls herself out of the pool, spurning the offer. 'Could you be any more annoying?'

The boy wades into the shallow end and emerges slowly out of the water like he thinks he's in an aftershave advert. He is a few years older than her daughter. Eighteen, perhaps. He is wearing red swimming trunks that fit well around his slim waist. It is clear that he cares about his body, that he runs or lifts weights or something.

269

'Maisie?' he says. He holds himself well: his face shines with health, his hands rest on slim hips and his smile is easy. 'I'm heading down to Camber Sands later, if you fancy it? After dinner, or something? Just if you're into it.'

'Sounds fun,' she says.

Maisie, in her tangerine bikini.

'Maybe when you turn sixteen,' says Becky to her daughter, ever so lightly. Even as she says it, she knows she'll pay for it but she sees the boy make the calculation. As she intended. Fifteen-year-old girl: that's a prison sentence.

Maisie looks away from her mother, at her feet and then at the boy. She rests her hands on her waist, above where the bikini ties at her hips in bows. 'Maybe see you later then,' she says to the boy. 'I'm sixteen at midnight. Maybe I'll come and find you on the beach at 12.01.'

'Sure,' he says, though he seems embarrassed, caught between mother and daughter. He lowers himself back into the water.

Becky's vision dims. 'What did you mean by that? You're not going out tonight.'

'What did *you* mean by telling him I'm fifteen? I'm not stupid. You might as well just write "It's illegal to have sex with me" in permanent marker on my legs. Or just draw a big "Stop!" sign over my pussy.'

'Fucking hell, Maisie!'

'Don't pretend you weren't doing that.'

'I don't want you skulking around on a beach on your own after dark looking for some sketchy guy you've known for all of two minutes.'

'I wouldn't *have* to do that if you'd let me hang out in the pool for a bit longer instead of dragging me off for cod and chips.'

'We're meant to be spending time together!'

'Don't shout.'

'What, because I'm embarrassing you in front of your serious long-term boyfriend?'

'What is *wrong* with you?' Maisie looks tearfully furious now, determined not to show it.

'You're being reckless.'

'I've got my swimming badges. I'm OK to be in a pool.'

'So why were you so keen to stay in?'

'God, do I have to spell it out?'

'Yes. Go on.'

'I think he's hot.'

Becky crosses her arms across her chest. 'And so what's your plan?'

'I haven't got a masterplan, Mum. Not everyone's as neurotic as you.'

'Any mum would find it worrying you're trying to get rid of us to be with some boy who could be anyone.'

'He's staying here with his parents as well. He has a name and everything.'

'It's not safe.'

271

Adam returns with an overly bright cocktail. 'Aloha!' he says, holding it up in a toast. Then, reading the atmosphere, asks Maisie, 'What's up?'

'Mum's being Mum.'

'I told her she couldn't ditch dinner to hang out with a stranger,' says Becky, matter-of-fact.

'Can we not do this here?' hisses Maisie, terribly aware that her boy is swimming short lengths behind her back.

'Back to the rooms?' Adam offers, all neutrality.

'Why do you always do this?' Maisie says. Now that they are dressed, and behind the solid door of Maisie and Becky's room, voices are raised, all the way up to how they're feeling, which is very loud indeed.

'I don't *do* anything,' Becky shouts. 'Do what?'

'Stop me from doing anything! You don't trust me to make any decisions. What have I ever done to make you not trust me? I don't smoke crack. I'm not whoring myself. I hardly leave the house without your written permission! Why don't you trust me?'

'I do.'

'You don't! What the fuck happened to make you like this?'

Becky takes a deep breath. 'I trust you, of course I trust you,' she says. 'It's boys your age I don't trust. They get drunk, they get out of control, they don't think.'

'You can't control everyone's behaviour.'

'It's my job to protect you.' For a moment Becky closes her eyes and in the darkness chides herself. She hadn't even been able to protect herself.

'I'm sixteen tomorrow and then your job is *over*. I can legally do what the fuck I like.'

Becky glares at her. 'Not while you're under my roof!'

'Then I'll find another roof! It'll be better than living in Shawcross prison!'

Becky collapses down onto one of the two double beds, suddenly exhausted, wishing Adam would hurry up and stop obsessing about the games console in his room and help her with all this: even just to intervene with a stupid joke to distract them both from this maddening, twisting journey down a rabbit hole.

Maisie glares back at her.

'Fine then,' snaps Becky. 'Go and live your life. Just don't expect me to pick up the pieces when you're gang-raped on the beach.'

Maisie looks utterly shocked. Becky feels like the words came out of her mouth without her brain's say so, all overheated and fearful and vicious.

'You've got massive problems,' says Maisie. She grabs her handbag, opens the door, steps through it, and is gone.

Becky turns her face into her pillow and sobs and sobs. She is radioactive with pain and shame and fury and guilt. And loneliness.

She pictures herself beating Scott to a bloody pulp with

her bare hands, until the individual features of his face are gone, smashed into a uniform pink mush, but it does nothing for her. Nothing will ever be enough for her.

She blows her nose in the bathroom. Washes her face with cold water from the basin.

Surveys the over-sized bath with Maisie's bikini discarded by the plughole and her vast collection of open tubes and pots of metallic-pink powder, creams, pastes and perfume arranged around the sides.

In the room, Becky perches on the peacock-blue bedspread still flat and made, the iron-smooth pillow dented once from a quick moment checking the hotel's TV channel. The dark gold curtains are open and quivering with the contrived cold of air-conditioning. She doesn't know what to do with any of this: the embossed complimentary stationery, the view . . .

Why won't Maisie just shout that she hates her? Instead she pities me, thinks Becky.

She flies to a knock at the door, but finds only Adam there, brandishing a packet of popcorn. 'I've got a really well-stocked minibar, if dinner's off the cards? *Chez* Adam or stay here? Décor is exactly the same though I prefer my paintings.'

'Maisie's not here. She went off in a strop.'

'Classic fifteen-year-old. It'll all be different when she's sixteen.'

'Adam.'

'She'll be fine. She's not stupid. She's not reckless. She's a really smart kid.'

'She went off without her room key card.'

'Well, you're here.'

'Shouldn't I go after her?'

'Maybe not?'

'I'm messing everything up.'

'No, you're not. You're a good mum. You're totally good, Becky.'

She folds herself into his arms. Hears him drop the packet of popcorn as his arms wrap around her.

After standing in the doorway together for a long moment, he disentangles himself to close the door, then turns back and holds her at a distance, gripping her arms lightly.

She feels his warmth soothe the fused and sparking ends of her adrenalized impulses. Feels his kind eyes glance at her collarbone and follows his gaze down the waves of hair covering her breasts. He looks at her again, as if to say: *OK? Are we OK about this?*

And she pulls his head to hers, kissing him. She can smell his deodorant and his skin.

She takes him to bed.

Afterwards, they shower, separately. They are shy with each other and dress hurriedly. Aware, too, that if Maisie returns then they must be dressed. And if Maisie doesn't return soon, they need to go and look for her.

As Adam darts around trying to find his T-shirt he says, 'Are we? You know was that all ri. . .? I thought it was . . .'

Becky goes to him and kisses him again and smiles. 'Yes. I am glad. Yes and yes. Now, Maisie,' she says. 'Hurry up.'

'She probably *wants* us to go looking for her.'

'You're not just saying that to make me feel OK about looking for her?'

'No,' he says, smiling. 'I want to find her as well.'

'You don't think something's happened, do you?'

'It'll be fine,' he says.

And a spark lights, scalding, inside her. She wants to say: *Stop saying that to me. You don't know that everything will be fine.*

But she says nothing.

As they walk down the hotel corridor together Adam says, 'Can I ask you something?'

'You will anyway.'

'Not if it makes you feel uncomfortable, the last thing I want to do is make you feel . . .'

'How I am supposed to know if you don't . . .'

'OK. Those things, on the inside of your thigh.'

'Oh.' There are three or four of them, neat blood-mark snips, high up, where you'd only find them if you'd been as close as he just has.

'Did you, you know . . . do it to yourself?'

276

'Yes,' she says. Ashamed, relieved.

He glances at her as they continue to walk. She doesn't need to look at how deep the concern has sunk into his skin, she can hear it in his voice.

'But that's worse than the bruising? I thought you said you'd stopped doing all that but, look, I don't want it to sound like pressure, I just wondered if all this Amber Heath stuff is making you a bit . . . I dunno, the stress of trying to keep your film afloat?'

'It hasn't been fun.'

He grasps her hand. 'You know I'll look after you if it falls apart.'

'I know. I just really want to make that film. I feel like I have to at least have that, after everything. You paid for me to do all the stuff that let me get my foot in the door. I can't walk away with nothing apart from a few years helping other people make their own things. I want to have *my* thing.'

'I understand.'

'If I get hit by a bus, I want Maisie to have something that she can say I did. Something I made happen, that I put all of myself into.'

'You could also try and avoid buses.'

'I'm trying to stay alive, obviously.'

But then she remembers that of course he doesn't take that for granted. He has seen her not wanting to be alive. He heard her admit it and then he tied himself to her, so that if she went, he'd be blamed.

They wait side by side for the lift in silence, heads bowed. She grips his hand tightly.

Had he loved her that much, even then? To hold her in the world like that, at such a cost? Even when she was broken, withdrawn, in hell, swollen with a baby she couldn't wait to be rid of, full of anger and hate. Her own father hadn't loved her through that.

Had Adam felt sorry for her? Or had he loved her? She supposed, one day, that she might ask him and now that day has come into view, and so chaotically. What had she meant, pulling him into her, wrapping her legs around him to lock him into her, feeling him come inside her, and wanting her whole skin to be touching his – what had that meant?

'You could put the job aside for a bit,' he says quietly.

'It can't just be any old film. It has to be *Medea* and it's not the time to walk away. Projects have a moment. If you miss it, it becomes something that didn't get off the ground. Nobody wants to be a part of one of those, something everyone else walked away from. It's just how it is. If I don't make it now, it'll die. I know it.'

They pass through reception. They check the pool complex. Maisie isn't there. Fear pricks through Becky's body.

As they walk toward the bar to check if she's there, Becky wonders: what am I doing? There had been a few flings in the past, but she'd wiped them from her memory as quickly as they had happened. She can't wipe anything away now: Adam is by her side and she can feel his cum trickle out of her, an unfamiliar wetness. And then she is back there, remembering all those years ago as she looked down into the crotch of her knickers and found semen there. Suddenly she is dizzy. She holds Adam's arm. I'm going to pass out, she thinks.

He looks at her. 'You need to eat something.'

'Let's find Maisie first.'

Maisie is not in the bar, or in the games room either, and they are running out of rooms in which to find her.

'She might have gone back to the bedroom,' says Adam. 'We could go back and leave her a note.'

'Let's keep looking.' Their conversation has dried up. What more is there to say, other than: *Where is she? Is she OK? Is she safe?*

They head into the hotel grounds. Uplighters pick out the shapes of topiary hedges arranged around a wide lawn. Adam and Becky walk in silence over its sprawling softness. It is a warm night, a light breeze pushing clouds out of the way of the stars. Night-singing birds call to each other.

Becky decides, then and there. If Maisie is found – if she is not drowned, stabbed, strangled or otherwise destroyed – then she must be done with her questions. She has to know.

She had hoped that time would close the gap in her.

Well, that hasn't worked, she thinks with a hard, unsparing voice. All it's done is chew her up and spit her out again.

But she is definitely ready now. She will face it and fight it. Let it be agony. Let there be violence. Let the stitching show afterwards, but things cannot stay the same. She cannot go on damaging herself and those around her.

Give me back my girl, and I will seek out Scott in real life.

No more digital toxicity, no more distraction, no more procrastination, no more weakness. She will take the risk, risk it hurting, and so start to heal. That is the deal she cuts with the universe.

Then, things will be different.

'I told Kate that I'm in love with you,' says Adam, taking her hand. 'She said she already knew that. She said she thought we'd all been kidding ourselves for a long time.'

Becky puts her hand to his chest to quieten him. There – close by – voices.

'What will you say to her?' says Adam.

'I don't know.'

'Try not to kill her.'

They move in a wide arc and Adam speeds up toward the sounds.

'Wait,' says Becky, holding him back, taking his hand and guiding him past great topiary animals, to where black and white flagstones make a hedge-rimmed chessboard. Maisie and the boy from the pool are sitting on it, cross-legged, facing each other. In the starlit darkness, the end of a joint flares as he inhales then passes it to her. Becky watches her little girl take it and smoke it with assurance. She has done this before. Obviously she has. There are no coughing fits. Maisie licks a finger and damps down the side of the Rizla paper where it is burning too fast.

'We were doing exactly the same at her age,' Adam whispers. 'Come on, shall we go get her?'

She hesitates.

'No,' she says, gripping his hand. 'Let's leave them. I have to trust her.'

And I don't have to be governed by my past.

When Adam lets go of her hand and puts his arm around her, kissing the top of her head, she knows she can do it. She believes with every breath, in every cell, that it is time to trust herself again.

When Maisie returns to the room, Becky is tucked up under the covers and watching a film on TV, eating from the bag of popcorn Adam dropped on the floor earlier. She had kissed Adam goodbye at his door an hour ago and it had felt exhilaratingly teenage and special, the idea that she would see him again soon, as if there was only History and double Geography to get through.

Maisie drops her handbag on the floor and sets off toward the bathroom.

Becky switches off the TV and kicks her duvet away. 'Mais, wait. I'm sorry.'

281

Maisie turns around and fixes her mum with a blood-shot gaze. Her face is crumpled and smudged and Becky thinks she can see blades of grass in her hair. An image of her daughter and aftershave boy tumbling on the lawn spreads quickly in Becky's mind like ink dropped on blotting paper. But she bids it leave. A blank page. She must trust that her daughter dealt with whatever happened in the best way she knew how.

'You look very stoned,' says Becky, smiling.

Maisie still doesn't say anything and Becky wonders whether she is almost too stoned to speak. 'I'm truly sorry for earlier.' She tries again. 'I messed up. Just because I'm scared, doesn't mean you should be, in fact I want the opposite for you. I want to make sure you've got everything you need for the world of adults, I . . .'

'Do you think you might be finding it a bit hard to let go?' Maisie asks gently.

'Yes,' Becky blinks back her tears. 'You may have been an adult for all of eleven minutes but in my eyes you're still my baby.'

Maisie walks toward her mum. 'I grew out of bootees, like, years ago.'

'You never really wore them. Always kicked them off. You liked to have free feet. Happy birthday, darling.'

Maisie perches on the edge of the bed. 'Thanks, Mum. Are you not now incredibly pissed off with me that I'm stoned?'

'No. Just incredibly jealous. Did you have a nice time?'

'I had a fine time. Seb is fine but, turns out, not all that.'

'I love you,' says Becky. Maisie jumps onto the bed and lays her head down on Becky's stomach. That's where you came from, thinks Becky, as she strokes her daughter's hair. I was your first home.

Chapter 22

Becky wakes before Maisie. Her daughter is sixteen now, asleep in the adjoining double bed, looking like she did when she was a baby, her cheeks smooshed into the pillow, peaceful.

Becky runs her hands over the bedsheet beneath her own body, feeling for the small patch where the cotton hardens, as if glued. It did happen, after all. She did it with Adam. And today they are going to walk around Dungeness and get fish and chips for lunch. She is looking forward to seeing him. She is starving hungry. A bag of popcorn for dinner was not enough.

Daylight streams through the top of the curtains. She wonders how late they have slept. Have they missed breakfast already?

She reaches for her phone, charging on the bedside table, and discovers both that it is 10.15 a.m. and that Amber Heath has been taken to hospital following a suicide attempt. She is in intensive care. Her family have asked for privacy. None of her friends have gone on the record. Calls to her agent have not been returned.

Becky tries to read everything, but nobody has more information.

Twitter has anger – raging calls for Matthew to face justice, as well as plenty of comments along the lines of 'she lied, she got busted' – but no new information.

Maisie stirs and opens her eyes.

'Are you OK?' she asks. 'You're really white.'

'No, I don't feel great,' says Becky. 'I think I've got a bug or something.'

'I'll go and get Dad.'

'No. Go and have breakfast with him. Have a nice time.'

'What about Dungeness?' says Maisie.

'You and Adam might have to go without me.' She is craving having the room to herself. So that she can pace, or throw up, or curl into a ball or cut, cut, cut at her legs.

Maisie leaves and, under the covers, Becky thinks of Amber wired up to machines, one that has pumped her stomach and another that helps her breathe.

Would Amber have ended up like this if Becky had spoken up about what she saw?

Becky is to blame, surely she is to blame. All she can think about is that night in the playground, those moments before Adam came for her, and how she had thumped her legs, how she had stopped short of thumping her stomach as blame ran so hot through her blood she thought her soul would melt. Her fault for ending up that way.

Now she cries, and she tears at her scalp and hair, wanting to tear out chunks, to disfigure herself, make herself bald and ugly and naked. Claws at her legs and arms like a cat defending its life from a predator. What about Amber's family? What of the sickness and blame sitting inside Amber's mother, that she raised her daughter all wrong – in a way that made her so vulnerable to damage?

Amber should not be the person to die. This is not her fault.

Amber is Medea is Becky is Medea: but the goal was revenge, not death.

Becky cannot bear to be with herself any more. Clambers out of bed and pulls every miniature out of the fridge. She lines them up on the bed and unscrews the tiny top off one, then tips the stinging stuff down her throat, swallowing and gagging. She looks at the others but doesn't touch another, she already feels so sick.

She lies on her back on soft maroon carpet and thinks of Maisie and Adam in Dungeness: how these beloved people will be stepping between the vast makeshift shacks and daffodil-yellow wooden houses, over the pebbles – perhaps discussing whether Becky is all right, if she's really all right. She can see the lighthouse and the waves and the cut-out shapes of cacti in her mind's eye, all set against the grey backwash of a sky that's lost its sun, clouds assembling, tumbleweeds spinning. And in the far distance the nuclear power plant dominating, all white and peppermint-green matrices gated up in thin metal. A black burnt-out house frame against the horizon. Pylons holding out their arms, offering nothing: these will surely remind Adam of the place they were both raised, a trigger to tell Maisie how hard it was for her mother then, how dreadful it was to feel so alone with something so new and yet so precious.

Perhaps Adam will think of last night, and regret it.

They have only been gone an hour, promising to come back for her as soon as she starts to feel right. She has declined their offer of going straight back to London. There will be paparazzi on her doorstep again, won't there? Maisie will want to know what Becky thinks about the news but she is not ready for that.

Colours mix and the staid lines of the room blur around her. She needs to get to the bathroom.

She vomits into the toilet bowl, straining her insides like she wants them to come unstitched from her, lungs and heart streaming out blood before their tubes and flesh splash into the water beneath.

There is one thought she cannot bury.

If you are the woman who saw me, you can call the police direct if you don't want to speak to David. Please, just don't say nothing.

The eyes are the windows to the soul, she tells herself, as she looks in the mirror and washes her mouth out.

Her thoughts swim back and back, heart thrashing in her chest, a sick rush back in time, but she digs her fingernails into the present – *don't take me there, please don't take me there* – by running the cold tap again and sticking her mouth under it. Rinsing and spitting. She pushes the bathroom door closed, there isn't a lock. Notices that perhaps she is sore down there and pushes her underwear down to around her knees, sits heavily on the toilet, cradling her head on her hand, arm resting on her thigh, and sees the crotch of her pants – lace, a bold magenta – stiff now. Feels around her pubic hair and yes, it is there too. Like glue.

And she is being sick again, even before she knows it, all across the marble floor, losing the strength she needs to stop what is now certainly happening – God, no, she remembers nothing after her eyes rolled back, lying back into the coats with Scott and he said *I'm so fucked Becky, I'm so fucked, are you?* And she was too gone to say anything at all, she was just thudding with drugs like she was underwater, pummelled, pinned under by the waves. Waking up, nothing, nobody who can tell her who—

Chapter 23

Hampstead, London
14 September 2003, the morning after the party

She is lying down, is all she knows – lying down in a bed, but she doesn't know where, at first. Arms by her side, she pulls something up between her fingers, like pulling up grass, but she is not in a field of living green stuff, she is somewhere un-alive where the air smells stale with smoke and sweat. She looks down. She is holding the coverlet she had seen earlier, so pretty and pink and swirled like the silken inside of a conch shell. She has fallen asleep at the party.

She doesn't know how she got there. In that moment, all she thinks she's lost is time.

She sits up and tries to swallow, but without enough saliva the movement hurts her throat. She feels around the sore edges of her mouth with a dry tongue. Next an aching pressure down the length of her spine – the way she had been sleeping, perhaps. Bolsters herself with both hands, legs out straight. For a moment she feels little and young, like a child in ballet class doing the exercise with toes pointed up, toes pointed down – good toes, naughty toes, good toes, naughty toes.

It is then that she feels something warm escape from between her thighs. She looks under the pink coverlet, too dark to see though. She feels afraid and ashamed at the thought that perhaps she has wet herself or, worse, is spilling dark menstrual blood onto their beautiful covers. She thinks this is the worst she will feel, she does, so appalled at the thought of soiling other people's things she tears pillowslip from pillow and rams it between her legs, eyes filling with tears at the thought of a parent's reaction to such damage. Injury, accident or stupidity?

She gets out of the bed and staggers stiff-legged past the walk-in wardrobe where she had spent half the night with Scott. He was fun. That was nice. Now she feels like shit. She goes into the bathroom: towels rippled in piles on the floor, bottles knocked over.

Faced with a full-length mirror now, a ceiling light illuminating her naked white legs, she stands pale in her pink cotton pants and T-shirt. She doesn't remember undressing. She doesn't remember leaving the wardrobe. There is an angry smear of blood down her thigh almost to her knee, some dark, some fresh, it has moved like a slow and quiet river out of her. She swallows, digesting this violent image of blood against skin where previously there had only been sun cream and chlorine.

Her thoughts snag and begin sifting back through time. It hadn't been that long since her last period, a week or so at most. A family lunch, old friends, she'd played Happy Families with the child closest her age, then visited the toilet. How silly she'd been not to bring sanitary towels, couldn't find anything in the cupboards, had to make do with a rolled bunch of rough recycled toilet paper. And now her body is bleeding again and there is obviously something wrong with her stupid body that it is bleeding again so quickly.

Then she sees a red mark across her ribs like a cat has clawed at her, and she has to step forward to examine herself closer in the mirror just to check it isn't crayon or pen. It doesn't wipe away and she wonders why. Part of a game with Scott, perhaps.

She drinks water from the tap and then sits on the toilet to have a wee. She feels too bad to care that there's no lock on the door. The house is quiet anyway. It feels like early morning. If people are awake, they're downstairs. The loud music has gone.

Knickers round her knees, she wonders why the seams of her blood-stained pants are wrong. They're facing outwards. The label at the back is hanging into space behind the waistband of her soft pink cotton knickers. Why has she done this? Was she so drunk that she took them off to wee and put them back on the wrong way round?

She stands and takes off her pants, then nearly trips in the leg holes. She starts turning them back the right way but even with her eyes half-closed, focusing on trying not to be sick, she notices that something is not right. There is a whiteness mixed in with the blood in the crotch area.

She cannot believe it. It cannot be right.

She crouches a little and pushes a finger into her vagina, which feels sore, then examines it. Amidst the blood smell of iron is the chlorinous smell of semen. It's not new to her. She had given Dave Lowden a hand-job at the Spring Ball and afterwards wiped away the rest of it in a toilet cubicle and, curious and unwatched, smelt it, just so she knew.

But how is that here?

She throws up. She vomits green bile and pale liquid onto the tiled floor, then retches and retches.

Where is Scott and did he do this to her?

She does not remember anyone doing anything to her and this is the moment she knows she did not dress inside out.

She would never *choose* to turn herself inside out.

She holds the pants, still half inside out – at a distance, as if they are someone else's entrails.

She lowers herself to the floor, cowers, curls into a ball, hiding herself from the reflection in the mirror, afraid to see how much of her has been lost, taken.

And then she loses more: over and over, vomiting onto the bathroom floor. She is all the colours of the rainbow, what with the pearlescent-white semen and rose-red blood and infected green bile and girly pink scraped skin. All the colours of the rainbow, and yet none of them.

Her skin hurts like the ripples at the start of skin peeling from flesh and frame. She puts palms to ribcage and feels upward to where her heart is, then down and across to the place where her lungs lie, side by side. Feels where her stomach sits, and around the circumference of the ribcage to the lower back, where her kidneys are. These organs that have grown with her and served her so well, they are all still there. And yet, she thinks she can feel each one of them cower in pain, the bruised edges and centre of each, trying to recover from the moment that someone has been inside her and jostled, in search of what they want.

She needs to be dressed and gone but on crawling into the bedroom she can't see her own clothes, just a heap of parental clothes, spilling out of the walk-in wardrobe – the stiff-collared blue office shirts of Dad, the pencil skirts and tulle-frilled tops of Mum, all pulled off the rails, trampled and mangled between wood and wire hangers.

Becky is crying quietly, vision blurred, when she finally locates her jeans, folded neatly beside the bed, her shoes placed next to them, as if she'd just taken a swim in a beautiful lake. Was this some kind of parting gesture intended to make the aftermath easier? She pulls on the jeans – far too tight and close now for a frame that is so bruised and sore. She steals a soft plain jumper from a shelf and puts it on.

She isn't crying now. She isn't hysterical. She feels unsteady and ill, but her actions are precise. She needs to go.

She creeps downstairs.

There are people asleep on the living-room floor: a mess of bodies lying piled and entwined, heavy and asleep. Music plays at a low volume. All the shutters are closed. She sees nobody who is awake.

She opens the front door and steps out. It is very early morning. She notes this, another fact that lies outside of her.

As she walks the streets back home that morning she feels the edges of herself blur. She needs to find an anchor before she disappears entirely, needs to know whether she has lost something or whether she has been stolen from.

One is carelessness, and one is a crime.

One she blames herself for and one she can blame another for.

For all she knows it is not a crime. For all she knows she is the one who said, *Yes, take me, fucking take my body.*

But she doesn't know for sure.

And she is sick, again and again. Where? She does not remember. She does not care.

If she goes to the police they will look at her face and beads and her spaghetti-strap top first, and listen to her voice second.

Did you have sex with someone you knew? Do you know for sure that something was stolen and not simply lost? Making an accusation? That's someone's life you're playing with!

But whose life? And what will become of her life?

Even if she goes to a police station she will not be able to answer a single question: no *who* or *when* or *how*. She does not know anything. She can guess, but she does not know. Not for sure.

And if she reported it, and the story got out? *Slag* and *slut* is what they would say of her in the corridors at school. They would say they saw what she wore that night, that they saw the look on her face and heard the game she was playing, all that time, behind closed wardrobe doors.

Bringing it on herself, the slag.

Making it happen, the slut.

She arrives home, and takes a hot shower, and then goes to bed, where she cannot sleep.

After midday, Mary texts her to report that she and Brendan had sex and to ask where Becky got to. *Was it Scott??!!*

She lies under the covers and feels a dull ache somewhere in her arm. She holds her hand up to the light and sees that a chaotic line of fingerprint bruises has appeared round the top of her wrist, like a bracelet of small grey pebbles.

Was it Scott? Becky asks herself. Was it Scott?

She holds her wrist lightly, covering the pebble shapes with her hand and fingers. Closes her eyes but she still can't sleep. It is like there is a high-voltage buzz in her head. She feels high, like adrenaline is making her alert to everything.

She draws her hand into her stomach and curls round it, and soon enough she falls asleep this way.

When she wakes into another day, in some ways nothing has changed. There are no new facts or anything like that.

But she remembers it as a new formulation now: I

passed out and while I was unconscious somebody stripped off my clothes and had sex with me and then put my pants back on me and then left.

The numbness of shock has gone. Now the blame burns a boulder-sized hole into the middle of her.

Some weeks later, when she's back at school, Becky runs into Scott in an empty corridor. He is in front of her before she is even aware of him. He smiles at her.

'I heard about this,' he says, indicating her stomach. 'That's a pretty huge thing.'

She pushes past him without replying. He tries to catch her arm and she evades it. She spends an hour shaking in the girls' toilets.

She worries that when she gives birth to the baby she'll be so full of hatred that she'll grab it from the doctors and swing it by the ankle so that its head breaks on the delivery-room wall.

Where do these ideas come from? She has been polluted. Changed. She is a ruined person. Scott isn't. Scott still mooches along with his friends.

A few days later, Mary asks again if Becky was all right at the party all those weeks ago. She keeps asking because Becky just hasn't been her normal self since then. Becky shrugs and then Mary says she wasn't going to say anything but she heard that Scott said they got off with each other and were maybe going to do more but then they both got so off their tits on these strong pills he'd got that they could barely sit up straight let alone do anything else.

'I think Scott really liked you,' Mary tells Becky. 'At the time.'

Becky sees Scott just one more time before she gives birth.

She finds him sitting alone out on the school playing fields. She has gone to find him, and she has. She knows she only has days to go, and then she might never come back here.

He looks up at her as she approaches.

She looks him in the eye. 'I just want to tell you that I know about you, OK? *I know*,' she says.

'Please don't tell anyone,' he says.

She wants to stay. She had promised herself she'd have the whole thing out, but she'd expected him to deny it. He looks pathetic. Frightened. And she can't do it anyway. She turns and walks away from him, her foetus – *his* foetus – awake and kicking hard.

'Becky!' he calls after her, but no, she won't come back. A sob bubbles out of her throat as she wobbles away. She still wants to kill herself.

She almost hates Adam for what he has done, binding her to being alive.

She doesn't go back to school again, except to sit her exams. She is in and out.

* * *

The day she brings Maisie home from the hospital, she opens her bottom drawer and takes out the pink pants she has wrapped in a plastic bag, and throws them away. She fills the drawer with spare nappies and wipes.

Adam and his parents are off buying a cot and clothes for the newborn.

There is no more room for questions. She has a daughter now.

She breastfeeds her girl, and waits for peace to fill the hole that was burned in her.

Chapter 24

'Please don't tell anyone.'

Please, just don't say nothing.

Becky has spent the day in silence.

By the time Adam and Maisie find her back at the hotel, curled up and shivering under the duvet, she has showered the worst of the vomit away. They fuss and flap over swollen eyes and pale skin and dry lips. *Time to get you home*, one of them says in motherly tones. Adam calls for Matthew's car to drive them home, forgoing their planned second night at the hotel.

She falls asleep on the way back and wakes in her own bed, early the next morning – disorientated and hot, under layers of blankets. The morning light is still low and the birds are waking at once quietly, and then loud – their songs tumbling and bumping into each other. She has the sense that her body has become unmoored in space and yet, in time? She is more clearly orientated than she ever remembers being: the day she has been holding off is here now. At the office they will think she is still on holiday so for the meantime she is safe to go about her business unquestioned. So long as she is careful.

The house smells of fresh laundry – Adam must have hung a load that night after their return. She finds him curled up like a guard dog at the foot of her bed on a blow-up mattress.

Silently, so silently – she must be careful not to wake him – she folds back the duvet, skin bristling with early morning cold. The reflection she catches in the mirror is smudged and tangled, hair standing on end like field stubble, but her skin shines white and her eyes are bright. The person she sees is both someone she recognizes and someone she has not seen before.

Her toes bend softly on the floorboards as she makes her way toward the doorway but she stops a moment before leaving, turning to see the shape his face makes.

Adam would have had such a different life without her. He might have travelled to South East Asia and Australia. He might now be married with a baby, be on his third business enterprise, instead of paying two sets of utility bills and visiting a family he doesn't live with, loyally servicing a sixteen-year-old lie.

She no longer wants him to make sacrifices for her. She wants him to be free.

She wants to be free.

Enough, now.

* * *

On the bus into the city, sitting with her eyes closed, she can smell the dry cleaning chemicals of skirts and jackets whipped out of their polythene body-bags, and the cloying hand-washing florals of silken City shirts, and body odour, and perfume, and stale shoes.

She feels inside her pockets for her tools: for the empty and folded, gum-edged envelope, flat and clean and ready to be filled. For the nail scissors: nicely sharp at one end, handles smooth and round as a child's rattle the other, ready to be used. She has cleaned them. They are the same scissors she must stop cutting herself with.

She grasps her phone tight in her palm and checks her social media feeds every minute. Refresh, refresh, refresh, until she knows exactly where she is going.

Scott always posts what he eats for breakfast, and where. If he does repeat a breakfast choice – *Variety isn't always possible, even for the most organized* – he'll be sure to include some life advice like *Smile, and the world smiles with you!* He likes to treat himself with positivity and kindness. He calls it self-care, like it's something he invented. These are the posts that make Becky want to hurl her phone through a window, because she hates the freedom of it. It is not a freedom that should belong to him. It has been paid for, day after day after day, as she sublimated and ignored and blamed herself for his crime.

This morning he has *cared for himself* by going for an open water swim in Hampstead Ponds. Hashtag-blessed and fuck you, she thinks. And then he has further self-cared with a 'good breakfast' of almond milk flat white and acai granola. Picture: spoon half in, half out, glazed pottery bowl, sunshine, a café next to his office called *cafffine*, whose sign is totally Instagrammable what with the white Courier font on black background and their triple-F logo.

She gets off the bus and walks at pace. Checks her phone. A post, two minutes ago: *Second coffee of the morning. Too addicted, but I need a vice!*

She waits across the road. Leans against a red-brick wall. Some foul dark liquid has pooled and is drying in a treacling mass where the brickwork meets the pavement.

She sees Scott emerge from the café.

He was worn his duck-egg-blue trousers. Leather satchel, latest phone, the best hair – one coffee just isn't enough for a man with such an appetite for fashion and caffeine and other people's bodies.

She hates him and is a little afraid of him.

She feels unprepared for how quickly his digital pixel existence has become him in flesh and blood.

She tells herself, come *on*. This will be an end to not knowing, an end to never being certain. She needs to hear him tell her what happened.

She does not want to end his life. Not now. What she wants is for her chosen words to have the impact of a weapon, to be a blunt instrument that will cause irreversible harm to his psyche, his emotional wellbeing, his mental fucking landscape. What she wants is an apology. An admission. An explanation of the crime committed, in full, with nothing left out. Evidence and atonement and closure.

If he denies it, she will take the proof she needs.

She feels the scissors inside her pocket and crosses the road, looking directly ahead. She is so fixed on where Scott has disappeared into an office building three doors down, at the same time checking her phone for how many 'likes' his dull caffeine habit has attracted, that a taxi swerves to avoid her. A teenage girl in tracksuit and wellingtons grasps her phone flat to her chest, having stopped her call to look at the woman who nearly died. But when she sees that Becky is OK, that Becky seems barely to have noticed, she continues her conversation.

Becky steps through the revolving doors and says to the man at reception:

'Karin Styles. I have a meeting with Scott Allen, Simpson Financial?'

The man nods and calls through on a flashing landline, to an office upstairs.

She made this appointment yesterday. *Of course Scott will be delighted to meet with her to discuss how she might invest her spare capital.* It was easy.

'Third floor,' says the porter. 'Just head to reception there.'

On the third floor, Scott's PA shows her into a white and glass and grey meeting room. 'Just hold on a moment,' she says, 'Scott's just finishing up on a call. Can I get you some tea or coffee or water?'

Becky declines, sits and waits, leans her elbows on the glass meeting table then at the sight of a greasy smudge draws them away immediately, as if electrified. What if that streak of cells comes from Scott's greasy fingerprints? Or his elbows lathered in the Kiehl's body cream he so loves to buy in bulk in case it's discontinued? How disgusting, she thinks, to have him touch her like this, in such a manner that she can't control. And she nearly retches as another thought occurs, that he has been in this room many times before, perhaps recently, talking and breathing, and that it's possible she is now inhaling the sour spittle from his enthused conversations about Birmingham and Cannes and his life's fucking achievements.

She is overwhelmed and stands up to leave, unsure whether she can weather this assault, this way of taking him in after all these years. But then the door opens and he sweeps in, bringing a strong cloud of clean laundry and pepper-spiked citrus. Her heart stops. She knows this smell, has inhaled it on tester strips in the basement of Selfridges once, maybe twice: *Dior Sauvage*, his choice of aftershave.

But that smell is just strong enough to drown out the will to fly and instead light the touchpaper to fight, anger in her veins bolstered with the knowledge that confrontation is, and always has been the only true way to get him out of her system.

'Sorry!' he says, not yet seeing her, not properly. 'Having a mental morning already! Anyway . . .'

Becky stands and they shake hands, and Scott recognizes her while his hand is still in hers.

'Becky?'

'Hi, Scott.'

A long silence. She wonders if he will run, or call someone to drag her out. But instead he frowns, then laughs. There are no dark circles or creases under his eyes. Underneath the duck-egg blue of his jacket, this well-tailored jacket, is a white T-shirt – cellophane packaging removed only that morning, she bets, crumpled and discarded on the floor of his luxury apartment for someone else to collect and throw away. God she hates him.

'I was expecting someone called Karin. You haven't changed your name, have you?'

'No,' says Becky.

'OK. Well . . . this is unexpected! Um . . . Did you want to discuss investment stuff or . . .?' He leaves the question trailing for her to fill in.

Where does she begin?

'How long's it even been?' he says.

'A bit over sixteen years since I last saw you.'

'Wow. You haven't changed.'

'I think I have.'

'Well . . . you look good.' He is being bright and sparky, the Scott of a named house plant and pretty coffees and hangin' with his big sister Gemma. Still, she can see that he is unnerved. Well, good.

'Do you remember that party we were both at in Hampstead?'

He squints, remembers. 'At that girl Amy's house? Do you want to sit down?'

'No I don't want to sit down. I don't know whose house it was.'

'OK,' he says cautiously. 'The same party we did a pill in her parents' amazing wardrobe room kind of thing?' He has dropped his voice, like he might be overheard.

'Yes. I wanted to talk about what happened between you and me.' Her voice wobbles a little and she digs her fingernails into her palm.

'Like what?' says Scott. He has dropped all the peppiness. Now he is nothing but anxious. She can't quite bring herself to say it though.

'After Spin the Bottle.'

'Yeah, but *what*?'

'I mean what *happened*. Sexually.' There. That's as close as she can get.

Scott looks down, embarrassed. 'Christ,' he says softly. 'Did that really upset you?' Then, 'Is that what you want to talk about? Now? Look, I don't remember everything. We were pretty fucked up.'

She nods, unable to trust herself to say anything more. There are tears in her eyes, and she lets them gather there, blurring her view, before she wipes them across her cheeks. She feels make-up stinging the inside rims of her eyes and knows it will have smudged coal black across her face, making her look polluted and messy and out of control.

'OK,' he says. 'Well . . . I did actually think about it afterwards and I felt bad about it.'

'Bad about *what*, Scott?' Say it. Say it to my face.

'We'd kissed for what, like, a few seconds or something? And then I went straight to trying to get into your pants. I opened your jeans and I was going to put my hand down there but then you obviously didn't want to, so I stopped. I'm really sorry if it upset you. I was just . . . To tell you the truth, I just wanted to do it so I could say I'd done it. I didn't even really want to.' He looks at her, concerned. 'Can I get you some water? You don't look good.'

'Keep talking.' She can taste something sour in her mouth. It is bile rising from deep inside her, or it is something bitter that has been in the membranes of her mouth for as long as she can remember that releases itself now that she is biting down hard.

'Um . . . then we did a pill each and things got really messy. I mean, they were really strong. I got them off my sister's dealer. I hadn't done one of those before. It was fun, but then we both got sort of spaced-out. I think you were quite pissed when we started? I don't know. It seemed to hit you a bit harder.'

'And then what?'

'I don't know. We hung out in there for ages. And the rest of the party went downstairs. I think Amy kicked everyone out of the bedrooms but she didn't find us so we were like . . . own private Narnia. We had fun.' He reaches for her hand and she flinches back. 'I am so sorry if I crossed a line, doing what I did.'

'And then what?'

'What do you mean?'

'Tell me everything that happened.'

'You basically passed out. I think mostly from the booze. I was still up and quite awake. And then I needed to go home so I was like, do I leave you there on the floor or what? So I put you in the bed in the main room.'

'Don't miss things out. Did you take off my clothes?'

'Becky, what—'

'Come on.'

'Yes, I took off your jeans so you'd be more comfortable. I tucked you in. I think I put you in the recovery position in case you threw up. And then I went downstairs. I had a bit of a dance and a smoke and then I just started to feel a bit wrecked so I went back to Bento's house with him. His parents were away in their cottage so we could just chill all day.'

'Is that it?'

'That is literally everything. And can you please tell me what this is about now, because you're really worrying me.'

Her heartbeat is pounding in her ears. He is so smooth. So convincing. Making out like unbuttoning her jeans was the worst thing he'd ever done. Apologizing for *that*! He's just like Matthew, she thinks. Making her doubt everything except *him*. Has he forgotten his confession? Can he possibly think she has forgotten it?

'On my last day at that school I came and found you. I said something to you. Do you remember that?' spits Becky.

'Yes.'

'What did I say to you?'

'You told me that you knew about me and I begged you not to tell anyone,' says Scott. 'And so far as I know, you never did. I don't know why you said it to me. I've wanted to ask you that.'

'I told you that I knew!' She is louder now.

His face is pale, blank, there is no flicker, so shine, no register, no nothing.

How dare he! She wants to smash the bones beneath his skin, and make black and purple bruising inside him, to make him sting and break and cry and fucking die the same way she did.

The pretence of good humour has burnt off him now and his words are chopped and sharp. 'OK, I think maybe we're done. Nice seeing you again.'

'Stop fucking with me!' Her grip tightens now, curling round the scissors, pressing deep now.

'Jesus.' He turns away from her. She realizes that he's going for the door. She jumps up and puts her body in his way.

'You bastard!' She is weeping now. She tries to hit him. He catches her wrists. He works out three times a week. He easily grips her. 'You fucking bastard! How could you do that to me?'

'Do what? Do *what*?'

She thrashes to get at him, to beat and punish him.

'You admitted it! You asked me not to tell anyone!'

'I know!'

'So say it!'

'That I'm gay? What the fuck is going on? I don't understand!'

The wind goes out of her. She crumples, her wrists still gripped by him, so that for a moment she hangs like a broken marionette, arms aloft, head hanging down. Thick wrenching sobs.

She expects him to step over her and call the police. But instead he lowers her to the floor, crouches down with her.

'Becky, please, tell me what you're trying to say.'

She can't speak. A low moan tunnels out of her.

'Becky?' He gently lifts her up, so that they are face to face. There are tears in his eyes. 'I thought maybe I said something to you that night? Or that maybe you figured out because I was happy to stop trying to do anything with you . . . You worked out I was gay. You looked so disgusted with me. I just panicked.'

Becky has built a foundation on hating him. And now it is crumbling.

'I was so desperate. I thought everyone could see it on me. I just wanted people to know we'd gone off together. Maybe think we were a thing, so they wouldn't start wondering. And then we had a really good time. Or at least I did. I just don't understand what *this* is.'

'You didn't do anything with me after that?'

'God no. I told the guys the next day that I fingered

310

you. I'm really sorry. That was so gross of me, and it was utter bullshit. I just wanted them to think I had.'

'You just left me sleeping in that bed?'

'Becky, what happened? Seriously?' He sits back, thoughtful. 'That party was in September right?' His thoughts coalesce. 'Did you get pregnant *that* night?' She nods. 'With Adam Thewlis, wasn't it?'

'No. I don't know who got me pregnant. I don't know who . . .' She chokes and his face clouds with understanding.

'Oh. Oh *shit*. Oh fucking hell.' Scott is crying freely now. A splayed palm at his heart, eyes welling with tears again. What she sees is a man who hates to be thought of badly. Who tries to be good. He is telling the truth. She knows it in her bones.

'You thought I'd raped you?' he says.

She nods.

'You've thought that for . . .?'

'Since that night,' she says.

'Oh Becky. Oh fuck. Oh, I'm so sorry.'

'You were the last person I remember.'

'I could *never* have . . .'

'I believe you. I'm sorry.'

'You know how I said I went home with Bento? Ben Towbridge? We'd been sort of trying things out with each other for about a month. Both in the closet. Barely even out of the closet with each other, even giving each other – well, anyway. I mean, I was always gay. My parents though . . . They were – they still *are* – massive homophobes.

I'm just waiting for them to die before I'm out-out.' He helps Becky off the floor and into one of the meeting-room chairs, sitting down next to her, hands clasping hers. 'What happened?' he asks her.

'I thought it was you,' she says. 'I've never known what happened. It's been killing me.'

'And you had the baby?'

'Yes. She's sixteen now. She's the best thing in my life.'

'Fuck me, that's complicated though.'

'Not to her. She doesn't know. Nobody knows. Apart from Adam. She thinks Adam's her dad.'

'And he took that on?'

'I was going to kill myself. He told my parents and his parents that he was the father. It gave my parents someone else to be angry with and . . . then I couldn't do it. Because he'd have been blamed and that wouldn't have been fair. I was going to give the baby up. But then I held her and . . . well . . .'

'And he carried on? Saying she was his?' Scott wipes his eyes. 'That is love. Fuck me, that is love. Tell me you got married?'

Becky shakes her head. 'I've been a real mess. It really fucked me up.'

'Of course it did.'

'At least I had you.'

'What?'

'I had you to hate. And now I don't have anything all over again.'

They sit there, holding each other's hands. She feels like a cork lost on the ocean. She has imagined killing this man. She has wanted him to suffer. And now her hands are in his, and he is crying over her pain.

He tucked her in, in the recovery position in case she was sick.

'I know it sounds weird,' he says, 'but in case you start thinking it must be bullshit and I must be lying . . .'

'I believe you.'

'Just listen. I think you should, like, get a DNA test of me done, or whatever. Even if you think it's crazy. It's good you believe me, but have the proof as well.'

She thinks about the scissors in her pocket and how hard she has been gripping them. How crazy her plan feels now. That she was going to shear the evidence from him. And here he is, offering it to her.

He sticks his head out of the meeting-room door and calls out: 'Yol, could I have some scissors and some tissues in here, please?'

When Yol brings them, looking curious but saying nothing, he snips off a lock of his hair, and swabs the inside of his cheek with one of the tissues. 'If you want me to do a blood test or something, I'll always say yes, OK? But at least you've got these.'

She takes them, knowing she'll never use them.

'You've had quite a ride,' he says to her. 'Holy shit, Becky.'

*   *   *

They hug one last time as she leaves Scott's office. In the lift, Becky squeezes her hand into a fist in her pocket and feels sticky blood from where the scissors have punctured a hole in her palm. She wonders if one day she will be so punctured that nothing will remain of her.

And yet, despite feeling damaged, she does not feel drained. She feels something new. A feeling that is quick and sharp and predatory and she is so afraid of it that she begins to run.

There is a darkness building inside her with the realization that she has lost the last of her power. She lacks even a name, now, to test against her pain.

She runs as if there are flames licking at her feet: home, down sun-drenched pavements, past lines of narrow-windowed, residential houses punctuated with baby-blue, grey, baby-pink and pale lime paint-jobs. She runs through estates, cutting across playgrounds and through triangles of green, skirting buggies and slaloming slow-walking toddlers and shoppers. She runs until her legs tingle and lightning bolts drive themselves through her chest cavity each time she stumbles. She runs fast, so fast from the fear that she may have passed the man that travelled into her and stole from her, a thousand times over. She may have passed him on the street striding, pausing, walking, standing still on a corner, glancing up from a phone. He may have been flicking through receipts and notes in a wallet at the corner shop as he held a big carton of milk under his arm like a small dog. All he'd have to do was angle his face a little, allow his hair to fall a little, to peer through its curtain and observe her height, taller than most, her nose, more slanted than most, and her long, long Rapunzel hair.

She is being watched by a face that is bigger and wider than she ever imagined. There is no specific twist or grimace or red-scaled skin. She is being watched by something that holds all skin colours and creeds and religions and there is absolute chaos in the universality, in the possibility of him being anyone. Of his having ebony eyes or snakeskin covering him or a long body or short legs or no hair, a waxy head, an inked head, one of those faces that can look at one moment awful in a photo and at another time beautiful. A son or father or brother or criminal.

He has become *everyone*.

There will be no more *justice deferred* to cling to; she has lost that today. The dock is empty. And yet Maisie lives.

Chapter 25

When she returns home, Adam is still in the clothes he slept in, his boxer shorts and a frayed Ramones T-shirt. 'There you are!' he says. 'I thought you'd gone to work.' He ruffles his hair, still bleary with the morning. 'I'd have saved you some pancakes if I'd known. Maisie took the rest of them for her lunch. She's gone in for a revision session thing.' He pauses. 'Hey, are you OK?'

She walks a few steps and collapses into him. He pulls her close to him, her ear to his chest. She can hear his heart beating.

'What's happened? Are you all right?'

Adam walks her through to the living room, his arm looped loosely and carefully around her waist. He sits her down on the sofa and drapes a tartan blanket around her shoulders, as if she has been in an explosion and is recovering on the kerbside. He kneels down opposite her and she follows his gaze as it checks her hairline, eyes, cheeks, ears, neck, shoulders for signs of damage and distress.

'I'm not hurt,' she says. 'I went to see Scott this morning.'

Adam knows what this means. He is very still, listening to her.

'I couldn't take it any longer,' Becky says. 'I had to know why he did it. But he didn't do it. It wasn't him.'

'How do you know that?'

'He's gay. And I could tell as soon as I got into it. For him it was just some party. He thought . . . Oh God, he thought I was angry because he tried to go to second base with me.'

'What would have happened if he'd admitted it?'

'I'd have had an answer.'

'He might have wanted a relationship with Maisie. Did you think about that?'

'I wasn't thinking about that.'

'Well, we have to. Imagine finding out your father was . . . someone who did that. It'd completely and utterly destroy her, Becks. I know this means a lot to you but we have to weigh these things.'

'I know.'

'Does he know about Maisie now?'

'He won't say anything. I know he won't say anything. He's a nice guy.'

'What's going on? I mean, confronting Scott?' He holds her face in his hands.

'I know, I know, I just wanted to know . . .'

'After sixteen years, does it really matter? Like, enough to jeopardize everything else you've got? Look at your life. I know there's been some shit, but there's also you and me and Maisie. You're making a film. You're loved.'

'Maybe it was that boyfriend of Mary's. Brendan? He was always a bit weird with me, even when Mary was around.'

'He's been dead four years. You're not going to get answers from him now, are you? I know it's hard. I know it's not fair. But if it's a toss-up between letting one bad moment destroy the rest of your life, against trying to let it go?'

'It didn't happen to you.'

He takes his hands from her face and rests them lightly on her hands.

'I could track down the people who were playing Spin the Bottle in that room,' she says.

'How would you even do that? Did you know who they all were at the time? And if Maisie ever found out. If she ever heard even a vague rumour . . .'

'I know, I know. I know I can't.'

Her breaths overlap and she is beginning the sky-high tumble into a terrible panic.

'This is about Amber, isn't it?' he says.

'Yes.'

'Is it . . . what's the word they use . . . "triggering"? Has it stirred stuff up? Because you were doing so well. You were off at Cannes, conquering the world.'

'I had a panic attack on the beach, Adam.'

'You were managing all right. Mostly. So what changed?

And how do we get you some help so we can get you past it?'

'I was the woman in the kitchen. At Matthew's house. I went there to deliver a present. I was there. I saw them. I'm the person she asked to come forward, and I haven't done that. And I think it's a problem for me. I mean, I think I know it's a problem for me.'

Adam sits back, taking his hands away from hers. He's a smart guy. Becky can almost see him crunching this new information, trying to make the best plan for them.

'This will be OK,' he says.

'What should I do?'

'Can you be sure of what you saw?'

'No.'

'So you're not much help to her as a witness. I don't mean that nastily. I just mean in practical terms, in terms of a possible prosecution, you not coming forward wouldn't change much. Given you're not even sure what you saw.'

'But she asked for that person to come forward.'

'I know that. We're just trying to weigh it all up, Becks. The other thing is, you've denied it was you, haven't you?'

'I didn't really mean to do that.'

'All the same, you're in the papers as denying being "the woman in the kitchen" or whatever they tried calling it. And you've definitely given quotes to journalists since then about what a good guy Matthew is. How do you get around that? On top of which it's been quite a while since she appealed for that witness to come forward. If you do that now, it'll look really bad. The papers will tear you apart for not coming forward immediately.'

Becky doesn't respond. What is there to say?

'And *Medea*?'

'It'd be over.'

'So on the one hand you've got stepping forward, which won't make the blindest bit of difference as to whether Matthew gets convicted or not. Plus you don't even know what you saw so what would you be trying to say? And then on the other hand you have getting to make your film, and not becoming a hate figure in the press for covering for your boss instead of coming forward immediately?' He weighs up the choices with the palms of both hands.

'I know, I know,' she says, though she doesn't quite feel it. 'Do you think I'm a bad person?'

'No, I don't. Not at all. This is about Matthew and Amber. Nobody else.'

'I can't live with myself.'

'Yes, you can. You've lived with worse. Becks, this is what I do every day with my businesses. I weigh up the opportunity, the cost, the risks, the benefits. You have to step back and try to see the big picture. It's not about one decision, it's about your life. Your future. Our daughter's future. All those things matter as well.'

'What should I do?'

'Be a good person? Try your best to be kind and

generous? Give people a chance? That's how you make the world a better place. Not by throwing yourself onto the fire because you feel like you owe something to a woman you've never even met. Who you've done nothing to.'

'She tried to kill herself.'

'You didn't do that to her. You didn't do anything. And, more to the point, even having seen it, you don't know what you saw.'

Becky nods. She wonders if she can do it. Just absorb it. File it away. Forget about it. Let the red carpet roll out. Smile, and thank Matthew from the podium if she wins.

'You didn't seem that surprised when I told you,' says Becky.

'What, about Matthew?'

'Yes.'

'I suppose I'm not that surprised. I think shit like that happens every day.'

'And I'm supposed to let Maisie loose into all that . . .?'

'Yes. You have to. *We* have to. It's what good parents do.' He smiles at her. 'Hey, I'll be right there with you stalking her boyfriends and threatening them with a baseball bat if they don't make her feel amazing every single day.'

'I am so going to be that person,' she smiles. He always makes her feel better with his reasonable thinking and jokes. If only she'd said something sooner.

'I know you're going to be that person. And so does

Maisie. It's fine. We'll still love you when you are. I do think you should think about changing jobs though. Maybe once *Medea* is filming? You don't want to be working next to someone you're afraid of.'

'I'm not afraid of Matthew. I think he made a terrible mistake. I'm not sure . . . I don't know what it was, but I don't think he's a bad person.'

'There you are then.'

'There I am.'

'Ready for some breakfast alcohol?'

'Can I have a pancake instead?'

'Always.'

She kisses him. Somewhere in the city, Amber is lying hooked up to multiple machines, everyone trying to keep her alive against her wishes, and here is Becky, realizing that, if she is honest, she has fallen in love with Adam, or has finally admitted that she has always loved him. How can this be fair? But how can it be otherwise?

They spend the rest of the morning under their own glass dome, breathing each other's air, moving in the warmth of their own microclimate. They lie in bed, legs flung over each other, talking, laughing and remembering: *I thought you were annoyed with me that time . . . But then I caught you looking at me . . . At first I thought it was just my new haircut . . . I saw it in your eyes . . . Felt it, yes . . . But couldn't be sure . . .*

That afternoon, the rumbling crashes of a summer storm

make Becky so nervous she can't settle. *You have a choice*, she says to herself. So she chooses to ignore it. But the thunder rolls and it feels like her heart and stomach are being flattened by heavy stones. *You can always do something*. So she shuts the windows tight, turns the music up and her phone off. She throws her arms round Adam and they kiss each other.

You have a choice, you can always do something.

Chapter 26

Becky sleeps fitfully, waking near dawn but then quickly falling back into a viscous dream where she is standing at the bottom of a bank of spiked hedgerows, on the hard shoulder of the motorway. An unending stream of lorries and cars pass her at terrifying speed. A man walks towards her holding a breeze-block in his arms. Becky knows that he is coming to smash her brains out, in front of everyone. She cannot move her feet. She screams but no sound comes out. Why does nobody stop? She tries to beg him to spare her. He comes closer, raising the block high above his head.

Only the blow never comes – instead he tosses the block sideways into the nearest lane, where it caves in the windscreen of a family car. The car swerves, clips a van in the passing lane, and spins and flips. Cars, trucks and vans collide, piling up, flinging off their wing mirrors and tyres high up into the air, sending engines spinning across the tarmac like flaming tumbleweeds. Becky stands transfixed. She is alone, watching the vehicles smash and pile, making a pyramid of shattered panels, spilled oil, broken glass. It is like ballet. She finds herself crying because of how beautiful it is.

She comes to, disorientated, in the grey yellow light of early morning.

Maisie will still be asleep and Adam has gone home now, leaving a rumpled and cold space in the bed beside her. She feels afraid and alone and longs for Adam's warmth and chatter as she senses the dark and silent approach of the many questions she has been trying to stifle.

How should she now think of all that time spent obsessing over Scott's potions and fashions and the holidays and words that inspired her thoughts, her plans and narrative? If he inspired her Medea film, does that make her passion for the subject somehow less truthful? And what of the last sixteen years?

What of that time (Maisie must have been six or seven) when Becky had arranged to meet that man in the garden of a local pub? He'd drunk four pints of cider, she'd smoked a lot of cigarettes and they had talked about soap opera and Big Brother. She wasn't attracted to his thoughts, his voice, his thin nose or rubbery lips but she still travelled with him in a bleach-smelling lift up to the eleventh floor of a council block overlooking Canary Wharf, and she still willingly took her jeans off while seated on his faux leather couch. She thought she was ready. She'd told herself in the run-up that sex post-rape could free her if only she was strong enough to achieve it.

But she wasn't ready and so, being thrown back into

the very past she was trying to escape at the cider and boiled-sweet smell of that man's skin, had felt like a failure. The fact of his body coming down hot and heavy on hers, ridiculous to think it now, but she had felt she was as close to death as if she were trapped inside a sandwich toaster. She had asked to leave before things went further, and he let her.

At home she had destroyed ten years of her old school exercise books in a bonfire, incanting Scott's name as she watched charred black feathers of paper rise to the sky, as if somehow these actions might cauterize the places he was still growing inside her and grant her peace.

It was several years before she tried sex again, that time with a media studies student, still horrible but with greater success – but now, lying in her bed at home, Becky struggles to know whether the last sixteen years would have been any less traumatic had she imagined a faceless ghoul pumping away inside her instead of Scott.

Scott had been like a co-ordinate on a map. He'd given her a diseased kind of security.

Becky comes back to herself remembering Adam. How gently he holds and touches her during sex, how safe she feels safe with him. Perhaps there is no need to reframe her whole past? Perhaps all is well in the present. Perhaps her love of Adam is all she needs now to heal completely. She can choose to think this way and so she does.

* * *

Becky arrives at the office and senses immediately that something is wrong. Siobhan glances up briefly and returns to her work, without a word – intent on clearing and sorting, making piles. The next time Siobhan glances up she looks so angry that Becky's insides ripple, ghost over grave.

'Is everything OK?' says Becky, arranging her coat and bag in the crook of her arm.

'He's waiting for you in the boardroom. With champagne. Financing is agreed. Contracts ready to sign,' Siobhan says, opening her desk drawer and yanking it off the runners with a crack.

'Are you coming too?' says Becky.

'No,' says Siobhan.

'Please come and have a drink. Emilia was your idea.'

'I don't want to.'

'What's going on?'

'Just . . .' She purses her lips and holds her palm up, flat and final. 'I can't talk to you right now.'

'Have I done something to you, Siobhan?' Becky's insides lurch and she begins to feel a queasy combination of exhaustion and nausea, like the draining aftermath of extreme motion sickness.

'Of course not. You'd better go in. Your champagne might get warm.'

Becky finds Matthew sitting at the head of the boardroom table. He looks up as she enters. He looks healthier than the last time she saw him. Taut and shining, like somehow he has shed wrinkles, shaved away years.

'Come and sit down,' he says, motioning her to a place at the table, laid with a freshly copied version of the *Medea* script and a pile of contracts marked with coloured Post-its. 'You need to read the draft agreements. As producer you have some legal duties you'll need to be aware of. It's all boilerplate stuff. FilmFour sent some script notes through as well. But first . . .' He reaches for a bottle of champagne and two glasses. He opens the bottle and the cork hits the ceiling with an air-pellet pop.

Drink Me.

She takes the proffered glass and holds it mid-air.

'You look well, Rebecca,' he says. 'Success evidently suits you.'

'Thanks. But can we get Siobhan in on this too?' she says. 'Make her a part of this?'

'I don't think so,' he says. 'She resigned this morning. About five minutes before you came in.'

Becky puts the glass down and sits back on her seat. 'Why?'

'She joined at the same time as you. You're going places and she's not. She'll find a job elsewhere without much trouble. I've said I'll help her out there, obviously. I'd do the same in her position. She's read the writing on the wall and made a move. We'll hire some more people. I'll need a PA. You'll need one as well. And we should get a development person who can report to you.'

'It's a shame. She's been here ages.'

'That's why she needs to move on. Don't feel sorry for

her. She's doing the right thing for her career. You'll probably end up working with her on things. It's a small industry. You might ask her if she'll let us throw her a leaving drinks?'

'I'll definitely do that.'

His phone rings and she waits for him as he talks, until he holds up a hand to her, indicating that this call might actually go on a bit. She excuses herself, leaving her champagne glass behind.

Becky walks out into the office again where Siobhan is filling a cardboard grocery box full of her personal stuff.

'Aren't you working out a notice period?'

'No. I said I didn't want to. He said that was fine.'

'Have you got another job?'

'I don't know what I want to do next.'

'I just don't understand why you're leaving if you're not going anywhere.'

'Well, I am.'

'Come on. We've known each other for years. Why have you resigned? Tell me. Is it just because you're jealous?'

'Yes, that's it. I just wish it was me toasting my nearly green-lit, massively hypocritical film.'

'Wow,' says Becky. 'That's kind of rude.'

But Siobhan won't meet her eye. 'Don't worry. I'm not going to make a fuss. I'd like to get a reference out of this and I know how things work.'

'What's wrong with you?'

Siobhan plucks files out of her drawers and hurls them

in fanned piles onto empty production desks. 'I can't work at this company any more.'

'Is this about Matthew?'

'No. It's about you. I did your expenses. While you were off in Kent being "treated" by the boss.'

'Thank you.'

'Going through your Uber business account was interesting. You know there's a map of every bloody journey you ever take? It shows the time and date and a line showing which route you took. You, Becky, got an Uber from your flat to a wine shop very near Matthew's house on a Sunday afternoon recently. Ringing any bells yet?'

Becky stands very still. Tries not to give Siobhan anything.

'Which Sunday, you ask,' Siobhan continues. 'Yes, the same Sunday that Amber Heath says our beloved leader pinned her down on his kitchen floor and raped her. What's next for Becky's Uber account that evening? Less than ten minutes later you're in a different one, taking off about a hundred yards from Matthew's house, heading home. Almost like you'd popped in, and then made a very hasty exit. Almost like you walked in on something and ran away pretty sharpish.'

Becky wills her muscles to be corpse-still, her eyes pond-still, but she feels the tremors – feels the concentric ripples on her surfaces.

'I went over to deliver a bottle of wine, to thank him for his support,' says Becky. 'I went to the front door but the lights were all out. So I took it away with me. I took it back home. I didn't go inside at all.'

'Somebody did.'

'Allegedly. Wasn't me.'

'If you say so.'

'Leave me alone, Siobhan,' says Becky slowly. 'You don't know what you're talking about.'

'I am leaving you alone. Look at me. I'm filling my box. I am getting the fuck out of here.'

'Matthew wants to know if you'd like a leaving drinks?'

'Ha. Yeah, I don't think so. I might have one too many and end up in a room with one of you poking me while the other swears blind that it isn't happening.'

Becky slaps her open palm hard across Siobhan's face. Siobhan holds her own hand against her cheek like she is checking it is still there.

'If you come after me, Siobhan, I will destroy you. Do you understand?'

Siobhan looks nothing but sad. 'Of course I understand that. I know exactly who you are, Becky. But in this moment, I can choose to leave and there is nothing you can do about it. I will not be an accomplice in your stinking, fake success. I will not stand by and watch a film about a strong woman being made by a woman as weak as you.' She looks down at her cardboard box. 'I don't even want any of this shit. Just send me my money.' Siobhan throws her key-fob into the box, turns and leaves.

Chapter 27

When Becky gets home she locks the front door and closes all the windows. She sits cross-legged on the bed with her laptop open. Later Adam's parents, Maisie's grandparents, will come over to celebrate Maisie's big day. They've agreed to do all her presents then. Becky loves Grandpa and Grandma T. She loves how much they love her daughter and she admires their calmness and their deep devotion to each other. Those are the foundations for a man as thoughtful and kind, as loving and generous, as Adam.

Becky turns over Adam's arguments about Scott. The recklessness of confronting him. She knows he's right, of course he's right. She tries to picture the moment: Maisie discovering that Adam is not her father. The unknitting of an entire childhood. The destruction of half her story – who she got her sense of humour from, the shape of her nose, the bend of her calves, her intolerance for tree pollen, her capacity for hard work. This from Dad, that from Mum. The two halves that make her: all tainted, all broken.

Becky hates that there are secrets. Whose fault is this? Is it hers? Did she somehow prey on Adam? Did she use him? She blinks at the memory of those early days of feeling so exhausted and so sad that she could barely make it out of bed, let alone make any kind of decision. Adam had put the idea to her. An easy path. A lie told out of love. His gift and his choice. Surely his parents would love him more for such a kind and selfless act? But might they love Becky less, this girl who'd taken most of a life from their too-kind son? Who'd robbed them of children with Grandma T's eyes, with Grandpa T's youthful head of curls, and all the history that they carried in their blood, the connections made from life to life in a chain of descent that Maisie should have carried beyond them, bearing a spark of them past their deaths and into tomorrow. All gone. Perhaps they might still love Maisie, the habit of love too ingrained to be erased, but what of her liar-mother?

But they are here, aren't they? And they look like a family now, and how easily the final change is happening. Becky can see the going to sleep and waking up together, under the same roof, day after day, week after week, month after month, year after year. Her arms around Maisie, Adam's arms around Becky.

She deletes Facebook and Twitter and Instagram and the password-protected folder called 'Household' which is really filled with words and images that she has collected from Scott's life.

It's time to start again.

* * *

The table is laid for cake and fizz, around an Aladdin's cave pile of presents wrapped in silver and gold metallic paper. Streamers and balloons have been draped across every photo and picture frame and a thin plastic banner sags over the door.

BIRTHDAY GIRL

Becky steps into the kitchen, cardigan wrapped tight round her body and over her fists, despite the warmth of the summer day. Adam and Maisie are already seated at the table, waiting for proceedings to begin. And soon, Grandma T, blue-eyed and bird-like, and Grandpa T, GT for short, named by Maisie after his favourite drink, join them from the hall after hanging coats and sorting shoes.

She can see the joy, its warm fireplace colours, pass between the grandparents as they hug their beloved and only grandchild: holding her tight, commenting on her lovely height and how much she has shot up in the three weeks since they last saw her. And Becky knows in that moment that although she can easily recall the exhaustion of those early days, she cannot inhabit that place again where she was prepared to give her daughter up for adoption. To think of a life without this gorgeous, funny, happy girl whose arms are folded around her grandmother, comparing each other's heights. No one in that kitchen can imagine a life without her: not her, not Adam, not the grandparents who plan their summer holidays just so they can spend time with their beloved granddaughter.

Adam yanks at a champagne bottle's cork and the wine

bubbles and spills like water from a garden hose, and there is laughter in unison at the indulgent waste and the humour and mess of it all. Adam passes everyone a glass as they take their places at the kitchen table.

'Thank you,' Becky says, taking her glass, her body tired but her mind restless, roaming, rebellious. She thinks of her family and her film, a new beginning, and she sips her champagne. From boardroom to kitchen, has she had a glass in her hand all day? Is this the happiest day of her life?

Becky's phone beeps – a text message, from Matthew – and her heart leaps with anxiety. Agreements now ready for signature. Boardroom meeting first thing Monday. 'Sorry,' she says. 'I'll turn it off.'

'Spielberg calling?' says Adam, scooping himself a marshmallow square.

'We all think you're doing so well,' says Grandma T, pulling a hair out her mouth. 'We told Audrey about it and she said that the chance of making a film is lower than the chance of . . . of, what was it?' She turns to her husband to corroborate a thought, complete a sentence. 'A comet hitting earth?'

'Honestly, Margot. Stop exaggerating. I think it was higher than the lottery . . .'

'No, she didn't say that . . .'

'It's a huge achievement anyway,' says Adam, knowing that the conversation is more likely to end in a cul-de-sac about Audrey's knees rather than something conclusive about a film being made. 'Presents?'

Maisie applauds, a lasso of streamer curling out of a lightly bunched fist, and her grandparents laugh.

'Family first, or Any Other Business?' Adam says. AOB is what they call presents from people who aren't family. It's a funny little Adam-thing from one year when he ran Maisie's birthday like a corporate meeting, just to amuse her. AOB has stuck and it became the way they've always done their birthdays. An inheritance for Maisie. Will she do AOB with her own children one day?

Becky's head isn't really here. She tries to wrench it back.

'AOB,' says Maisie firmly. 'Let's sort the wheat from the chaff!' Becky swears her daughter's love of attention is only getting more pronounced. Will she end up commanding a boardroom or an audience from the stage? Becky often finds herself wondering whether her daughter's life will be anything like that, or nothing at all like that. What would Maisie have been like with young brothers or sisters? Does she have half-siblings now, somewhere, unknown? Has Becky's assailant made a life for himself, with a wife and children and a job and the rest? Has he ever done it again or was she somebody's one-off, their great and last mistake? Or have they forgotten her?

Did Becky say *yes* that night?

Maisie tears open a shiny, metallic-papered package from Lily. It's a garish, deliberately ugly knitted jumper with the words *Hot Sauce* written in Comic Sans font. Maisie laughs delightedly. 'She remembered! This is awesome! Look at that font. I totally love it. I'm wearing it forever.' Maisie wriggles her way into it.

'You'd look good in something like that, love,' says Grandpa, turning to his wife. 'I still think of you that way. Hot Sauce.'

'Oh, enough!' Grandma says, pleased and smiling. 'You look gorgeous, Maisie.'

'I thank you!'

Becky grasps her champagne stem. She can't concentrate. Her mind is on Siobhan now. Will Siobhan really drop it? And will it matter if she doesn't? What if she goes to the police? Becky thinks about raising it with Matthew: perhaps they should say that *she* came to him, after the story broke, and told him then that she'd walked in on them? That she'd offered to be his witness but he'd told her not to bother feeding the fire. That he'd declined because he trusted his own innocence absolutely. There was no crime to bear witness to.

His story fitted with everything she knew, after all. She had been moved by his candour. His confession of ugly behaviour, albeit with the desire to show Amber a hard truth lying beneath it all. He was trying to show her the truth: wasn't that what he had said, in so many words? Done for her sake as much as his. And now Amber is in hospital, because she has tried to end her life.

She listens to the burble of Adam and Maisie riffing off each other about another present opened; she barely registers what it is. A prank present from a friend, perhaps. Here is her beautiful, accomplished daughter on the verge of the exams that will launch her into the next exciting phase of life. She has everything laid out ahead of her . . . This is a good day and yet she feels on the other side of the glass: smiling along, nothing really touching her.

And yet. Becky has weathered the storm, has she not? Siobhan will get her reference and keep her silence. Amber will live or die, and that's not up to Becky. The stories in the papers, already fading, will vanish altogether. Her film will pick up more cast members, more money. She will choose her staff and, unlike Siobhan, they will be grateful for the opportunity to work hard for her. To learn from her. Everything can now flower into life.

'Sorry,' she says, when she realizes someone must have said something to her, because everyone is looking to her like they're expecting an answer. 'Still haven't got my strength back from Camber. What did you say?'

'Only should we put the pizzas on?' says Adam. 'It's OK. Let me take care of things.'

'I think I just need some coffee. I'll make it.' Becky gets up and puts the kettle on. 'Any other takers?'

'I like my coffee like I like my women,' says Adam, in a husky bass tone. 'Served in a mug.'

'I like *my* coffee like I like my men,' replies Maisie instantly. 'Strong. And yet decaffeinated.'

'Open another present,' says Grandma T, rolling her

eyes. She knows that left unchecked they might do this routine for another five minutes.

Becky heaps two spoons of coffee granules into a mug. The idea of making proper coffee is too much.

'Next present,' declares Adam. 'Who's this one from?'

'This is from Jules.'

'Who's Jules?' asks Grandma T.

'A boy who likes Maisie,' says Adam.

'Dad! Back off.'

'What?' cries Adam, doing his outraged New York Jewish matriarch bit. 'A boy shouldn't like my beautiful girl? Boys shouldn't write poetry about this beautiful face of hers?'

Maisie squirms.

'Adam, you're embarrassing her,' says his father.

'That's my job! Maisie, tell him!'

'It's his job, Grandpa, and he's extremely good at it.' Maisie shoots pretend eye-daggers at Adam.

Becky sits back down with her coffee. 'What's this one?' She can't seem to hold anything in her head.

Maisie tears open an A4-sized envelope. She pulls out a folder. And bursts out laughing.

'What is it?'

'Oh my God, I can't believe he actually did this!'

'Did what?'

'OK,' says Maisie to her grandparents. 'So me and Jules have this joke that I'm a Viking or from Denmark or something because I'm tall.'

'What?' says Grandma, perplexed.

'It's just this stupid joke. With my eye colour and everything, I must have come from Viking stock. We do this whole thing with me feasting instead of eating at school lunch, and any time I go off he's like, *Maisie's off pillaging. Lock up your livestock and clay jugs.*'

'But you're tall because your mother's tall. It's something to be proud of, it's . . .'

'It's fine, it's just a joke, Grandpa. Anyway, he did this thing where he was like, *I'm going to prove it once and for all*, and he swabbed my cheek with a cotton bud thing and said he was having me analysed by the Viking institute. But he's actually done it. I mean, there isn't a Viking institute. He's done me one of those ancestry service thingies.'

A ripple of ice-water seems to run through Becky. She catches Adam's eye. His gaze darts, sharp and quick, away and back in the direction of Maisie. She knows he is thinking the same thing.

'I'm sorry, I don't quite follow,' says Grandma T.

'They take the DNA in your saliva,' says Maisie, 'and then they compare it to millions of other samples and then they can tell you your family history. Like, on a genetic level. Not names and stuff, but where your lineage is from over thousands of years.' She opens up the booklet. It is full of charts. Her eyes shine as she reads. 'This is so cool!'

'Over thousands of years?' says her grandfather. 'And all from some spit?'

'From some cheek cells.' Maisie beams.

'That's unbelievable. Fantastic,' he says. 'What's next? Day trips to Mars?'

Maisie laughs.

Becky is urgently trying to catch Adam's eye again. This has to stop, and now. 'Do you want to read it later?' asks Adam.

'We've got a pile more presents to get through,' adds Becky. 'And honestly, I might have to head to bed in a minute.'

'It's really detailed,' says Maisie. 'I have Irish heritage. Like, thirty per cent of me is Irish genes.'

'That's my dad,' says Becky, her interest piqued, despite herself. 'His mum and dad were both from Wicklow. Is this one of the ones that gives you medical results? I'd be interested in that.'

'No, you can get those too but this one's just ancestry,' says Maisie. 'Ha ha! I can't believe this.'

'What?' says Becky.

'He's written here that I'm still a Viking even if these results say otherwise. He's written that I've managed to get my own DNA wrong. That's funny. He's really funny.'

So she likes him back, thinks Becky. He has teased her into loving him. Well, he wouldn't be the first.

'Next present,' says Adam, handing her a big box. The photo album had finally arrived. There will be enough in there to distract Maisie from the rest, for a good long while: Becky has gathered and printed photographs from all their recent trips away together. 'This one's from me and your mum.'

Becky pushes the box further forward.

'Thanks,' Maisie says, still reading the sheets. 'I'm, like, fifteen per cent Greek,' she says.

'That's right, you're from immigrant stock,' says Grandpa. 'Along with your height, that's another thing to be proud of.'

'Yes but look, it's so specific. It's not even Greece, it's like, *Southern* Greece.'

'That's right,' says Grandpa. 'My family side are from Sparta. Never mind your Vikings, the Spartans were real warriors. Put me in an arena with that Jules and I'd have him in a headlock in a second.' He flexes his arms.

'I'm not telling Jules about being from Sparta! I'd never hear the end of it.'

'Sorry, what was all that?' says Becky. An impossible thought is assembling itself, through the fog of too-many-other-things. 'What did you say?'

'I said put me in an arena with that Jules . . .'

'No, the bit about Maisie and Greece.'

Maisie leaps up and comes round the table to sit next to Becky, pointing to a pie chart. 'So this is me. I am the pie. And this is all the gene pools that I'm made up of. And this is over, like, a thousand years. They take tiny little mutations and average patterns and loads of science stuff and it says what you're made up of. Like, there's a bit of Jewish genes there, like three per cent?'

'That's my great-grandmother!' says Grandma T happily. 'She married out. Big scandal. This is wonderful!'

Becky looks at Grandma and Grandpa T. Her daughter. 'And can it be wrong?' she says. With every breath from her lungs and beat of her heart she hopes, wishes, prays it is wrong.

Becky can't look at Adam but from the corner of her eye she can see he is looking fixedly at the table.

'It's just data,' says Maisie. 'But you know, I just *feel* so Greek. I often prefer to eat olives when crisps are also a choice.'

'I like this present,' says Grandpa. 'Your people grew olives outside Kalamata. My own grandfather used to talk about them being big as apples. Does it say about Kalamata?'

Becky stands, legs weak underneath her, edging past Maisie, gripping the back of chairs as if they were crutches. 'Sorry,' she says. 'I'm not feeling well. I have to lie down.'

'Should we wait?' says Maisie.

'Help her, Adam!' says Grandma T.

'No!' says Becky, the trembling spreading through her body like a fever she will never be rid of. Adam doesn't move. 'No. Go on without me.'

Becky hears a roaring in her ears as she runs up the stairs. It is the sound of the universe ending, of hell opening.

She finds herself standing motionless in the doorway to her bedroom, absorbing the surroundings as if recently killed and now standing outside her own body, hanging onto the last images of life: the rose-pink walls painted in eggshell. Curtains held back with lengths of nautical rope. Shelves refitted twice so they wouldn't slant. All Adam's DIY.

He has touched her here, in this room, and now everything that he has ever touched, those shelves, her ribcage, her neck, is damaged.

She hears the sound of the grandparents and Maisie gathering in the hallway, and the click of the front door, and finally those voices receding down the street.

Then a knock on her bedroom door, before Adam steps in.

If he is there, armed with a long-rehearsed emergency explanation, it fails him at their first moment of eye contact. She has known the paralysis of shock, the caving-in feeling of bad news making her legs buckle, but this is different. Why is he here, in her bedroom, when he should be far away and never returning?

At first she cannot speak and it kills her that she can't get her words out because she wants them to fly out of her, like daggers, landing in his flesh, cutting him into parts.

'I can explain,' he says.

She rushes at him with arms raised and, feeling the white heat of grief and anger fill up the space inside her, forms boxer's fists. Then, for the first time in as long as she can remember, she uses her physical strength to harm someone other than herself.

She pounds away at Adam's half-covered head as he

ducks down, like he is a stake she is trying to bury deep in the earth, her fists like mallets, only stopping when she is exhausted and has not managed to destroy him, has not buried him out of existence. Then she stumbles back, away from him, the bed between them as protection. She stands trembling with her spine pressed to the wall, panic swelling up through her breathlessness. She claws at her own throat, and all she can say is, 'It was you it was you it was you.'

She sinks now, his mirror image on the far side of the room, on her knees, overwhelmed by the pure misery of love curdling and blackening. Her heart . . . ! Oh God, how it hurts.

For long minutes they stay that way, the room's length between them, Adam racked with sobs, Becky fighting a new urge to be sick, to be empty, to become a void again, capable of feeling nothing.

It was him. He did this to her and he kept silent. Sixteen years of obsession and hatred and harm – and he said nothing.

Everything becomes stillness. And then finally she can speak. Her heart cooling into iron, closing to him. Speaking to him from a dead place.

'You let me suffer,' she says.

'Please . . .'

'You knew that I needed to know. I had to know what happened to me and you knew and you didn't tell me. Because it was you who did it.'

'Becks . . .'

'Don't call me that.'

'Oh shit . . .' Adam topples forward, his face pressed into the carpet, a picture of destruction.

'Sit up,' she says.

Now there is only room in her heart for the practical things that need to be done. 'Maisie will be back soon because she'll want to know how I am, and I don't want her seeing this.' Becky wonders whether she will be able to control herself when it comes to it: to hold herself back from the impulse to destroy Adam by telling Maisie everything. 'Come on, sit up,' she orders him again. 'We need to decide what to do.'

And he obeys her, eyes red against his pale face.

'If she asks why we look this way,' says Becky, 'it's because an old friend of ours died today and we just found out. Someone from school. No one she knows. I left the room because I didn't want to spoil her birthday while she was happy opening her presents. If she asks, his name was Ben. We haven't seen him for a long time. It was just a shock.'

'Will you let me explain? Please?'

The face she had touched with her fingertips only hours before, communicating something warm like love, is nothing more in that moment than a flesh and skin arrangement. The mask that once convinced.

'I want you out of our lives,' she says blankly.

'Would you please just let me tell you what happened?'

Becky sees it so clearly then – this pattern of men calling themselves good men, sitting her down to explain how all the things that she *might* have seen, or even things that she has had done to her, were in fact nothing. Trivial matters that are easily dismissed, if only she can agree to let their explanations blossom until they fill all the spaces left by her questions. *Let me tell you. Allow me to explain. This is the way things are.*

Adam begins whimpering then, like a dog or a child. 'Please, just hear me out.'

Even as her curiosity gets the better of her, even as she tells him, 'Fine, explain,' she doesn't believe that she'll be given the truth. Not if the truth costs him more than the price he's prepared to pay for it.

'I was in love with you—'

'So you lied to me for sixteen years.'

'No!' he says. 'That's not what it was. Please. It's important you know I loved you. I've always loved you.'

She stands up then, to make herself bigger, wanting to cower over him in his crouched position, to make him feel as small as she had once felt. But she does not walk towards him, she is not ready to be an inch closer to his body. Instead she lowers and loudens her voice.

'If you say the word *love* again,' she says, 'I will kick you out and I'll tell Maisie the whole truth, as soon as she's back. And your parents. What you did was not *love*. Don't you *dare* use that word.'

'I'm sorry.'

'Get on with it,' she spits. 'Tell me what you did.'

'I came back. I came back to the party in Hampstead because I wanted to see you. I thought . . . I just . . . I won't use the word, but I just wanted to be with you. And I thought – or at least I hoped – that you maybe liked me too. The way we talked to each other, I was in love with—'

Becky flings the nearest object – a mug left by the bedside – hard, at his head. It smashes on the wardrobe door less than a foot from his head. She wants him out, he is as repulsive to her as a murderer. She wants him damaged and impotent, like she has been for half her life.

'I came back to the party to see you,' he says, holding himself still, upright yet foetal, legs held to his chest. Glassy eyed. 'And when I got there it was late. I think it was about two in the morning. I had to be back at home the next day for my dad's family but I was really high and . . . I don't know. I thought I'd come and see you and maybe we'd . . . Anyway. I looked for you and you weren't downstairs where most people were, and Mary had apparently taken off with that guy she was seeing, so I checked around the house and then I found you.'

'Like Sleeping Beauty.' Her voice wavers as she tries in vain to sharpen her words so they will slice him, but she finds only a withering, disappointing sarcasm to express her sadness for the girl in the bed, asleep and unaware that she is about to be invaded. 'Waiting for my prince.'

'You weren't asleep. You were in bed but you were awake.'

'I don't remember a single moment that I was awake with you.' But even as she says it, she finds she cannot trust that she is right. Maybe he is right. Perhaps she woke briefly. 'I was never awake,' she says again, holding her own hands to stop them from shaking.

'You were really out of it. Like . . . I'd done a pill and I'd had some beers and a joint as well downstairs. And you were in bed in the dark and I put a lamp on and sat down, and I swear it was just to ask if you were OK, and you said to get in and so I did.'

The world tilts. He is going to make it her fault.

'I didn't say that,' says Becky. 'I didn't ask you to get into my bed.' Becky puts her hand to her mouth, then wonders if the movement has betrayed her.

'I got in with you and you sort of snuggled up to me and I thought, or at least I think I thought: oh my God, she likes me that way as well. And then I kissed you and . . . you were obviously really wasted, but so was I and, I don't know, I really honestly thought . . .'

'Get to the good stuff, Adam.' She cannot take much more of this scene setting, this underpinning and drapery. She just wants him to say it now.

'I don't remember if we said much. I just remember really, really wanting to be with you and thinking you wanted that too. And so we took off our clothes.'

'*We?*' She presses her fingers firmly together, imagining Adam's skin caught in her pinch.

349

'I took them off,' he says sheepishly. 'But you didn't seem unhappy about it.'

'Unhappy? So, what, I was smiling? Opening my legs and asking you to fuck me? Is that what I was doing?' Now her words land like daggers in him. And she wills herself not to cry.

'You didn't seem unhappy. I swear to God. I swear on my life.'

'At least swear on something I give a shit about.'

'On Maisie's life then.'

She holds onto the bed-head then, for balance. 'Hurry up, you're making me want to vomit.'

'Then we had sex. And afterwards we cuddled up.'

'*We* cuddled up? So I put my arms around you?'

'No, it wasn't that exactly.' His face strains. 'You just, you kind of fell asleep in my arms is what I'm saying.'

'I don't remember that, we didn't do that.'

'You were so wasted. But we both were.'

She swallows down her words. She never wants to hear him speak again, and yet she wants to hear it all, every last detail.

'And then I realized how late it was,' he continues, 'I had to go home. So I put your top and pants back on you.'

'You tidied up your mess. What a polite boy,' she says, her teeth clamped, like gates holding back the hungry, decimating energy inside her. She wants to tear his fucking head off. She imagines the grey fleshy structure of his

350

brain lying under her foot, the maggot shapes it would make pressed outward under the pressure, a series of little grey balloons holding sixteen years of his memories.

'The next day I thought maybe I should call you, but then I was really worried you'd say you'd regretted it. So I thought I'd see you at school and in my head, if you were happy about it, then I'd know we were maybe going out together. And if you avoided me then you'd be letting me down gently. That kind of thing. And I tried to come up to you. Don't you remember that?'

She does remember. A half-wave from Adam in the hallway while she went lesson to lesson, living a waking nightmare of having been a nameless somebody's black-hole fuck. A piece of meat built for someone to ejaculate into. Yes, he had waved.

'So I thought, OK, she doesn't want anything to do with me, and I was heartbroken, to be honest.' Adam tries to look her in the eye. 'I just assumed for ages that you were being weird around me because you hated that we'd had sex together and you were trying to forget about it. I felt . . . It doesn't matter what I felt. But I thought I'd made you hate me.'

'You have.'

'It wasn't like that.'

'I'm sorry, it wasn't like *what*? Not like fucking *what*? Say it.'

He is flustered. 'Not like . . . I mean, until you told me you thought you'd been raped I had no idea that you

351

didn't even remember any of it. I remembered it even though I was really high. For me it was the biggest thing that'd ever happened to me. It was the best thing and then—'

'The earth moved for you, did it?'

'And then after you blanked me it hurt. Becky, it was like the biggest thing in my life.'

'Me. Fucking. Too.'

'I didn't think it was *that*, I really didn't. I'm telling you the truth.'

'You didn't tell me the truth though, did you?' she shouts, spittle exploding into the air, sticking to her chin.

'I was sixteen.'

'You didn't tell the truth.'

Adam takes a long breath. Staring at her, like he has suffered some great injustice and is doing very, very well to remain so patient with her as he explains. Or is he frightened? Or is he telling the truth, now, at last? Becky's head swims.

'The girl I was in love with slept with me and then ignored me. That was bad enough. And suddenly I was going to be her *rapist*? I was never that. That's not who I am. And that's what you were going to think of me if I said—'

'No, Adam. That's not enough. When you knew I couldn't remember, you chose not to tell me. Fucking say it.'

'Part of me was scared of going to prison after what you said, but more than that, I just . . . I honestly, in my head, in my heart, I really hadn't done that. I could never do that, to you or to anyone. And once you'd said that and I already hadn't admitted it, I hadn't told you what happened, after that I realized, oh fuck, how do I go back? How do I tell her *now*? And the longer it went on I just . . . I was a coward about it. That's true. But I couldn't face the idea of you thinking that about me. And once I knew you were going to put the baby up for adoption I thought, well, this is terrible, but I can at least be a friend to her. If she needs someone to take the blame for it, let me . . . And then, and then . . . Ever since we met . . . I've always been my happiest when I'm with you. I've never loved anyone else like I love you. And when we got together?' He blinks like he might cry. 'It was the happiest I've ever been.'

'What about my happiness, Adam? All those times I was so grateful to get any scrap of what you could give us, all the time thinking: he's doing us a favour. I never asked for more. Never asked you to stay with us and help while you were off at festivals getting high with your friends because *it's not like you were her father*. But you were! You fucking were! And you let it look like charity. Buying all that *stuff*. All the times . . . You let me get eaten alive by not knowing what happened. You found me looking at Scott's Facebook page and when I told you why I was doing it, you didn't give me an answer. You didn't let me have the truth. You fucking let me drown!'

He looks down at his hands. 'I know,' he says, so quietly that Becky must strain to hear it.

'Why did you do that?'

'Because it was you. And it was Maisie. I couldn't lose you. I couldn't do it. I wasn't brave enough at the time. And then later I couldn't see how to tell you the truth and not seem like a liar.'

'But you *are* a liar.'

'I didn't mean to be one.'

'I said, out loud, I wanted to know what happened. I asked you, who do you think did it to me? There were bruises on my wrist the morning after. Was that you? Did you hold me like that? Did you *hurt* me like that?'

His eyes fill with tears. 'I don't know, I honestly don't know . . . I don't remember every little bit.' He blinks. 'I've tried my best to make up for it,' he says.

'I know. You've paid a lot of utility bills. Never child maintenance. Never because you brought her into this world, without my consent. Only because you were the guy who made all the sacrifices. So *fucking* selfless.'

'How could I have done it any other way without telling you?'

'Listen to yourself! Can't you hear what you're saying?'

'I've told you the truth now and you hate me.'

'I needed the truth *then*. I needed it the next morning, Adam, when I woke up alone and there was semen inside my underwear and part of me had been fucking stolen.'

'Oh God.' Adam rests his head in his hands. Then he

354

seems to shrink before her as his limbs fold in on themselves and he sobs loudly into his lap. 'I was always looking for a moment to tell you. When you weren't suicidal. When it wouldn't risk pushing you over the edge. And then you gave birth to Maisie and you fell in love with her. And so did I. It was our daughter, Becks, lying in your arms. And I wanted . . . It was never a sacrifice. And if I let you believe it was a sacrifice, or at least something I didn't need to do, then I'm sorry, that wasn't my intention. I just wanted to be with the two of you, looking after you both for the rest of my life. Only . . . you didn't love me. And so I tried to see other people.'

'I hate you,' she whispers under her breath.

'It was always you. I always held out hope because you never got that involved with anyone . . . and it was hard, because I know that on some level you found the whole dating thing difficult because of your history . . .'

'Because of the fact you *raped* me.' Her teeth grind together, her fists bunch again.

'Stop saying that! Let it be what it was, which was two really wasted teenagers . . .'

And then she roars. She roars at him, in deep, thick, solid, ravaged breaths. She roars at him, wanting to singe his hair and burn his skin with the size and volume of her voice. She roars until his eyes are wide with panic and fear, so that spittle showers him and his neck retracts like a lizard.

'Stop it!' he shouts.

'Did you, at any point, ask me if you could have sex with me?'

'Stop it.' He is crying now.

And still she roars, intoxicated by the look of terror on his face, as if for a split second she had made him feel her pain.

'Did you ask me? Yes or no?'

'No,' he screams. 'I did not ask you.'

The silence is so thick, so clogged she can hear both their struggling breaths.

'And you didn't ask me,' he says, with a voice that is both choked and perfectly clear. 'You didn't say yes and you didn't say no. And then it was you who forced me to lie.'

'*What?*'

He unfolds himself from his kneeling position on the carpet and stands up.

'You said you'd been raped that night,' he says. 'And that wasn't true. But I didn't have any way of proving it. Maybe if you'd said you couldn't remember, or that you'd done something stupid while you were blacked-out, then I could have said: "no, that was us, that was you and me. Don't you remember?" But instead you said you'd been raped. And by the time I got my head around that, I couldn't come back from it. You never let there be a question about what had happened. You said you were raped and that was it. So that either made me a rapist or not. And I wasn't a rapist. Not then, not ever. I don't blame you for anything. I really don't. But can't you see how what you were saying made things impossible for me?'

The world recedes. Becky tries to hold onto what is happening. Can he possibly be asking her to apologize to him? Is that where he thinks this might end, sixteen years of agony tied off with an admission from her that yes, perhaps she had been over-hasty and backed him into a corner.

All her fault, really. When you think about it.

He continues speaking, filling her silence with his words. 'I'm not saying you did anything wrong, Becks,' he says. 'Not at all. I should have told you what I remembered, as soon as you said anything. I just want you to understand how it was. From my side of things.' The view from his side of the bed. 'What you thought happened, didn't happen.'

'Is that what you'd tell Maisie? That you listened to me say I wanted to kill myself and you said nothing, because what, I'd got it all mixed up in my *pretty little head*?' Her stomach is hot with acid, the spit cold on her chin. 'That my version of events was, simply, according to you, *wrong*?'

He says nothing.

'That you fucked an unconscious girl,' she continues, 'and when she woke up alone, with her pants turned inside out, you thought it was best not to say anything, on the off-chance I was trying to . . . what was it you said? "Let you down gently"?'

He stares down at his kneecaps.

'Are you honestly still trying to make me believe you're a decent man?' she says, her words short with anger, incredulity.

'I am,' he says, and she watches his hands travel to his waist and his elbows bend and his chest widen a little. 'I know I am a decent man.'

The sound of familiar voices in the road outside hauls Becky, drained and disoriented, back into the present. Time has gone quickly. Adam hears them, too.

'What about us?' says Adam. 'What happens now?'

The doorbell goes and Becky, now dazed, leaves the room to answer it.

Maisie's face creases with worry. 'Mum! What's wrong?'

'Something happened to someone we used to know,' says Adam, from up the hall behind Becky. 'Someone from a long time ago. It's nothing you need to worry about.'

'From how long ago?'

'School days,' says Adam. Becky can't speak. She can only hold Maisie and try not to break into pieces.

The next day, Becky goes to the local police station.

The woman behind the counter is hunched, pressing a pen onto a pad, midway through writing a sentence, when Becky leans in and says, 'I want to report a crime.'

'I'll be with you in just a minute,' says the woman, glancing up. Blue shirt, black pullover. Practical blue. Police black. Black and blue covering every part of her.

But Becky does not move until the woman looks up again and this time she speaks clearly and slowly and too loud for the size the room. She speaks the words that will change everything for her.

'I want to report a rape.'

Chapter 28

Hackney and Islington
One year later

At two in the morning Becky wakes with butterflies in her stomach thinking, *No, I can't go through with it.* But then, by daylight, in her little kitchen up on the third floor of this ex-council block overlooking the park, after coffee has been drunk and fingernails picked at, she thinks, all right then. It is another deep breath, in a year that has been full of them.

It is a warm, bright day. In the park, the leaves on high branches catch the light and sway softly. Morning dog walkers make conversation with each other as their dogs sniff and wag. Nobody is in T-shirt and shorts quite yet. She'll dress for a light breeze, she thinks. This flat is half the size of their old place, but has twice the view. Is that a kind of parity? Might she really have lost nothing after all? Enough time has passed that she can half-smile at the thought.

Maisie's friends think her new neighbourhood is awesome. It's where any number of struggling music producers and would-be fashion moguls have moved, in search of cheap rents while they chase expensive dreams. The neighbourhood is beginning to get written about in those pockets of the internet seemingly made to be unfindable by anyone over the age of twenty-five. To Becky's eye, these stories are somewhat overselling a remote, scuffed corner of Hackney, where the shops sell milk and noodles and table tennis bats. Still, she has seen octogenarians with hard East End vowels queuing in the post office alongside wasp-waisted girls with nose rings and asymmetric hair, so perhaps it's true. Or becoming true.

What matters to her is that the flat is hers. There will be no help with the bills here.

She dresses in front of a door-hung mirror.

She looks different to the Becky of a year ago. Her limbs have lost their pale and sinewy skittishness. She has become rosier, rounder, even dimpled in places. She has been cooking, making slow stews and sugar-dusted cakes with which to welcome her daughter home. 'Like something out of the 1950s,' says Maisie, only where is the pipe-smoking paterfamilias proudly washing his car in the driveway?

Becky sets out for the first bus stop that she'll need. The cinema that she is heading to is not the closest cinema, but it's the nearest one still screening *Medea*, so it's where she must go if she wants to catch it on the big screen which, she decided only this morning, *is* something she wants. She suspects it will hurt, and with further hurts

361

undoubtedly in store for the late afternoon, why not get it all over with? A full day of horrors, but ones she has chosen.

She walks rather than runs now. She has tried running softly and slowly but she can't connect to this way of moving, not after seventeen years of pushing her body to the point of agony. The urge to burn until she is spent is no longer there. Still, with her newfound ardour for cooking hearty dishes, her jeans were getting tight, and she couldn't afford a new wardrobe, so she has taken to walking, which is just as well considering the irregularity of the buses.

Walking has taken her long miles around their new area and she already knows it better than their old patch. It's harder now, because she is working again and the daytimes no longer belong to her, but as the evenings lighten and lengthen, on those days where after-school things keep Maisie out late, she still tries to walk home, picking a new route as often as possible. Sometimes she thinks of nothing as she strolls through the streets beneath the pointed and mirrored buildings of the City of London, feeling only the sting of particles in her nostrils as she turns on to the pollution-choked A-road in the direction of home. And sometimes, more often than she would like, she feels the still-warm embers in her marrow as she winds through a market selling blackened bananas and haunches of meat wreathed in flies, as her thoughts return to Medea. Was it enough for Medea to watch her husband collapsing with grief at the loss of his children? Did it satisfy, even fleetingly?

On a good day Becky tells herself it was enough that she walked into the police station to give them her story. Sometimes that feeling lasts for hours, sometimes more than a day. On other days, when doubt and recriminations flood in, she tries to lose herself in the easy tedium of office work. She is doing admin in a small solicitor's office and she likes the simplicity of it. It requires her to be efficient and organized and conscientious, but nothing else. Nobody needs, or asks for, her ideas. She will not change anything here. Her name goes on nothing. She is useful and she is appreciated for it, and the pay is sufficient so long as she and Maisie never do anything expensive. Nobody demands lifelong loyalty from her here. One day she will look further, cast her net for other ways to spend her days but, for now, it is exactly what she needs. For now, it is enough.

On her lunch breaks, Becky sits on the green near the office and watches people talk. She allows herself to zone out, watching how tree branches bend and dip in the breeze. She allows herself to be bored. There is no pressure in this job. No one is emailing her or phoning or texting her any more. Instead there are starlings, turning as one above her, and rats slinking around the sides of a canal, and pretty purple-flowering weeds that spout from a clogged drainpipe.

She has taken to wearing only those clothes that feel

good on her skin. On the rare occasion that she buys something new, it is all soft cottons and skirts that float and fall long – styles that may age her but, unlike her old black trousers and button-up shirts, make her feel less held-in, or more softly held.

Her hair is cut to a short bob. People have commented on how it brings out her rosy cheeks and beautiful eyes, but it is the colour she loves: dyed from mouse to mahogany it glosses for the darker seasons and glows warm in the summer months. And it changes the shape of her face. She is no longer so readily identified as the woman from the trial. In the office, where it's only six of them, it has never come up. Nor has she raised it. And it's not a drinks-after-work kind of office. They disband at five, each heading off to their own low-key life.

After twenty minutes on the bus, Becky has made it to Islington. She passes the Queen's Head pub. Scott took her out drinking here a few months ago, pushing a vanilla-scented cocktail into her hand before they both sunk deep into a cracked-leather sofa.

Scott likes the way Becky never tells him he should come out to his parents. Everyone else is mad-keen that he do it, he says, to 'really rub the gay in their faces before they croak'. He's just not sure that it's very *kind*, is it? Bad enough that he's torturing them with a lack of grandchildren. But nor does he want to be a Bad Gay, letting the side down. 'The thing is,' he tells her, 'they bought me theatre tokens for my last birthday and said maybe we could all go and see a West End musical together, even though that's really not my thing, so I think they're basically trying to tell me they know and they're fine with it. Don't you think?'

She has unpicked all her hatred from his face. His eyes no longer appraise women's bodies for opportunities to drug then abuse them. His smile conceals nothing. If he frowns, it is not a sly flash of his true self – instead it is some passing discontentment, nothing to worry about. In fact, she has become fond of his face. It is open and animated. Scott cries easily. He throws back his head when he laughs. He likes to hold her hand when they're talking, and she likes that, too.

Scott has a boyfriend at the moment. His name is Ryan. *It can't last*, whispers Scott when Ryan is well within earshot, *he's too pretty and too lovely and he makes incredible hummus!* Ryan thinks Becky ought to start dating again. 'You're wearing too much billowing velvet,' he tells her. 'Eventually you'll be mistaken for a chaise longue and then that'll be it. You'll be stuck in some old fruit's drawing room for the rest of your life. You're fucking *fit*, Becky. You need to get out there and get some!'

'No,' says Scott. 'I don't want to share her with *anyone*, let alone a heterosexual!' They carry on in this fashion, teasing her and so taking care of her. Maisie says the same things about dating. Becky is thirty-three now. That's a third of a life, Maisie tells her, with the blissful entitlement of someone who believes anyone she loves will live a hundred years or more.

Does Becky want another child? And someone to have that child with?

Not yet. She doesn't think so.

Not yet – her watchwords of the last few months. Her mantra. A 'no' withheld or postponed. A possibility untested and untaken, but not yet refused.

Becky steps into the cinema foyer. It is an elegant old art deco picture house that smells of filter coffee and musty frayed velvet. She has timed her arrival so that there will be very little hanging around in a lit theatre; in fact, the adverts are already playing.

She buys popcorn and a bottle of Diet Coke. Why not? She has taken a day off work for this, one of her precious 'annual leave entitlements'. Why not enjoy it? She reconsiders and buys a shiny plastic bag of chocolates as well. Because God knows she is about to need them. Isn't she?

She picks a seat off to the side and towards the back. It's midweek, in the middle of the day, and the auditorium is nearly empty, just three other people, all alone, sitting beneath the dancing projector beam. Despite everything, Becky feels a little kick of magic. She loves the smell of the place, the darkness, the way everyone is turned in the same direction. The scale of the pictures. How the sound is loud enough to vibrate in you.

Becky takes out her phone to turn it onto airplane mode. There is a message for her, confirming her meeting for later in the afternoon. Her stomach tightens. She realizes that she is biting her fingernails again. She taps in a quick reply, confirming.

They are to meet on a bench on the north side of the garden in Arlington Square. It's a school day and they'll have the place to themselves.

Becky looks up as the official certification card is shown. *Medea*, rated 15. Becky wonders if they went back and forth to get it there, if anyone ever actually walks out at the warning of strong language and violence, and if she should do it now. But then the film begins.

As the opening titles play, there is the sting, no less keen for its anticipation, of seeing the name of her director – no, not *her* director, simply *the* director – float into view.

A film by Sharon McManus.

Everything inside her feels it is flapping and fluttering like a pigeon being chased by a stamping foot. She eats four chocolates in a row, as if they will give her ballast.

They have kept her idea for the opening credits, letting names in a canary-yellow font float against stormy waters.

A Bottom Line film
In association with FilmFour
Emilia Cosvelinos

Becky notes that Sharon's name has been added alongside that of the original screenwriter. She is a co-writer now, as well as director. *So that's how it went after she left the job*, thinks Becky. Perhaps it was part of the price extracted for Sharon's staying on the project? More credit, more money.

But after the titles fade so does the sting, and she finds herself enjoying it more than she'd anticipated. Mostly she is pleased that it works, this artfully modernized tale of a woman who exacts revenge on her husband by murdering their children and who then, intoxicated by the ease of it, murders the husband for good measure.

Most of the last script Becky saw has made it to the screen.

Medea buries her husband's body and takes control of her husband's business, and then the town, absorbing and supercharging all his old business relationships, not least the one he had with his best friend who Medea now sleeps with.

Medea understands perfectly well what her legacy will be when she is found out, which she knows must happen, but still she refuses to run. Up on the big screen, Emilia/Medea is surrounded by a group of men decrying the ways in which she has betrayed them. Medea counters that she spent a lifetime being betrayed and, in tolerating it, betraying herself. She is magnificent in her contempt for them, even as they close in on her, intent on their revenge.

Becky waits for Medea to be strung up by the men. Only Sharon must have changed the script because now the men paw and rip at Medea's clothing, groping and slapping her flesh, screaming at her to repent. And Medea doesn't give them anything they might want from her, no fear or contrition or submission or shame. She scorns them. She pours fresh humiliation on them, naming their shortcomings as they cover her with their hands, half of which punch and slap, while the other half grab for breast and crotch. Their violences overlap, arms pushing against arms to get at her, clenched knuckles smashing down on the spread fingers of their brothers.

She is the question they cannot solve and it maddens them. They see their own wives in her, in those moments of disdain they catch and ignore but cannot quite forget. She is the short-skirted shop-girl who mocks their hungry glances. With their fingers crowding and cramming up inside her they still cannot have her. She has killed her husband's children, the children she bore him, and yet she refuses to appear insane. Where are her tears? Why doesn't she beg? With punches to her ribs and mouth they look for the contrition that will let them sleep easily again, by their wives and mistresses, and across the hallway from their daughters, but finding nothing, and losing hope they walk away loudly naming her a *Crazy Bitch*, in the hope that it might after all be true.

Medea's body turns in the wind. She seems foreign to Becky, in a way that is new to her. She had been so certain, once, of the meaning of the Medea they had crafted from draft to draft, refining and testing each turn until the character's pain and complexity and her terrible crime was all worked through and mapped, scene by scene. It had made sense then, on paper. But all of that has gone now. The camera lingers on Medea's face, her eyes still open, pooled with blood from her injuries, yet seeming still to see. She looks dead ahead, scanning the horizon as if she is looking for someone. But who? She knows where her children are. Those that were coming for her have arrived and departed. The leaves on the tree above her bow and ripple. Her body turns to distant rooftops, a church spire, a young girl in the distance, looking at her.

'I want to report a rape,' Becky had said.

Becky remembers the sharp pivot to soft kindness in the officer's voice when she said, quickly, 'I'll go and get someone.'

Moments later Becky was seated in an interview room with white-painted cinderblock walls and cloud-grey linoleum floor.

A detective had entered, 'Detective Inspector Whitecross,' she'd said, but Becky didn't say anything in response. All she could focus on was the fine telephone wire of dried tea on the rim of the Detective's mug. She was thinking about Maisie. How would Maisie cope when she found out? Would she have to find out? Might she be spared?

DI Whitecross offered her tea, by way of a gentle reminder that there was talking to be done in this room. Becky shook her head.

'I witnessed a rape and I'd like to give a statement,' said Becky, because if she hadn't spoken quickly, she might have lost her nerve.

I was raped, Becky said to herself. *I was raped. I know I was.*

And now I am in the five point seven per cent of people who report rape. I am five point seven per cent.

'Let me just turn on the recorder, if you're happy for me to tape this? Saves a few pencils.'

Becky nodded and started talking before she lost her nerve.

'The woman was out of it. I didn't recognize her at the time. I found out later on that she was an actress called Amber Heath.'

I was out of it for years. My name is Rebecca Shawcross.

The chief inspector wrote in her pad as the recorder ran.

'I wasn't sure what I was seeing. But it didn't look happy. I don't think it looked consensual, though I know you can't tell. All I can tell you is that I was there. I saw them. I saw her.'

My arms and legs and lungs and stomach, all of me has hurt every day since I was sixteen.

'The man's name is Matthew Kingsman,' she said. 'He is my boss, at a film production company called Kingfisher Films.'

The man's name is Adam Thewlis. He was once my best friend.

I am in the ninety per cent of people who know the identity of their rapist. I am ninety per cent.

'It happened less than two weeks ago. The fifteenth of May. I went to drop off some wine at his house and I saw them together and then I left.'

It happened sixteen years ago. Very late one Saturday night, or early one Sunday morning.

'I know she made a statement saying she'd been raped. She thought there was a witness and she asked them to come forward. I made a statement to the press where I said I supported my boss. I denied being there. I should have said something sooner. I should have come forward.'

I woke up and someone had had sex with me. There was nobody there. Nobody said anything to me afterwards. But it happened. Maisie is proof that it happened.

'You're here now. That's what matters,' said the detective, smiling a smile that wasn't really a smile, and then she asked more questions: time of day, clothing, before, after.

He knows the truth. He knows that I need the truth, but then he's always known that, and he kept it from me. He was there. I barely was.

'Did anything prompt you to come forward now?'

Becky sat in a long silence.

Finally the detective said, 'The matter will be joined up with the sexual offences unit and you will be informed if anyone is charged with the offence. You might be required for any court case that arises.'

The tape recorder clicked to a close. And Becky was free to go.

Scott asked her later, 'Didn't you know what would happen?' He meant the headlines. Those scathing think-pieces that labelled Becky a Judas, a betrayer of women, an enabler of misogyny. A woman who lied to defend her rapist boss. A woman who let an actress spiral down to attempted suicide, disbelieved and pilloried as an attention-seeker, for the sake of her own glittering career. All the photos of Becky and Matthew together in Cannes. She hadn't been aware so many were being taken.

'Yes,' she had said. 'I knew.'

The question the papers asked again and again: *why did she come forward now?* Why speak up unless she'd been found out, or had let it slip to someone, or had been nailed to the truth by some last-minute piece of CCTV?

There was no doubt left in the public mind; a woman had said she was raped, and there had been a witness. Therefore it had happened. And that meant Becky had beyond doubt witnessed a rape and had chosen to say nothing. She had instead supported the man who paid her wages and promoted her. You'd know when someone is being raped, wrote one commentator. If there was doubt, you'd say something. What is worse, a little embarrassment or letting an attacker go unchallenged? Sometimes the articles made Becky doubt what she knew. Had she coldly calculated the cost-benefit of letting Amber suffer?

Someone from the hotel in Camber recognized her picture and sold their story – Matthew's payment for her no-expenses-spared weekend away. The spoils of a war on women, in which she was a collaborator. That sealed things in the public mind. And it did look bad, she knew it. 'The *optics* were bad,' said one journalist.

She tried to hang on to her truth. And eventually she stopped reading the articles.

She had chosen to live with it. She gave no interviews, no comments, no quiet inside-briefings to defend herself. There was going to be a trial and, having elected to give Amber the truth, at the cost of near everything, how could she jeopardize Amber's chance of getting justice? Why try to save herself?

'Was it worth it?' Scott had asked her.

'Yes, it was. I think so.'

Then Scott had asked her permission for him to give her a hug, which sounded so quaintly old-fashioned that she almost asked why on earth he'd ask that, before she remembered exactly why he might ask first, and then she was so moved by his thoughtfulness that she couldn't let him out of her arms, not for five long minutes.

The film is nearly over, but Becky knows that two more people are yet to visit her from the screen. In an interview ahead of the film's premiere, Emilia had spoken about how Sharon convinced her to stay in the role, disclosing a new plan for the film's final scene. It had 'moved me deeply, as a piece of art. It puts life in all its pain into the heart of the story', Emilia had said.

That scene now begins to play.

Becky has read enough reviews to know that the moment is coming, but it still kicks her in the gut when Medea's grave is visited by her grieving sister, Chalciope.

Played by Amber Heath. A theatrical metafictive flourish.

On screen, Amber lays flowers then a tender kiss on the freshly dug ground.

Becky suddenly wishes that she had not seen the film on a day like today, when she was sure to feel even worse later on. That she had allowed herself some time to recover from seeing Amber's face, beamed ten feet high on the cinema screen, tearful and reproachful, mourning the world's women lost to betrayal and despair.

The credits begin to roll and – there she is – Becky's second visitor.

Siobhan's name has ended up in the credits for *Medea*, thanks to her taking a new job as Development Executive at Julia Peppard's company, Bottom Line. Siobhan joined them only a few days before Bottom Line announced their deal to acquire all rights in *Medea* from Kingfisher Films.

When the news broke, Siobhan had texted Becky: I didn't plan that one btw. It was the first contact between them since the day Siobhan resigned.

In a year of thinking things over, it is the slap to Siobhan's face that still makes Becky feel sick with shame. Its viciousness. The fear behind it. The desire to crush and intimidate anyone who might expose her. She has gone over that moment many times, but still, her inability to take Siobhan's censure on the chin, instead assaulting her, is something that she cannot forgive herself for.

The only silver lining is that it gives her a vanishingly small moment of fellow-feeling with Adam. That slap was not the totality of who she is. It is not her whole truth. And so when Adam had asked her to please believe that what he did to her is not *who he is*, now she at least understands what he means. It doesn't change much, it doesn't excuse anything, but she knows what he means.

A few days after Siobhan texted, Becky had taken the strength gained from a rare good night's sleep, and the comfort of her daughter sleeping close by, and the sun beaming through a gap in the curtains, and decided to call her. So, without breakfast, without allowing herself time to doubt and unpick the instinct, she picked up the phone and dialled.

Siobhan had answered after two rings. 'All right?' she said, a response so unexpected that Becky was silenced. 'Beck, are you there?'

And then the words had poured out. 'I'm calling because it matters to me what you think. And I want you to know that of all the bad things I've done in the last year, the thing I most regret was hurting you. I can't take that back and I'm not asking you to forgive me, but I want to tell you that when things started happening with Matthew and Amber, I made some really bad decisions. I was afraid of what might happen and what I might lose. I didn't want my life destroyed by something I hadn't done. But that was wrong. I should have been braver than that. And I'm so sorry I took it out on you.'

Enough silence had fallen for Becky to think Siobhan

had ended the call until she heard her say, 'Bit heavy for eight a.m. on a Tuesday?'

Becky had laughed, sniffing back tears.

'Seriously,' said Siobhan. 'I'm feeling sorry for you right now. Some of the stuff they're saying about you . . . especially as I know you loved your work and you worked hard. And you did come forward, in the end.' Becky felt tears on her cheeks and she was glad Siobhan couldn't see them.

Becky wanted to tell her more: to drape and underpin and contextualize everything with the details of her own story, to do as Matthew and Adam had, garlanding their actions with good reasons, solid explanations, great excuses, and a bulletproof sense that they ought never to be judged for any pain they had caused. And yet, with Siobhan, she tried to let her apology stand unreserved.

'I'm making my film, Becks,' said Siobhan. 'You know the one where, like, if *Watership Down* was actually a laugh? I honestly think I might get Aniston. Like, comedy Aniston. The best Aniston.'

'I'm pleased for you,' she said, believing it too.

The industry had felt like another country then. Its vanities, its ways, its hungers – they had dropped away. On the surface, at least. And Becky had left that behind. So when Siobhan asked her what her next move was going to be, and the reply was that she had been taking long walks, Becky had to work to convince her ex-colleague that this was actually true.

'But you were doing so well!' said Siobhan.

Then Amber's face, drunk or drugged, out of it and miserable, trapped, on its side against Matthew's rug, stared back at Becky.

'No, I wasn't,' she replied. 'Not the way I should have been.'

It was only later that Becky realized she might have sounded like she just wasn't moving up the ladder fast enough but then she thought, Siobhan will get it. They hadn't made plans to see each other. But nor did it feel impossible that, one day, they might.

Becky watches Emilia's credit float up the screen.

The film has attracted four-star reviews across the board. Emilia is a name in the Best Actress race, although some pundits have debated whether the 'Kingfisher scandal' will still bite her in the ass when it comes to the voters.

Emilia has been canny. Of course she has; her advisors are well-paid to help her navigate things like this. In interviews she has been at pains to emphasize that she refused to do the film while Kingfisher was involved, but after they exited she felt able to at least discuss it with Sharon, who she credits as a 'visionary director and an unequivocally feminist voice'.

The divorce of Kingfisher and *Medea* had been messier in real life. Once Matthew's trial was announced, the project was dead so long as he was attached to it. Becky had been fired for gross misconduct. Matthew's legal fees must have been extraordinary, thinks Becky. The company's back catalogue and existing projects were quickly sold off, no doubt much of it going on the divorce from Antonia, all done within a few short months.

And then there was whatever he paid his exceptionally-skilled barristers to defend him from the rape charge. All in, it probably cost him more than *Medea*'s total budget.

The day Becky received an email from Kingfisher Films' lawyer informing her that she was no longer in its employment she had dug out her old contract and struggled through terms and conditions she didn't remember ever having read. A contract signed at a time when she was simply grateful to have the job. She had gone through the four-page document with quivering hands: a trial three-month period, during which either party could decide to terminate . . . A salary that was paid monthly into her bank account . . . Standard terms and conditions. She might have caved and taken her termination lying down, had she not been acutely aware of a stack of bills to pay, and her iron-clad refusal to ask Adam for help. She would not let the first neutral words spoken to him be ones asking him for something. So she had knocked back a neat gin and called the lawyer back, stating in very simple terms that she expected a proper redundancy package. She had named her price. And she wanted a guarantee that if *Medea* was made, she would receive the full bonuses promised to her. The lawyer had outright laughed at the idea *Medea* might survive this shit-storm, but Becky had been adamant. She said she'd sell her story to the press if the money wasn't in her account, and a deal memo agreeing *Medea* payments in her hands, by the end of the day.

She'd hung up. And to her surprise and relief, she received both. And of course the *Medea* demand had worked out very well.

Was it blood money? No, she told herself. She had earned it legitimately. By the time she co-signed the agreement between Kingfisher and Siobhan's new employers, she had her own lawyer on board. She signed away any right to have her name in the credits, in exchange for a substantial cheque. That cheque had been the deposit for her flat with the view of the treetops.

Becky spills outside, blinking into sunlight after the darkness of the cinema. She stayed until the end credits finished. A small part of her had hoped that maybe someone might have sneaked a coded thank you to her into the 'Special Thanks' section. She might have been alluded to somehow, a wave of recognition made in disguise. But no. Her erasure is complete.

And what does she think of her film? Or rather, the film.

No. *Her* film.

She thinks she likes it. She thinks perhaps one day, when she can bear to tell the story as a dry account of some things that happened, instead of a searing *mea culpa*, then maybe she will refer to it out loud as her film. She is glad at least that it exists, to let go of it this way.

And tomorrow she will go back to work in the solicitor's office, and set about checking, filing and posting.

She checks her phone, flicking off Airplane Mode. Amber Heath has texted to say she is running five minutes late to meet her.

Chapter 29

Becky kills time, sitting on the steps of a shopping arcade near the cinema, with a cup of coffee, hiding behind her sunglasses.

She watches as a rowdy group of teenage girls, probably skiving off school, jostle over a phone screen, shrieking with laughter, giving each other endless grief for some slip of the emotions over a boy, a photo, a friend, just *life*. They are still at the beginning of so much. Becky tries not to nakedly stare at them. The sunglasses help.

The past year has been hard on her own sweet teenager.

When the news broke that Amber Heath's longed-for witness had a name and face, Maisie had asked Becky the question, and Becky had told her, *Yes, it was me*.

'You were *there* when it happened?' Maisie said through her tears. 'All that time you sat on your hands and didn't say anything?'

'Yes.'

'And you defended him! You said what a good man he was!'

'Yes.'

'While everyone called Amber a liar for making up a witness?'

'Yes.'

'Mum, she fucking tried to kill herself!'

'I know.'

'And you were there?'

'I saw two people having sex and I left straight away. I didn't really understand what I'd seen, other than Matthew on the floor with someone who wasn't his wife.'

'But she asked you to come forward.'

'I know.'

'And you didn't. You lied and said it wasn't you.'

'I've told the police everything.'

'When did you do that?'

'A couple of days ago.'

'But I don't understand. Why didn't you say something straight away?'

'I wish I had.'

'No, answer the fucking question! Why didn't you say anything?' And with that, Maisie had broken: the forensic questioning gone, and in its place an angry blizzard of accusations and condemnations. 'What if it had been me? How would you have felt if someone put their fucking stupid career ahead of helping me out while I got raped on a floor somewhere?'

What could she say to save herself?

She might have said: listen. I might have had a different

383

life, if Adam hadn't raped me and then lied to me for sixteen years.

I might have been less frightened of losing the things I had.

She might have said: I spent sixteen years believing that I was lying to you when we told you Adam was your father. For most of that time, I blamed a man who turns out to be gay and kind and horrified that I thought that about him. I used to fantasize about killing him.

I might not have been so warped and wounded.

You might not have existed.

I ended up owing too much to two men.

Two men who knew exactly what they were doing with me.

And I lost everything.

Would Maisie have carried on tearing her apart then?

Becky has rehearsed the moment many times, picturing Maisie as she learns that her father – the man she loves most in the world, who gets her humour, who makes pancakes with her, who kisses her hello and goodbye and with whom she feels safe – broke into her mother, and then lied. And lied and lied.

No longer the child of two kids who were once in love enough to *do it*, and then kept her because they loved her, and still love her together. Instead, a child born of violence. A nearly-given-away child. A lied-to infant, daughter of a deceived and broken mother and her manipulative rapist. Her baby face searched for evidence of her paternity.

What happens when your story collapses? How do you fill the gaps that you are left with? Becky knows something about that, and it is the last thing she wants for her daughter. But it is the price that would be paid for justice with Adam. There is no way around that. If she wants to keep her child as she is today – happy, loved, and whole – then there is no place for the truth.

And so she makes a choice.

She chooses her daughter, who in this moment is screaming at her and calling her a terrible person and angrily claiming that she will never forgive her for having done this to another woman.

Becky chooses her daughter.

Let Maisie scorn her. Let Maisie reject her. Let Maisie hate her, if she must – but Becky knows she will never reach for Medea's knives and poisons.

She will let Adam have Maisie, only for the sake of letting Maisie have Adam.

She will not knowingly raise her daughter, part of a new generation, to feel broken, at fault and ashamed.

When Adam stopped coming round to their flat, Maisie of course had her narrative. Becky was the cause and Adam's absence was the effect.

Maisie was furious. She demanded that Becky make things right. Unlike Lily, whose parents could apparently not be within a thousand yards of each other, she had a Mum and Dad who hung out. Who liked each other!

'I'm sorry,' Becky had said, again, as Maisie set off for Adam's flat, enraged at the new distance.

Becky had cried. Not for her daughter now, and not for Amber either, but finally for herself.

Adam had lost nothing but Becky. How could that possibly be fair?

Maisie's whole school knew about her mother. Overnight she flipped from being someone who was making a cool feminist film with rising star Emilia Cosvelinos, to a hypocrite, career-prioritizing, woman-trashing, liar-bitch. The woman in the kitchen. The woman who did not come forward (at least not straight away).

One night, soon after the news broke, she heard Maisie come crashing and tripping back into their flat.

She waited for her daughter to fall asleep before she poked her head around the door. She smelt the acetone traces of alcohol. She picked Maisie's school blazer off the bedroom floor and smelt the sharp and sweet herbal scent of weed on it. But what authority did she have left?

She tiptoed back to her own bed and sat, head in hands.

Two days later, Becky was waiting at the school gates after a meeting. She'd spent nearly half an hour in the headmistress's office laying out the case for her daughter as a talented and deserving scholarship candidate, who was going through a rough patch. The headmistress had been supportive. Maisie had never been a problematic student before now. Then Becky had decided to wait at the gates for Maisie, risking the cold shoulder, a stony silence, head in her phone as they made their way home. And so, when she saw Maisie break away from her friends and walk towards her with a not-unwelcoming smile, Becky was surprised.

Even more surprised when Maisie began talking to her as if she was picking up from a conversation they'd started earlier that day. 'Jules's mum showed me pictures of the women living in shacks who look after their kids by selling their bodies to truckers,' she said. 'She said you're a victim of a patriarchy that pressures women to support men. I think that's what she said. I was a bit stoned. She also told me to stop getting stoned in term-time.'

'What did you think about that?'

'She seemed really shitty that I was angry with you. And she's really clever. So, I don't know . . .'

'You don't know what?'

'I don't know. Maybe I'm wrong? I don't know. I sort of want to be wrong.'

Marry Jules, Becky had thought. Marry him for his mother.

It's not like it was all bad. Some old friends came out of the woodwork to support her. She even got a postcard from her schoolfriend Mary wishing her well. A few industry contacts reached out and told her that it didn't sit right that 'yet again' a powerful man's downfall also took out the women around him. You may be down but you're certainly not out, they told her, though nobody went as far as offering her a job. Nobody was *that* stupid, bringing that kind of heat to their own doorstep. But there were at least hints that, when things died down, it wouldn't be impossible for her to find her way back. If that was what she wanted.

Matthew didn't get in touch, either before or after the trial. For all matters relating to Kingfisher, Becky spoke to lawyers.

In fact, apart from in court, Becky hasn't heard Matthew's voice in a year. She has seen him in the papers a few times, looking pale and overweight and bone-tired.

She feels sorry for him, despite everything. How must it be to hold your children and still hope to feel loved by them when the world knows you as a rapist?

He sold everything he could. He chose to leave rather than attempt to rebuild. He probably calls it retirement, but really it was flight – from the film festivals that would no longer host him, from journalists who could no longer be relied on to write hagiographies, from actors who'd refuse to be seen having a drink with him.

He at least has his money. He has his awards statuettes and his film credits. Somebody will love him again, somebody foolish enough might even trust him. But it's a grim shadow of what he had.

It is time to go. She wonders, briefly and absurdly, if she ought to buy something for Amber – a gift, like flowers? She drops the thought as soon as it arrives. It's not a moment she can pad out with gifts and other such evasions.

At the trial Amber had said, 'I felt like I was going mad. Everyone thought I was making it up, just to sound like I could prove it. And after a while I thought maybe I had made it up. Like nobody had ever been there. And I was this crazy drunk bitch who didn't know what was real anymore.' Becky read the full transcript afterwards. As a witness, she hadn't been allowed to watch Amber giving evidence, not that she could have borne it.

A *crazy drunk bitch*. Becky could have spared her that.

Becky finds herself slowing down as she walks past beautiful Georgian terraced houses, their black-painted rails pristine against white-painted façades. Amber hasn't given any indication of what she expects from their meeting, only that she wanted it to happen. Becky tries to think if there is anything at all that she could tell Amber about that night that she hasn't already disclosed at Matthew's trial. What more can she offer her, other than an apology, face-to-face? Becky is reminded of Adam crouched against her bedroom wall, shards of shattered china on the floor beside him, looking caged and desolate. Did he want to run then, like she wants to run now?

Adam had sixteen years to think about what he might say, if the day came when he had to account for Maisie's paternity. And what had he managed, when that moment arrived? He had given an account wherein he was wrongly accused, and of something so monstrous that he was

389

bullied into a lifetime of silence, trapped in a lie. Poor Adam. The victim of her assumptions.

He had a story that he could live with, maybe even one he could defend to other people, if Becky ever forced him to. He had spent sixteen years finding ways to not be in the wrong. He wouldn't unpick them now. Not for her. But she could at least unpick herself from him. And she had done.

To begin with Maisie had blamed it on the Amber story, the sudden gulf between her parents. But as time passed, and Maisie learnt from Adam that he didn't at all blame Becky for what she'd done, Maisie's questions grew sharper. She wanted their old life back, and it wasn't happening, and nobody seemed able to tell her why; Becky understood all that, but still hadn't thought of a way to explain her bone-deep need to be far, far away from Adam.

'So what is it? Why won't you tell me?' Maisie had said.

'Our friendship's changed. It's just time for us both to move on.'

'Move on from what?'

'Just move on. Try to meet people that we might have a future with.'

'That's bollocks. You're not even dating.'

'Can you just leave it?'

'No! Why do I have to see Dad on my own just because you're "moving on" even though you're actually not doing that? That's really shit.'

Becky thought: yes, but I can live with that. And I can't live with the way things were, not now.

So Maisie came and went between school and home, weekdays and weekends, seeing Adam when she could – until Becky began noticing that Maisie was returning from each visit less animated and more subdued. When gently questioned, Maisie reported how pancake-day had turned to cereal and then, lately, nothing at all: no groceries in his fridge, hence no offers of food. He bought her take-aways now, if she said she was hungry. And then, uncorked, Maisie talked about Adam's unopened post and the foetid smell in his apartment, and about how much she missed the old Adam and their jokes and, finally, directed with full force at Becky, how angry she was that Becky wasn't doing anything about it.

And all Becky had said was, 'This isn't about me. He's not like that because of me.' Fuck being held accountable for him.

'Mum, I know people have called you about him. Everyone's worried and you're meant to be his best friend and you don't even care!'

Becky's answers were always a variant of the same neutral thing: she didn't know for sure what was wrong with him, hadn't seen him much herself recently, in fairness he wasn't really speaking to her either.

Then one morning, Maisie begged. 'Please visit him. I don't think he'll listen to anyone else.' And the look on her daughter's face caught her out. All Maisie's affected teenage-weariness was gone. She looked like she had when she was toddler, bereft at some catastrophe but still hoping and believing that her mother might fix the world. Fit a dropped scoop of ice-cream back into its cone. Find a lost stuffed giraffe. Ungraze a knee. 'Mum, I'm really worried he's going to kill himself.'

Becky felt a tight and bewildering knot of righteousness and grief forming. She had let Adam keep his freedom, let his parents keep their pride in him, let him have his daughter's love and respect. She'd let him keep it all for the sake of Maisie. All she had asked was to be cut free of him so that she could graft herself to something new and grow again.

She could have stayed home that day, ignored her daughter's requests and the looming threat. And yet, she found herself travelling up twenty-three floors in a whisper-quiet lift to the door of Adam's apartment. The truth was that she could live with him being dead to her, but she could not live with the idea of his death forever on her conscience any more than he could with her, sixteen years ago.

His death would leave so much destruction in its wake. Her own sacrifices. A heartbroken daughter, blaming herself for not being enough to keep her father wanting to stay alive. Some of her own grief, perhaps.

She would blame herself for it. And she was done with blame. She had to be.

Adam answered the door dressed in a ratty navy dressing gown. He looked authentically terrible. A sour smell hung off him and it looked like he hadn't slept in weeks. She hadn't called to let him know she was coming.

'I want to talk to you,' she said.

He turned and walked back inside. Below the floor to ceiling window panes, the city spread out, cut through with a river.

'You need to stop this,' Becky said. 'You need to sort yourself out. You're upsetting Maisie. It's not good enough.'

He turned to her, red eyes welling up. 'I've tried.'

'So try harder.'

It occurred to her that it was possible that Adam's actions in the last month, the worry he was causing his family and their friends and their daughter, might all have been orchestrated to bring her to this moment. Brought here so that she could bear witness to him paying a price. A calculated offering of despair and atonement, manufactured to satisfy her. She realized that she would never know for sure. And also that, in truth, perhaps it didn't matter.

'I can't live with it,' he said eventually.

'With what?'

'With you thinking about me like *that*.'

'You can't change that.'

'I know.'

'Maisie loves you. And you love Maisie. That should be enough for you to get on and do your job as a father.'

'But you think I raped you.'

393

'Yes, and you say that you didn't. I don't want to hear it again. I'm only here for Maisie.'

'We have to.'

'Have to what?'

'Go over it again. I'm sorry, but I can't live knowing that you think that about me. That's why I couldn't – that's why I didn't – for you to even think that about me . . . I can't live with it.'

Becky had gone to the kitchen island then, and taken down two mugs, and boiled a kettle to make them coffee. Black, for want of milk. He had sat, stubbled and lank, on the edge of his armchair. She had felt his eyes on her but she did not look up to meet them. She knew he wanted her to throw her arms around him like a movie heroine proclaiming that they could move on and build something new.

But there would be no heat or ice or raised voices and healing embraces from her. He was a collection of bones, he was flesh, he was a badly wired brain and a heart without a beat now. Her heart had closed to him. She pitied him. That was what she wanted him to understand. And beyond that she was only here to protect what she held dear: a future self unburdened by blame, and a daughter whose skies were clear and bright, unclouded by grief.

'We were so close.' He talked to the polished concrete floor.

'I know we were. Now,' she said briskly, all practicality.

'You need to take your rubbish out. And you should call your mum. She's worried about you.'

'Can you please stop talking to me like that?'

'Like what?'

'Like you're a social worker or something. Like we've never met.'

Becky handed him a mug of coffee. 'What do you want, Adam?'

'I want to go back. I want to find you the next day at school and tell you that last night was the best night of my life and that I love you and that I'm desperately hoping you feel the same way.'

'I want to go back and never go to that party. But here we are. And we have a daughter who needs both of us.'

He couldn't meet her eye. 'I'm begging you to believe me.'

'That's not how it works.'

'Then I don't know what to do.'

'Ask me how you can make it up to me.'

And then he did look up at her. 'How can I?'

'Have a shower. Get dressed. Make pancakes with Maisie again.' She felt each item on her list land like a blow. 'She loves you. She respects you. Be there because she needs you.'

'But you don't.'

'No. I don't need you. But I do love her.' Becky gripped the coffee mug a little tighter. 'I'll make things work with the three of us, for her sake. I'll invite you over at some point, and you'll accept our invitation. We'll have dinner. It'll make Maisie happy. You'll go home after we've eaten. That's how it will go. That's what I want from you. All this . . .' Becky gestured to Adam's stained dressing-gown, to his haggard face and the clothes dumped on the floor, 'This does nothing for anyone.'

'What about you though?'

'You can't offer me anything I want that I can't get for myself.'

Becky turned and watched a small aircraft lift itself out of the Docklands. Sunlight caught its portholes as it banked. She tried not to cry. She had once let herself love him and it had left its mark on her. Despite everything, for a moment she felt the urge to put her arms around him and to cry on his shoulder, for all of the things they had managed to lose together. For all of the damage done and the impossibility of finding a way around it.

But she let the urge pass.

'You were really wasted,' Adam said softly. 'The next day when I woke up, I threw up and then I remembered . . . and I wanted to believe you'd wanted the same things I did. But I couldn't be sure that was true. I wasn't sure. And I didn't ask you. I just hoped.'

Becky's stomach lurched. Adrenaline made her skin tingle.

'But that's not enough, is it?' he said. 'And so maybe it's true. Maybe that means that I raped you. That's what it means, isn't it? To not ask. To not know for sure. And whether it's true or not, I'm sorry. I ruined so many things for you. I did that. I loved you, and I fucked up your life.'

She steadied herself, not letting him see it.

'You . . .' he raised his hands to his head and began to cry. 'I'm so ashamed of what I did. Never letting you know.'

She tried to fold back time, to imagine seeing Adam at school on the Monday that had followed. How would that have been? If he'd told her then that their night together had been amazing, a shared adventure, despite both of them being so out of it? Would she have believed him then, if he had looked both afraid of rejection and full of hope, and so surely like someone who had committed no crime, who could never want to hurt her or take from her? Would her underwear, clumsily rolled back up her legs, have felt like a sweet, half-arsed attempt at leaving her decent when he had to leave in a hurry? Would she have believed him then?

Becky looked at Adam again and tried to tease him apart, to will him into somehow being different men: her lover, Maisie's father, her partner in collusion, her friend, her counsellor, her rapist. But none of them had given her the truth.

She won't forgive him and he won't forgive himself. They now have that in common, along with a daughter. It will have to be a new wound, one that fits perfectly where she once nursed her questions.

'How do you feel now?' Becky asked.

'I feel trapped,' Adam said. 'Like I'm in a prison I'll never get out of. I don't feel like I can survive it.'

'I did,' said Becky. 'You will too.'

Then the tears ran down both of their faces; his turned to the floor, hers to the window, her gaze tracking the path of the Thames, snaking to the horizon.

Chapter 30

Becky enters Arlington Square through one of its four gates and stands a while looking out across the flower beds – Union Jack reds, blues and whites – and along the benches lining the central path. A woman sits, reading a book with one hand, pushing a pram back and forth next to her. An elderly couple, in sunhats, summer chinos and dress respectively, sit hand in hand, enjoying the sun.

She checks her phone. Perhaps Amber has changed her mind? There is a WhatsApp thread from Maisie and Adam debating what kind of a cake to make for his mum's birthday. Back and forth their messages go, each one like a stitch binding their minutes together.

Becky looks up and sees Amber at the end of the square, seated on a bench next to a paved area, partially shielded by an olive tree. Becky plots a course along a line of fudge-coloured flint and beach stones buried into the concrete, and thinks about how Amber could pass for any young, slim Islington professional, maybe someone who has just moved into her first house, paid for by a collection of parents: oversized sunglasses propped against her

Rapunzel-golden hair, dressed down in cropped jeans and loafers.

Actors so often look smaller in real life than they do on screen, but when Becky saw the magazine pictures of Amber exiting court after her testimony, she wasn't just small, she was downright thin, utterly vulnerable, childlike. The facts of Amber's last suicide attempt had pushed at Becky's thoughts. It wouldn't take much to end a life as fragile as hers seemed in the pictures of that day on those courtroom steps, under a winter sun.

But she looks better today. There is colour in her cheeks. She seems slim, not skeletal. She has been working; Becky knows this from following her on Twitter, on the account she once used to spy on Scott, back when he had been her rapist. Amber has been heard and believed. She is not a lunatic after all.

They won't prosecute, Adam had told her, way back when the question of what she might owe Amber had seemed in the balance. And yet they had taken it to court, despite the paucity of evidence. In fact, Matthew's own arrogance had seen to that.

The trial had begun in winter, on a day when the heating had broken down in the courthouse.

It was here that Becky learned that the day after Matthew had given her his side of events, he had volunteered a statement to the police. He must have been sure, at that point, that Becky's silence was sealed. He had her loyalty.

Perhaps then he felt he could afford to rewrite the narrative, with Becky's place in it wiped as surely as his CCTV footage.

There was history between Amber and I. An affair. A few separate nights in London at my club and one, perhaps two, weekends, out of London. I ended it soon after the Hampshire weekend because she was needy, a little unstable. The girl needed a boyfriend and some therapy. I'd said I would be happy for her to seek my advice any time, because the film business is capricious and tricky to navigate. It chews people up and spits them out. I like to be able to help.

I called her up the following weekend to say the kids were out of town so she should come to the house to sort things once and for all. I thought I could give her some useful numbers for people. A psychiatrist, for one thing.

He told the police: *We drank a lot. I was having a nice time.*

He said: *She sat on my lap. She wasn't wearing any knickers. It was a seduction.*

Amber, in her evidence, instead offered: *He came and sat next to me on the sofa. Put his hand up my skirt and tried to pull my knickers off. I told him no, but I did kiss him. I wanted to leave but I didn't want to be rude.*

Matthew said: *She kissed me and I said something like:* Hold on, I've already said no to all this. *But we got carried away. We'd had a lot to drink. We kissed on the steps all the way up to my bedroom, nearly didn't make it. And then we were in the bedroom having sex on my bed. I'd never have sex on a floor, let alone a kitchen floor.*

Amber said: *He got me onto the kitchen floor. He raped me.*

Matthew said: *Of course there is no 'witness'. It never happened. And there would have been nothing to see. Two people drinking too much wine. That's all.*

And Becky?

Becky, shivering with both cold and nerves, had given her evidence: a red and black shoe. A thigh pinned down. A look on Amber's face. What look? Distress. There was a time she thought it could have been ecstasy but no, she thinks now distress. Had Becky ever been asked by Matthew not to say anything? No. Do you vouch for the character of Matthew Kingsman? Not any more. Can she be sure that what she saw was rape? No. All she can say is that she was there. In the kitchen.

And now she was here.

Becky sits down next to Amber.

Amber Heath, publicly torn down, disbelieved, called a slut and slag and liar.

'Hello again,' she says.

Outside the courtroom, the photographers had surged at Becky like baying, drunk football hooligans. Up in her face with their questions and microphones. Camera flashes dazzling her.

Matthew had the best barristers that money could buy. He was acquitted. Of course he was. He and Amber had met before, slept together before. She went there, knowing that his wife was away. They drank wine. And if he denied having sex on the floor, it was because it was a humiliation too far. To be thought of that way.

Amber puts her arms around Becky and hugs her for a long time.

Afterwards, they sit next to each other on the bench, Amber holding Becky's hand.

'I'm sorry I didn't come forward when you asked,' says Becky. 'I'm sorry I didn't say anything sooner.'

'But you did say something.' Amber turns to face her.

'But he was acquitted. It might have been different.'

'I doubt it.'

'They wouldn't have called you a liar,' says Becky.

'Some of them still would have.'

'Stop being nice. You tried to kill yourself. You thought you were going mad, and I let that happen.'

'You didn't know me. And you didn't owe me anything.' And then, 'Why did you do it? In the end?' asks Amber.

'I thought I owed you an answer. You needed an answer and I had it. I could at least give you that.'

'I don't think I'd have come forward. I'd have kept quiet.'

'You don't know that,' says Becky. 'Are you not angry with me, Amber?'

'You burned down your whole life for me, when you didn't have to. I'm not angry with you. You're my hero.'

The two look at each other then. Amber squeezes Becky's hand.

'It really helped. Please believe me.'

'I do,' says Becky. 'I believe you.'

Acknowledgements

As an ex-agent myself, I'll start with my old peer-group. Thank you to Veronique Baxter for her ongoing support, ideas, gift for perspective and downright brilliance. Many thanks also to her tireless colleagues Sara Langham, Alice Howe and everyone in the foreign rights department at David Higham Associates. My gratitude to the always erudite and fabulous St John Donald at United Agents for his work on the film and TV side.

Thanks to everyone at HarperCollins for their enthusiasm for this book – Abbie Salter, Jen Harlow, Liz Dawson, Holly Macdonald, Fionnuala Barrett – in particular my editor Martha Ashby, whose notes I always look forward to. Outrage, determination, amusement, analysis, joy, tears: her talent and humanity are present in every conversation and track-change. It makes working with her an absolute joy and privilege.

My friends continue to be an essential source of support, love and knowledge. Thank you to the women who have shared their stories of workplace and home. During my research a number of friends offered their particular expertise across various technical matters: Rupert Russell on court procedure, Melissa Case on criminal and family justice policy and imposter syndrome, Marianna Turner on medical general practice, Heather Brearey on the workings of both the police force and the teenage mind. Thanks also to Negeen Yazdi and Damien Jones for sharing their insights into the film industry, from international film financing to the colour of the beach umbrellas at Cannes. Any mistakes are entirely my own.

Many others supported me during the writing of this book. Zofia Sagan and Emily Pedder both deserve a particularly extended virtual-hug of thanks.

Family, always. The unerring belief and enthusiasm and love of the Begbie family: Mum, Dad, Louise – thank you. And all the Edges for their support and love. My best friend, Melissa, for always talking things through, around and over.

I gratefully acknowledge the works of several authors whose books I read in preparation for writing: Rebecca Solnit, Laura Bates, Jessica Valenti, Rose McGowan, Deborah Frances-White and Brené Brown. And last but not least, a big thanks to Euripides, dead for a long time but still bitingly relevant.

A huge, warm thank you to my two sons Jack and Griffin who, when I emerge from writing, exhausted and sometimes disturbed, manage to ground me with their hugs and talk of martial arts and Minecraft. And finally, kisses to my husband – my buddy, my sounding-board and story-breaker, lifetime co-pilot, supporter-in-chief, partner in everything, Tom.